CHILD TAKEN

DARREN YOUNG

CHILD TAKEN

Waterford City and County Libraries

RedDoor

Published by RedDoor
www.reddoorpublishing.com

ISBN 978-1-910453-30-8

Female silhouette designed by Freepik.com
Male silhouette from www.openclipart.org

A CIP catalogue record for this book
is available from the British Library

Cover designer: Clare Connie Shepherd
www.clareconnieshepherd.com

Typesetting: WatchWord Editorial Services
www.watchwordeditorial.co.uk

Printed and bound by Nørhaven, Denmark

*For Luisa, Alessio and Emilia; who gave me
everything I needed to do this*

*And the rest of my family for helping me
to become someone who could*

Prologue

I want to tell you what happened that day.

Tell you my side of the story. It won't be easy for you to hear. It might help if you put yourself in my position. So I need you to imagine you are me; and I need you to imagine you're at home.

Home, if you can picture it, is a large, sprawling 1920s house that sits alone atop the cliffs on a remote stretch of the North Devon coast. It's a picturesque place, but in need of some love and attention that you never quite have the time to get around to giving it. On a good day – and the day you are imagining is a ridiculously hot one in August – the views are stunning, but the place can appear a little ominous when it's dark or rainy.

You have lived there since you bought it on a whim a few years ago, knowing full well it would become a money pit that you'd never get around to finishing, but she loved it at first sight, so you put in an offer. *She*, by the way, is your wife. She's out at the moment, so imagine you are sitting all alone, in the sweltering heat, waiting for her.

Just popping to the shops, she said when she left over an hour ago, but you know that she never 'just pops' anywhere, and it's already past midday. But she won't be much longer because she knows you worry about her when she's away from the house. You love her dearly and you can't wait for her to get home, but you're worried too. You always are; she's been through a lot and you'll be glad when she's back. That's why you're here, after all. It's why you took that day, and a few others, off work. To keep an eye on her.

You know she isn't perfect; but how many of us are anywhere even close? You know she has her 'moments'; you see them all the time. It's been like it ever since… Only two hours ago you said the wrong thing at the wrong time and spent the next ten minutes picking up cereal from all four corners of the kitchen floor and wiping milk from the walls and tiles, getting a tiny fragment of the shattered ceramic dish in your finger. But it doesn't make you love her any less.

You begin to tidy things so she doesn't think you've just sat there worrying – you put a magazine in the rack, and slot the remaining breakfast dish and two cups into the dishwasher. You have missed her for every single second she's been gone: from the moment she stepped out of the door, got into her car and you heard it disappear into the distance.

Imagine you hear it again. The car pulling back on to the drive, tyres slowly rolling across loose gravel. There's that tingle of anticipation that some relationships might eventually lose but not yours. You look at your reflection in the kitchen cupboard's glass door and you run your hand through your hair because she prefers it to be a little untidy.

There are footsteps on the gravel; imagine you hear a key turning in the door and her walking in, a reddish sun-kissed tinge on her pale skin, vest top and shorts, her brown hair bobbing up and down on her shoulders; the most beautiful thing in the world. But when you look at her face, into her big brown eyes, they're full of concern – you'll quickly come to realise it's guilt – and you look down and with her, hiding behind her legs, is a small child. A young, pretty little girl with blonde curls and a face that would melt even the frostiest of hearts. Imagine it if you can. Your wife, standing there; a child you've never laid eyes on, holding hands with her as if their being together is the most ordinary, unremarkable thing in the whole world.

Well, that's what happened to me.

What would you have done?

4

I want to tell you what happened that day.

Tell you my side of the story.

You see, if it wasn't *my* story, or if I had been one of the other mothers on the beach that day – an observer rather than in the centre of it – I think I'd have been saying what they were surely all thinking. That I couldn't believe a mother didn't know where her child was.

But at least hear what I have to say before you think it too.

Of course no one on the beach actually said those words. It might have been absolutely chaotic on that sand, people everywhere, noise everywhere – completely overwhelming, to be honest – but all these strangers kept coming up to me, telling me we'd find her and that she couldn't have gone far, even though they had no idea how far she might have gone. But they were so convinced – and convincing – that I went along with it and became one of them, doing what they did. Calling, shouting her name, reassuring myself that it would all turn out just fine, as they reassured me it would.

They were all so active, so sure, so purposeful and so damn orderly, in the way they set about finding her, that for a time I got swept along in their overconfidence. Most of them were so good at giving orders, marshalling extra resources and spreading newcomers, that they could have been headmistresses, organising their staff and pupils in the playground when the whistle blows at the end of break time. They had found this common purpose on that beach, some of them tuned into a kind of shared sense of duty as a parent; but there was no hiding the fact that it was a task, and one that would eventually end. One they'd go home from, back to the normality of their lives.

I wouldn't. Part of me is still on that beach. Maybe it always will be.

I'm embarrassed to admit it, but at the moment they got busy searching for her, despite going along with it, all I actually wanted to do was lie down on the sand and scream until either my lungs burst or the tide came in and covered me over. I had already broken down inside; I could have burrowed with my hands like a rabbit into that sand and then got everyone to cover me up using the kids' buckets and spades.

But of course I couldn't do that, could I?

So I dutifully followed the others. Shouting, looking, asking. Trouble was, we weren't even searching in the right place. The swarm of helpers, even Todd, bless him, were close to the sea, on the sand that was closest to the sea, but for some reason my eyes were being drawn away from the beach, across the promenade and the sand dunes, across the full-to-the-brim pay-and-display car park behind it and to the road that snaked up the hill and over it towards the dot of a town on the horizon.

A voice inside me, right away, said that it was those places, not the beach itself, where we should be looking. Even before the first police officers arrived, I felt it so strongly.

But the others wouldn't have listened anyway. They kept searching among the people on the beach, on the sand or in the water. And I watched them do it. Watched them as they looked at me with those pitying eyes as we all desperately cried out her name, over and over.

If I'd been one of them I'd have thought the same thing. *How could such a thing happen?*

But it did happen. I wasn't one of the others, observing. It happened to me.

And as my eyes wandered again, across at the road that led off the car park and up the hill, I had this sinking feeling that we were already too late.

I might not have known where she was.

But I knew she'd been taken.

Thirty minutes earlier...

'Hello sweetheart, are you lost?'

Jessica was too young to really know what *lost* meant, but as it happened, at the moment the question was put to her, her family were little more than fifty yards away to her right.

A silhouette had asked the question. A tall, black shape, blocking the midday sun and the girl's view of the ice-cream van ahead. The silhouette crouched down on one knee, at the girl's eye level. She could see the silhouette's face now that she was close up. Her face was as soft and warm as her voice.

'Well, we can't have you walking all alone in this crowd,' the woman said. 'Where's your mummy?'

The child didn't answer but looked instinctively towards the packed beach. It was different now somehow; lots of people – people she didn't know – were now between her and her parents, moving in all directions. Some were headed for the sand and others away from it. She knew that somewhere among them, behind them, her mother was there; they'd been together only a few seconds earlier.

But that was before she had seen the ice-cream van.

The woman followed the young girl's gaze. Two weeks of continuous sun, cloudless skies and higher-than-usual temperatures had brought thousands of people to the beach, and it was as full then as it had been at any point that summer. Young children, some just like the girl, others older, ran around playing and shouting; bat and ball games were in full flow. Dotted across towels and sunbeds were exhausted parents just glad not to be at work.

'Can you see her, sweetheart?'

The girl looked at the swarm of activity and noise and shook her head. She looked as though she might cry but was trying her hardest not to. The woman took her hand, leaned in closer and whispered, 'Don't get upset. We'll find her.'

The girl wrinkled up her nose. The woman's warm smile made her feel safe, and she looked towards the van again.

'Tell you what, why don't we get you a nice big ice-cream and then go and look for your mummy?'

The girl looked at her and back into the crowd, expecting her mother to come out of the masses at any moment with a face like thunder and ready to give her the biggest telling-off of her young life. She'd never expected to get as far as she had, but with each step, anticipating being called back at any moment, there had been nothing, and by the time she had got close to the van it had been too late.

'Don't worry.' The woman held out her hand and the young girl gratefully took it. They walked towards the ice-cream van, but instead of joining the queue they walked past it. The girl hesitated until she felt the woman's hand squeeze hers and they continued walking. After a few more steps, the child glanced back at the van.

'I know a much better one.'

They walked off the concrete promenade, past the beach café and shop and across the sand dunes to the car park behind it. There were about eighty cars crammed on, some in legitimate spaces, and others pushing the boundaries of car park etiquette – and physics – to the very limit. They reached a small blue hatchback in the corner and the woman opened the driver's door. The young girl stopped and looked anxiously around, every not-yet-fully-formed instinct in her body telling her that something wasn't right. The woman knelt down again and put her hand on her shoulder.

'It's only a short drive, to the best ice-cream ever,' she said excitedly, 'and then I'll take you straight to your mummy, OK?'

She lowered the back of the chair and helped the child into the seat behind it and leaned in to fasten the seatbelt. The young girl wasn't completely sure what had been said to her, but she had heard enough words in the sentence to placate her. Besides, she needed her new friend more than ever now, because she knew she was in a lot of trouble for wandering off as she had.

The woman smiled and ran her hand through the girl's mop of blonde curls and grinned at her. 'It'll be OK.'

Then she put the driver's seat back into its original position and climbed inside. The car was warm and the seats sticky. The steering wheel was almost too hot to touch, and the inside of the vehicle began to smell of sun lotion.

The woman turned the key and the engine kicked into life; she wound down her window to let in some cooler air. In the distance she could just make out the sound of a woman shouting. Shouting out a name; each cry sounding more desperate than the one before.

It was coming from the beach.

Part One

Twenty years later…

1 | Danni

'Can you check the amount and enter your PIN, please?'

The customer looked at her, confused.

Danielle Edwards checked the screen and quickly worked out why: she was asking the woman to do something she had already done. She had to press a button now, so that a receipt printed off. Her head throbbed and her vision was blurry as she did it, and she felt as though she was swaying in a strong wind. It didn't help that the customer had just had two separate fillings, one in each side of her mouth, rendering almost half of the alphabet impossible for her to pronounce.

'Sorry,' Danni said, and handed her the receipt. 'See you in six months.'

The customer said something that sounded a little like *thank you* and left the waiting area for the door to the car park. Alone, Danni took several deep breaths and put her head down on the reception desk. When she lifted it, there was a forehead-shaped pool of perspiration in its place, and when she put her finger on the back of her neck it was wet and hot to her touch.

When the dentist, who was also the owner of the practice and her boss, finished with his next patient, Danni quickly sorted their payment and next appointment before admitting how ill she felt, and was immediately sent home.

In under half an hour, her car was slowing down outside her house where she lived with her parents and she was looking forward to an afternoon of nothing more taxing than pulling the bedcovers over her head and sleeping the fever off. But, as she pulled on to the drive, her mother's estate car was in its usual parking spot, alongside the neatly manicured hedge where there was just enough room to put a car and still open the door to get out. Danni frowned – her mother was supposed to be at work all day; she'd seen her leave that morning. She parked next to the estate car, got out, and opened the front door with her keys.

'Mum?'

There was no reply. The house felt empty and cold; no lights on, no sound. Danni listened carefully and called again. She kicked off her shoes and stood still, listening, and heard what she thought was the very faint sound of water and someone crying.

She ran up the stairs two at a time, and as she got closer to the bathroom, its door slightly ajar, she heard it much more clearly: sobbing, and the noise of water, dripping on to the floor.

'Mum?' she called, a little louder, and knocked on the door, but there was no reply. She pushed the door open and saw her mother lying in the bath, her head just above the clear water. The bath was full, almost to the very rim, so that even the slightest movement created a tiny ripple that sent a droplet of water over the edge and on to the white ceramic tiles below.

'Mum!'

Danni's mother didn't seem to hear or see her or even know that she was there. She seemed listless, almost unconscious, except she was crying, or had just stopped; she stared ahead at the taps; her make-up had left grey lines down her cheeks as it ran into the water.

Danni's first thought was to look around for pills or alcohol but there was nothing obviously out of place. She put her fingertips into the water. It was tepid, and had been run at least an hour ago, maybe more, and she quickly pulled up her sleeve and plunged her arm into it to take out the plug and begin to drain the water out. She grabbed the biggest bath towel off the rail and spoke softly to her mother. 'You'll catch a cold.'

She put her hands under her arms and tried to lift her, but to begin with her mother didn't budge and she was impossible to move like that, so Danni kept talking, gently encouraging her, and finally she began to respond so that she could lift her to a standing position and wrap the towel around her body. Then she carefully helped her step out on to the tiles and sat her down on the toilet seat. She began to pat her dry.

'Danni?'

'It's OK. You're OK.'

Patricia Edwards mumbled incoherently as Danni finished drying her, stood her up and led her into the master bedroom and helped her into some thick pyjamas. They both heard another car pulling on to the drive, and for the first time since she'd arrived home Danni saw her mother begin to find her bearings. A look of genuine horror spread across her face. They listened as the front door opened.

'Pat? Danni?'

Danni went to the top of the stairs and looked over. Her father was standing at the bottom, looking up. He wore corduroy trousers and a dark jacket, complete with elbow patches, over a casual shirt, making him look like a college lecturer.

'We're up here, Dad,' she called down.

'What's wrong? I stopped at the shop but they said your mum had come home.'

Danni glanced back at the bedroom, where her mother was sitting on the bed, watching her, listening to her conversation. Her face was begging Danni to say nothing.

'She's feeling sick. I've been sent home too; we must have the same thing.'

'Is she all right?'

'I've just got her into bed. But I'd stay away from us both unless you want it too.'

He took off his jacket and hung it over the banister. 'I'll make some tea.'

Danni went back to her mother and helped her under the bedclothes. She didn't ask, and her mother didn't offer anything by way of an explanation either, but she nodded a silent *thank you* as Danni plumped up a pillow and put it behind her. Then Danni went into her own room and began getting undressed and into her own bed. In the commotion she had forgotten how poorly she felt herself, and she lay under the covers as a wave of nausea swept over her.

The door knocked and her father brought in a cup of tea. 'How are you feeling?'

'Not great. But I'll sleep it off.'

He kissed the top of her head and left her, telling her he was working in his study and to just shout if she needed anything. Danni nodded and tried to sleep, but it proved difficult. All she could think about was what might have happened had she not come home when she did. She lay awake most of the night and had every intention of asking her mother about the incident the next day.

But when she woke, late and after barely an hour's sleep, there was no opportunity before Patricia left for work. And that evening, and for the rest of the week, her mother managed to avoid her or change the subject if they did end up alone together. It was strange for Danni – they'd always told each other most things; they were more like friends that way – but she could see her mother's obvious discomfort, so she waited. Before she knew it, another week, then a month, then several months had passed, and Danni began to wonder if she had blown it out of proportion. By the time a year had gone by, she had all but forgotten about it.

But she was about to get a reminder.

2 | Danni

'I just want you to leave me alone!'

Danni slammed the door of the taxi, narrowly avoiding taking the tips of his fingers with her, and gave her address to the driver. As the cab pulled away, Euan Corbett ran alongside for a few seconds until the car gathered speed and left him behind.

She sighed. The evening had turned out to be even worse than she had expected.

Euan was a little over two years younger than she was and had been what she described as her 'sort of boyfriend' for ten months, an off-and-on relationship, until a fortnight ago, when she'd ended it; or at least tried to. Ten months ago, she'd been carried along by the new-relationship excitement and semi-regular sex, and neither had wanted things to get serious, but then Euan had changed, while for Danni the novelty had already worn off. The age gap, or, more pertinently, the difference in maturity between them had become a problem. Danni had tried, as a compromise, to keep things as they were, but he had wanted more, wanting to see her almost every night. When she'd spent time with her best friend, Sam, or simply on her own, he had become moody, and if she even mentioned another man's name, however innocently, he became inexplicably jealous, and so eventually she'd told him it was over.

But he had refused to leave it there, and had begun to harass her with text messages and calls until she'd ended up switching her phone off at work, and sometimes outside work too. Then he'd taken to turning up outside the dental practice when her shift finished, and after one such occasion she'd allowed herself to feel sorry for him and agreed to talk over a drink.

'You're wasting your time,' her mother had said when she saw her putting on her favourite dress, and Danni knew she was probably right; but she also had this hope that she might be able to get him to change back.

'He's just a lad,' her mother told her. 'He needs to be a lad. He's not ready for a relationship, even if he thinks he is.'

Danni knew he wasn't. She'd known it from the minute she'd said yes originally, back at the start, when he'd pretended he wanted to find a new dentist as an excuse to talk to her. But, despite her mother and Sam trying to get her to see sense, she had found early-days Euan to be fun and charming; the boyishness was part of the attraction, and she'd allowed other parts of her body to rule her head. She had also enjoyed being a part of his world, as it had given her a brief break from hers. She would see him two or three nights a week, which was perfect for her, and, even though he could be immature, she just figured he'd do his growing up in the relationship.

But the fun had turned to petty arguments and then begun to border on obsessiveness – and the age gap felt more like ten than two years – so Danni had acted decisively.

But now Euan was suggesting she'd been too hasty.

'You don't need a girlfriend,' she'd told him as they sat in a neutral pub earlier this evening with a bottled lager and a wine. She'd realised she didn't need a boyfriend either.

'It'll be different,' he'd promised, his words coming out machine-gun rapid as they always did when he was nervous. 'I'll be different.'

She doubted it. But he was using every last ounce of his charm to win her over, so she had agreed, reluctantly, to have another glass of wine. Except, when he went to the bar, he had got into an altercation with a man whom he accused of looking over at her, and Danni had put her coat on and left before he realised what had happened.

Outside, she had flagged down one of the taxis that frequently rolled by, and, as it pulled up at the kerb, Euan had come running out and tried to stop her getting inside.

'Euan, please!'

He'd tried to convince her to get out, and that was when she had told him to leave her alone. It had sounded harsh, as though he were a nuisance-causing stranger rather than a spurned boyfriend, and she felt bad during the taxi ride home.

But enough was enough.

So, it was only a few minutes after nine o'clock when the taxi dropped her opposite her house. At least, she thought as she paid the driver, the relationship was definitely over now and she could move on. She was even looking forward to laughing about it one day with her mother.

The house was a four-bedroomed detached property on the outskirts of the village. Her parents had spent a fortune on it, to bring it back to life, after the previous owner, an elderly man well into his eighties, had died after allowing it to fall into a state of disrepair. Her mother, especially, had spent years putting her stamp on the place, decorating and redecorating every room several times and filling it with stylish furniture, paintings and flowers, and, Danni had always thought, warmth too.

But when she got to the front door she felt an unfamiliar chill, and thought she heard raised voices from inside.

She stopped and checked her phone in case she'd missed a call from them, but she hadn't, so she stepped closer to the door. She heard her father speaking, more clearly now, and she tried to listen to what was being said. Then her mother's voice argued back – Danni couldn't remember them having a cross word before – and the situation sounded quite heated. She realised she was leaning forward with her ear pressed to the front door.

She stepped back.

They weren't expecting her at this time. They didn't know that her evening with Euan would go downhill so quickly, and she hadn't called or texted them to tell them.

She wanted to know what they were arguing about, but she couldn't stand on the step eavesdropping for much longer. And she didn't want them to think she'd been listening, so she was about to rattle her keys in the door and make it noisily obvious that she was back home when she heard her father shout over the sound of the TV.

'Bloody hell, Pat.'

Danni stepped back from the door instinctively. For Thomas Edwards that was extremely strong language; he absolutely detested swearing and didn't allow it in the house. She put her key slowly into the lock and turned it until she heard a tiny click, then she put her hand on the door and carefully edged it forward until there was a small gap and she could hear them properly. She tensed her body, leaned into the gap and listened carefully.

'Don't talk down to me, then.'

'But we've been over and over this.'

He sounded more frustrated than angry to Danni. She knew she should stop listening but she found her feet stuck firmly where they were and her curiosity getting the better of her.

'*You've* been over it, you mean,' she heard her mother say loudly, and with an equal measure of frustration in her tone.

'We both have. And I thought we agreed.'

'So, what if I've changed my mind?'

'It's not just about *you*, though, is it?' her father said.

'No, it's not, it's about us all.'

'Yes, and I said no.'

'She'll find out one day.'

There was suddenly silence, and Danni was concerned that they might have heard her or that one of them was going to storm off into the hallway and see her, but the voices started again, calmer this time.

'Look, we're going round in circles,' her father said.

'I know.'

'Let's sleep on it and see how we feel tomorrow.'

There was a break in the background sound from the television at the exact moment her mother let out a defeatist sigh. 'OK,' Danni heard her say.

She was conscious that the conversation was ending and if she walked in now they'd worry she had heard, so she took a step back, carefully closed the door and then turned her key and made a more dramatic entrance, cursing under her breath and throwing her handbag to the floor.

'What's happened?' her mother said, rushing into the hall. Danni stood on the mat and angrily kicked off her heels.

'If I ever say I'm going to give Euan another chance,' she said, 'please shoot me.'

Her mother smiled sympathetically. 'He's too young for you, Danielle,' she said, trying, but failing dismally, to hide the I-told-you-so in her tone. She was the only person who called her by her full name.

'He's history now,' Danni said, and they smiled at each other.

They both walked into the living room. Her father was sitting on the sofa pretending to watch the TV, although the sound wasn't on anywhere near high enough for him to be really listening to it.

'So,' said Danni awkwardly, 'what have you two been up to?'

'Nothing,' her father said with an unconvincing shrug. 'Just watching this.'

Danni looked at the screen, where a brightly coloured bird was feeding a nest full of young chicks while a man's mellow voice described it with panache. She couldn't remember her parents ever watching a wildlife programme in her entire life.

'Well, I'll leave you to it, then,' she said and walked towards the door. 'Goodnight.'

'Night, love,' they both called after her in unison, a little too rehearsed.

Danni spent the next two hours sitting on her bed replaying the conversation she'd overheard, analysing every word but coming back to that one sentence – one that possibly had nothing at all to do with her. *She'll find out one day.*

But who was this *she*? And what would *she* find out one day?

Danni climbed under the covers and switched off the light. She had an early shift in the morning and knew it wouldn't hurt to get a full eight hours' sleep in for once. As she closed her eyes, the image of her mother in the cold bathwater, tear-lines on her face, resurfaced in her mind. That incident, almost forgotten, suddenly seemed significant again.

There was something her parents weren't saying.

Not to her, anyway.

And she was going to ask her mother what it was.

3 | Patricia

'C'mon, move over.'

The road was more than wide enough for two vehicles and it was probably wide enough for three, side by side, but in the darkness, with the rain that had been falling since midday lying all over the road surface and covering most of the white lines that ran down its centre, it seemed much narrower.

It was early evening, but it had been dark since mid-afternoon. The rush-hour traffic had cleared and there were fewer cars, and therefore less spray from their wheels, and that made driving a little easier. But it was still a horrible night, and you had to take extreme care, keep your wits about you and your eyes on the road. If you did all that, then it shouldn't have been too difficult.

But the oncoming vehicle had a driver who was doing none of those things. Their car was straddling what could be seen of the white lines and they were going much faster than a safe speed. Their headlights were old and dim; she could barely pick them out in the gloom; she just knew they were getting closer and closer.

'For goodness' sake, move over,' she said, concerned but not overly. But the distance between her car and the one coming towards her was getting shorter and two of its wheels were on her side of the carriageway. She flashed her main beam but it seemed to have no impact.

The wiper blades on her Ford estate car were doing their best, at full speed, to keep her windscreen clear, but the rain was so heavy that every droplet they removed was replaced by dozens more. She was blinking and moving her head from side to side to try to get a better angle through the zigzag of water running down the glass when suddenly the oncoming car put its headlights on full beam, and the dazzling brightness forced her to shield her eyes with her left hand.

'One minute I can't see you,' she seethed, 'and now this.'

She was just a hundred yards away now, and she began to wonder if the other driver knew she was there. Or even cared. She put her hand on the horn and pushed it firmly down, but it had never been the loudest of horns, and with the sound of the storm outside the car it was probably barely audible.

For the first time, she was afraid. They were too close now to just hope for the best. If one of them didn't do something, one or both of them was going to be involved in an accident.

Seventy-five yards. She had to make a decision.

At that stage, thinking quickly, she saw two options. She could cross on to the opposite side of the road herself, the side where there was slightly more room and which was away from the cliff edge. But it wasn't without risks; she knew that if the other driver corrected themselves at the last moment she'd hit them head on, and it was impossible to second-guess what they might do, especially under pressure or in a panic.

The alternative was to carry on and hope to squeeze through the small gap that existed between the oncoming car and the steel safety barrier. It would be tight, but she had to presume that when the car got that close it would see or hear her and the driver would realise their error and correct their position. It was what she would do.

Fifty yards. Surely they can see me by now, she thought.

She decided it was safer to stay on her own side of the road. She pressed her palm down on the horn as far as it would go, keeping it there. She flashed her headlights once too, for good measure, and watched for signs of the onrushing car adjusting its direction and speed.

But it didn't.

If anything, the marginal move it did make was further on to her side, and it didn't seem to slow at all. She was suddenly aware, as she slowed down to less than twenty miles per hour, that the other driver wasn't going to do anything. Its headlights poured in through the windscreen, momentarily blinding her, and she knew that she had nowhere to go; her options had gone. Even the gap she'd hoped to get through had narrowed, and there was no hope of squeezing through any more. It was the other car or the barrier; she was definitely going to hit one of them.

She screamed.

Instinct took over at that moment and, as the other car loomed in front of her, she pulled the wheel to the left, swerving into the safety barrier with an impact that jolted her body from side to side. Her car's front wing ground against the metal as she tried to turn back on to the road, but, with nowhere to go, she slid along the next barrier too. She tried to correct herself by pulling right, but her tyres had already gone over the edge; the third barrier gave way and her bulky estate car battered its way through it as though it wasn't there.

On the other side was a slope, steep and unforgiving.

For a split second, her car left the ground completely, then the wheels reconnected with the bank with a heavy thud and then gathered pace as it rushed downhill until it clipped a tree stump and flipped in the air, coming down on its roof. It continued to slide, now upside down, and she screamed again as its side windows shattered and the fragments flew about around her. The Ford's headlights lit up the ground in front, affording her a brief glimpse of what was ahead in the darkness: a steep grassy bank, punctuated by trees. Her car slid between two of the bigger ones and reached the bottom of the bank, where it flipped again and rolled three times before juddering to a halt, on its side on the edge of a ravine.

The stench of fuel filled the air and she lay in shock as the car teetered above the drop, wheels spinning and rain pouring in through the glassless windows. It seemed for a second that it might stop there, but one last gasp of forward momentum carried the car over and it fell again, hurtling quickly downwards until it hit the bottom of the ravine and could fall no further.

The car ended up at an angle rather than completely upside down but the woman could see the floor was still above her head. She felt liquid on her neck, dripping from her body above her, and searing pain. The liquid ran down her chin until she could taste blood on her lips. She tried to cry out but no sound made it through. Instead, shock was enveloping her whole body, and in the faint glow from the car's headlights she looked up and saw that her legs, although she couldn't feel them, were almost completely crushed by the mangled seat.

She was sick, vomiting on to her own forehead. The smell of fuel almost overwhelmed her, and as rainwater fell in through the glassless windows she was sick again as the smell of petrol and the taste of her vomit mixed at the back of her throat. Her hands scrambled around for her phone as the pain began to come; it was probably her only chance of survival. But even after opening her seatbelt to give her more reach she couldn't find it, and she realised her bag had been flung out during the descent.

She tried to drag her body forward but the pain from her torso was too much to bear and she had lost all feeling in her legs. She lay back against what remained of the driver's seat and cried for a few seconds, unable to think of anything else she could do.

It was then that she smelt it.

Smoke.

Despite the rain coming in through the broken windows and the car sitting in almost a foot of water at the bottom of the ravine, something was burning; the acrid smell of smoke was filling her nostrils, making her cough and begin to lose consciousness. Smoke was suddenly all around her and she made out the unmistakable sound of flames, licking as they took hold of the flammable fuel around it, coming from what felt like somewhere behind her, and getting closer. She looked up again at her crushed legs and didn't bother to try to find out what was on fire but breathed in the toxic fumes quickly, sucking them into her mouth and nose as much as possible.

Patricia Edwards closed her eyes, gripped the seat and prayed the end would be quick.

Then the car exploded.

4 | Danni

'She'll have stayed at the shop to help them tidy up.'

Danni watched her father as he paced up and down impatiently. He didn't appear to hear what she said but she knew he had and had chosen to ignore it. She also knew he didn't like any mention of the shop.

He'd never liked her working there. He saw himself as breadwinner and didn't care that it might be an old-fashioned approach to life; although Danni teased her parents about it endlessly, saying they were a throwback to married life in the fifties. He earned enough as a writer for her mother to not have to think about working. He'd become very accomplished, first with a popular magazine and then, when he could afford to go it alone, as a freelancer, writing for several publications and part-time ghost-writing for people who wanted to write but couldn't. It paid well, they lived very comfortably, and he had encouraged his wife to take up hobbies to fill her time.

But she wasn't built that way.

Patricia had tried everything from gardening to cycling but nothing had caught her imagination or kept her occupied enough. It wasn't that she needed to work; she *wanted* to work, and, by chance, she had found what she was looking for.

She had done a spring clean that had cleared the house of all the clothes they no longer wore, and she ended up with a car boot full of bags, which she took to the local charity shop in the village. As she had stood in a long queue, the one member of staff rushed off her feet dealing with everyone,

28

she saw a poster pinned to the counter asking for volunteers to work there, and by the end of that week she was a new member of the team. Her husband had been horrified at the time.

'Why isn't she answering her phone?' Danni's father said, looking out of the window.

'If she's driving, you know she won't pick up.'

Her father continued pacing. Danni smiled to herself because he was always like this when her mother was back a little later than usual: acting as if the world was about to stop because the woman of the house wasn't there to put his dinner in the oven. The truth, uncomfortable as Thomas found it, was that his wife loved working at the shop and would have done more hours if she didn't think it would cause such a rift between them; she already did as many as she could get away with. When the shop had joined a nationwide appeal to raise money for a water crisis in Africa, they had set up a fundraising function with the help of the local MP, and Patricia had offered to work late until the function finished. Because the MP had arrived late, and the event had also attracted a lot of people, the function had extended into the early evening and they had done very well. Danni had received a text message from her mother earlier in the day to tell her how successful it looked like being, and it was just a shame that it had coincided with the worst weather they had seen that year, otherwise there would have been even more people there.

But it also meant that it was much later, and dark, when Patricia was due to set off, and the rain was falling heavily as the skies darkened. With thick black thunderclouds rolling in off the sea and the odd bolt of lightning in the distance but getting closer, Danni and her father watched the clock and the sky with concern. What was a fifteen to twenty minute drive on a good day could be at least double that on a night like this.

When the clock reached half-past six, Danni became more concerned. Her mother would normally call ahead if she was going to be this late. She let another fifteen minutes pass and then she left a message and sent a text, but neither received a reply.

'I told you, she must be in the car.' Danni tried to sound reassuring, but she could hear in her own voice that she wasn't as sure as she had been, and after another quarter of an hour she was as worried as her father.

All the time, the weather had been worsening. The lightning bolts lit up the sky every few minutes, while a deep growl of thunder followed each one quickly, telling them the storm was now directly above them. Thomas left his wife a third voicemail.

As the minutes ticked by, Danni realised that she didn't have any telephone numbers on her mobile phone for the shop or any of her mother's colleagues. She found the shop's number on the internet but, when she called, the out-of-hours message clicked straight in, so she ended the call and thought about what to do next.

Then she remembered something.

She went into the hall. There was an antique wooden console table with a handset on top for the home phone, which only her father used, and then only to say *no, thanks* to nuisance callers. Underneath was a large wooden drawer: her mother's drawer, full of useless items that only Patricia ever got around to sorting out, usually once every two years or so.

Neither Danni nor her father had any reason to go in there, but a few months ago Danni had looked in it for a takeaway menu, and she recalled seeing her mother's old address book.

She opened the drawer and began taking things out until she found it, with its leather-effect red cover and gold lettering, sitting at the back underneath a two-year-old pizzeria menu and one for a Chinese takeaway that had since closed down and reopened as something else. She swept some of the dust off and opened it at the first page, with A on the left-hand side and B on the right. She turned over the page and scanned the names under the letter D, quickly finding Dot, a retired lady who volunteered three days a week at the shop and someone her mother had always talked of fondly. She dialled her number, a landline.

Dot answered the phone and was concerned when Danni explained why she was calling. She had said goodbye to Patricia at a quarter to six and they had both headed for their cars. The weather and the roads were not good, Dot said, but she had still got home in well under thirty minutes.

Even allowing for them living a mile further out of the village than Dot, and the road conditions, the journey should never take more than an half an hour. Danni made sure her father couldn't hear her and made a discreet call to the local hospital, but they weren't aware of any accidents and hadn't admitted anyone in the last hour.

She took the address book and made room at the back of the drawer to put it back as she found it, but, as she forced it in, the back cover began to bend: it was being pushed against an object she couldn't see. It became wedged against the top of the table and she pulled it back towards her to try again.

A folded A4 leaflet, stuck inside the back like a bookmark, fell into the open drawer. Danni was too concerned about her mother to take much notice of it, but, as she straightened the address book's spine and back cover, something made her look at it.

It was a very faded information sheet from a charity. A missing persons charity, with contact telephone numbers. From its condition, Danni guessed it was several years old, and noted there was no internet address on it, which gave a further clue to its age. On the front were three photographs: a teenage boy, a woman in her late twenties, Danni estimated, and in the middle of them the standout image. A young, pretty blonde girl. She was smiling and probably about two years old, with a caption below that read:

MISSING: JESSICA PRESTON

Danni put out her bottom lip, staring at the girl's face. Then she folded the leaflet back up, placed it back inside the address book, and pushed it as best she could back into the drawer.

When she went back into the living room, her father was dressed in waterproofs. 'I'm going to look for her.'

Danni quickly scooped up his car keys off the sideboard and tucked them into her pocket. She looked at the rain-lashed window as another forked prong lit the sky and the whole room. 'You can't go out in this.'

'Your mother's out in it!'

The only roads in and out of the village were narrow and winding, and not the kinds of roads you drove on at night when the weather was like this.

'She's probably waiting for the rain to ease.'

'She would have called.'

'The storm might be affecting the signal. Or the mast might be down again.'

Danni was clutching at straws and knew it. The last time the mobile phone mast on the hill had stopped working was three years ago, and in a storm much more ferocious than this one. But Thomas did listen to his daughter's cautionary warning and they waited, sitting in near darkness except for when the lightning struck and illuminated the room, until the storm began to ease off and eventually, after another twenty-five minutes, finally stopped.

'We need to call the police,' Danni said as her father put his jacket and boots back on, but, as he was heading to the door, there was a loud knock on it and they looked at each other.

The next twenty minutes were a blur. Two police officers, soaked to the skin even in heavy-duty raincoats, came in and talked to them. They explained what had happened but shock hit Danni long before they finished. She only heard their first few words.

Her mother was dead.

If she had listened as her father did, she would have learned that a sharp-eyed motorist had spotted one of the roadside barriers missing on the clifftop and had called the police to notify them. When a patrol car had gone to investigate, they had seen the remains of the Ford estate car at the bottom of the ravine.

It had taken another thirty-five minutes for more police to arrive and make their way down to the wreckage, identify the car and its owner from the numberplate and find the remains of a body inside, and only after that were they able to dispatch officers to the house.

Danni couldn't recall the police leaving, or the following day when her father had to collect her mother's items, or when they went to the Chapel of Rest the next morning. She only remembered they had both fallen apart, and she had no idea how they got through those next seventy-two hours.

But somehow they must have.

And after that, her father disappeared to his study and the next time she saw him, for longer than five minutes, was at the funeral.

5 | Danni

'Bye, Mum.'

Danni mumbled the words through heavy lips and moved to her left so that her father could throw down the single rose he had been holding all morning. As he did so, he stood looking down at the hole in the ground, utterly bewildered, and Danni steadied him with a hand on his forearm because she was worried he might topple or, worse, jump into it. There was no knowing what he might do.

He had been that way pretty much since the car crash had happened two weeks ago, and Danni had tried her hardest to break down the barriers he had erected, to grieve with him; but he had spurned her efforts every time and retreated to his study in a way that made her worry if he would even make it out of there for the funeral at all. It was one of the few reasons to be grateful for the delay that had been created so that the police could finish their extensive enquiries and the coroner could record his verdict of accidental death. *A tragic waste of a life on a country road in hazardous conditions*, the coroner had written in his report, and the time he took to reach that conclusion had given Danni and her father a little more time to come to terms with their loss.

So Thomas had made it to the funeral and displayed a convincing stiff upper lip as her mother's friends and colleagues had come to the house in the late morning to follow the cars to the church. Danni had watched as he stood stoically, back straight, and sang the hymns she had chosen and listened to the prayers. Danni had even read a verse from a song by her mother's favourite singer.

As she finished the last line, her father had smiled and nodded appreciatively at Danni as she sat back down. It was the first time since the accident that he had made any real attempt to communicate with her, and she hoped that the funeral, as hard as it was, represented a form of closure; or at least the opportunity for them to begin taking tiny steps forward.

She couldn't bear another two weeks like they'd had, anyway. Not only had her father locked himself away but he had put on a ridiculous front, one of a man who was wondering what all the fuss was about. *I'm fine* was all he said to her when she enquired through the study door as to how he was, and he had tried to convince her that he was busy with his work and glad of the distraction. Yet she heard him sobbing late at night on more than one occasion.

Danni had reminded herself that he was an intensely private man, even at the best of times, and they had never enjoyed that close father-daughter relationship the way others did. From what her mother had told her, his parents – both long dead – hadn't showered their only child with love and attention either. He seemed like a throwback to a time where fathers played with their children for one hour a week, usually at the weekend. So she wasn't surprised that he chose to grieve alone, away from fuss and well-meant sympathy.

She knew he'd have struggled to cope with it too. She had taken on the tasks that needed doing, including the funeral arrangements and little things such as cancelling her mother's hair appointment and informing the bank and local council. Everyone had been so nice, so helpful and so bloody understanding, she thought, that she had wanted to run as far from them as possible. There had been a limit to the number of pitying looks and condolences she could take, and she had reached that limit surprisingly quickly.

But she had never felt lonelier in her life. She had told her friend Sam, in a call the previous evening, that it almost felt as though she had lost both of them, not just her mother. She wanted to share her pain with her father and, although she was an adult, she still needed his support. This was the first significant loss she ever had to deal with, and she had hoped that, after losing the most important person in her life, the second most important would be there for her.

But she realised it just wasn't going to be like that.

He could be a difficult man, she thought. Her mother had always brought out the best in him; she had been a warm person, not afraid to show emotion, and she had helped her husband to stop hiding behind his seemingly cold and unfriendly exterior; within the marriage, he was a warmer, more approachable person.

Until the argument the night before her mother died, Danni had always believed her parents' marriage had been near-perfect and thought that he was a great husband.

He had also been a great father too. He might not have known how to give her a hug at just the right moment, or tell her he loved her, but he had been supportive in whatever she did, and protective too.

And she hadn't ever wanted for anything. But Danni was worried, now, that her mother had been the glue that had held it all together; without her, she was concerned what might happen to them.

Yet at the funeral he had rallied a little, finding strength or at least putting on the bravest of faces. At the cemetery, Danni had been surprised at how well he had coped, shaking hands with sympathetic attendees and even engaging in brief conversation with some of them. It seemed as if half of the village had turned up, and Danni would never have managed to speak to most of them without her father's help. She hoped that he had just needed these two weeks of solitude to be able to do this. But when the congregation had drifted away and left him standing with her at the graveside, looking into the abyss, that little-boy-lost expression had quickly returned.

Danni hugged him, pulling him close, an unspoken *It's OK, Dad. We can get through this together.* But the embrace felt awkward and she could feel his body trying to escape her clutches; and, when he did, he closed back up for the rest of the day. He didn't say more than a few words at the wake, preferring to stand in the corner, looking out of the window in a pose that said *leave me alone* to anyone who thought about approaching. He left Danni to thank people for attending, while he disappeared back to the sanctuary of his study as soon as he felt he'd shown his face for long enough.

Danni watched him go, and knew all she could do was be there for him, until he was ready to open up or until he needed her as much as she needed him.

It was what her mother would have wanted.

6 | Danni

'How you holding up?'

The question made Danni jump even though she knew who it was asking it. She had retreated to the kitchen to begin loading some of the dirty plates into the dishwasher so that there was less to do when everyone had gone. There were just a few people left now, in the living room finishing off the last of the buffet and recounting tales about Patricia.

'Euan,' she said. 'I didn't hear you come in.'

She knew she sounded disappointed he was there, and wished she had concealed it a little better. She'd thought he had already left; a discussion with him was the last thing she wanted now.

'I know you don't want to see me, but I couldn't just leave without at least saying hello,' he said from the doorway, where his six-foot frame filled most of the space. 'And I really liked your mum, Dan.'

Danni bristled. Only her best friend had permission to call her that and she hated it when anyone else did, but she was too tired to say. Neither did she say that her mother had never liked him back, and her father even less so.

'Is Carol still here?' she asked. 'I haven't spoken to her yet.'

'She had to get back to work. She sends her love.'

Danni had enjoyed a better relationship with Euan's mother, Carol, right from the day they met. She was a very young mother, so she was in her mid-thirties now and by her own admission making up for lost time, so she'd always called

Danni to meet for drinks or a coffee after work. They'd become friends, and, had it not been for Carol, she wondered if her relationship with Euan might have been considerably shorter.

'I'll call and thank her for coming.'

The last of the guests were hovering in the hallway, readying themselves to go, so Danni went to see them out while Euan took her place in the kitchen and put the rest of the plates in the dishwasher. All of her mother's colleagues from the charity shop had attended – they'd closed the shop for the day out of respect – and Dot, the first to arrive and last to leave, hugged Danni warmly and told her to let her know if she could do anything. She told her she would and closed the front door behind them.

'You didn't need to do that,' she said, walking back into the kitchen.

'It's no bother.'

Danni moved towards the door and, although she tried to avoid making it obvious, she glanced at the clock. Euan either saw her or sensed what she'd done and smiled.

'I'd better be making a move myself.'

She felt guilty. She wanted him out of there, but, as soon as he acknowledged it, she felt she didn't want him to go, if only because she didn't want to be alone. 'I'm sorry. I just—'

He put a comforting hand on her shoulder. For the final weeks of their relationship she had dreaded being with him, but he had always had a gentle, caring side that just didn't come out enough.

'You don't need to say anything,' he said with a smile, 'I'll see myself out.'

Danni nodded and smiled meekly. She found herself holding her tongue, wanting to say something but knowing she shouldn't. She closed her eyes and, when she opened them, Euan was already in the hallway.

'You don't have to,' she called.

He turned. Confused.

'Go, I mean.'

She was at her most vulnerable, but she had been alone for two weeks and it felt a lot longer.

He walked back in the room. 'I thought—'

'Don't think,' she said, an overwhelming urge rising up in her body to feel something and be with someone. She realised she wasn't really fussed at that moment who that someone was; anything was better than the numbness she'd experienced in the last fortnight.

He stepped close to her and she gripped his shirt and pulled him to her, and kissed him as hard as she could, releasing more built-up anger than passion. His hands wrapped around her and she reached down and pulled his shirt out of the waistband of his suit trousers.

Then she stopped, took his hand and led him through the house, up the stairs and past her father's study. She put her finger to her lips as they passed the door, not really sure if she cared whether he heard them.

They reached her bedroom, and she closed the door behind them and pushed Euan down so that he was sitting on the edge of her single bed. She was in control now and, although she was far from sexually experienced, she knew he wasn't either.

She stood in between his feet and turned so her back was to him. 'Unzip.'

He did as she asked. Danni slipped her knee-length black dress down over her shoulders so that it fell to the floor, and turned around to face him. His eyes widened and she opened the clasp on her bra and let that fall too, momentarily instinctively covering her breasts with one arm but then, feeling more confident, dropping it down by her side. Her heart was beating quickly but she felt no emotion; nothing except that, at that very moment, she wanted Euan for no better reason than that he happened to be in the right place at the right time.

Danni stepped forward so that he could touch her and he pulled her forward, pushing his head against her body and kissing her belly and then her breast, his teeth gently gripping her nipple. She felt a rush of exhilaration and began to undo the top button of Euan's shirt, and then pulled it roughly over his head and arms, but the cuffs were too tight and he had to help her. They both giggled like naughty children.

At the other end of the hallway there was the sound of a toilet flushing that made them stop and look at each other. They heard the bathroom door close and then the study door slam shut.

Danni wondered if it was her father's clumsy attempt to remind her that he was in the house, but she dismissed it and pressed her body back against Euan's, and he put his hands on her sides, running them down over her hips until they reached the material of her knickers. He paused, as if he was waiting for permission.

Danni knew that if his hands moved another inch there was no turning back, and the last thing she'd expected to be doing on the night of her mother's funeral was having sex. But now, in the moment, it felt right, or maybe not as wrong as she would have imagined it would, and she kissed the top of his head, silently acknowledging that he could continue, so he slid her knickers down over her thighs and past her knees and they fell to the ground at her feet. As Euan moved his head down and forward to kiss her between her legs, she gasped, and a pang of guilt ran the length of her body.

Danni wasn't sure if she felt bad about what she was doing because they had only just buried her mother, because her father was but a few yards down the hallway, or because she was shamelessly using Euan and had absolutely no intention of it going anywhere beyond the night.

She put her hands on the back of his head, grabbing his hair and pushed his face into her body. She was going to look after her own needs for now.

She'd worry about the rest in the morning.

7 | Laura

Laura Grainger hated Tuesdays.

She hadn't always, but the resentment had grown, and now it was the day of the week she dreaded, especially in the winter.

Tuesday was dog-walking day and started early, well before it was light and more than an hour before she usually got up. On a bleak January morning like this one, there was very little she could imagine that was worse.

She didn't need an alarm on a Tuesday. Her dog – on any other day he was the family dog, but he was very much *her* dog on a Tuesday – was already whining and pawing expectantly at the back door of the house, waking her in the bedroom directly above. Laura groaned, checked the clock and switched off the alarm she had set on her phone. She slowly climbed out of her warm bed and pulled the bedroom curtain to one side. The only light was the faint orange glow from a lamp-post, only just visible through the sea mist that was hanging over the road. A crisp frost had settled over everything, but at least it was dry, she thought, as she pulled on three layers of clothing and trudged downstairs.

Ten minutes later she stood at the bottom of the coastal path, at the point where the path turned back on itself and the steps down the beach began. She wasn't going that far, it was too dark beyond that point, so she stood waiting for her dog to do what he had to.

'Come on,' she muttered.

Her dog was a King Charles spaniel that had been a present for her eleventh birthday, a reward for persistence after many years of asking for a puppy. It had been a dream come true, and she'd promptly christened him Mimark, a word she'd heard once on TV and liked even though she had no idea what it meant, and had resolved to give as a name to her first pet. When her father brought him home, he had sat there, all big drooping ears and oversized paws that it would take him the best part of a year to grow into, and she'd put a pretty red bow on him and promised her parents she would always take care of him.

Her dog was now an old boy with a greying chin, who dragged one of his hind legs behind him and had the weakest bladder imaginable. He did everything at his own pace and exactly when he wanted to; so if Laura needed him to be quick – for example, on a freezing winter morning when she was probably going to be late for work – then he would almost certainly do the opposite.

'Please, Mimark.' She even thought the name sounded idiotic now. The dog looked up and carried on sniffing around the foot of the tree stump. Laura rubbed her hands together and then pressed them against each other tightly, as though she was praying, which she could easily have been.

Every other day, her father did this routine, but on Tuesdays the job was hers because there was an early-morning staff meeting at the hospital where her father worked and he liked to stop at the petrol station for a bacon sandwich he thought no one knew about. Her mother had long ago refused to take Mimark anywhere after he had excitedly tried to chase a rabbit down the coastal path and pulled her so hard she had twisted her knee.

That dog, so full of energy and strength, was hard to imagine now. Laura watched as he plodded around, sniffing bushes and knocking frost off with his nose, while she stamped up and down to warm her toes and stop them going numb.

'Just get it over with, will you?'

Finally the dog did what she asked, and Laura clipped on his lead and desperately tried to hurry proceedings by pulling him along behind her until they reached the house. It was only just after half-past seven, and her father had left barely forty minutes ago, but the house was dark and cold when she got back and she quickly made herself a drink and some porridge while Mimark drank his water and ate the biscuits she'd poured into his bowl. Then she rushed upstairs into the shower, dried her hair, put her make-up on in double-quick time and dressed as quickly as she could, constantly checking the clock; if she was lucky she'd only be five minutes late for work.

As she manoeuvred her old but reliable red VW Polo off the drive and drove down the hill into the town centre, she cursed several times as not one but three dustbin lorries held her up in quick succession – another reason why Tuesdays were not her favourite day, especially if you were in a hurry to get anywhere before eight forty-five. That was the unusual start time for work at the town's weekly newspaper, the *Gazette*, where she worked as a junior trainee – and her boss was a stickler for punctuality. As it was closer, she swerved through the entrance to the small staff car park, one she hardly ever used, and found a space in the corner that few cars would attempt to fit into, but she had neither the luxury of choice nor any concern for her car's bodywork; it already had more scratches than she could keep track of. She anxiously checked her watch as she ran up the stairs and hoped that David Weatherall, editor, owner and basically the only person with any power, wasn't in his office.

But, as she walked briskly into the modest second-floor offices to join the rest of the newspaper's overworked staff, it was already past ten to nine, so she put her head down and made a beeline for her desk.

'Morning, Laura.'

David was sitting at his desk, and he looked at the office clock on the far wall rather than at her when he spoke.

'Morning. Sorry I'm late,' she called, already unbuttoning her coat and throwing her leather satchel so that it landed heavily among the clutter on her desk. Tuesday was never a good day at the paper if you were the most junior member of staff, because the stories that had built up over the weekend had already been allocated, and that meant you got the leftovers or, even worse than that, the dull administrative tasks no one wanted.

David Weatherall was the driving force behind the publication, having the absolute final say on everything and anything. He was revered by the rest of the staff, so much that when they talked about him it was always using his full name, never just David. When Laura had been taken on, she had quickly realised that everyone who worked at the paper was either scared of him or in awe of him, usually both. After just one week, Laura had certainly known she was.

As she had got to know him better, or as well as anyone could get to know such a man, she'd realised he had only two moods. He was always either miserable or annoyed; and sometimes he managed to combine the two. He was in his early sixties, with a healthy head full of whitish-grey hair and neatly trimmed moustache of the same shade. He was proudly old-fashioned but he harked back to the 'good ole days' a bit too much for Laura's liking, talking about the halcyon days of newspaper publishing as if they were better than sliced bread, while treating the digital age like a blight on society. When she had first joined the paper and suggested they send out a tweet about that day's main headline, she'd thought he was going to have a stroke.

As Laura hurriedly opened up her laptop, his head appeared from his office door and looked over in her direction.

'Laura, I have some filing for you.'

'Can I just check my emails first?'

'When you arrive on time you can check emails first. The filing, please.'

Laura went to his office and collected the files he'd been working on, three cardboard boxes' worth, and pushed them in a trolley to the Records Room, a dusty, stale-smelling room in the building's basement. It was the kind of place you would send someone you didn't like, which was about right, Laura thought, as she began putting the files back in their rightful place.

She had no expectation of David's ever becoming her biggest fan – he hadn't wanted to recruit her in the first place – and unless he suddenly decided to retire and hand over the reins to someone else she knew she was unlikely to further her career at the paper, and she would be stuck doing jobs like this for a while yet. But, she reminded herself, it was a *job*, and not everyone was finding one of those after graduating.

She spent the rest of the morning putting paper into cardboard folders; only in her daydreams could she picture being asked to follow proper leads, and being the reporter behind a real story, and then reality always kicked back in.

Her thoughts turned from journalism to the weekend because, unusually for her, she was going out. She had arranged to meet some friends for a drink, two girls she'd met during her university years, and she was really looking forward to it.

It was another reason for hating Tuesdays. They were far enough away from the previous weekend that you had all but forgotten it ever happened, but so far from the next one, it felt as if you would never get there.

8 | Laura

Laura's red VW Polo climbed the hill and turned into the small side road that didn't look as though it led anywhere but the sea.

She drove to the bottom, past the field and the stile that led to the path to the coast, and turned into a tiny cul-de-sac with just four houses nestled in the hill that sat above the beach. She got out wearily and opened the iron gates at the furthest house, then drove up the driveway and parked next to her mother's car, checking she'd left enough room for her father to squeeze past and put his car in the garage. Tuesdays were a long day for him, with the staff meeting, another meeting with the department heads and then his actual shift, and Laura knew he would be lucky to be home before seven.

Helen Grainger was standing in the kitchen making the evening meal when Laura trudged in through the back door. Mimark briefly raised his head out of curiosity as he lay in his basket, and she bent down and ran her fingers through his fur.

'Hi,' she said, and gave her mother a kiss on the cheek, smelling the red wine on her breath, and in return received a hug that was usually reserved for people she hadn't seen in years; Laura had to extricate herself out of her grip to sit down.

'Good day?'

It had been one of the least good days she'd had at the *Gazette*, and there had been quite a few to compare it with. But Laura preferred not to spend any more time talking about it on top of actually being there, and she hoped her mother would take the hint.

'Fine,' she shrugged as Helen put a glass of wine in front of her. 'Bit early, isn't it?'

'If you don't want it…'

There was a glint in Helen's eye as she said it and Laura smiled, picked up the glass and took a sip, and realised it was exactly what she needed. She sat and watched as her mother multi-tasked around the kitchen, firmly pressing the edges down on a meat pie she had made that afternoon. If she did nothing else in a day, she would diligently prepare a family meal for them, timed to perfection to coincide with her husband walking through the door at the end of his shift; he would call ahead from the car with an estimated time that was rarely out by more than a minute. If you wanted to miss the meal – and Laura rarely did – then you needed a very good excuse and to give plenty of prior notice.

Robert Grainger was one of the most prominent surgeons at the nearest hospital, a relatively large one with a big and densely populated catchment area. As well as some of the key specialist units, it also had the largest A&E ward outside of one of the county's main towns. He was an industrious worker, and it wasn't a surprise to see him clock up as many as fourteen working hours in a day.

'So, not such a good day?' Laura's mother pushed the pie to one side and took an egg from the fridge.

'It was OK.'

'I thought you liked your job.'

'I do.'

Her mother put the offcuts of pastry into the bin and Laura knew exactly where the conversation was going.

'You know your father had to pull a few strings to get you in there,' she reminded her for what seemed like the thousandth time, as she broke the egg and beat it in a bowl.

'I know, Mum. It's fine, really. I just spent all day filing, that's all.'

'Ah – instead of writing front-page stories?'

'Don't take the piss.'

'I'm not,' Helen protested with a smile, 'and mind your language.'

Laura smiled.

'But I'm just saying. Filing comes with the territory, doesn't it? For a trainee?'

Laura shrugged. 'Of course.'

'So you have to get on with it. You've—'

'Got time on my side, I know.'

Her mother began brushing the beaten egg over the pie, and looked over her glasses at the recipe book perched up on the worktop. Laura thought she resembled a wise old owl when she cooked. Hair tied back, putting ten years on her, and the glasses adding at least another five, she worked meticulously while still finding time to dole out advice and sip from a large glass of Cabernet Sauvignon.

'I bet even – I don't know, the best journalist in the world started out doing some filing.'

Laura nodded without really listening. She wanted to tell her that she doubted she would ever do anything much more exciting than filing if it was up to David Weatherall, but her mother showed so much confidence in her, she thought better of it.

Laura had to tread carefully when it came to her career choice. Her parents had both tried very hard to talk her out of journalism, citing the unpredictability, instability and even dangers involved, and she had fought them every step of the way. Her father had been determined to convince her to take a better path, maybe into medicine like him, but she'd dug her heels in, and eventually they had been the ones who'd conceded.

So she could hardly complain now. But she had expected so much more when she completed her GCSEs with good grades and two A-levels before enrolling on a media studies degree course and after that another media course and then a separate qualification specific to journalism. It had taken four years, and her parents had become increasingly supportive as the time went by.

But, when she finished studying, the excitement had been knocked out of her by the reality of the job market. The recession had hit the media sector hard, and when she went for a job – for even the most junior roles at small publications – she was one of hundreds of media studies graduates or unemployed journalists who applied, and in the first year she managed to secure only a handful of interviews, none of which ended with a job offer. She'd ended up taking part-time bar work to make ends meet.

She knew it would have been easy for her parents to say they told her so, but instead they rallied behind her, buying her a car and not taking any payment for her keep, so that she could get herself a foothold. Her father, whose own parents had told him to forget his fanciful ideas of becoming a surgeon, even went to the local newspaper that had rejected her application six months earlier, and put in a word with the editor. Unknown to Laura at the time, David's wife had undergone an operation to remove a cyst a few years earlier, and complications had set in during what should have been a routine procedure. At the time, late at night with a skeleton staff, the situation had escalated and she could easily have died, had it not been for a surgeon who had already left for the day but answered an emergency call and returned, refusing to give in until he'd pulled her through and, in all likelihood, saved her life.

The surgeon was one Robert Grainger, M.Ch. and, although he was not a man to call in favours lightly, he had gone against his principles and done so on this occasion, prompting David to offer Laura a job as a trainee, on a low wage and with absolutely no guarantees but it was the foot on the ladder she craved. It was one of the reasons she didn't object too strongly when the editor gave her so few leads and so many admin tasks. He was a proud man, and he wouldn't have enjoyed having his arm twisted like that. And her mother was right: everyone did have to start somewhere and, unless you were amazingly lucky, that somewhere was usually at the bottom. And it had only been six months. If nothing else, it had given her a solid grounding and an insight into the less glamorous aspects of the role.

'You'll appreciate it more when you do make it.'

Laura watched her mother put the pie into the double oven built into the units of the spectacular kitchen. Despite his struggles to convince his parents he could, her father *had* made it, and the house was testament to that.

She sighed and took another sip of her wine. Having her father get her a job had been no fun for her either. It felt as if she had to prove herself to him and David, and as if she had to work harder than her colleagues to get the respect she deserved.

She wanted to show her parents what she was really made of. If only David would give her a break from the dusty basement and hand her a real story, she'd show him too.

She just needed that one chance.

9 | Laura

If Laura was going to get a chance to shine, it wasn't that week.

If the filing on Tuesday had been an unpleasant part of her junior role, by Friday she would gladly have taken any amount of boxes into that basement and spent all day there. Saturday evening couldn't come soon enough for her.

Wednesday started badly. Sue Montgomery, David's trusted personal assistant and the only person in the world, Laura thought, who could possibly put up with him for as long as she had, came into the office with a face that was a ghastly shade of Wicked Witch green and by ten past nine she had already been sick twice in the toilets. This prompted David to ask Kelly Heath, one of the *Gazette*'s senior reporters, to drop her home on the way to her next meeting.

Laura had never known Sue to be off other than the odd holiday, when she would organise a temp to cover her absence. But without warning David was lost without her, and he asked Laura to help him with some of Sue's tasks. She quickly established that this meant taking on the less glamorous parts of Sue's duties, and David started by dictating a letter he wanted her to type out, but did so at full 'Sue-speed' and Laura couldn't keep up. She was too afraid to tell him, but when she had typed it and printed it for him he promptly tore it up and made her start again – and that, unfortunately, was as good as it got for the rest of the day.

The following morning, Sue called to say she felt even worse, and Laura ended up with the editor again, despite her protests that there must be better options. Thursday was the day Sue put the weekly performance statistics together, and it was an exercise that should have taken no more than an hour. But it took David almost that hour to explain what he wanted, and when Laura started compiling the data it went fairly well until she made the mistake of suggesting an improvement that she thought might also save some time in future. David lost his temper, and she had to finish it off with a tense atmosphere hanging over them that lasted for the rest of the day.

By Friday, the editor had become utterly miserable and seemed to be on a mission to make everyone suffer. Two reporters had called in with the same sickness bug that Sue had, which worsened his mood, but mercifully, Laura thought, Sue was back at her desk, although not looking at all well; an obvious fact that David pretended not to notice.

Laura found herself in his office just before lunch when she took in some work she had finished off from the previous day, and he kept her there to explain, in precise detail, how disappointed he was with her recent performance. When she tried to argue that she had been covering Sue's absence and should be judged on her own work, he said he was referring to that as well, so she gave up, took her medicine and got an empathetic smile from Sue on her way back to her desk. Laura had learned, early on in her employment, that you didn't engage in a debate with David when he was in this kind of mood. It was well known that he liked to give someone a proper dressing-down to make himself feel better, so Laura had at least spared everyone else in the office an afternoon of criticism, and she got a few nods of approval from them afterwards.

'Thanks for taking one for the team.'

Laura hadn't noticed that Kelly Heath had come back to the office while she was in with David. She smiled. 'Glad to help.'

'Want to help even more?'

Kelly was a rising star at the *Gazette* and could do no wrong in David's eyes. She always seemed to get the best stories and, even if she didn't, she often turned them into better ones than they started off as being. Laura asked her what she needed. 'Jane's off sick and we had a few interviews lined up for tomorrow,' Kelly told her.

Jane was Kelly's usual partner on any stories that required more than one reporter.

'Tomorrow?'

'Means giving up a bit of your weekend. And David's not the quickest at paying for overtime.'

'Doesn't matter. I'll help.'

Laura noted that Kelly seemed surprised. 'Great. I owe you one.'

Laura smiled as Kelly gave her the details for the next day and left the office. Laura watched her suspiciously. People like Kelly Heath rarely did anyone any favours unless there was something in it for them.

The next day was a more sobering experience than Laura had anticipated. She had always read Kelly's stories with a sense that she lived the life of a proper journalist: close to the edge, skirting danger and meeting lots of interesting characters. But they spent half of the day hanging around waiting to interview people who didn't want to talk to them, and the other half waiting for a protest march that was cancelled at the eleventh hour after last-ditch talks between the local residents and council officials.

'Does this happen a lot?' she asked as they walked back to Kelly's car.

'What? Non-stories?'

Laura nodded.

'More than you'd think,' Kelly said as she opened her door.

Laura got in the passenger seat so that Kelly could drop her off at her own car. 'Really?'

'It's not as exciting as you thought, is it?'

Laura shrugged. 'At least it shows David I can handle more than filing.'

'I'm sure he knows that.'

'He thinks that's all I'm good for, and if it weren't for my dad I probably wouldn't even be doing that.'

Laura had never mentioned her father's influence in her getting the job, and she presumed the others didn't know either. Kelly smiled but didn't press her to say more, and Laura was grateful. She already regretted saying as much as she had, about her father and her job. Kelly was such a favourite of David's, she couldn't say with certainty that anything she said wouldn't get back to him.

'Well, if you want a long career at the *Gazette*,' Kelly laughed as they pulled away, 'you'd better get used to days like this one.'

10 | Laura

By the time Laura left Kelly and made the short drive home, she was already running behind schedule, and she gave her mother her phone and asked her to send a text message to her friends to tell them.

'I'll run you in,' Helen called to her as she ran up the stairs.

'I can get a cab.'

'It's no problem.'

Laura almost ran through the shower rather than spending any time under it and quickly got changed into her least journalist-looking clothes; she had never been one for dresses or anything flashy, so she made do with a black sweater and jeans.

'They said they'll be in Gordon's,' her mother shouted over the drone of the hairdryer as she finished getting ready. 'Is that the new wine bar they've just opened?'

Laura smiled. She knew her mother liked to think she knew all the places in town but if she was honest it had been ten years since she'd set foot in any of them, and this 'new' bar had opened more than twelve months ago.

A few minutes later they were in Helen's car and driving down the hill towards the small town centre. It was a very quiet place every other night of the week, but it had garnered a reputation as a good place to go on a Saturday, and hundreds of people between the ages of sixteen and sixty flooded in from the surrounding villages. Since the relaxation of pub opening hours it had become quite a lively centre, and there were large groups in the streets as Helen tried to find a spot to drop Laura off.

'There's a lot of lads about.'

'It's Saturday, there always are.'

'Well, be careful.'

'Mum!'

They pulled up in a parking space outside the mini-supermarket so that Laura could get some money from the ATM before she walked the short distance to Gordon's, a refurbished bar that had once been called a wine bar but now considered itself far more sophisticated; it also had by far the most expensive price list in town, so the plan was to have one drink there and move on afterwards.

'I mean be careful who you talk to.'

'I'm not twelve, Mum.'

'I'm just saying.'

Laura had known the offer of a lift into town would not be without motive. Her mother wasn't that keen on her being out at night, and the longer she could spend with her and know she had arrived safely, the better she would feel. As it was, Laura rarely ventured out in the evening, and into town even less, preferring to stay home and read or go to the cinema on the retail park. But she had also promised her friends that she would have a night out with them and she couldn't cancel again – she'd done it twice already. And with the week she'd had, she was actually looking forward to some girl talk and putting her job to the back of her mind.

One of the problems with the town was that there were so few people her age living there. Nearly all her schoolfriends had left for jobs or further education and not come back after university. One of her favourite remarks when asked about the town by outsiders was to say the busiest place was the funeral directors; there were three of them in a row on the high street, just to prove her point. At work, the next-youngest person was six years older than her, and nearly all the staff were married with children or about to start families. She found she had very little in common with any of them. So she enjoyed the rare opportunity to catch up with people her own age and recall some of their university antics.

As planned, they had one expensive drink in Gordon's and then moved to a student bar that sold cheap cocktails all night, before settling at a third place, a large pub that played music into the early hours and attracted a large crowd. They decided to stay there until closing time or when they'd had enough; whichever came first, but, as they weren't seasoned drinkers, by midnight all three of them were showing signs of being ready to go.

'Let's have one more,' said Laura, letting the alcohol in her do the talking. It was also her turn to buy and she didn't want them to think she didn't pay her way, so she went to the bar to order another round.

'Laura,' a voice said from behind her as she stood trying to attract the bartender's attention. 'I thought it was you!'

She turned, but she already knew who the distinctive and overly confident Australian accent belonged to. Brian Hales had been one of the more interesting aspects of her media studies course and she'd sometimes spent a quarter of the lecture or more just observing him. He was a few inches over six feet, with naturally wavy light brown hair and a smile full of glistening white teeth. His mannerisms could be mistaken for arrogance but, as Laura had watched him and later got to know him, she had realised it was simply confidence. He had an annoyingly strong ability to always know what to say, and was always the centre of attention. He towered above most people, and his smile could light up rooms on its own.

'Brian!'

They hugged a little awkwardly, or certainly it felt awkward for Laura, as she realised, mid-hug, that he had seen her naked on probably more than a hundred occasions.

'What are you doing here?' she said, blushing.

She had been attracted to him from the first lecture, and her friends had been too, but none of them had spoken to him until three weeks into the course, when he had come over to her in the canteen and introduced himself and then begun flirting outrageously with her, and she'd found herself reciprocating against her better judgement.

And just like that they had clicked, skipped their afternoon lectures and gone to the cinema and then back to her student flat. After that, without having a conversation about it, they had developed a mutual understanding that they would meet once a week at Laura's flat after her last lecture of the day and Brian's rugby training session and have sex, usually in the shower, as there was more room than in her single bed.

They had never become a couple and the relationship had never developed beyond that arrangement, even though they enjoyed each other's company when they were together. Laura had known she had way too much on her plate for a full-blown relationship, and Brian was arguably even busier than she was, as he combined studies with playing so much sport. When they graduated, the arrangement had ended, again without them talking about it, and they hadn't stayed in touch.

'Rugby match,' he shouted over the music, and nodded to his right, where a group of young men with perfectly toned torsos were play-fighting in a much-too-small corner of the bar and making a lot of noise.

'Did you win?'

'By forty points.'

'Naturally,' Laura said. Brian Hales didn't lose at many things. She watched as two of his team mates downed their pints with ease.

'Who are you here with?' he asked, and she pointed over at her friends.

She tried to keep the conversation going above the shouting and music, but it wasn't easy although Brian managed to tell her he was doing well at a mobile communications company and had been promoted to a new post in London. Laura nodded, a little impressed but more confused at what that had to do with media studies and a little jealous too. Brian was a male version of Kelly Heath, for whom being successful came very easily. If he'd wanted to be a journalist, she thought, he'd probably have had a great job with a great publication land on his lap rather than have to work his way up by doing years of filing. He asked about her job, so she told him about the paper but found herself talking up some of the details so that it sounded as though she was Kelly's main rival for the top stories, and then she realised her friends were waiting for their drinks and went back to them before he could ask any more questions.

At just after half-past midnight, the three girls stood outside the bar and said their goodbyes as the next taxi rolled forward from the queue. They had told Laura to get in, but, as she gave them a final hug, Brian Hales called her name.

'You go,' she said. 'I'm just going to say goodnight to Brian.'

They looked at her, pulled knowing faces, got inside instead and waved as the taxi drove away. Brian was a little more drunk now, and flirting again, and they picked up their conversation, talking about university and who they'd kept in touch with: Brian, virtually everyone who played sport, and Laura, just the two girls who had just left in the taxi.

'Good times,' the Australian said, nodding.

'Mmm.'

'Pity you haven't still got your flat.'

He laughed and winked, his way of pretending he was just having a joke with her, but Laura knew him a little better than that and he had never been as subtle as he thought he was. But she wasn't offended. There was enough history between them for neither to be embarrassed. She wasn't the girl on campus he could just meet up with for sex any more, but she was still single and still very attracted to him.

'I only live ten minutes away,' she said. 'If you don't have plans.'

'Didn't you say you lived with your folks?'

She felt her cheeks get hot. 'Yes. But I have my own room and everything.'

Brian laughed.

She took his hand as a taxi pulled up at the kerb and they jumped in and took the short journey to her house, his hand gently squeezing her thigh for the entire journey.

The cul-de-sac was dark and silent, with just the orange light from the street-lamp in the distance showing them where to go once the taxi had pulled away. It was nearly one o'clock, and Laura giggled nervously as she walked down the drive and found her keys and tried, several times, to put them into the door. Then she took Brian's hand again and led him into the hall.

'Laura?'

A light came on and her father was standing at the top of the stairs in his pyjamas.

'Dad!'

She instinctively let go of Brian's hand.

'I thought I heard someone,' Robert said, rubbing his eyes but not fooling his daughter one bit. She knew he had been awake all the time, waiting for her to get back, probably watching out of the window, she thought. He didn't look very impressed.

'Sorry, I didn't mean to wake you.'

'I was just nodding off.' He smiled as he walked down the stairs still looking sceptically at the boy with her. 'Are you going to…?'

Laura took a second to register what he meant.

'Sorry, this is…er, Brian. A friend from uni. I told you about him, remember?'

She knew she almost certainly hadn't, but it sounded better that they shared a past, and her father didn't know, or need to know, that the past they shared had only fulfilled one basic need.

Robert eyed the tall Aussie up and down and held out his hand. Her father was at least four inches shorter and two stone lighter, but she could have sworn she saw Brian take a tiny backward step, and for the first time it seemed the charm and right words had momentarily escaped him.

'Well, Brian,' he said as they shook hands, 'thank you for getting Laura home safely.'

'No bother, Mr Grainger.' Brian nodded and smiled, glancing at Laura, who half-smiled back; both had quickly established that their brief reacquaintance was over.

'Goodnight, Brian,' her father said.

'Night,' said the Aussie with a nod, and closed the door behind him.

Robert looked at his daughter. 'He seemed nice.'

Laura nodded and watched as her father walked back up the stairs.

'Night, love,' he said at the top.

'Night, Dad,' she said, and followed him up.

Part Two

The day after she was taken...

It felt as if I was waking up with a hangover after a heavy night.

I opened my eyes; the room was hazy, sun creeping in through the gaps in the Venetian blinds and laying pencil-thin lines across the duvet with laser precision.

There was a split second – maybe not even that long – when it felt as though it might have just been a dream. A weird, warped dream, so vivid and intense, but a dream nevertheless; all I had to do was wake up from it. But I was already awake, and the realisation of the awful truth quickly found its way to the forefront of my consciousness.

We had done it.

It was real.

I opened my eyes fully and looked at the alarm clock. It was a few minutes before six o'clock and, outside, it looked as if another gloriously sunny day was in store, but inside our bedroom it was bleak, as though we had our own little black cloud, just for us. It wasn't hard to see a storm was brewing, somewhere off in the distance but moving towards us; a storm that I knew was only going to get worse and from which there was no escape.

I let my eyes close for a moment and saw them, those two shell-shocked parents on that beach, wandering around with jerky movements, turning this way and that, as if they were lost, and with not a clue which way to turn next – but all the roads led nowhere anyway.

I quickly opened my eyes again.

We'd barely slept. My wife had tossed and turned through the night; I couldn't say if she'd managed to drift off for even a second but she hadn't cried any more and that was something, although it may have been because she'd run out of tears at that point. When we'd put the child in a makeshift bed in a hastily arranged spare room, she'd stayed with her for twenty minutes, stroking her hair and humming softly until she went to sleep.

The child.

That was what she was at that moment. Little more than a commodity; like one of those dolls you could pick up from the shop on the promenade for £4.99. She didn't even have a name, let alone an identity. Yet even without them, even as a commodity, she had fixed the damage to my wife that had until now seemed irreparable, and in that alone she had already achieved something I'd not been able to do.

Did my wife even know it yet? Did she feel as if she was no longer broken? I rolled over to her side of the bed to face her.

She wasn't there.

I got up, worried at first and then not; it was so obvious and I knew exactly where she'd be, so I tiptoed across the bedroom and on to the landing and put my head slowly around the half-open door of the next bedroom, a spare room that wasn't spare any more.

She was lying in that tiny bed, fast asleep, all curled up so that her legs didn't protrude from the end. In front of her, also asleep, was the little girl; their breathing in unison, my wife's arm wrapped over her, keeping the bedcovers in place. The sun was creeping into this room too, and lit up their faces.

That image, on its own, made it worth the risk; even though I knew there was every chance we wouldn't make it. I suspected that one day – maybe the next day, next week, maybe years down the line – a misplaced word could bring it all crashing down on our heads. I knew that one day someone might ask the wrong question – or the right one, depending on your perspective – at the wrong time and we'd have nowhere to go and this little girl might learn the terrible truth about us.

But that was for another day.

That child became more real then and no longer a £4.99 doll. She became this beautiful thing that would glue everything back together and make the future very different from the one I'd foreseen less than twenty-four hours earlier.

I took one last look at them and left them to sleep. My wife, without even knowing it, looked happy again, not broken any more; and, for me, it was the moment I knew I'd made the right decision not to call the police.

There was no longer any doubt in my mind.

That child was ours now.

That next day, I found myself lying in a strange bed.

There was a tiny moment among all the sleeplessness and crying when I must have drifted off through sheer exhaustion, and I awoke with a start and with the briefest, and cruellest, sliver of hope that it might have all been a really bad dream, and not real.

One look outside reminded me it was very real. At least a dozen vans and cars belonging to television news outlets were parked up on the seafront hotel car park; and I remembered they'd put us up there so we could be close to the beach in case she turned up.

Having hardly slept, instead watching a seemingly endless loop on the local news until the early hours of the morning, I started that next day with a thunderous headache, a sore throat that let out barely more than a pathetic croak, and the horrible sensation that millions of pairs of eyes were looking at me, even when I was alone.

Todd was no help at all. He said he was sure that, if she had been taken, whoever did it would come to their senses and bring her back. 'You don't just steal a child!' he kept saying – but then, he didn't really think she had been taken. Not by a person anyway. He was sure it was the water that had taken her, and I knew that because, every time he said her name, he would instinctively look in the direction of the sea. I wanted to punch him when he did that, and when he sat feeling sorry for himself and asked if he could have been a better father and I wanted desperately to tell him yes, he could have been. If only he'd spent as much time with his kids as he had under those bloody cars, or if only he'd been as interested in what Jessica was doing as he was in those bloody sports pages.

Then maybe they wouldn't have to be looking for her.

The police liaison officer was even less helpful. 'No stone will be left unturned' was her go-to line, but all I could see were divers scouring the water and people combing the beach for clues, and, when I asked if they were knocking on doors and stopping cars, she just reverted to her default position. I was so angry, yet I couldn't make them understand.

Looking back, I should have been more rational – spoken to someone higher up the chain – but instead I let them convince me that they knew best, knew better than a mother and her maternal instincts, and I stood by and watched it unfold right in front of me.

The only person I shouted at, quite ridiculously, was my son, Stuart, as if an eight-year-old could be responsible for what had happened – but that didn't stop me. Why hadn't he been looking out for his sister? Why hadn't he told us she wasn't with him?

Why this? Why that?

I was just looking for someone to blame, and he was the easiest of the targets available to me. And my asking *why* was just to give me a break from all the *if only*s. You see, the hardest thing, in those moments when the whole world is spinning around you and you just want to find the button to press stop and get off, is the feeling that it could all have been avoided if you'd just done things differently.

If only I'd not read that magazine. If only I'd taken her to get an ice-cream. If only I'd not taken my eye off her. If only I'd seen which direction she was headed. If only we hadn't decided to go to the beach. If only it had been raining. If only we'd been happy with one child.

But the distraction of blame wasn't masking the sense of inevitability that I felt so strongly. There was an indelible conclusion that Todd, the police liaison officer and probably everyone else had already reached at that point, but just wouldn't say to my face, probably for fear of breaking me completely.

My daughter wasn't coming back.

11 | Danni

Danni wasn't making any headway with her father.

A week had passed since the funeral, a week Thomas had spent cocooned in his study, carefully avoiding her by keeping irregular mealtimes and pretending he was busy or that he hadn't heard her. Rather than fight him, she was waiting for him to come round in his own time, although she hoped he'd hurry up.

By contrast, Danni herself was coping better than she expected.

She wasn't sleeping well – her dreams kept waking her in the early hours and leaving her mind scrambled – but she had managed to go back to work the day after the funeral. She manned the reception desk at the dental practice that her family had used since she was five years old, and, when she got home each evening at twenty past five, she cooked and left a meal outside the study door and then did some housework. It had quickly become a ritual – a new one for her because her mother had always insisted on taking care of everything, but one that kept her suitably focused, and distracted.

It also took up most of her time. Although her father was virtually invisible, she didn't like to leave him, so she stayed at home any time she wasn't at work. She had never had a very busy social life, but even the one she did have had gone out of the window, and she hadn't seen anyone outside of work since the funeral, including her best friend. They had spoken a few times on the phone, and she had made excuses about having so much to sort out and looking after her father, but eventually she had let slip that everything felt as though it was on hold until she was confident of leaving him on his own. The following evening there was a knock at the door, and minutes later the two friends were sharing a bottle of wine.

'You didn't need to do this,' Danni had protested at the door.

'You need it,' her friend had said, and brushed past her.

Samantha Newbold was Danni's oldest friend, the only friendship that had lasted beyond the secondary school where they had been inseparable. Now Sam was a supervisor at her uncle's footwear company in the next town, and she had remained a loyal and dependable friend, and they always turned to each other in times of trouble – times like this. Sam had been a rock in the days before the funeral and also during it, and Danni felt guilty for not seeing her since.

'I'm here, trying to move forward, and he's dragging me back down all the time.' Danni used her hand to demonstrate.

'It must be hard for him, but he is an adult.'

Danni wasn't in the least bit surprised by her friend's less sympathetic stance. Sam was a straight-talker who rarely minced her words. Danni had always teased her that she never used any sentences where the word count reached double figures, and she had often thought that, if they hadn't been friends from an early age, she would probably have been intimidated by Sam and found her too abrupt. It was only by knowing Sam so well that she realised she simply had an old head on very young shoulders. She was also physically intimidating at almost six feet tall – height she inherited from her Canadian father – and strikingly beautiful like her West Indian mother.

They had become friends when they were eight, plonked together by a teacher at primary school and quickly forming a bond, but Danni had always been in Sam's slipstream as she catapulted through life taking any obstacle in her stride. She was the tallest girl in their year, captained the netball team – while Danni was usually reserve and carried the drinks – and represented the county at several sports; she was never, ever pushed around by anyone. But she never let anyone push her friend around either, and Danni grew accustomed to, and even comfortable with, being in her shadow. As they got older, Sam had been the first girl in their year group to have a proper boyfriend, and the first one to get a job when they left school.

Her maturity played a big part in this. Although now only twenty-three, she spoke like someone who could pass for twice that age. But she'd had no choice but to grow up quickly: she'd endured a turbulent home life, and her parents' volatile relationship, until her father had left home. Danni often wondered how she'd have coped if their lives were somehow switched, and always reached the conclusion that she probably wouldn't have. It had made Sam very wary of people, though, especially men, and Danni knew that was why she was giving her father very little slack.

'You can't always be here for him. You have your life too.'

'I'm worried he's having a breakdown and doesn't know it,' Danni said.

'He's just grieving, Dan. And he's stronger than you think.'

They continued talking but they kept arriving back at the same place: it was something for her father, and not Danni, to resolve – and he would, Sam insisted, but in his own time.

'I just feel guilty that I'm not in the same place he is.'

'Is that where you want to be?'

'No.'

'Is that where your mum would want you to be?'

'Of course not.'

'So enough guilt, then.'

It sounded like an order and Danni realised it probably was one. Sam didn't let her mope, and she knew her mother wouldn't want to see her doing that either; she would have expected her to move forward. She'd always been that kind of person, one who dusted herself down and got on with things.

'Shall I open another bottle?' Danni asked, but her friend shook her head and told her she had a meeting in the morning and it was expected that she would say something about next month's sales targets.

'With a hangover, I don't think I'd do it justice,' she laughed, and they had a black coffee instead before Danni walked her home, a short journey of less than half a mile to the next estate, even though Sam kept insisting she could walk alone.

'I need some air,' Danni told her. 'So stop bitchin'.' She laughed and gave Sam a gentle shove. She liked being the only person Sam let into her inner sanctum, beneath the strong veneer and hardened shell. She decided to tell her everything that had happened after the funeral.

'He took advantage of you.'

Danni had to work hard to persuade Sam that it hadn't been like that and that she'd instigated it as much as Euan had, if not more.

'You weren't thinking straight.'

'I knew what I was doing,' Danni assured her. 'Besides, it was a one-off.'

'Does he know that?'

Danni had always kept Sam fully in the loop about Euan's behaviour when they split, and had showed her the messages he'd sent.

'He'll have to.'

'Does your dad know he stayed the night?'

'God, no. But these days I could have a whole roomful of men in there with me and he'd not notice.'

'I'm shocked enough that you had one!' Sam laughed as they reached the house.

'I just want to talk to him. Dad, I mean, not Euan.'

'Then find something to talk about. Work, for instance.'

'I don't want to talk about work.'

'And he doesn't want to talk about your mum. Work is a neutral subject.'

'It's also a boring one.'

'So say you have a problem you need help with.'

'I don't.'

'Then make one up.'

Danni thought about it. 'It might work,' she said.

'He can only say no.' Sam shrugged. 'But I bet he won't.'

Danni left Sam at her gate and rehearsed the conversation on her way home. When she walked in, she made a cup of cocoa and put it outside the study door on her way past and called her father to tell him it was there. To her surprise he opened the door and, seizing the moment, she mentioned that she had a problem at work and he immediately wanted to know more. It was the first time she had seen a sign of life in his eyes since the night of the accident.

'I'm tired, Dad. Can we talk properly tomorrow? Over dinner maybe?'

Her father agreed straight away and said he would do whatever he could do to help her. Danni suspected he had been looking for this kind of opportunity to talk.

It was a step forward.

And, for the first night in quite a while, Danni slept soundly.

12 | Danni

'I just wish you'd stop fussing.'

There wasn't quite the progress Danni had hoped for when her father arrived at the restaurant, more than twenty minutes late and clearly preoccupied. He was in the clothes he had worn all week, unshaven, and his demeanour was colder than the previous night; he brushed away her questions about his welfare and clumsily moved the talk on to her work 'problem' at the first opportunity.

'We can talk about it later,' she told him, trying to take his hand, but he was acting like someone who had been coerced or even ambushed into a discussion he didn't want to be part of.

She thought about telling him about a real problem: that Euan had sent her three text messages that day, each giving the distinct impression that he thought there was more to the night he'd spent with her than she did. It would stop her having to lie, but then her father had never seen eye to eye with Euan, so she knew he would almost certainly react badly. And she'd have to say more than she wanted about what had happened after the funeral, and she already felt bad about that night on several levels – not just for leading Euan on, but for doing it so soon after her mother had been laid to rest.

The thought of her mother made her try again to get behind her father's façade, and for a second his eyes turned watery and she thought she might have succeeded, only for him to sense his own vulnerability, cough, and close up again, as if he had been about to say something and thought better of it.

'What?' she asked, encouragingly.

'Nothing.'

'You can talk about her, you know…'

'I don't need a counsellor, Danni.'

'Maybe that's exactly what you do need.'

He looked angry with her and Danni gulped, not expecting the reaction. She had considered suggesting some professional help after the funeral but she was glad she hadn't now. She waited for his anger to subside.

'I don't need to see anyone. What would I say? That she was such a wonderful person? That I'm upset she died? That I miss her? Big surprise.'

'Dad!'

He apologised and took his daughter's outstretched hand and held it in both of his. 'I'm just not ready to talk about it yet.'

'It?'

'Her. It. The accident. You know what I mean.'

She squeezed his fingers and smiled.

'Now what's this problem at work?'

Danni had concocted a reasonably plausible story about one of the dentists at the practice, but it seemed inappropriate at that moment. 'It doesn't matter.'

'I thought that was why we came here.'

She nodded and told him it was just a personality clash and nothing that she couldn't handle herself now she'd given it more thought.

Her father smiled. 'I wouldn't be much help anyway,' he said. 'It's been years since I've worked with humans.'

Danni smiled too. That was true: her father's freelance status meant he did most of his correspondence by email. Other than the odd interview as part of some field research, he hardly spoke to another person during his working week, and it had been a long time since he'd had to deal with anything approaching office politics.

'But thank you for offering to help.'

'No problem.'

But there was a problem. Without a topic to hide behind, Danni could see his uncomfortable state return. When their food arrived, his relief at having a distraction was clear and they ate in near silence. Danni wondered how much of a corner they had turned, but she knew it wasn't nearly as much as she had hoped.

'Do you mind if *I* talk about Mum?' she asked as her father finished his dessert.

Thomas shook his head, although Danni could see it was reluctantly. But she needed to talk. He might not be ready to, she thought, but he could listen, even if just to help her. Danni tried to put some of her thoughts, jumbled as they were, into words. When she finished, she realised they all boiled down to one thing. 'I suppose I'm just missing her,' she said. His eyes became watery again. 'I feel I've been cheated. That I didn't get to tell her the things I wanted to.'

She waited for her father to speak but he didn't.

'Do you feel that too?'

He nodded, but as he started to speak – she could see the words forming – he stopped, seemingly not trusting himself to let them out.

'I can't believe she's gone.' Danni shook her head. 'There are so many horrible people in this world, and she was so – so perfect, I guess.'

She looked at her father but he looked away. She felt a chill run down her spine but wasn't sure why; she just knew that she didn't like the feeling. 'Wasn't she?'

'Of course. More than you know.'

Danni felt uneasy. His words were fine, but there was something in his eyes, something she wasn't sure she wanted to explore, but knew she had to.

'Then talk to me, Dad.'

Her father let go of her hand, and loosened the neck of his crisp blue shirt as if it was cutting off his circulation. Danni waited for him to speak, but he looked as if he was trying to think of a way to do anything but.

'I told you, I'm finding it hard,' he said.

'Hard to talk about the wonderful things she did? How can that be difficult?'

He shrugged.

'So is there something I don't know?'

The question had been there all along. It had been on her mind since her mother's death. If she was honest, it had been there for much longer, but she hadn't expected to bring it up, because, until Patricia's untimely passing, Danni had always thought that her mother would be the one to answer it. Now that that was impossible, she knew that her father was the only one who could. She thought back to the conversation she had overheard and shuddered. He didn't know she'd heard it, and she almost felt sorry for him; he was heading for an inevitable collision he didn't even know was coming.

For Danni, it was now a matter of when, not if, she would have to tell him.

'Of course not.'

Danni wasn't an expert on body language but she had watched enough people in the waiting room at the dental surgery hiding their real fear behind a brave face and false bravado. Her father was in that waiting room now: knowing he was getting closer to going somewhere he didn't want to, but with an inevitability to it all the same. She stared at him until he was forced to look back.

'I said no.'

He was stern, bordering on hostile, and demonstrating quite clearly that he wanted the conversation to end there. She knew she had to tread carefully in case she sent their relationship spiralling further in the opposite direction and forced him back to the solitude of his study, and she was prepared to wait for another, more suitable moment.

'OK. I'm sorry.'

Her father dismissed her apology with a wave of his hand, cleared his throat and drank the remaining coffee in his cup.

'So anyway, what's happening with you and Euan?'

Until then she had been sure her father hadn't seen them together after the funeral.

'We split up, remember?'

'I know, but didn't I see you talking the other night? At the—'

Now Danni wanted to end the conversation quickly. 'You did, but it was nothing,' she said and looked away. 'Still split up.'

The mood had changed completely in that brief exchange. Danni felt embarrassed that her father might have seen them after all and, God forbid, heard them in her bedroom. It horrified her to imagine it; they'd always been a family where sex, in any context, was not a topic for discussion, especially for her father. In twenty years, she couldn't remember her parents kissing in public, never mind any other physical sign of attraction.

She thought about the night of the funeral: the short but satisfying outpouring of emotions. The way she had then let her hormones overpower her, and the way the grief in her had somehow exaggerated that desire, leading her into bed with Euan against her better judgement. She had been aware enough not to make lots of noise, but she hadn't specifically tried to make none at all, if that were even possible.

Danni felt herself getting uncomfortable, picturing her father sitting in his study drowning out the sound of their meaningless sex, on the day his wife's body had been laid to rest. She blushed and felt her cheeks burn hot enough to reheat her drink. She finished it, hiding behind the cup, and then changed the subject to less important ones, like her plans for the weekend and her father's next writing assignment.

The mood had changed enough for her not to want to talk about her mother any more.

Danni suspected that that was exactly what he'd intended.

13 | Laura

Laura went into work on the Monday morning determined to enjoy a better week, which wasn't that much of a stretch given how bad the previous one had been. But she had no idea how much more eventful it would turn out to be.

Although she took no delight in Sue's sickness bug sweeping the offices of the paper, she wasn't unhappy that three of the more established reporters had succumbed to it over the weekend, leaving the editor short of staff and with a glut of leads from the weekend that needed attention. When Laura walked in, twenty minutes early, he called her into his office and asked her to follow up on one of them and write a piece on a local farming dispute. Short and simple, he said, and, although she nodded, her head was already racing with ideas and angles, and by the time she was at her desk she had envisaged the headline on the front page.

That headline – in fact, thoughts of any headline – was quickly quashed when she reached the farm that was the centre of the story. She climbed out of her car, her sensible shoes already squishing into the dark brown mud, and walked up to the dilapidated farmhouse where she met the owner, a farmer named Bob, who had been accused in an anonymous call to the council of covering up a disease in some of his animals. Laura found Bob a pleasant sort; on the surface at least he seemed very sincere and apologetic for the state of the house, and not a little surprised that the paper had even felt it necessary to send anyone to cover it.

A non-story was how he referred to it at first, and Laura thought about Kelly's warning, though she was determined to judge it for herself. But it quickly became obvious that he was right. The inspectors from DEFRA had already visited and given the farm the all-clear, and when Bob explained that the anonymous tip-off came just after an acrimonious meeting with his soon-to-be-ex-wife and her solicitor, which was the latest instalment of a nasty and protracted divorce, things fell neatly into place. When he also told her that the police had been sent to the farm twice previously after similar unsubstantiated claims, it became clearer still.

'It's costing me so much, I ain't got enough left to live on,' Bob told her with a defeated shrug, and she looked around at the crumbling walls and clear neglect and lost her appetite for the headline, feeling sorry for him when she left with barely a page of notes.

When Laura got back to the office, and after she had salvaged her shoes as best she could in the ladies' toilet, she set to work on her 'story' and quickly established that she could write it in five minutes and it might, if she was very lucky, find a place in that week's edition, but that it would be buried somewhere on page twenty-one, maybe above the story about the council increasing parking meter charges and below the picture of a family of cats who all had one blue eye and one green, she imagined. As she typed, she became more despondent, as the story was every bit as uneventful on her screen as it was in real life, and she even considered including a line about the farmer's wife but deleted it as quickly as she typed it because she had no evidence other than Bob's word, and she wasn't going to put the paper into a libellous situation. Not that David Weatherall would ever let it get past him anyway.

She finally settled on a more factual, evidence-based piece but, as she checked it, she thought about the subject a little more, and became increasingly angry at the way Bob was being treated. She could put the facts straight, at least as far as the disease was concerned, but if it was on page twenty-one how many people would see it, compared to those who had heard the whispers?

No smoke without fire, they would say, even some of those who saw her article, and she quickly decided that it didn't do anything like enough to redress the balance or highlight how an innocent and honest man's livelihood and life's work could be potentially destroyed by a vengeful ex-spouse. The more she thought about it, and about the state of the farmhouse Bob was having to live in, the more she wrote, straying closer and closer to the divorce case without slandering anyone.

Backed up by some Google articles on similar cases, although not involving farms, she finished the longer article and checked it, feeling pleased with herself not only for setting the record straight but also producing quite a strong commentary on the way the world could easily chew up and spit people like Bob out. But with David's brief also in her head she emailed him both the shorter, factual version and the longer commentary piece and suggested he choose which one to publish.

An hour later, he called her into his office, and it was immediately clear from his expression that this was one of his angry rather than miserable days, and that she had definitely contributed to it. As she walked in, he was staring over the top of his glasses at his computer monitor, eyes narrow and gleaming with several frown lines above them, so she sat down and waited for him to speak.

'Interesting take on the farm story.'

'Thank you.'

His forehead creased even more. 'That's not praise,' he said. 'I was surprised you even *thought* I might like it.'

'I just—'

'Let me help you out, in case you ever think of writing a piece like that again,' he interrupted.

Laura gulped.

'Not. In. My. Paper. If I wanted drama, there are plenty of people I would go to before you. But I don't want drama.'

'I just—'

'People in this town like facts. Want facts. This is just speculation and opinion, much of which has nothing to do with Bob Greenway or his farm.'

'I'm not—'

'It's simple. DEFRA were called. People who buy his meat will want to know what's going on. He got the all-clear. People will want to know that. Bob would want them to know. What's so difficult about that?'

Laura squirmed with embarrassment like a child again, sent to the headmaster's office for pulling her skirt up in the playground. Her parents could make her feel small at times, but this was taking it to a whole new level.

'Nothing. I just—'

'Nothing. So then, I'll delete the second version, we'll pretend you never sent it and then you can do a quick edit of the first one and we'll get it to press, OK?'

'Yes, Mr Weatherall.'

She hadn't called him that since her interview but she was too afraid to be any less formal. He looked at her as if he was already wondering why she was still there and then looked at the door, so Laura stood up and walked out, head bowed, tail firmly between her legs, as she crossed the office to her desk while the rest of the staff, the ones who had made it in, fell silent and watched her walk of shame.

It was another reason for her to be pleased that half of the office were sick.

14 | Laura

Laura really wanted to dislike David Weatherall but, as hard as she tried, she found it a difficult thing to actually do.

She sat at her desk, staring at her screen, occasionally glancing over at him behind the glass wall and wooden door that was his office, and muttering under her breath. But she couldn't find any words that conveyed her exact thoughts; her feelings about her job had reached a new low, but she still had enough respect and admiration for the editor to stop short of throwing in her notepad and pen and walking out.

What she really needed was for someone to make light of it, and break the cloying atmosphere that had settled over the office since she'd walked out after her dressing-down. But of course, she thought, none of them would. They'd be too busy just watching her, glad not to be on the receiving end themselves and careful not to let David think they were taking her side.

Not that he cared either way, she thought. He was too long in the tooth to be concerned with the opinion of anyone who worked there, with the possible exception of Sue. David Weatherall simply *was* the *Gazette*. Nearly two decades earlier he had taken on the task of resurrecting the publication when it had fallen on hard times and the owners had wanted to cut their losses and find a way out. After a distinguished career with a national paper, David had been one of the high-profile casualties of spending cuts and had been made redundant. Laura had been told that several other newspapers had offered him jobs, but he had lost confidence in himself and lost his affinity with the corporate side of journalism and instead took a gamble on the *Gazette*, his home town's newspaper, and purchased it for a song.

Whereas most people would have given the ailing publication a wide berth, David made it his mission to return it to its former glory, even with the growth of online competition and the changing landscape that newspapers faced. He dedicated his every waking hour to making it a source of local pride rather than the advertisement-laden deadwood it had become, and he hired the best people he could find to help him.

As long as they were fairly cheap.

With the help of his redundancy cheque and a local bank loan to get the finances in order, he set about increasing sales, and had managed to exceed targets and expected sales year on year ever since. Early on, he had leaned heavily on his 'local boy made good' image, but eventually the paper was able to stand on its own: a local, trusted institution that could be relied upon for factual local stories, interesting well-composed articles, and interviews that readers actually wanted to read.

Within five years he'd convinced most of the people in the town to buy a copy every week. But Laura knew that it hadn't come without sacrifice. It was a well-worn story, but not without foundation, that his first wife had left him sixteen years ago and he hadn't noticed for nearly two weeks. He also struggled to adapt to rapid change, and the rise in prominence of the internet and social media had been a constant challenge. In fact, he had told Laura that it was partly down to her age, and ability to use technology, that he had agreed to hire her, bringing the average age in the office down at a stroke. He might not have liked it, but he accepted that the growth of the digital side of publishing wasn't going to go away, and he had actually managed to increase hard copy sales while the paper's online readership continued growing.

What was less known about was his younger life as a journalist, but Sue had told Laura he had once been the impetuous young reporter in search of the big story, and it was only time, and experience, that had worn him down and made him favour factual reporting over more thought-provoking and challenging pieces. But, as Sue often reminded them all when they whinged about it, it was his newspaper, and he'd earned the right to decide what went in it and what didn't.

Laura watched him through the glass as he sat drinking his afternoon cup of tea – a ritual he never missed – and read back copies, his own brand of quality-checking to ensure that the tone of the paper remained consistent. Then, as if knowing she was watching, he quickly turned to his side and looked directly over at her. Laura jumped, trying to look busy, and pressed the Send button on the email containing her freshly edited article.

David beckoned her over, and she hesitantly stood, feeling the eyes of her colleagues on her. She walked slowly to the editor's office.

'That rewrite should be in your inbox.'

'Good. I'll have a look in a minute.'

'It won't take that long. It's only ten lines,' she said, trying to hide the sarcasm.

'That's all it needs. Thank you.'

Laura eyed him with a certain suspicion because he rarely thanked her for anything, and for a moment she had a horrible feeling that he wanted her to cover for Sue again, as she had been complaining of still feeling unwell from the moment she'd walked in.

'Anyway, I have another story for you,' he said over his glasses.

Laura raised her eyebrows. The editor opened his desk drawer, took out a brown manila folder and put some papers from his desk into it. He wrote LAURA on it in a thick black marker pen and handed it to her, although his hand held on to it a little longer than was necessary and she had to yank it from his grip.

'It's a bit bigger than you're used to,' he said.

'I can handle it.'

'Hiring you was a risk, Laura. I don't have money to waste. I need you to step up.' He looked over the top of his glasses.

'I understand.'

Laura opened the folder and glanced at the A4 sheet inside. Her eyes widened and she looked at the editor in a way that suggested he might have handed her the wrong folder.

'Well, go on. Time is money and all that.'

'I'm glad you think I'm ready for this.'

'I didn't say you were,' he said, 'but I've had two more people go home sick since lunchtime and we are down to the bare bones. So you're all I have.'

It hurt a little, but Laura realised she didn't care; nothing was going to dampen her enthusiasm, not even a vote of little confidence.

'I won't let you down, David,' she said, and put the sheet of paper back in the folder.

'I hope not,' he said, already on to his next email.

Laura walked across the office to her desk, clutching the folder tightly. Her back was straight and her chest out this time as the rest of the staff watched her intently.

They didn't know it yet, but Laura had just taken a step up the career ladder.

15 | Danni

Danni thought they were over the worst of it.

Another week had passed and her father had finally begun to use other parts of the house rather than confining himself to the study. They were also talking more – only sporadically, but it was better than nothing at all, she thought, and her father had never been the most talkative of men, even before the accident. He worked a lot, most evenings, and she'd always had her mother to confide in and they'd spent hours drinking coffee and gossiping, and that was a part of her life she was missing the most. She didn't have that kind of relationship with anyone else other than Sam, and she was wary of taking up too much of her friend's time.

Danni valued friends as much as she did family, so she didn't enter into friendships lightly, but over the years, as people had moved away from the town to work, if they had begun to drift away she had let them, until she had lost touch with everyone but Sam. She knew she'd never let that friendship go the same way as the others.

But although she could talk about anything to Sam, it wasn't the same as with her mother. For one thing, Sam liked to get straight to the point, whereas her mother could talk for hours on almost any subject and had had a habit of asking the right questions. It was something she knew she wasn't going to find with her father.

But she had developed a way of filling part of that gap in her life.

Her father was out, so she lay on her bed and closed her eyes, as she had started to do often since the accident. It was a form of meditation she'd invented, and if she freed her mind enough she could imagine her mother was with her. It didn't always work, but, if she was able to clear the tangled thoughts inside her head, she could feel her mother's presence with her in the room.

After a few minutes of lying completely still, she felt a familiar warmth beside her – not actual body heat but a sense of wellbeing that she'd have found it hard to describe to someone else, even Sam. She turned slightly as if to face her.

'Are there things I don't know about you, Mum?'

She lay still and waited; she knew her mother couldn't reply, but it didn't matter, because Danni could sense what she would say and exactly how she would say it. They had talked for so long, about so much, when she was alive, that it was easy, as long as she was prepared to speak for both of them. But she still became impatient.

'Well?'

'*Your father said there wasn't, didn't he?*'

Danni smiled to herself. She might have said the words, but it could have been her mother. It was an uncanny impression.

'It wasn't what he said. It was how.'

'*How did he say it?*'

'Like he was hiding something.'

'*That's what you read into it. You don't know,*' said Danni in her mother's exact tone, a voice of reason. As she'd always been in their conversations.

'I know when someone is holding something back, Mum.'

'*So what do you think it is?*'

'I don't know. But there's something.'

'*You know your father. He's not the most open of men at the best of times.*'

'Do you think I should just ask him?'

'*Didn't you do that already?*'

'Push him for a proper answer, I mean,' Danni asked.

'*Do you WANT a proper answer?*' Danni's impression of her mother replied immediately, and she had to think about what she wanted.

'I know I don't want to keep wondering.'

'*So that's your answer, then.*'

'But I've only just got him talking.'

'*It's up to you, Danielle. If there is more, you have to decide if you want to hear it.*'

'Do you think I'll regret it if I do?'

'*How will you know until you do?*'

Danni was so engrossed, she hadn't heard the car pull on to the drive. Her father had hardly left the house since the funeral, but that morning Danni had persuaded him to take a trip to the library, a place he could go and be out, without having to interact too much.

'Is it to do with the conversation I overheard?'

There was no response. Patricia smiled, or at least the crystal-clear vision of her in Danni's head did.

'Danni?'

Danni opened her eyes. 'Mum?'

'Danni?'

It was her father, outside her bedroom door. She got to her feet and opened the door to find him still in his coat, flakes of melting snow in his hair and on his collar.

'Who were you talking to?' he asked.

'No one; I must have nodded off. How was the library?'

'You know – full of books.'

'Did you see anyone you knew?'

'I kept my head down, to be honest.'

Danni nodded. Since the accident, if she saw someone she knew, or her mother knew, she found it hard to know what to say to them, especially as the other person would tilt their head in pity and start asking questions she didn't want to answer, so it had become easier to avoid them; she'd become adept at pretending not to see people.

'It's a first step,' she said.

'And I feel better for it.'

Danni got up from her chair and gave her father a hug and a kiss on the cheek. It felt nice, and she didn't want to ruin it by asking any difficult questions.

If she was going to have *that* conversation, it was going to have to be another time.

16 | Danni

No one could have slept through the storm that night.

The rain, horizontal and heavy, hammered against the doors and windows and at times felt as though it was strong enough to break through them; and it seemed to go on for ever. Danni had lain awake listening to the bombardment for an hour, but when it showed no signs of abating she went downstairs to make herself a hot chocolate. In the kitchen, she found her mother doing exactly the same thing.

'Can't sleep?' she asked.

Danni shook her head and her mother got out an extra cup. Her father had gone to London on a two-day research trip.

'Your dad said it was the same where he is. Baileys?'

Danni nodded and they sat on the kitchen stools drinking and watching the rain run down the kitchen window. Normally they would have talked non-stop, a rat-tat-tat-tat of comments about anything and everything, but Danni found her mother unusually quiet.

'Everything OK?'

'Just tired,' she said, and boiled the kettle again to make a second drink.

Danni sipped it, not really wanting another mug but using it as an excuse to stay with her mother and find out what, if anything, was wrong.

They sat in silence for several minutes. Then Patricia spoke.

'Danni.'

'Uh-huh.'

'You know I love you, don't you?'

'Of course! What's brought this on?'

Danni was about to laugh but quickly sensed her mother's seriousness. She looked as if she was about to cry, and, as she went to speak, Danni saw her stop herself.

'What?'

Her mother smiled and shook her head. 'I just don't tell you enough.'

'Of course you do.'

Danni had a horrible sensation – that her mother was about to tell her she was seriously ill or even dying – but instead she put her hand on her shoulder and laughed. 'Sorry, it's just one of those moods I get in when your dad's away…'

Danni opened her eyes. There was no rain, no wind, not even a gentle breeze outside. She switched on her bedside light and sat up. It had felt so real, but it was the first time she had dreamed of her mother like that since the accident.

She tried to remember what she had said, but it was already becoming fuzzy.

But she knew it wasn't *just* a dream; it was a recollection of a real conversation they'd had, on that stormy night a few months ago, and at the time had seemed a little strange but not that significant, and Danni had gone to bed and all but forgotten it afterwards.

But it felt significant now. Whatever it was that was bothering her mother, it wasn't a mood, and she was usually fine when her husband was away.

The more Danni remembered it, the more convinced she became.

There was definitely something her mother had wanted to tell her.

17 | Laura

'Keys, pencils, pens, pad, spare pad.'

Laura mentally ticked off the items that she knew were in her bag as she ran to the car park, the manila folder tightly clutched to her chest. When she reached her car, she laid the folder on the passenger seat and opened it again, just to check it still had the paper in it that she'd read in David's office.

There was a sheet of crisp white A4 paper. On it, at the top was the typed address of the shopping centre in the next town with a woman's name, also typed, and Sue's scribbled note next to it that simply said (MOTHER) in brackets. Underneath were handwritten notes by David's PA.

> *Child missing, female, Seasons Shopping Centre, approx. 2.15pm. Police arrived – treating as possible abduction – DS Knowles is at customer service desk. No further information.*

Laura still wasn't sure she should have it. She wondered if David had given her a file he had intended for Kelly Heath by mistake. Or maybe was it a huge, elaborate prank that the whole office was in on? Because, if it was real, it was a big leap for her. This was a proper story, the kind that Kelly and the other established journalists were given and she only read about later. She knew David's hands had been tied by the illness sweeping through the ranks at the *Gazette*, but at that moment she didn't care if she was the editor's second, third or even twentieth choice.

It was her story.

The Seasons Shopping Centre was in the next town, four miles down the coast, and was a sad-looking late-sixties-built building whose best years were definitely behind it. How it had survived the recent recessions no one was quite sure, but, even though many shops had closed or changed hands, the one main department store had decided to stay, and continued to attract just enough custom to make it worthwhile keeping the whole place open.

The drive only took ten minutes in the middle of an afternoon, and Laura was soon parked in the multi-storey car park next door to the centre. She ran down the stairs two at a time, eager to get started. The entrance via the car park was an unwelcoming set of double doors with flaking paint and a faded sign. Laura had only been there a handful of times because, unless you specifically wanted to go to the department store, there was little else there for someone her age. She made her way to the customer service desk at the far end of the ground floor, with every shop along the way – those that were still trading anyway – displaying huge SALE signs in their windows.

The desk stood on its own in the middle of the concourse, with HMV on one side and a boarded-up unit on the other and a poster that said NEW STORE OPENING JUNE – so the opening was either very delayed or they were giving people plenty of notice. As she approached, even at quite a distance it was obvious who the missing child's mother was. A twenty-something woman in a padded blue coat was anxiously looking around through bloodshot eyes, while a female police officer tried to talk to her. A uniformed member of staff with a *The Seasons* polo shirt and name badge stood at the desk making a phone call, but she ended it as Laura approached.

'Can I help you?'

'Laura Grainger. The *Gazette*,' Laura said confidently, holding up her staff pass the way she'd seen reporters do on television. The woman at the desk looked at it with indifference, and the police officer checked it and nodded. The child's mother stared at Laura.

'I understand there is a child missing,' she said quietly to the police officer, who shot a glance towards the desk. The woman standing at it gave her an *it-wasn't-me* shrug.

The police officer stepped to one side to remain out of earshot of the woman in the blue coat. 'We aren't certain the child is missing at the moment.'

'So you know where they are?'

The police officer glared at the trainee reporter, and Laura had to work hard to hold her nerve and not apologise. The officer put her radio to her mouth and spoke to someone, and Laura heard her name mentioned and a minute later a woman walked out of the HMV store.

'Detective Sergeant Knowles,' she said, and shook Laura's hand as she addressed the police officer. 'There are two assistants in there who I might want to talk to again – can you get their contact details in case I do, please?'

The officer looked at Laura and walked over to the store. Knowles smiled at Laura as she took her notepad out of her bag. 'We think the father might be involved.'

'Think?'

'We're trying to contact him.'

'Is she in any danger?'

DS Knowles seemed mildly irritated by the question and ignored it.

'Can I speak with the girl's mother?'

'I don't think tha—'

The woman in the blue coat stepped in and looked at the detective. 'The more people who know, the better, right?'

She looked at Laura, expecting an answer, but Laura just opened her notepad as Detective Sergeant Knowles stepped aside to allow the woman to stand next to her. Laura took the sharpest pencil from her bag and got some basic details from the woman, including her name and that of her daughter,

Rebecca, or Becky as she said everyone called her, who was four years old. She asked her what had happened.

The mother fought back tears as she explained that she'd been in the card shop, had been standing in the queue waiting to pay with her daughter next to her, but, when she had paid for her cards and bent down to put her purse in her bag, her daughter had gone.

'Gone?'

The woman looked guiltily at the detective sergeant. 'I only took my eyes off her for a minute or two.'

'She didn't say anything?'

The woman shook her head and looked at DS Knowles again; the detective raised her eyebrows as if to silently say to her, *you wanted to talk*.

'Has she ever done this before?'

'Never.'

'You didn't see anyone who might have—'

'My ex. Becky's dad. We've been seeing a solicitor about custody. He isn't allowed to see her.'

Laura scribbled on her pad. 'And you think he might have taken her?' she said, looking at the detective as she said it.

Knowles frowned and stepped between them. 'Look...Laura, isn't it? I get you have a job to do, but we don't have any facts yet, so can we not speculate, please?'

'Fair enough.'

DS Knowles leaned in closer so only Laura could hear her. 'Am I on record here?'

'Not if you don't want to be,' said Laura, and lowered her pencil and pad.

'Rebecca's father has got a bit of history. He came second in the custody battle and we think he might be trying to scare her.'

'Looks like he's succeeded.'

They both looked at the girl's mother: she was shaking, and every passing minute seemed to add another crease to her forehead.

'He hasn't done this before, but that was before the last hearing. They had quite a bust-up by all accounts.'

'Do you think he'll do anything stupid?'

'No. Chances are he'll turn up in an hour and it'll all blow over.'

'And?'

'We'll detain him overnight, probably charge him while they have time to get a court order against him. That's the way it goes, I'm afraid.'

'What if he doesn't turn up?'

'Then you have your story,' Knowles said with a half-smile, and for the first time Laura suspected it was the detective who had called the paper, hoping to control the story.

'And I can quote you if that happens?'

'If it gets that far – and I'm sure it won't – you can quote me all you like. But for now, help us do *our* job, and then I'll help you do yours.'

Laura nodded and closed her notepad. Kelly had told her that the police often preferred to keep the press on-side by feeding the story they wanted to tell, rather than risk losing public confidence. This was the kind of story where public relations was especially important, and they agreed that they would keep each other updated with any new information. Laura handed the detective a business card and thanked her for her help.

'I'll keep you posted,' Knowles told her, but Laura knew she'd only get what the detective sergeant needed her to know. And her expression seemed unconcerned, as if she'd seen it a hundred times before. Laura thought she'd probably also seen the wide-eyed keenness she'd arrived at the centre with, the hope that this might be her big break, and wanted to manage her expectations.

Now, as she trudged away from the detective, Laura was expecting it to turn into another non-story by early evening.

18 | Laura

Laura decided to find something to do while she waited for an update.

The shops would be closing in less than an hour, and on a cold midweek night the town centre would be desolate and she didn't want to stand around outside. She thought about David Weatherall and considered what he would do.

Anticipate what will happen next, she muttered to herself. He was always saying that, and, even though she thought he was a miserable sod who mistrusted anyone under the age of twenty-five, he knew a thing or two about following a story.

His oft-repeated mantra during her first twelve months was about thinking where the story might end, and being prepared, so that, if it did, you were already ahead of the competition. There didn't seem to be a lot of competition on this one – Laura had noted that she seemed to be the only member of the press who was even aware of Becky's disappearance – but she also knew that would change quickly if the girl didn't turn up soon.

If that happened, then it would be a major news story, with lots more police and a huge amount of public interest. She'd need to be ready because the window she would have in which to break the news would be tiny, even if Detective Sergeant Knowles was as good as her word. She hoped the girl was OK, but she also knew it was an opportunity.

She left the shopping centre and found a corner seat in the coffee shop over the road – the only one that was open until eight o'clock – whose large floor-to-ceiling windows afforded her a clear view of any comings and goings through the main entrance.

She quickly plugged in her laptop and began to type an article – so far, one full of holes and missing information, but at least it was an outline, although she was careful not to make the mistake of jumping to conclusions. DS Knowles and Becky's mother might be confident about who took her, but they didn't know for sure, and if she wasn't found tonight then, in theory, anything could have happened.

Laura found that the first five hundred words came very quickly, and she left gaps or red-font questions where she needed more. But when she read it back, even with the gaps filled, it still felt like an extension of the headline, which she wouldn't get to choose. It lacked context, quotes, and above all depth, so she began making notes of the people she would like to speak to if the girl didn't turn up, starting with the mother and any other relatives and friends. She needed people who could really shed some light on the situation, and maybe offer some theories on what might have happened.

Her phone rang and she snatched it from the table, but it was David asking for an update.

'Nothing much happening,' she said, 'but police reckon she'll turn up soon.'

He told her to keep him in the loop and, if she felt the police might be wrong, to let him know so he could send someone to help her.

'Will do,' she said, and ended the call. Laura knew exactly what that meant: he would send Kelly and she'd take over completely.

She decided to add some context to the would-be story while she waited, so she connected to the café's wi-fi and opened up a web browser and typed into it: 'child abductions northwest england'. There were plenty of results, but nothing that matched her search with much accuracy. The only connected matches were a false alarm five years ago and a family-related abduction three years before that. She got as far as the second page on Google and gave up and went back to the search bar: 'child abductions uk'.

She expected more, but the first page was entirely made up of the names of organisations that could help you if your child was missing or abducted. On page two it was full of national statistics, and she realised as she browsed that children went missing often but child abductions were incredibly rare, and almost always involved a relative or someone the child knew.

She moved on to page three and was just about to go back and try a different search when an entry, two-thirds of the way down the screen, caught her eye. It was about a missing child, not recently but more than twenty years ago – the article was marking the twentieth anniversary the previous year – and not a local story but one in the southwest of England.

Laura read the article and followed the link to a newspaper local to the incident, where she read the story of Jessica Preston, a two-and-a-half-year-old who had vanished from a beach on a summer's day and never been seen again. There were related links at the bottom of the story that gave more details, and the police clearly believed she had drowned, a theory that the girl's mother strongly disputed, claiming instead that she had been abducted, although Laura couldn't find any information either way and the coverage on the internet seemed fairly scant.

She continued clicking on to other links to follow the story, although there wasn't that much on it and what did exist was limited to extracts from newspapers at the time, but she became absorbed in it nonetheless. Although there was a good deal of repetition, she gradually filled in blanks and pieced together what had happened, or at least what people believed to have happened, given that there were no eye-witnesses and no evidence.

As she devoured any information she could find – such as the fact that the child's mother had suffered from mental health issues recently and that her other child had been taken into care – she found a story about the child's father, and was about to open the link when she was disturbed by her phone. She groaned, expecting David again, but it was a mobile number she didn't recognise.

'Hello.'

'Miss Grainger?'

'Yes.'

'It's Detective Sergeant Suzanne Knowles from Lancashire Constabulary.'

Laura's pulse began to quicken. 'Has she turned up?'

There was a pause.

'We are doing a press statement at seven,' the police officer told her matter-of-factly, then lowered her voice. 'So if you want to get ahead and break the story first, now's the time.'

'No word from the father?' Laura asked, genuinely concerned for the girl despite the rocket-fuelled boost this would give her profile at the *Gazette*.

'No. I still think she's with him, but we need people to start looking out for her. Right away.'

'Shall I quote you as a police source?'

'If you like, but they're sending someone from the city to take the case. Looks as though she's officially a missing person now.'

'Do you know who they're sending?'

'Jenkinson. That's all I know. Now if you'll excuse me…'

'Thanks for the heads-up.'

Laura ended the call, took one final glance at the page of the article she had been reading, bookmarked it and went back to her document on Becky's disappearance. She had phone calls to make, people to talk to and a very current story to complete – quickly, before anyone else got a sniff of it.

She would have to forget all about Jessica Preston for now.

19 | Laura

Laura had enjoyed her brief moment of glory, even though it was over before she had time to even tell her parents to look out for it.

She'd finished her article in the café, called David and run it by him, and within minutes the two of them were on a conference call to the *Gazette*'s website editor, who uploaded the story on to the paper's website with the headline that David had insisted upon: CHILD TAKEN.

Less than twenty minutes after the story went live, with Laura's name sitting proudly underneath, Detective Inspector Ian Jenkinson had started his press conference, where he asked for the public to help in the search for Rebecca Holden. It hadn't taken that long for the story to sweep across the internet, with the BBC, Sky and nearly all other UK news outlets putting the breaking story on their websites too.

Then chaos. As Laura had expected, the small town was descended upon by a media circus: reporters from several newspapers and TV stations arrived in vans loaded with crew, cameras, sound booms and artificial lighting. There had been nothing like it in the town before, with roads closed off, and a crowd gathered outside The Seasons that quickly grew into the hundreds even though it was a very chilly night.

David Weatherall had called in all available staff to field calls from other news outlets, and everyone was asking to speak to Laura, although David shielded her from the spotlight. He wanted her to continue to work at the scene and she had been allowed to ask the first question at the press conference, amid all the lights and flashing cameras. Laura didn't mind one bit that the attention was now all focused on the detective inspector; she'd put her name and that of the *Gazette* well and truly on the map, and David was quick to praise her when it had settled down.

The paper's website, accustomed to less than a thousand visitors per week, received ten thousand hits in the time between the story breaking and the press conference. Within the next hour those hits had gone past fifty thousand, nearly all of them landing on Laura's article. David had assigned Kelly Heath to the story at that point – she'd made a miraculous recovery after calling in sick the day before – and she joined Laura at the shopping centre just as the press conference was drawing to a close.

'Well, you certainly struck it lucky here,' Kelly said as Laura met her outside for a discussion on what to do next. Not that she needed telling, because David had made it clear when he'd last spoken to her that Laura was to assist Kelly; but the older woman quickly established the hierarchy too, in case she hadn't got the message.

'I'm going to talk to the family,' she said. 'You try to find anyone else who knew her and is prepared to share something.'

'Anything in particular?'

'Anything they're prepared to tell you. Family history, gossip, I don't care. Anything we can use.'

'Not dirt,' said Laura firmly.

'What's the difference?'

'They have a child missing, Kelly. They don't need us raking up stuff that's got nothing to do with that.'

'I'll judge what it's got to do with,' she said.

Laura made a mental note not to tell her anything she'd consider to be unconnected 'dirt'. But she knew she would also be feeding on mere scraps; Kelly wouldn't let her get within a mile of a family member or close friend if she could help it.

'I don't know if it's relevant enough, but I found a story that we might be able to use.'

Kelly frowned, but showed enough interest for Laura to continue. She gave her a brief précis of the Jessica Preston case.

'I know it's over twenty years ago, but it will help readers identify with what Becky's mother is going through.'

Kelly ran it over in her mind. Laura fully expected her to quickly dismiss it but her face lit up instead. 'Let's go with it. We can put it on one of the pages as a *look what can happen if she doesn't show up* piece.'

Laura nodded suspiciously and then realised it was a perfect 'win-win' scenario for Kelly. If it improved the narrative then she'd get the credit and, either way, it would get Laura out of the way for a while and allow her to completely take over the story.

'Well, go on, then.' Kelly was already wandering off to talk to the family and had no need for her. The area was cordoned off and only a few reporters were being allowed past the barriers – strictly one per news agency – so Laura slung her bag over her shoulder and made her way back to the coffee shop she had used to write the breaking story, to search again for more details on Jessica Preston. David had given explicit instructions to have all pieces ready for print early the following morning, so they could go straight into the first few pages of that week's edition and on to the website even sooner.

The coffee shop had stayed open after the story broke, and the owners had been rewarded by nearly a week's worth of custom in a few hours as the crowd and press used it as an unofficial refreshments station and place to get warm. Nearly every seat was taken, so Laura squeezed into a gap by the window, ordered a coffee and opened her laptop.

She went back to the story about Jessica's father, her brother, and some of the theories that had come out at the time and since from the authorities, mainly the police detective who had led the search until it was called off after five years.

It seemed that the majority of commentators had concluded that the police were right and that she must have drowned; only the child's mother had remained in opposition, and fervently maintained that it was an abduction. Even twenty years later, in the anniversary article, the mother had been adamant that Jessica was still alive, but Laura noted in one passage that she had been admitted to a mental health unit, not far from Weston-super-Mare, not long after the search had been officially called off, and, as far as she could tell from the limited information, she was still there.

She began to type some words but struggled to find a suitable link to what was happening now. This appeared to be a clear case of child abduction, whereas the Jessica Preston case did not. The Seasons Shopping Centre, cold and dark, felt like a very different place from a sunny August beach with a dangerous rip-tide. After half an hour, Laura found herself having managed only six lines, her mind constantly thinking about the mother of the child, Sandra Preston.

She found a picture of her, taken the next day when she'd made an appeal on the news. Her eyes were bloodshot and she looked bewildered, as though everything that was happening around her made no sense. That all she wanted was her little girl back.

She was the link. She looked exactly like the mother in The Seasons.

She looked at Sandra Preston's face, trying to imagine what it was like to have no closure, to always be wondering what happened. Laura felt guilty for wondering if she really believed her daughter was abducted, or if it was her way of hiding from the awful truth. She clicked through more images and found one of her, taken earlier when she was twenty-five, the caption said, and Laura noted how happy she looked, so unaware of what lay ahead.

She could feel her heart aching for the woman. She checked her phone for any updates from Kelly but there were none, so she searched for more on Sandra Preston and, as she did, she realised exactly what she wanted to do.

She put into Google the name of the unit where it said the woman resided. A telephone number came up on the screen and she typed the number into her phone and called it.

A receptionist answered within two rings, remarkably friendly and helpful given that it was so late. Laura apologised for that and explained who she was and, to her surprise, she was transferred straight through to the unit's general manager, a Mrs Stanton. She seemed friendly enough, but Laura still anticipated a negative reaction when she told the manager what she wanted to do.

There was silence, and Laura thought she'd put the phone down. 'Hello?'

'I'll have to call you back,' the manager said.

'OK.'

Laura ended the call and waited. The manager had promised she'd get back to her within the hour but she called back much sooner, barely fifteen minutes later.

'Normally I wouldn't do this without a risk assessment,' she said, raising Laura's hopes, 'but I've spoken to Sandra and she has agreed to see you tomorrow at two.'

'Tomorrow?'

Laura realised she had not been prepared for that answer. She'd expected to be refused or, at best, to have to try to convince the manager to agree to her having a telephone conversation.

'Is that OK?'

Laura sat looking at Sandra's picture.

'Hello.'

'Yes, sorry, just checking my diary.'

Laura pretended to press a few keys, and made a humming noise as if she was running her finger down against a busy schedule. 'Yes, I can do two o'clock,' she said after a few seconds.

'So we'll see you then,' the manager said.

'You will.'

Laura deleted what little she had managed to type of her article and typed a new working title: WHAT IS IT LIKE TO LOSE A CHILD? It wasn't going to make David's deadline, but she was pretty sure that this would be something that the editor would want to print, so she closed the laptop and ran from the coffee shop to the shopping centre to update Kelly on the developments. Then she collected her car and drove home.

She had an interview to prepare for.

20 | Danni

'That's another one!'

Danni removed the headset she always wore in the early part of her morning shift at the dental practice. Between half-past eight and ten o'clock she would spend most of her time fielding calls from patients trying to book or cancel appointments. Today it had only been the latter; three already and it was only twenty past nine. The second dentist at the practice was sitting in the reception with her; her latest appointment was one of the ones that had been cancelled. She shook her head.

'One of those days.'

'Looks like it.'

Another call came through and they looked at each other. 'Surely not,' said Danni, and put the headset back on. 'Madeley's Dental Practice – good morning, how—'

'Danni?'

'Yes.'

'It's Carol.'

It took a few seconds for Danni to register that it was Euan's mother. Her voice sounded different through the headset.

'Hi.'

'I had to ring you there. Your mobile kept saying it was unobtainable.'

'Oh, right. I changed my number.'

'That explains it. I was worried about you.'

Danni asked how she was and answered Carol's questions about the funeral and how she was coping. Despite their previous friendship, it felt difficult now: strained, and too much like hard work.

'Have you heard from Euan?'

Danni made an involuntary snorting sound, and hoped Carol hadn't heard. 'Sort of,' she said quickly, trying to cover it.

'What?'

There was a pause. The dentist had gone back to her treatment room, and when Danni checked the appointment diary there was at least twenty minutes until the next patient was due.

'That's why I changed my number.'

Now Carol paused. Danni waited for her to work it out.

'He hasn't!'

Danni told her about the calls and text messages: how they had peaked a fortnight after they split up, and then dropped off around the funeral but then started again. Euan's mother was silent, taking the information in.

'I'll speak to him,' she said softly. 'He mustn't do this to you, especially now.'

Danni took a deep breath. If she didn't tell Carol the whole story, and she found out from Euan, it would look as if she'd deliberately held it back.

'I'm partly to blame, Carol. I I spent time with him after the funeral. I never wanted to get back together or anything. I was just in a bad place.'

There was another awkward pause.

'Well, I'll still talk to him.'

'Listen, I have to go, a patient has just come in.' There was no patient, but Danni didn't want to talk about it any longer.

'OK, sorry love, keep in touch.'

'I will, bye.'

Even before there was a click on the line to indicate the call had ended, Danni knew that she wouldn't keep in touch

111

with Carol Corbett. It was a chapter of her life she wanted to put behind her.

She sat, her pen dangling from her mouth, as the practice fell silent. It was unusual for there to be no drilling or sound of voices from the treatment rooms, and she took advantage of the calm to think about what to do next about her father. He hadn't spoken to her much in the last few days and she had continually put off asking him any questions, so they had reached an impasse, one that was difficult to move on from.

As her shift ended that evening, after one of the quietest days she'd ever known at the practice, she left promptly and stopped off at the nearby shop and picked up a bottle of wine. Then she parked her car at her house and walked to Sam's, timing it perfectly to coincide with her friend getting back from her own job. It was something they had done a lot, before boyfriends had got in the way.

'You read my mind,' Sam said when she opened the door, still wearing her coat.

Within minutes they were sitting in the living room with a glass each. Sam had rustled up a plate of nibbles and they were taking it in turns to complain about their day. The television was on but Sam had turned the volume right down. A reporter from the BBC was standing in the light rain, giving a live update. Behind them was a shopping centre, almost in darkness.

'Terrible, isn't it?'

'What is?' asked Danni.

'A little girl's gone missing.'

'From round here?'

'No. Up north somewhere, I think they said. She was with her mother and just…disappeared.'

'Disappeared?'

'That's what they said. I only switched it on a minute before you knocked on the door.'

The TV began to show repeat footage of a press conference. Sam turned the volume up.

'What about the CCTV?' Danni wondered aloud as the police detective on the screen answered questions from a room of reporters – including one about the cameras, which it turned out had been switched off because of some faulty wiring within the ageing shopping centre.

The detective explained that the case was being treated as abduction. Then a picture of the missing girl's father was put on the screen, along with a hotline number and a request for information on his whereabouts. In the picture the man was smiling happily; it looked like a photograph taken at a family Christmas dinner.

'They think he's taken her.'

'That girl's poor mother must be going through hell,' said Danni.

'Especially as she was taken from right under her nose,' said Sam. 'Do you want to keep watching?'

Danni shrugged.

'I'll leave the picture on.'

Danni nodded and Sam muted it and put the remote control on the arm of the chair; but both found it hard not to keep looking at the screen for updates.

'So,' said Sam, offering Danni a crisp, 'what has your dad done now?'

Danni had told Sam, in an exchange of text messages earlier in the day, that their talk at the restaurant hadn't gone well. Now, face to face, she told her about her mother in the bath, the overheard discussion, and her father's reluctance to talk about anything. She noted her friend's silent disappointment. 'Sorry for not telling you before.'

'Why didn't you?'

'Half of me thought I was blowing it out of proportion, and half of me was...embarrassed, I guess.'

'About what?'

'My parents. I always thought they were this great couple.'

'They were.'

'I don't know what to think any more.'

'Maybe you're reading too much into it. If there were anything bigger, you'd have noticed it in other ways.'

Danni nodded. On the television screen a woman with bloodshot eyes was talking to the camera and her name appeared in a box below her face. She was the missing girl's mother. Sam grabbed the remote and turned the volume up and they heard the final part of the plea, where the woman spoke with a broken voice and appealed for anyone who had her daughter to come forward.

'How long as she been missing?' asked Danni.

'Since this afternoon.'

'I can't imagine how she feels.'

'She should feel terrible,' said Sam, and Danni winced at the coldness in her tone. 'I mean, how does your child just go missing like that?'

Danni looked at the woman on the screen, her red eyes surrounded by dark circles and the streaks where she'd been crying. She didn't share her friend's haste in apportioning blame. 'It probably happens more than we think.'

Sam didn't reply. The reporter came back on and then they went back to the interview room and a police detective named Jenkinson repeated the mother's appeal for people to come forward with information.

'The girl wouldn't have left with a stranger, surely?' Danni wondered out loud.

Sam shook her head. 'It'll be the dad. It's always someone they know.'

Danni looked at her. Sam shook her head. 'You've got to question what kind of family that kid's got.'

Danni said nothing. She knew how it felt to have no idea what your parents might be capable of.

21 | Danni

Despite Danni's protests, Sam had opened a second bottle of wine as their conversation had turned to work, then back to Danni's parents, and then the unfolding events on the news.

'Sounds like this is more than just a domestic.'

They watched as the story came back on the news channel roughly every thirty minutes; all evening it had been the leading item on the headline bulletin.

'I hope she's OK.'

Sam nodded, and Danni felt her eyes becoming heavy. She needed to walk home, but she sensed her friend was in the mood to go on much longer. She waved her away when she tried to refill her glass. 'I need my bed.'

'Lightweight.' Sam grinned. 'Shall I call you a cab?'

Danni was looking forward to the sobering walk and clearing her head a little with the fresh coastal breeze on her face, so she politely declined and put her coat on, giving her friend a warm hug. 'Thanks for listening. It was good to talk.'

'That's not talking, it's slurring,' laughed Sam.

'Well, thank you, anyway,' Danni laughed back as she opened the door and the sharpness of the cold night air hit her cheeks immediately; she pulled her collar up as high as it would go.

'I'm sure it's all going to be fine with your dad,' Sam shouted from the doorway as she walked down the path.

Danni smiled and walked into the headwind. It was only a mile to her house but she decided to take a slightly longer but better-lit route because it was so late. She turned and waved one last time. 'Shut the door!' she called into the whistling wind. 'You'll freeze.'

Sam lived with her mother but Danni rarely saw her. After a protracted divorce, Mrs Newbold had taken on three part-time jobs to be able to afford to stay in the house and sometimes it was after midnight before she got home, so determined was she that Sam's life wouldn't be disrupted. Sam had left school and got a job with her uncle's firm as soon as she was able, in order to help pay the bills and reduce the burden on her mother – not that Danni had ever heard Mrs Newbold complain about her lot. As a result, they'd always had a house to go to, rather than hanging about on the streets like other teenagers, and, when they got a little older, it was somewhere they could spend time and talk after a day at work. And now, Danni was again grateful to have a place to go that got her away from the house and from treading on eggshells around her father. But she knew she had to go back some time.

In the summer, when it was lighter and drier, Danni would cut across the Rec, a large, square patch of grassy land that was edged with trees and had a football pitch on one side and a children's playground in the centre. It cut the journey distance and time significantly, but it got quite boggy when it was wet and, because the trees blocked out the street-lighting, no one tended to go on it after dark, in case a dog-walker hadn't cleaned up after their pet properly. The alternative, longer route was to walk around the edge of the square, past a row of shops that included a post office, a hairdresser's and a fish and chip shop that stayed open until midnight to catch the custom from the pub on the other corner of the Rec.

As Danni approached, the owner of the fish shop, a Cypriot man whom Danni's family had got to know quite well and who'd been at her mother's funeral, was just seeing out the last customers of the night and closing up. He waved, then turned the OPEN sign on the door to CLOSED and switched off one of the lights. The customers were three teenage boys, now shouting and jostling over a bag of chips, outside the hairdresser's. When they saw Danni on the opposite side, one whistled and the other shouted drunkenly, 'Get 'em out for us, darlin'.'

Danni quickened her pace a fraction and didn't look at them. The village was quiet and usually trouble-free; it always had been, but at a certain time of night, like a lot of towns and villages, it had one or two problems with groups of young people hanging around in the street, often drinking, smoking and sometimes causing a nuisance.

'Fuckin' snob,' another of the group shouted, and she instinctively glanced over at them. 'Yes, that's right,' he said. 'I'm talkin' to you.'

She carried on walking, even faster now, and could hear them talking loudly to each other as they walked in the opposite direction. When she was far enough away that their voices had become muffled and distant, she turned to look, but could only see two of them heading around the corner in the direction she had come from. As she turned, the third boy appeared alongside her from out of the trees.

'Sorry 'bout them.'

Danni jumped, startled. The lad, a skinny six-footer with basketball shoes and a black, shiny coat that resembled a pile of car tyres, had cut across the corner of the Rec. She smiled politely and carried on walking, each step a little longer. Her house was no more than six hundred yards away.

'They're pissed.'

Danni smiled.

'I don't think you're a snob.'

Danni felt torn. If she ignored him, she would be exactly what he didn't think she was; but she didn't want to encourage further conversation, and she definitely didn't want him to know where she lived.

'Thanks,' she said. 'And no need to apologise for them.'

'What's your name?'

117

She didn't want him to know that either. She carried on walking quickly, but his long bandy legs had no trouble covering the ground, although his little stumble as they crossed the road told her that he had, like his friends, drunk too much.

'Look, I just want to get home,' she said, and hoped he would just get the message and leave her alone, but he seemed to take her brush-off as a challenge instead.

'I'm not stopping you. I only asked your—'

A car came up behind them and slowed quite deliberately, so that the skinny boy looked around and blinked in the glare of the headlights and had to shield his eyes. Danni carried on walking and heard the car edge slowly forward, until it pulled alongside her, and she heard the whirr of the electric window as it came down. She tensed.

'Danni.'

She looked, but already knew from the voice that it was her father, leaning across towards the passenger side so she could see his face. The lad stopped walking and watched them. Danni opened the car door and climbed inside, looking at the six-footer as she did. 'Night, Danni,' he said sarcastically. She smiled and slammed the door.

'Everything OK?' her father said. She nodded, and pressed the button to close the window.

'Let's go home.'

Her father glared at the youth for a second or two and then pulled away as Danni stared forward, relieved but also embarrassed. 'Have you been drinking?' she heard her father say, but she ignored the question. He didn't drink alcohol himself and, as with most things he didn't approve of, he didn't approve of anyone else enjoying it either. But she had wanted him to get back to how he used to be, so she didn't answer, just shook her head and hoped he couldn't smell the wine on her breath.

She'd told Sam that she wanted her father back in her life. And she was really glad he had shown up when he did.

22 | Laura

'Your destination is on a restricted access route.'

The female voice was sharp and to the point. Laura watched the portable satellite navigation unit she'd borrowed from her father as it calculated the journey to the destination, and came back with one that was a few minutes over four hours. That was fine: with some potential motorway bottlenecks to negotiate, she'd allowed herself more than five hours to get there.

She rechecked the items in her bag again, and then waved to her mother standing in the doorway. Helen waved back, her face beaming with pride. Both her parents had been so pleased for her when the story had broken, and when she'd asked the question at the press conference, that she hadn't told them that Kelly had replaced her as the main reporter on the story. She decided that she would get the interview completed and surprise them with it when it went live on the home page of the website that night, because that would remind everyone that she was still key to the *Gazette*'s reporting of the case. Besides, she thought, her mother would be worried sick if she knew she was driving so far on her own, so she'd told her she was doing a number of local interviews with the family of Becky Holden, and needed the SatNav to find their addresses. Only David, his PA and Kelly knew where she was really going. The editor had been very impressed with what she had done so far, and securing the interview must have been the icing on the cake, because she had rarely seen such enthusiasm from him. Sue had given her an expenses form and petty cash for the trip.

As she pulled off the driveway with a final wave, she felt the butterflies in her stomach, and they stayed there as she got to the main road and the woman's voice told her to take the third exit at the roundabout. She stopped to fill up with petrol just before she joined the motorway, then, as she was halfway down the slip road, her phone rang and she saw Kelly's name on the screen.

'Shit.'

She ignored the call and a minute later it rang again, but she was already in the middle lane of the motorway overtaking a lorry and didn't have a hands-free kit in the car, so she decided to wait until she reached the next services and call her back.

Her phone beeped to tell her she had a voicemail message.

She hoped Kelly was ringing her to wish her luck.

She drove another two miles, then her phone beeped again, this time to tell her she'd received a text message from Kelly. She carefully held the wheel with one hand, checked her mirrors for any police cars and read the message on the screen.

laura if on way stop becky found safe and well :) kelly

The car swerved, its tyres trespassing across the raised markings on the hard shoulder and making a grinding sound, and she straightened it back on the carriageway and threw the phone on to the passenger seat in frustration. 'Fuck!'

She banged her palm against the steering wheel. No one wanted anything other than a successful conclusion to the story, but she wished it had happened twenty-four hours later than it had. She pulled in at the next services and sent a cheery reply to Kelly through gritted teeth and went inside.

She realised she wouldn't have to call for an update. The story was the headline on the twenty-four-hour news channels on the big screens inside the services, and she watched as the breaking story unfolded before her.

As it happened, another twenty-four hours would have been problematic for Becky Holden, as she and her father had been picked up in Dover when a couple alerted police after seeing them at the port. Although it was unclear how he would have managed to get her on board a boat, with all the authorities on alert and everyone looking for them. If he had, the consequences could have been far worse. As it was, he had not put up a struggle when he was apprehended, and Becky's mother was already on her way to collect her. It had pretty much been exactly as DS Knowles had predicted, Laura thought as she watched the interviews and saw a clearly relieved DI Jenkinson answering questions; just over a slightly more protracted time period.

But it had still worked out well for all concerned.

Laura took her phone from her bag and made the call she was dreading. The receptionist at the High Cliffs House transferred her straight through to the manager.

'I'm afraid I have to cancel, Mrs Stanton,' Laura told her after they'd exchanged pleasantries, 'so would you be able to speak—'

'Whoa, hang on right there,' said the manager, her voice turning quite hostile. Laura stopped talking and she heard the manager call out, although it was muffled; she must be holding her hand over the phone. Then she was put on hold and classical music was pumped into Laura's ears for a few minutes. Finally, the music stopped.

'Hello.' The voice sounded frail.

'Sandra?'

'Yes.'

'It's Laura Grainger, We have an interview set up for this afternoon.'

'Two o'clock.'

'It was. But I'm going to have to cancel, unfortunately.'

Silence. Laura grimaced.

'The missing child has been found this morning,' she said.

There was an even longer silence, then, 'That's good.'

Laura could feel some of her pain, even from two hundred miles away. 'I'm so sorry to mess you about, Mrs Preston. Really I am.'

More silence.

'Mrs Preston?'

'It's OK. You don't have to explain.'

'I do. You see, my editor would never agree to me coming all that way to interview you now that she's been found.'

There was no reply.

'Mrs Preston?'

'Look, Laura,' the woman said wearily, 'I'm pleased she's been found. And I appreciate your showing an interest.'

'I want—'

'I could have done with reporters like you when she was taken.'

'I'm really sorry.'

'Don't be; it's not your fault.'

'But—'

'It's different now. These days, a child goes missing, the whole world knows about it within a few minutes. Every time the news is on, or you pick up a paper, it's there. And that's the way it should be. But tell me, when was the first time you heard about Jessica?'

Laura paused. 'Yesterday.'

'And that's more than most. Hardly anyone even knows her name. She went missing at the wrong time. It's probably just as well you didn't interview me. I doubt anyone would have read it.'

Laura stayed quiet.

''Cause they didn't care what I said then,' Sandra continued, 'so why would they care now?'

23 | Laura

Laura walked up to the double doors that led into the *Gazette*'s second-floor offices and took a deep breath.

It was mid-morning, and the first time she had been into the office since she broke the story of the missing child. Now, shaken by Sandra's comments and full of disappointment that she'd not been able to interview her, she just wanted to get to her desk and start something new.

'Here she is,' she heard a voice say quietly as the doors opened, and everyone in the room turned at the same time to look at her. She smiled, and a spontaneous round of applause broke out that accompanied her all the way to her desk. As she sat down, embarrassed, she looked over at David's office, and he nodded and just about raised a smile.

Over the next ten minutes, several members of staff shouted over to her or came to her desk to congratulate her on the story before she could put on her laptop and read the website article and Kelly's cover story on how Becky had been found. Then David's assistant came up behind her with a cup of coffee; another first in Laura's time at the paper.

'Shame about the interview,' she said softly, and pulled up a chair next to Laura. 'It would have been a brilliant angle.'

Laura smiled and thanked her for the drink, quickly realising that Sue had been assigned pep-talk duties by the editor. 'Better that she turned up safe and sound,' she said briskly. She had decided to put that positive spin on her disappointment, and it was true, she'd wanted that outcome from the start. But having

Sue console her did mean one thing: she'd made it into David's more trusted inner circle of reporters.

As the office chatter began to die down and everyone got on with their jobs, Laura found it harder to focus on anything except the interview, and at lunchtime she found herself staring at an empty screen and daydreaming about how it might have worked out differently. She called Kelly to talk about the Becky story and tell her how good she thought her piece was, but David's favourite reporter told her she was too busy to talk and cut her off abruptly. So much for her new-found respect, she thought.

At lunchtime, when David had finished eating a sandwich that Sue had taken to him, he called Laura into his office.

'Did I tell you how well I thought you'd done?'

'Yes.'

'Good. So you're free to begin work again whenever you want to,' he said over the top of his spectacles as he proofread an article.

'Huh?'

'The story. It's done. The girl's safe.'

'I know.'

'So you need to stop dwelling on it and move on.'

'I'm not…dwelling.'

The editor continued talking as if she hadn't uttered a word. 'There was some kind of dispute at yesterday's market. The police were called in the end but I want you to see if there is anything still there or if it's blown over.'

The town had a weekly market with two dozen stalls that got a lot of footfall if the weather wasn't too bad.

'The market?' Laura said, and immediately regretted the way it came out: as though it was too mundane for her now. David seemed to give her the benefit of the doubt and handed her his trademark manila folder with some details inside.

'Probably nothing in it, but the injured party thinks there is, so just see what you can find out.'

Laura nodded, almost feeling the bump as she came back down to earth. 'On my way.'

'And don't bother coming back,' David said as she was halfway through his door. She turned and looked at him blankly and he smiled, pleased with himself for getting the reaction he'd looked for. 'Take the rest of the day off when you're done. If there's a story, type it at home and email me.'

'Really?' Laura hovered in the doorway; this was not something he did as far as she knew, and certainly not for a trainee.

'You've had a busy week, and I don't want you coming down with that bug. So we'll see you on Monday, OK?'

He was already engrossed in the next page of the article he was checking, so she thanked him and skipped back to her desk, tucked the folder into her bag with her laptop and walked out of the office again with her head held high, enjoying her elevated position in David's pecking order.

The early-afternoon sunshine warmed her cheeks as she made her way to the car and checked the details on the paper in the folder. The person she needed to see lived on a road that was more or less on her route home, and when she got there and spent a few minutes talking to the man she quickly realised that the whole thing had been blown out of proportion and there was nothing for her or the *Gazette* in taking it any further. She made a few notes anyway, so that the man didn't get that impression. Laura wondered what the police had thought, being called out to what was little more than a shouting match over a garden ornament.

'Thank you for your time,' she said as she left the man's house with most of the afternoon ahead of her.

'Will I be in the next edition?' the man asked, and she smiled.

'I don't make that decision.'

She got back in her car and thought about Sandra Preston. If things had turned out differently, her interview and the article would have sat in a prominent position in the next edition, *and* on the website. A lot of people would have seen it, and her name under it.

She turned her key, and her car's engine spluttered and choked in the cold. She was about to do it again – it often took more than one attempt – when an image crossed her mind: a vivid image of a woman sitting in a chair, waiting for her, with disappointment and frustration etched across every inch of her face. The picture had been there since they'd spoken earlier; and the woman's words played over and over in Laura's mind.

She shook her head and went to turn the key again but the image wouldn't go away, and neither would the words. She took her phone from her bag and pressed a number on her 'recent calls' list. A woman answered, and Laura asked if it would be possible for her to speak with Mrs Preston. There was a pause, then the manager came on to the line and Laura repeated how sorry she was for what had happened earlier.

'I only agreed because I thought it might help her to talk.'

'As I said, I'm really sorry.'

'I don't know what—'

'Could I talk to her now?'

There was a silence. Laura didn't think Mrs Stanton would appreciate being interrupted, and she checked her phone to make sure she hadn't hung up on her. Then she heard a tired sigh. 'Let me ask her,' the manager said, and put Laura on hold, classical music filling the vacuum.

'Hello.'

The voice was familiar but frosty; Laura felt the chill down the line.

'Mrs Preston,' she said, 'I'm so sorry for cancelling our meeting.'

'You already said that.'

'I know I did. But if you'll still see me…'

Laura paused. Sandra was silent so she continued hopefully, '…then I'd like to come and do that interview on Saturday.'

Part Three

One year after she was taken...

We didn't know how to deal with information.

To begin with, it terrified us. We avoided news of any kind; it reminded us of what we had done. The television became little more than a decoration, sitting on a wooden unit, for display purposes only; it might as well have not had a plug. The radio was never switched on, and if we were in the car we played cassettes; I erased all the stations from the radio's memory. Newspapers were our biggest enemy and we steered clear of them at all costs. In the end it became easier to simply not go anywhere where information might be present, so for twelve months I rarely left the house other than for work, and my wife and our new child didn't leave it at all until after we moved house.

The move was central to our plan. I wanted to stay at the old house long enough that it didn't arouse any suspicion, then move. But that first year was hard, sneaking around, hardly having any lights on, peeking out of the windows, hiding the child whenever the postman came within a hundred yards and going into a blind panic if anyone ever knocked on the door.

It was the same at first when we moved to the new place. But we quickly realised that no one in the new location knew, or cared, who we were. They didn't know if we had children or not, so it became easier.

I wish I could say that about the move itself.

We bought this ramshackle old money pit, with a fair bit of land around it, no neighbours close enough to bother us and which needed a lot of work. But it was also available at a knockdown price – the owner had died and their children wanted a quick sale – and I paid for it in cash. So we moved in the dead of night: the three of us and everything we could shove into the back of a transit van. We told a couple of our old neighbours we were moving to be closer to my wife's mother because she was ill. That also explained why they hadn't seen her for months.

But they didn't care either, and why would they?

I took a short break from work, using the same excuse, and did the renovations we needed to make the house comfortable enough to live in. We hardly saw other people. No one visited, no one bothered us and I became something of an expert at DIY, but we never quite managed to live without the fear of a knock at the door.

But that knock never came.

And slowly information became more of a friend again. The house began to feel like a home, and we switched the television and the radio back on. We let newspapers back into our lives too, and we quickly found that the news was more than just a friend; it was our window to the rest of the world. We could follow the case, the updates and any commentary on the missing child, but we could also see that the story was slowly but surely taking up fewer column inches; eventually it vanished permanently from the screens and news bulletins.

Everyone had stopped looking for her.

My wife just blossomed, caring for our child, now almost four years old, and raising this incredibly cute, clever and confident young girl.

Now and again there was an appeal for fresh information but most of it was lip service. I remember clearly one breakfast bulletin when a police detective was interviewed and said in a resigned manner that he thought she had probably gone into the sea and been taken by the current.

It was also the same morning that the child began to call my wife 'Mummy', and it felt like the first day of the rest of our lives.

The hardest parts of the first year were the moments when I was caught off guard.

The rest I learned to cope with: the stares, the sympathetic nods, the way people shuffled across on the pavement so they could avoid having to walk too close in case they had to speak to me; as if I was begging for spare change. That bit was easy. Truth be told, I didn't want to speak to them any more than they wanted to speak to me.

No, it was the things that I wasn't expecting that got to me, and felt as though I had climbed a mountain and at the top there was no oxygen and I was doubled over, gasping for any drop of air as if it might be the last I ever tasted.

An example was when I was doing the laundry and I found one of Jess's socks, all balled up at the bottom of the basket where we keep the dirty washing. It was just one sock on its own, not a pair, and that hit me harder still because I imagined her, all alone too, out there in the big, bad world with no one to look out for her. I cried and cried and cried when I found that sock.

Cried until I couldn't muster one more solitary tear.

And there was the time I received a letter from the preschool I'd enquired about. I'd asked to go on their contact list so I could find out about the school and whether they had any places available when Jess was old enough. They didn't know they were sending a letter about a child who wouldn't go to their school after all, and I should have just thrown it in the bin when I saw the insignia on the envelope, but it hit me harder than finding the sock in the end. I read that letter until the words were almost worn off the paper and I could say them in my sleep.

Then I couldn't get rid of the damn thing because doing so would be admitting to myself that she wasn't coming back and she'd never take up a place at that school; so instead I kept it in a drawer so that if she did walk through the door I'd have the letter all ready to go. And, of course, I kept opening the drawer and seeing it, usually by accident.

But other times not.

When I did, at first, I gasped so desperately for that air, but as time passed I told myself that the next occasion when I felt like that, the next time I was at the top of that mountain and the oxygen had gone, and my neck muscles had all but closed my airways up, I wouldn't fight it but would just give in and let every last particle of air drain from my body and leave me with the darkness.

I thought that was the way out I needed.

But when it happened, when I saw that damn letter, I couldn't do it.

I think that, despite what everyone said about what had happened to her, because I knew that she was alive I also knew that I had to be there waiting if she found her way back to me.

And so I breathed.

24 | Laura

High Cliffs House was a privately run mental health unit that, as its name indicated, sat on one of the highest points of the road that ran along the most easterly corner of the North Devon coast.

Laura had parked her car in the small staff and visitor car park on the opposite side of the road, and she now saw why: the old car park was still partly visible, right next to the building, but the erosion of the cliff face had seen the corner of it fall on to the rocks, a hundred feet below, and the rest had been cordoned off by a metal fence, with streams of red and white plastic ribbon to warn people of the danger. The building, dirty white and imposing, sat further back, roughly seventy yards from the cliff edge, although Laura did wonder for how much longer as she walked up the pathway to the main reception doors.

With lighter weekend traffic on the roads, the SatNav had predicted her arrival time to within a few minutes, and having left plenty of time to spare she had sat in the car preparing for the interview, even though nothing that came from it might ever see the light of day.

As she reached the large front doors, she heard the crash of waves on the rocks below, and she took a look up at the ominous dark grey sky that had threatened rain all morning without actually delivering it. The sea the cliffs overlooked was as grey as the sky, except for the tufts of surf the fierce wind exposed.

Laura felt the salty spray in the air. It was hard to see where the sky stopped and the sea started, and the building felt cold, miserable and uninviting; nothing like any of the images on the website, which were the kind an estate agent would take, that made everything look bigger and brighter, and where the sun was always out, in a clear blue sky with a cobalt sea below.

The door was locked. She pressed the intercom button and announced her arrival and the receptionist let her in. The reception area was poorly lit, with a wide, sweeping front desk and odd sofas and chairs positioned as a makeshift waiting area in front of it. The receptionist appeared through the door behind the desk, greeted her with a warm smile and took her though the visitor procedures, then presented her with a laminated visitor pass on a blue cord with a large number eight in black on the front.

Laura sunk into one of the comfier-looking chairs and waited a few minutes until the manager arrived through another door and greeted her.

'Thanks for doing this,' Laura said, shaking her hand.

The manager nodded with indifference and asked for identification and inspected her *Gazette* staff card. 'Sandra will see you in the main room,' she said, ushering Laura towards the large double doors at the other end of the reception area.

'OK.'

'We do have visitor rooms, but Sandra prefers...'

She opened the doors to a much bigger room, a huge space with large sash windows all around it and a variety of chairs and tables around the edge, with a wooden area, that looked as if it might once have been a dance floor, in the middle. It was full of light, despite the depressing gloom outside, but its light grey paintwork was clinical and unfriendly. Laura stepped inside and followed her.

Spread around the room were fifteen people, and all but one of them, Laura quickly deduced, were patients, the other a nurse who was trying to watch as many of them as possible while her attention was being taken up by one in particular, a gangly six-foot woman in a long white nightgown who was trying to climb on to the sill of one of the huge windows.

Laura scanned the faces in front of her, but couldn't recognise any of them as being Sandra from the photos she had seen.

'She doesn't usually get any visitors,' the manager said as they made their way across the room, Laura following a step behind, mostly unnoticed and ignored, other than by one male patient, who quickly looked her up and down and then turned away. The nurse shouted across to another man who had started to open the button on his trousers, and that made everyone look over at him, including Laura, distracting her and almost making her trip on the edge of a thick and well-worn rug as she reached a table and two chairs in front of one of the windows.

Sitting in the armchair was a woman, her hair grey and straggly, her face pencil-thin; and she was dressed in a long cardigan and house slippers. Laura was shocked; she looked twice the age that she knew her to be.

'Your visitor, Sandra.'

Laura tried to hide her surprise, and held out her hand, but the woman didn't look at her, let alone shake it. The manager smiled and left them, and Laura stood looking out of the window. The views must be incredible on a good day, she thought, but today it was hard to see what she was looking at, although she could just see a patch of sand poking out from the rocks below as the tide began to go out.

'Horrible, isn't it?' mumbled Sandra.

Laura sat down on the wooden chair on the other side of the table and politely smiled as she removed her coat and took her notepad from her bag. 'Thank you for seeing me, Mrs Preston. I'm Lau—'

'You didn't answer me,' she interrupted, never taking her eyes off the beach below.

'Answer?'

'About this place.'

'It's not…'

Sandra chuckled to herself. 'You don't need to lie. You get used to it, believe me, but that first time you see it must be a bit of a shock for someone like you.'

'Like me?'

'Young. Bet you didn't know that places like this even existed, did you?'

Laura shrugged and pretended it was all in a day's work, but she knew Sandra was right: she hadn't been anywhere like this before; she'd never had a reason to.

'What with Bloody Mary trying to climb out of the window for the tenth time today already,' Sandra continued, 'and Old Tony playing with himself in the corner.'

'I really appreciate—'

'Trouble is, what else they gonna do? They get put here and they're lucky if their family visit twice a year. I can't recall Tony having a visitor since I've been here. No one cares, no one gives them anything to focus on. If they did…'

'I'm sure you're right,' Laura said slowly, and knew immediately that it sounded patronising.

'I'm not like the others, Laura. You don't have to talk to me as if I don't know what day it is. Or worry that I might try to climb out of the window.'

Sandra didn't turn her head when she spoke. She was perfectly still but her eyes were alert, darting around all corners of the beach below.

Laura smiled and put her pad on the table. The receptionist walked towards them with a tray and placed a cup of tea on the table in front of Sandra and another on a coaster on Laura's side, plus a small glass of water.

'You didn't say if you wanted a hot or cold drink, so I got you both.'

'That's great, thank you.'

The receptionist walked back to the main doors. Sandra's head was still close to the glass, studying the ground below as the receding tide began to expose more sand.

'How long have you been here, Mrs Preston?'

'Since they decided I was crazy.'

Laura held her pencil to the paper but wasn't sure what to write. She just settled on the word 'crazy' and put a large question mark next to it.

'But they don't only stick you in here if they think you're crazy,' Sandra said with half a smile.

'No?'

The woman shook her head.

'No,' she said ruefully. 'They also put you here if your child goes missing and you won't accept their version of events.'

25 | Danni

'He was bothering you.'

Danni put her hands on her forehead and sighed. She and her father had been talking for the first time since he had picked her up, and although at the time she had been relieved at his intervention, she hadn't been pleased to find out why he had turned up as he did. He'd already admitted that he had driven around to Sam's to see where she was and then followed her home.

'I'm not a little girl any more. I could have taken care of it,' she snapped back.

'You looked uncomfortable.'

'He was just a kid who'd had too much to drink. And I was virtually home.'

Her father sighed now. He had always hated confrontation. 'I was just trying to help you.'

'I don't need your help.'

'You're my daughter.'

Danni looked up, a fiery glint in her eye and one that told her father he'd said the wrong thing but that it was too late; it couldn't be unsaid.

'Your daughter, am I?'

'What do you mean?'

She looked right into his eyes. They held that uncomfortable expression again. 'I was just checking.' Danni almost spat it out. 'Checking you knew who I was, because you've barely said a word to me since Mum died.'

He looked down.

'And I've hardly seen you in that time either.'

'I'm sorry.'

Danni waved away his apology. 'What is *sorry* going to do? We both lost her, Dad. You shut me out when I needed you most.'

'I've handled things badly.'

'It's not a project. I don't want you to *handle things*; I just want you to be a father all the time. Not just someone who shows up when I get followed by a pissed-up arsehole.'

'Danni!'

She stormed off to her room, to get away from her father because she knew she was going to swear more if they continued talking, and that would set them off again. As she lay on her bed, she thought he might come in to attempt a reconciliation, but instead she heard him go into his study, and didn't hear him again until the next morning. They missed each other at breakfast and then, later that evening, he tiptoed around the house to avoid her, and when they passed at one point the best either could do was to grunt a goodnight that felt very forced. The next day was the same, and Danni found herself avoiding him too, looking for ways to be in different rooms or waiting until he had left a room before she went in. She finally decided enough was enough, and the following morning she intended to make the first move and clear the air.

But as she walked into the kitchen he was putting his coat on.

'Morning.'

'Can't stop,' he said awkwardly. 'I've a train to catch and I'm already late.'

Danni sat at the breakfast table as he gathered his wallet and keys and picked up his briefcase. He was an extremely organised man, one who didn't leave it too late to leave the house if he had a train departure to make. He must be using it as an excuse to avoid having to talk.

'I'm off, then.'

'Right, see you tonight.'

'You won't actually,' he said, checking his watch. 'I'm away until tomorrow night. Research. See you.'

'Bye.'

She watched as he struggled out of the door with his overnight bag in one hand and his briefcase and car keys in the other. When the car had pulled away and she could no longer hear the engine she put her head in her hands and began to cry. Floods of tears came out and she wasn't even exactly sure who they were for; it was the first time she'd cried since the funeral.

She thought a couple of days on her own might do her some good, and it was her day off so she lay on the sofa, watched daytime television and grazed on anything she could find in the kitchen cupboards, but by lunchtime she felt sick and was fed up and lonely. The house, big and draughty at the best of times, felt colder than she'd ever known it, even with the heating dial turned to maximum, and she put on a thick woolly jumper over her pyjamas.

The afternoon was worse than the morning. She found herself pottering around, unable to concentrate on any task for long or find anything that she wanted to do. She even took to digging out an old box of photographs and thumbing through them for pictures of her mother, until she realised it was making her feel worse rather than better.

She picked up one of her favourite photos, taken as her mother was about to leave the house on the evening of her fiftieth birthday, when they had all gone out as a family for a meal, and stared at it, recalling the occasion. Patricia hadn't wanted to go, she hadn't thought turning fifty was anything to celebrate, and a teenage Danni had snapped her as she put on her shoes in the hallway. 'Smile!' Danni had shouted, creeping up on her blind side, and her mother had tried to hide her face but Danni was too quick and the image had captured her mother as she always thought of her: beautiful, yet reluctant to be in the spotlight; much happier staying in the shadows.

She gazed at the photograph and felt a pain in her stomach.

She looked around at the walls: her mother had chosen all the décor and hung paintings and the whole place reflected her taste and sense of style. But Danni realised that, without her mother actually being there, it felt as though she was visiting an art gallery. It was all very nice – but she didn't want to stay there for ever.

She picked up her phone from the coffee table and called the one person she felt she could still trust implicitly. Samantha detected her despondent tone immediately.

'Things no better?'

'Worse, if anything.'

'Did you talk?' her friend asked, and Danni gave her a brief summary of the way things had gone since she had last seen her.

'That's not good, Dan.'

'I've had enough. I wanted to ask you a favour.'

'Anything. You know that.'

'Would it be OK if I came to stay with you?'

26 | Laura

They had skirted around the main topic since Laura had got there. Sandra still hadn't taken her eyes off the beach, which now had a hundred-foot-wide strip of sand that disappeared off into the gloom.

Laura had asked some background questions as she tried to find a way to talk about the woman's daughter. Sandra had toyed with her, being deliberately cryptic or simply man-oeuvring around a question with a swift change of subject. When she'd said she was here because she refused to believe the official verdict on what had happened, Laura had tried to press her gently to continue, but she'd started talking about Bloody Mary again and the moment had passed. But she had been there thirty minutes now, and it was time to be more direct.

'What do you think happened to Jessica?'

Laura looked directly at Sandra but her eyes remained fixed on the beach below. She looked down at the carefully prepared ice-breaking questions on her pad, none of which had been asked. The ice hadn't been broken yet. It hadn't been that kind of interview.

She waited as Sandra considered her answer. From the other side of the room, Bloody Mary eyed her up and down suspiciously, and Laura had to look away when their eyes met.

'I know she didn't drown.'

'How can you be sure?'

Sandra frowned as if she didn't like to be doubted, and took a while to find her words. 'Because someone took her.'

Laura had read about this in the articles on the internet. Even when just about everyone else had concluded that her daughter must have drowned, Sandra had stuck to the abduction theory, despite a lack of any witnesses in the several hundred people on the beach. She asked Sandra why no one had seen anything.

'They weren't looking for her, were they?'

'Wouldn't she have cried out if someone tried to take her?'

Sandra stared at the beach. Laura could see in her frown lines that it was something she'd contemplated before. 'She obviously didn't.'

'But surely *someone* would remember seeing her.'

'She didn't drown.'

Laura watched the woman's eyes, scanning the sand and waves below. If she lacked conviction in what she was saying, she didn't show it.

'I'm just doing my job,' Laura said quietly. 'I'm just trying to work out why everyone was so sure she'd gone in the water.'

'Her hat, I suppose.'

Sandra's head dropped. Laura looked at her, waiting for more. She hadn't seen anything about a hat in her research.

'They found her hat. It washed up on a beach half a mile away, about a fortnight later. That was enough for the police. Enough for most people.'

Laura scribbled shorthand in her notepad but didn't speak for a minute until she felt Sandra was ready for the question.

'So how do you think it got there?'

'I don't know.'

Laura rubbed her chin but Sandra was clearly discounting the damning evidence, selectively it seemed. She decided to leave it for now and move on. 'Tell me about Jessica.'

Sandra turned her head a fraction, not enough to look at Laura but her expression had changed, as if she had finally been asked a question she wanted to answer. 'I could say the things I said to the other reporters,' she said sadly.

Laura held her pencil against the pad.

'I could say she was this and that, but truth is she wasn't even three years old and I don't really know if she was any of those things.'

'How come?'

'I was too busy to notice.'

Laura wasn't sure if it was an excuse or if she was chastising herself.

'I was working two jobs, trying to be a wife and bring up two kids. I never seemed to have a second.'

'But you still raised her.'

'I was her mother for what seemed like ten minutes. Her brother was a handful, to put it mildly, never gave me a break, but Jess was much easier, so she'd get plonked in her pushchair most of the time.'

Sandra sniffed and Laura didn't know if she should push her further, but the woman blew her nose and continued.

'I didn't know how little I knew her until she'd gone. At the time, you just carry on, don't you? I never thought she suddenly wouldn't be there one day.'

'You could never have known.'

'It's easy afterwards to think I should have spent more time with her, but hindsight is wonderful, isn't it? Truth was, we had enough problems in our marriage as it was.'

'Like?'

'Money. Stuart. Todd always said we shouldn't have another child. He didn't think we could handle two. Guess he was right. For once.'

'What did you tell the other reporters?'

'That she knew her mind, that she was bossy, cheeky – you know, the stuff they wanted to hear. She might have been all those things for all I know. Or none.'

'Might have been?'

'When she was little. She's probably different now.'

'You're one hundred per cent sure she's still alive.'

Sandra blinked as if the question surprised her, as if she had never considered for one second that her daughter was anything else. 'They didn't take her to hurt her, I'm sure of that.'

'How?'

'She was very... sweet. People loved her. She had this way about her; you couldn't do her harm. The person who took her, they'd have loved her too.'

'Why does no one else think that's what happened?'

'It was easier for them all to think she drowned,' Sandra said quietly. 'And, in the end, it just began to upset people when I said she was still alive.'

'Upset?'

'Todd, Stuart, the police. They thought I couldn't accept it and had invented this story of her being taken as some kind of denial.'

'Todd said that?'

'Not in so many words, but he believed it. Other people just felt sorry for me – sorry that I couldn't face the truth.'

'That she had gone?'

'That I was a terrible mother,' said Sandra, a deep frown line stretching across her forehead.

Laura finished off her glass of water. 'Why are you sure she couldn't have gone in the sea?'

There was a long pause.

'Stuart was by the water. She'd not have gone near it without him, and he always looked out for her. And there were flags.'

'Flags?'

'Red flags. Danger. The sea was too rough that day and the lifeguards weren't on duty so I told the kids not to go in the water if the flags were red.'

Laura made a note on her pad. 'Could she have ignored you?'

'I was strict,' said Sandra, shaking her head. 'Too strict, probably.'

'But why do you think someone would take her?'

Sandra shrugged. 'Why does anyone do something like that? They had their reasons. I always wondered how they could live with the guilt afterwards. But they must have thought it was worth it.'

Laura made more notes. 'Why are you here? This unit, I mean.'

'I told you. I refused to do what they wanted.'

'Which was what?'

'Face reality. When they called off the search, and then when Todd passed, they said maybe I could find some kind of closure.'

'And you said...?'

'*How can I get closure if she isn't dead?* Then they said I had to consider the facts.'

'Facts? The hat washing up?'

'The hat – the fact that no one had seen her, that the sea was rough that day, that a child could be swept out and their body never wash back up – and the fact that people just don't walk off with other people's children.'

'I think people know that's not fact.'

'They do now, but twenty-odd years ago they said it was.'

'So you fought them?'

'Every day. The social workers they sent to help, they just got pissed off with me. I went through four of them in one year. Then I got so bad, they said I would be better off spending some time in a psychiatric unit.'

'Some time? How long have you been here?'

Sandra looked as though she was counting in her head. 'Fifteen and a half years.'

Laura winced. 'And you still have hope?'

'Not that I'll find her,' Sandra said softly, 'but I'm never going to give up hoping that she might find me.'

27 | Laura

'Tell me more about Stuart.'

Laura felt Sandra's hostility return and her eyes glistened with anger. 'I don't want to.'

'You lost him soon after your husband, didn't you?'

'If you know so much, why are you asking?'

'I don't want to upset you. I just want to understand.'

Sandra didn't look at her, but she relaxed in her chair a little. Big raindrops had started to fall, hitting the windows and running down in a haphazard fashion, and Sandra had to peer through the gaps between them to see the beach. The tide was almost out now, leaving brown sand with huge salty puddles in its place. Laura looked where Sandra was watching, the shoreline that stretched way into the distance. On a clear day, Laura thought, she would be able to see the whole beach until it reached the cliffs a mile or so away; she would have a perfect view of it, whereas today, she could only just pick out the sand right below them.

'He was all I had,' Sandra told her in a quieter, softer voice, the edge removed from it. 'I'd lost Jess and then Todd.'

'Why did they take him?'

'They said I wasn't fit enough to take care of him.'

'But you were his mother.'

'They probably thought, *she's lost one already so we can't trust her*.'

'They said that?'

Sandra looked down.

'They wanted me to get help, proper treatment. So they wanted to put him in care and then see how things went.'

'And what happened?'

'I told them he would be better off if they found him a new family. Permanently.'

'What?'

'It was for the best.'

'Not for you!' Laura almost shouted.

'It doesn't matter about me. Stuart needed a family that could give him the attention he needed. I'd lost a child, and a husband. I was fighting anyone and everyone over Jess and they wanted to put me in here. Where do you think was the best place for him?'

'Was there no family who could have taken him in?'

Sandra shook her head.

'I read about Todd,' said Laura. 'But what really happened?'

'What did you read?'

'That he died. From alcohol poisoning.'

Sandra laughed. 'Is that a polite way of saying drank himself to death?'

'I guess.'

'I think he blamed me half the time and himself the rest. Eventually it was easier to drink a bottle of scotch than face it. And he never talked about it.'

Sandra continued to look at the window, continually clenching and unclenching her fists, unsettling Laura, but she pressed on with her questions.

'Because he couldn't or wouldn't?'

'What's the difference? I never knew what he was thinking.'

'What do *you* think?'

'The drowning option was better. More final. If he believed she might still be alive, then he'd feel like he hadn't done enough to find her. When Jess went, a piece of him went too, I know that. He'd worked too much and spent hardly any time with his kids, and never realised it until she'd gone.'

Laura nodded and let her continue.

'He drank until the pain went. I think that one day the pain wouldn't go so he just carried on drinking till it all went away.'

'Did he try to get help?'

'I dragged him to the doctor once and he told him that if he carried on it could end up killing him.'

'And?'

'I think it just gave him ideas.'

Laura smiled sympathetically and Sandra blinked back a tear.

'So why are you really here?' Laura surprised herself with the question. It was just in her mind; one of those things you wanted to say but usually stopped yourself.

'I told you.'

'I mean why are you still here?'

Sandra seemed irritated. She made a circle with her finger next to her head. 'I'm crazy, remember? You need to keep up.'

Laura put her pencil down and glared at Sandra. 'You're no crazier than I am.'

She watched the woman's face. A half-smile formed, as if she was pleased with herself, although Laura wasn't sure what for. Maybe for fooling everyone else for so long.

'Even if I wasn't before, I must be by now.'

She motioned towards the rest of the room without looking at it. Laura watched Old Tony sitting in the corner watching the television, his hands thankfully nowhere near the waist of his trousers. The nurse was telling Bloody Mary off for climbing on the window yet again.

'You know you don't belong here, Sandra,' she said softly.

'Is that your qualified medical opinion?'

'I've been speaking to you for less than an hour and, qualified or not, I know you shouldn't be here. It would only take a doctor a few minutes to...'

Laura looked at Sandra, who had her head a few inches from the rain-spattered glass with her mouth slightly open.

Her hair hadn't been brushed, probably for several days. In appearance, there wasn't a great deal of difference between her and Bloody Mary, who had just began to climb on to the windowsill again as soon as the nurse's back was turned.

'You *want* to be here. Don't you?'

Sandra snorted.

'You want them to think you're *crazy*.'

Sandra didn't answer.

'You could be looking for her,' Laura said, almost in a whisper.

'And where would I start? Who would help me? Who would even believe me?'

'I believe you.'

'I told you on the phone,' Sandra said sternly, 'no one wanted to know then and they won't care now.'

'So you sit here, just watching the beach?'

'No one bothers me. I fit in here.'

'Now *that* is crazy,' Laura said a little too loudly causing some of the patients to look over at them. 'You can't just give up.'

Sandra sniffed. 'What I'd have given for someone like you twenty years ago. But it's too late now.'

'I thought you were never giving up?' said Laura.

'I said I won't give up hope.'

'But wherever she is now, she has no idea she's Jessica Preston.'

'You think I don't know that?'

'So unless you *do* something, you can watch that beach every day,' said Laura, 'but you'll never find your daughter on it.'

28 | Danni

Sam had told Danni that she was welcome to stay as long as she wanted to, so she was packing a bag with enough clothes to last a week. That would be enough time to decide what to do next; she had no intention of imposing on her friend any longer than that.

She heard her father's car pull up and the front door open. She had planned to be gone by the time he returned, so to avoid a scene, and then let him know where she was later that evening. But his earlier-than-expected arrival had scuppered her hopes of a quiet exit, so she finished putting her things into her small case.

There was a quiet, apologetic knock on her door.

'Danni?'

She told him to come in. Her case was open on the bed and practically full, while a few items were scattered next to it that she still had to find room for.

Thomas put his head around the door and looked at the bed. 'Just wanted to check you were OK,' he said.

'Yeah.'

'I can see you're busy. I'll leave you to it.'

He closed the door and Danni bit her top lip and cursed under her breath. She pushed the remaining items into the top of the small suitcase, forced it shut with all her strength and took it down the stairs and straight out into her car. Then she went back inside and called through the study door.

'I'm going to Sam's for a few days.'

Her father opened the door. 'Can't we talk?'

'She's expecting me and I'm already late,' she lied.

'When will I see you next?'

Danni couldn't remember ever seeing him look so beaten. 'I'll be back tomorrow to pick up a couple of things.'

She gave him a kiss on the cheek and went back to the car, afraid she was doing the wrong thing. They'd done nothing but argue or fight, but she still felt as though she was letting her mother down by walking away.

The drive took less than two minutes. Sam was waiting at her front door and excitedly grabbed her bag and took her to the spare room, which she had made as cosy as possible, setting up a sofabed, and then they went downstairs and sat half-watching an American police drama on TV, while Sam questioned her about her father's behaviour and then ordered in a takeaway. After they finished it, they shared washing-up duties and then spent the rest of the evening watching re-runs of old programmes, mostly comedies, at Sam's insistence, to cheer Danni up.

The next morning was clear and frosty, and Danni lay under the duvet in her temporary bed listening as first Mrs Newbold got up and left for work, and then, an hour later, Sam. She went back to sleep, and when she woke it was just after ten o'clock and the sun had come out and melted all of the frost.

She hoped she could time it so that, when she arrived home, her father would be busy in his study or, better still, out altogether, because she didn't feel like talking yet and she knew he'd want to. But, when she reached the house, not only was her father's car on the drive but another one too, and she had to leave her own car on the footpath outside.

In the kitchen, a man with a light grey suit was talking to her father as she walked in; they both stopped and her father made some awkward introductions.

'Danni, this is Mr Graham. This is my daughter, Danni.'

He didn't offer any explanation as to who the man was or why he was there, and Danni nodded a curt hello as her father ushered him from the kitchen and into the hallway.

'Well, Mr Edwards,' Mr Graham said as she walked up to her room, 'let me know if you decide you want to proceed with the letting.'

Danni heard her father hurriedly get the man out of the house; she stormed back down the stairs and they collided in the kitchen.

'Seriously?' she said, glaring into her father's eyes. 'Mum's only been gone a few weeks.'

'Please let me explain.'

Thomas persuaded her to sit down and filled the kettle with water. 'I'm just looking at a few options,' he said, and made them both a cup of tea. 'That's what I wanted to talk to you about yesterday.'

'Unbelievable.'

He put her cup in front of her but she waved it angrily away.

'I just think a smaller place would be better for us.'

'Us?'

'Yes, a fresh start.'

'I don't want a fresh start! All of our memories of Mum are here.'

Her father sat opposite and tried to hold her hand but she pulled it away. 'I know,' she said. 'But she isn't. And it's hard to be reminded of that every day.'

Danni shook her head with disappointment.

'Besides, this is too big for me.'

'What about me?'

'I thought you were at Sam's,' he said, and she realised her moving out had played right into his hands.

'For a few days! To get some space.'

'For now. But you'll leave properly one day for a place of your own.'

'You've really thought this through.'

'You said I needed to move forward.'

Danni glared at him again. 'Or move on completely?'

'Danni.'

'Mum's been gone a month and you want to go, just like that.'

'I just think it's for the best,' he said.

'The best? Destroying everything you and Mum built together?'

'That's not fair.'

'I can't imagine what she's thinking. You know how much she loved this place. I thought you both did.'

Danni stared into his eyes until he had to look away.

'I'm not selling it.'

'No, just letting strangers trample all over Mum's memory instead?'

Her father glared at her now. 'I can't win with you, can I?'

'One of us has to remember her.'

His hands were trembling now, and when he looked at her she felt a chill run down her spine. 'Don't you dare question my memory of her.'

'Then stop making me.' She stood up and he did too. 'I've got to go,' said Danni.

He sighed and sat back down. 'The last thing I want to do is to upset you,' he said, more softly now, the anger subsiding.

'Funny way of showing it.'

'I'll put the estate agent off until we've talked properly.'

'Don't bother. It isn't just the house,' said Danni. 'It's us two. We can't be in the same room at the moment.'

'I'm trying.'

'What, by hiding in your study? Or moving out?'

'It's been hard,' he said, and stood up again, picking up his empty cup to put in the dishwasher.

'Too hard to be a dad?'

'Don't be ridiculous!'

'Is it?' Danni asked.

'That's enough!'

Danni stared at him. All the things she wanted to say were on the tip of her tongue and she knew she wouldn't get a better opportunity.

'You can't just shut me up like you did Mum.'

Her father's face went bright red and the look in his eyes made Danni uncomfortable; it was one she had never seen before. She took a tiny backward step.

'What?' he said.

'When she said she wanted to tell me your secret?'

He looked at her and she stood firm, her heart pounding, and stared into his eyes. It was clear to her that he was uncomfortable but was trying to hide it with confusion. 'Secret?'

'I heard you!'

'I don't know what you heard, but—'

'Bullshit!'

He hurled the cup.

It wasn't at her; she could see in his eyes that he was being careful about that. It flew into the wall to her right, narrowly missing a picture that hung there, and spots of tea lay along its trajectory as it shattered into dozens of pieces that showered down on to the kitchen tiles.

For a moment, time stood still. Danni stared at her father, unsure what to do. He looked at her and then at the wall and down at the pieces of porcelain scattered across the floor.

'I'm sorry.'

She looked at him, feeling her eyes welling up. She walked past him and out of the house, climbed into her car and pulled away, not even looking to see if there were any other cars around.

It felt as though she was halfway to Sam's before she took her next breath.

29 | Laura

Laura hadn't planned on spending the night away from home.

She left High Cliffs House and Sandra Preston in the middle of the afternoon, feeling the drop in temperature and seeing the first white flakes as she got into her car. She was hungry, but the sky was a white blanket of snow and she knew her best option was to leave for home as quickly as possible. But, even by the time she reached the main road a mile and a half from the building, the snow had begun to fall heavily and a radio report said it was going to get worse the further north you travelled.

In the distance, she could see brake lights coming on. She pulled over to check the weather app on her phone and it was full of yellow warning signs. A lorry went past her and, when it came to stop a hundred yards ahead, its wheels skidded on the fresh snow and it slid momentarily from side to side. It was enough to convince Laura that it was too much of a risk to try to carry on, so she turned around and went back in the direction of High Cliffs House to find a hotel in the nearest town.

There was only one, and when Laura got there she took the last single room they had and went straight into the restaurant and ordered a meal. When she went up to her room an hour later, it was a small corner one with a tiny desk and portable TV that had terrible reception because of the weather, so she took out her laptop and began turning the pages of notes she'd made from the interview into something resembling an article.

She knew that David would have no use for it, and the local papers had already run a basic piece on the twentieth anniversary less than eighteen months earlier, so she thought hard about a fresh perspective that didn't just tell people what they already knew.

Laura intended to send her article to the local papers in the town where Jessica had gone missing, and, if it was good enough, she hoped they might want to use it and pay her a freelance fee – which would come in useful, as the *Gazette* wouldn't cover her expenses and the overnight stay had just doubled them. Eventually, after several false starts and deletions, she settled on a way to tell Sandra's story and typed out the article before falling into her bed at around twenty past midnight, only stopping to call her mother and tell her she had decided to stay at a friend's house for the night.

When she woke, the Sunday morning rain and warmer temperatures had cleared the snow from the roads, and she made an early start, her thoughts turning to Sandra Preston several times during the four-hour drive. The interview had been thorough but she could still have sat there longer and gone much deeper; Sandra had seemed happy to sit and talk all day and Laura had eventually had to make an excuse to get away. But, it was perfectly understandable, she thought, because it didn't seem as if Sandra got any real opportunities to talk about Jessica. Laura doubted that Bloody Mary or any of the other patients would be good listeners, and the staff had been working hard just to keep things under control. She also knew that she'd only done the interview because she'd felt sorry for Sandra, and that it was time to send the article off and move on.

The next day, further evidence of her new position in David's thinking came when she was invited for the first time ever to the Monday morning meeting, and handed a new lead to follow. The lead was about some leakages in the town's water pipes. Some locals had set up a Facebook page where they posted photographs of cracked or leaking pipes. The idea, as far as Laura could tell, was to shame the council, and the water company that owned the pipes, into fixing them. The social media page was claiming that the issue was putting an extra twenty pounds on to the average water bill and, as tended to happen with this kind of thing, it had already garnered over a thousand 'likes' and nearly a hundred comments saying how disgusting it all was. It felt to Laura like a million miles from missing children stories, from shopping centres or beaches, and she found it hard to take it seriously, especially when a five-minute call with a water company employee told her that such leaks were very common, had no impact on bills at all, and that the company had actually budgeted to lose more water than they did each year from damaged pipes.

Despite the calculations and accusations that were all over the internet page, it really was an insignificant story and she knew it, but she did the local people the courtesy of making a few calls and getting some quotes. She knew that the people who had posted on Facebook wouldn't want to let the facts get in the way of a good story, and the council and water company would insist on the paper getting the details right and setting the record straight, but when she checked some of the figures she had been given by the water company against some published OFWAT data it merely added weight to the corporate argument, as the lost water volumes were, comparatively, some of the lowest in the whole country.

In the end, she decided to write a story that was fair to both parties. She would include all the facts and figures but also highlight that there were pipes leaking a lot of water and that was a waste no matter how positively the water company spun it. As she began typing, she knew that it would be lucky to make the website, let alone the front page.

Her mind kept wandering back to Sandra and some of the things that she had said during the interview. She took out a second notebook she'd used for Sandra's interview, and began making some notes about further questions she might ask and changes she might make to the article she was going to send out that evening. When the clock reached the time when she usually went for her lunch break, she saw she had committed twelve lines to the water article and spent at least two hours looking at pages on Google about Jessica Preston.

'You coming to lunch?'

The question made her jump. She had never been asked before if she wanted to join the others on their lunch break; she was clearly one of them now. She told them she'd catch them up and quickly deleted the history on her browser just in case David decided to check it.

If he had, he would have found numerous searches relating to the police activity, reports that had been made public and articles in the press at the time. Laura was shocked how little Jessica's story had been reported nationally; after the first few weeks it had virtually disappeared from the news in much the way as the little girl had disappeared from the beach. There had been no body found, yet as soon as her washed-up hat was discovered, the police detective in charge, and the assorted media, had settled quickly on that conclusion. Laura had researched drowning and found that although a body not turning up was possible, it was still relatively rare for it not to happen eventually.

When she got back from her lunch – a sandwich in the building's canteen with half a dozen of the *Gazette*'s staff – she focused on her article about the water dispute for a few hours and emailed the final draft to David, and then watched as he reacted to the 'incoming mail' ping on his computer and opened her document and began reading it.

Laura felt she'd finally been accepted. The editor smiled and she imagined he was impressed at the way she'd diplomatically served both sides on the issue.

The trouble was, there was now only one story on her mind.

And it wasn't that one.

30 | Laura

'Does Angela like her new job, then?'

Laura sat in the kitchen, about to put a spoonful of vegetable soup in her mouth when her mother asked, and for a second she wasn't sure what had prompted the question. Then she remembered: as far as her mother knew, Angela was the friend she had stayed with on Saturday night, and she'd recently taken up a new role with a fashion magazine in Manchester.

'Uh-huh.'

Laura's mother sat down at the table with her own bowl. Laura watched her sprinkle pepper on to her soup and look up at her. 'What's up?'

Laura hated lying, especially to her mother. 'I didn't stay with Angela on Saturday.'

Helen looked at her with a puzzled frown. 'No?'

Laura swallowed and shook her head. 'It's a long story,' she said, 'but I wanted to surprise you and it didn't quite work out as planned.'

'So where were you?'

'Devon.'

Her mother stopped eating and put her spoon down. Laura knew she wouldn't be happy that she had done that kind of journey on her own, or without telling them beforehand.

'I was doing an interview…for a story.'

'In Devon?'

'I knew you'd worry if you knew I was going.'

'Why would the *Gazette* want you to interview someone in Devon?'

Laura explained how it had transpired, how she'd had the idea for the piece and how she had taken on the interview herself after Rebecca Holden had been found.

'Goodness.'

'I couldn't just cancel on her. Not after what she's been through.'

'I can't believe you lied about it.'

Apart from the odd tiny white lie Laura hadn't been dishonest with her mother before, and she could see the disappointment in her eyes.

'I'm sorry,' she said, 'but I thought you'd try to talk me out of going.'

'Why would I do that?'

'Because David didn't agree to it? Or because I had to pay my own travel?'

Helen sighed. 'I know you don't earn enough to do what you did.'

'I just thought it was worth it. Are you angry with me?'

'Angry? No, of course not.'

Laura thought she looked angry.

'I wish you'd told us. You could have taken your dad's car and we could have got you a better hotel.'

Laura smiled apologetically. 'Sorry. And there's only one hotel anyway.'

Helen began eating her soup again and her expression softened. 'Just promise me you'll tell me in future.'

Laura promised she would and they continued eating. Her mother cut them both a slice of home-made bread. 'Now, tell me about this poor woman.'

Laura gave her mother a brief summary of the interview with the girl's mother and of the disappearance of Jessica Preston. 'Do you remember hearing about it?' she asked.

Helen thought about it for a few seconds.

'Not really. It's a long time ago. I might have seen it on the news but I don't remember, if I'm honest.'

'I don't think many people do. That's what Sandra said. It didn't get the coverage it would now.'

'Times have changed.'

'It's such a sad story.'

Helen nodded. 'I can't imagine what she's gone through.'

'Still going through,' said Laura. 'She pretends she's strong, but she can't face it really. She's staying in the mental health unit to avoid facing reality.'

'That the girl died?'

'More that she lost her. She's convinced she's still alive.'

Helen raised her eyebrows.

'I know. But she's certain of it. She thinks someone took her.'

'Took? From a beach? With people around?'

'I know,' said Laura, 'but there's no proof she drowned either.'

'So why isn't she looking for her?'

Laura put her hand under her chin and stared at her mother. 'That's what I said.'

'And?'

Laura shrugged.

'She's tired of the heartache, I think. But, if she's right, then her daughter could be out there somewhere and doesn't even know it.'

'After all this time?'

Laura nodded.

'She could be anywhere in the world.'

'But just imagine if someone tracked her down. Talk about the story of the century.'

Helen smiled, as if she'd read her daughter's mind. 'The police couldn't find her. What chance has anyone else?'

'But if they did.'

'Who's they? Anyone I might know?'

Laura smiled. Her mother had always liked to tease her, and it was such a long shot, it was barely worth thinking about.

'You never know, Mum.'

'I know that it's big. Too big for David.'

'Tell me about it.'

Her mother looked sad and Laura asked her what was wrong.

'I said this would happen,' Helen replied, 'when your dad put a word in for you at the paper.'

'Said *what* would happen?'

'The *Gazette*. I always said it would hold you back.'

'We all have to start somewhere – you said so yourself, remember?'

'I know I did. But it's obvious that you want more than it can offer. The *Gazette* won't even pay for your petrol to Devon.'

'It's not a local story.'

Helen got up and began putting their bowls into the dishwasher. 'I wanted to send you to a top university. In America.'

'You never said.'

'We talked about it, at the time.'

'You did?'

'But you wanted to do it on your own.'

'I did. I do.'

'I know you have. But I can't help thinking that if we'd pushed you, if we'd helped you go to America, you'd be writing bigger stories now rather than having to chase million-to-one shots and pay your own travel costs.'

'It's a big *if*,' said Laura, 'but I have a job, things are looking up and I'm really enjoying working on this article.'

'You're still working on it? I thought it wasn't local.'

'I've written up the interview. And I'm sending it to the papers in Devon, see if they want to publish it.'

Helen looked surprised, or impressed; Laura couldn't quite tell which. 'Good for you.'

Laura smiled at her. 'Well,' she said, 'I've got to pay for that petrol somehow.'

31 | Danni

Danni felt more at home at Sam's than at her own house.

It had only been a few days, but she was comfortable and they were enjoying each other's company. She knew that it would be easy to extend her stay, but she mustn't. She needed to begin making some plans of her own.

'You know you can stay as long as you want?' Sam asked when she told her this.

'I know. But it feels like I'm putting off moving forward. And Leo will be back soon and I'll be in the way.'

Leo was Sam's new boyfriend, whom she'd met at work. He worked at a sports management company – Danni had no idea what that meant – and travelled a lot. His latest project had taken him to the Middle East and he'd been there for six weeks, during which time he'd been back in the UK on two occasions. He was due back permanently in a fortnight anyway, but he'd tried to get Sam to travel to Dubai for a weekend and she'd resisted, something Danni had not understood.

'I just want to see how it goes first,' said Sam, 'before I start flying across the world to see him.'

'But think of the shopping!' Danni laughed.

'Where will you go, anyway?'

'Dunno. Home at first, I suppose. Wherever that is.'

'I can't believe he wants to leave that house,' Sam said, and opened a large box of chocolates that she insisted had to be emptied before the evening was over.

'He emailed me today.'

'Is that his new way of avoiding arguments?'

Danni smiled. 'He said all he's trying to do is get a smaller place – an apartment – and rent the house out as a holiday home.'

'Cosy.'

'I had an email about an interview too.'

'What? Where?'

'Southampton.'

Sam looked at her, demanding more information. Danni explained that a company that supplied the dental practice had asked her to come for an interview. Their sales director had been at the practice during Danni's shift a few weeks before her mother died, and when his appointment with the practice manager had been delayed he had watched her handling patients and started talking to her about a new position they had coming up. 'He said I would be great for it. So he took my email address and said he'd let me know after they advertised.'

'Sounds more like he was hitting on you.'

'Not everyone thinks like you! Anyway, they put an advert in the paper two weeks ago and they're interviewing on Thursday.'

'Did you apply?'

'He said I didn't need to.'

'Are you going?'

'I wasn't sure,' said Danni, 'but the way things are, what have I got to lose? I like my job, but it would be really good to move into something with more prospects, and with a bigger company. And the job they're hiring for has far more responsibilities – and better pay.'

The next day she went back to the house to collect her favourite blue suit for the interview and her father came out of the study to apologise about throwing the cup.

'I was just frustrated. About a lot of things,' he said, blushing. 'I've never tried to shut you up. You or your mum.'

'I heard you talking,' Danni blurted out, 'that night I split up with Euan.'

He frowned and gazed out of the window, trying to recall.

'You and Mum were arguing,' she helped. 'And I heard you.'

'I'm sure what you heard, Danni, was just a minor disagreement. We did have them from time to time, you know.'

Danni wasn't sure they did. 'What was it about?'

'I can't even remember. It can't have been that important.'

'Mum said something like *she'll find out one day.*'

Her father smiled. 'I think it was about someone at the shop, if I recall correctly.'

From his expression, Danni wasn't sure, but he sounded confident enough and she felt silly again – as though she was dreaming up some big conspiracy that sounded less and less plausible the more she said it. She changed the subject and told him about the job interview.

'It won't do you any harm to broaden your horizons,' he said.

'And it makes you feel less guilty.'

'What?'

'For taking my home from under me,' she said, and instantly regretted it; at the moment, she couldn't stop looking for ways to have a confrontation with him.

'Please don't find underlying meanings in everything,' he said. 'I just meant it would be good for you to explore something new.'

Danni nodded. 'Sorry.'

'And the new place I've looked at is big enough for both of us. But I suppose you'll move to Southampton if you get this job.'

'It's just an interview, Dad. There are probably loads of candidates.'

When he'd sent the email earlier, her father had attached a few photographs of an apartment he'd found. Although she hadn't acknowledged them, she had taken a look and it was a nice place, a new-build, with two storeys, in a beautiful position on the beachfront with sea views from the living room and both bedrooms. Her father said in his email that he had secured first option on the top-floor apartment – a perfect place, as he put it, to get inspiration for his writing, and it would need virtually no maintenance, unlike the family home.

'Where will you put all Mum's stuff?' she asked him.

'I'll have to put some in storage. It's a decent-sized place but there are very few cupboards.'

Danni pictured her mother's things sitting in a cold, dark storage unit with a big yellow logo on the building. It was not an appealing thought and she told her father so.

'Well, if you want to keep some of her things out, you'll need to do it next week,' he said. 'And we can give some to charity. To the shop. She'd have wanted that.'

She nodded and they carried on talking – the first time in a while that they hadn't ended with a disagreement. He wished her luck with the interview when she left an hour later.

The next morning, she stood at the train station in her best suit, listening to an announcement that told her that the train to Southampton was about to arrive. It was dark, and a swirling wind was blowing across the tracks. It was that hour before the sun came up and frosty underfoot, and she held a takeaway coffee cup in one hand and a newspaper in the other, feeling like a proper commuter when the train slowed to a stop and she stepped on board.

A minute or so later, the 06.10 to Southampton was ready to depart and Danni sat with her feet next to the heaters, trying to warm them up. As she sipped her coffee she opened her newspaper, and began thumbing through the pages until an article on page ten caught her attention.

It was about the mother of a child. A child who had gone missing more than twenty years ago.

Does Life Really Go On?

As the twenty-first anniversary of her disappearance approaches, the mother of Jessica Preston is no nearer to finding closure, *writes Laura Grainger.*

Twenty-one years ago, two-year-old Jessica Preston went missing from a crowded beach in Devon and was never seen again. Anyone old enough to remember, and who lived in the area, won't need reminding of the harrowing events on that sunny August morning, or the hours, days and weeks afterwards as the community tried to come to terms with what had happened.

It is hard to imagine it today, with twenty-four-hour news cycles, social media campaigns and high-profile child abduction cases very fresh in the memory, but back then the story was only a national headline for one or two days, and even locally it quickly moved from headline story to the sidebar and eventually only warranted a mention on a significant anniversary.

Life quickly moved on, as it does. Even those who helped police to search the beach, coastal paths and nearby woodland after Jessica went missing soon went back to their daily lives. The police search went on for longer, but they were so sure that the little girl, a few months from her third birthday, had drowned, that the search was eventually called off and the case closed in all but name. Of course, the official line is that anyone with information should contact the local police, but the reality is that no one has called that helpline for more than fifteen years.

So what of the family Jessica left behind?

Her father, Todd, died soon after the fifth anniversary of her disappearance, from alcohol poisoning, after becoming addicted to drink to numb the pain of losing his only daughter. Her brother was taken into care and eventually adopted by his foster parents.

Which leaves Jessica's mother, Sandra, for whom life hasn't moved on at all. She sits, all these years later, still clinging to the hope that her daughter will one day return. Shortly after losing her son and husband in quick succession, she was admitted to a psychiatric unit, and she remains there now. Waiting and watching through a large glass window, her only 'view' of the world which has treated her so harshly.

She has been told that she must find closure – move on and accept the fact that her little girl died that day in the rough and unpredictable sea – but she believes, vehemently, that the police and coroner's theory is simply not the case. She remains convinced that her daughter was taken and has been raised by someone else, so there has never been a funeral or memorial service for Jessica in the twenty and a half years since her mother last saw her.

'Unless anyone can show me her body, I'll always maintain she is alive and was taken by someone. It was my view on the day and nothing has changed,' she told me when I visited her earlier this week. 'So I console myself with the fact that, even though she isn't with me, and I've missed her growing into a young woman, she is hopefully still happy and loved.'

Whichever version you choose to believe, it is a tragic story.

On one hand, a mother's life has been torn apart and no one has been able to provide that tiny crumb of comfort by telling her what happened that day.

But if Sandra Preston is right about her daughter's disappearance, and she was taken that August day, then her daughter would have been too young to have any recollection of it and will have grown up never knowing, or even having any idea of, her real identity. Unless the people who took her decide to give themselves up, or ever tell her what they had done, she will be completely oblivious to the truth.

And even if she is right, where does that leave Sandra now? Two decades later she remains hopeful but also realistic. We do not know what Jessica might look like today, or if she is alive, if she is still in the country or was smuggled abroad. Even the most sophisticated facial recognition techniques are based on probability and assumptions. The description of Jessica as a two-year-old might apply to ten to fifteen per cent of the UK female population, and then she might have significantly changed her appearance anyway.

So, with that in mind, her mother has accepted that, although she won't ever give up hope, the chances of her ever seeing her daughter are incredibly small.

But, with that tiniest glimmer of hope, she sits alone in the unit looking out on a beach just like the one her daughter vanished from. Whether it was a terrible accident or a callous crime, whether you blame her for not looking after her daughter better, or think of her as a victim in every sense, she won't mind. No one will ever blame her more than she blames herself. More than twenty years later, she has little to fill her days except the waiting. Her family are gone; she has no friends and no visitors. Her only 'relationships' are the ones she has forged with the staff or fellow patients.

And that is probably the life that awaits her for the rest of her days.

But, 'If I give up on her,' she told me as she watched the empty beach below from the huge windows, 'then what happens if she finds out who she is and comes looking for me? At least, with me here, she'll have someone waiting for her.'

People use the expression 'life goes on', don't they? But, when they say it, I'm sure they haven't just spent an hour in the company of Sandra Preston.

Part Four

Two years after she was taken…

It had taken time – a whole two years – for us to stop looking over our shoulders.

Two years before we finally knew that that knock on the door wasn't going to come at any minute – and we had lived over a million of those minutes – the knock that would destroy it all in an instant. And we began to relax. Not completely relax, you understand, but when you've spent two years wound as tightly as a spring, waiting for something to happen, it was so good to at least not have that feeling any longer.

Two years was the point when we stopped thinking of ourselves as fugitives, and started thinking of ourselves as parents. Parents to a beautiful little girl.

It's actually your perspective that changes in that time. She was always a beautiful little girl, of course we knew that, but one whom we saw differently from anyone else. For those first twenty-four months we talked about her as if she were something we had picked off a supermarket shelf or ordered from a website. So it was good to be able to think of her as a child; one we were now fully responsible for and who loved us unconditionally.

My biggest worry, to begin with in those first two years, was whether she knew what we had done. I studied books in the library and they all said that a child wouldn't be able to remember their life before the age of three, but obviously we could never ask anyone to confirm it so we had to trust what the books told us. But I always wondered, when I looked in her eyes or caught her watching me; she had this look – not fear or anger but disappointment, as if some part of her instinctively knew but she just didn't understand it.

But, after two years, that look had gone.

The news that had been so helpful in keeping us fully updated on the story now began to also tell us that the story had almost bled completely from the public's consciousness. It had become a footnote every now and again in the media, only mentioned on the anniversary and when there was a very rare case of mistaken identity.

Time allowed us to become parents, and my wife thrived in the role. It was like watching a new person form in the space where the old one once stood. Heartache had gone without a trace and had been replaced with confidence and pride. After two years, she began to take her out in public and no one in the village batted an eyelid, for there was nothing at all unusual about a mother out with her child.

'Isn't she big for her age?' people would say when they saw her, and my wife would agree – and this was crucial in the way we integrated into our new lives. We had false records and documents that showed we had a daughter who was a few months younger than the one that went missing.

So time, and the changing of it, helped us cover our tracks too. We were the proud parents of a young girl in a place where no one knew us, in a world that had all but forgotten what had happened on that beach.

Two years ago, when they'd walked through that door, it had been impossible to imagine a time when we would be able to show our daughter off in public without the constant threat of being found out. But we, like the world, had moved on.

How our daughter's real parents were moving on was something I tried not to think about too much.

Two years? Is that really how long it's been?

I hadn't even realised until a local reporter knocked at the door early in the evening and asked if I would answer a few questions. Todd was asleep on the sofa, and if I were being kind I'd tell you he'd had a hard day at work, but I'd stopped being kind after two years. He had passed out; he'd started drinking earlier than usual that day, and, when I let this reporter in, it was for some company as much as anything else.

We sat down in the kitchen and I made us a cup of tea. 'So, it's two years today,' he said by way of an opening to his questions, and I looked at him, confused, angry that he'd not even got his facts right; annoyed that he was so sloppy. In my head it seemed much less than that, and I could hardly remember there being a first-year anniversary. But then, I'd spent most of that time in a self-imposed daze; just getting through each day was an achievement, never mind remembering them.

The poor man must have wondered what on earth was wrong with my face – he hadn't even reached the first question in his notebook – and then I started to tell him he was wrong, but, as the bitter words started to slip from my mouth, I stopped. It was me that was wrong, not him. The seasons all merged into one long bleak winter for me, but spring had duly arrived, and now it was summer again; I just hadn't noticed the date.

She had been gone for two years.

What I could remember was the way people changed towards you. At first, people I thought I knew, but who did not have the first clue how I was feeling, told me how I should act and the things I should feel. *Stay positive*, they said to begin with, but that message became mixed over time and then changed; stay *strong*, they began to tell me, which was just another way of saying *prepare for the worst*.

Only they had no idea what the worst was. Was, for example, the worst finding her dead, or never finding her at all and not knowing if she lived or had died? I realised that, however well-meaning they were, their words were meaningless; after all, none of them really knew what had happened to Jessica.

Then, over time, they stopped saying anything at all. I was supposed to have grieved, come to terms with my loss and moved on. The police said it, the counsellor said it, and the people I thought of as friends probably said it too.

Only I wasn't ready to move on.

But it became easier to nod in the right places and pretend I thought they were making some sense, rather than keep fighting them. And my friends? They stopped coming around and calling me anyway when I couldn't move on. That was when I needed my husband most, to handle things like this, support me and help me through anniversaries and answer difficult questions in interviews, but the man snoring off his stupor in the next room had nothing to offer me. If he'd thought she was still alive, he'd have been out there looking for her.

And now the reporter began asking his questions and using the past tense in a way that told me he was sure she was dead too. I thought about telling him what had really happened to my daughter but they'd all heard it before, and by the look on his face it wasn't what he'd come to hear today. He only wanted a grieving mother so I gave him exactly that: the tears and incoherent mumblings of someone who was slowly coming to terms with her loss.

It was just easier than fighting all the time.

32 | Laura

The editor of the *Herald* had posted Laura a compliments slip with a handwritten thank-you and cheque for two hundred and fifty pounds, plus five copies of the paper containing her article.

In an email he had told her how pleased he'd been with it, and of the positive response since it had been published. When she'd sent it to him, a few days earlier, it had been with no real expectations, and he had given no guarantees of using it and certainly not of paying her for it, so it was a real bonus that he had covered her costs, with some change, afterwards. She thought about framing the cheque, as a motivating reminder that her talent had been recognised beyond David Weatherall's office, but after checking her bank balance she'd cashed it instead.

Her mother had been so proud when she'd shown her the article in print, although also worried about David's reaction.

'Won't he be upset?' she asked over breakfast.

Laura had been concerned too, but the *Herald* was a very local paper, just like the *Gazette*, and wouldn't have a readership far outside its circulation, so she had put her worries to the back of her mind and she told her mother to do the same.

'I just don't want you getting in trouble.'

'I won't. I doubt they shift more than a few hundred copies.'

'So what next?'

'Back to the day job, I suppose.'

Laura was quite relieved to say it. Sandra might not have any closure, but she was looking forward to it; the travelling she'd done had already eaten into a lot of her spare time and when she'd looked in the mirror that morning she had been shocked by the fatigued appearance of the twenty-something girl who looked back at her. The missing child had provided her with fifteen minutes of fame; it was time to start building on it.

'Got to happen some time,' her mother said with a smile.

'Just imagine *if* Sandra was right, though.'

'It's a helluva big *if*.'

'But imagine it. Finding her, after all these years. Now that's a story...'

Helen stood up and looked at the clock on the microwave. 'C'mon. If you're not quick, you won't have a day job to be late for.'

Laura was pulled abruptly from her imagination; she took a last bite of her toast and then rushed out to the car, making it into the office with a few minutes to spare. But all morning she found her mind wandering, asking questions, and her fingers typing words into Google searches that were all about Jessica Preston and nothing to do with her day job.

What if there was even a one per cent chance of finding her?

It was her way of justifying her actions, but by lunchtime she had to admit that there didn't seem to be anything even close to a one per cent chance. The trail had gone cold long before the police had called off the search; and that itself was more than fifteen years ago. After that, other than the odd reference or comment in the local press, there was nothing new that had been added to the story in all that time.

She glanced over at David's office. He was sitting in his chair and it looked as though he was dictating a letter to Sue even though all three of them knew he could type perfectly well. It was his way, Laura thought, of just holding on to the past for a little longer. He paused and turned her way and she looked back at her screen, embarrassed, and trying to work out how he seemed to sense it every time she watched him. But the jolt made her concentrate on her *Gazette* duties for the next few hours, and she was grateful it did.

But little by little Sandra Preston slowly found her way back into her consciousness, and the image of her sitting at High Cliffs House, watching the waves crash on the rocks below, became sharper.

And then, from nowhere, her mind moved on to the water. She imagined the day: clear and hot, no clouds and only a gentle breeze off the sea; but still the water didn't take its cue and waves continued to roll, heavily at first when they were thirty yards away and then breaking white as they closed in on the sand. A red flag fluttered in what little wind there was. The lifeguard's high chair was empty, and would be for at least another hour or so.

She saw a little girl, summer hat on her head, with blonde curls protruding from under the brim, walking near the edge, looking out at the oncoming waves. Her bare feet pattered in the waves as they broke on her feet.

What if a bigger one came in?

What if she stepped out further than she should?

Laura shook her head. But for the first time she began to reassess how sure she was of Sandra's assertion. She had done the research on rip-currents and knew how dangerous they could be for an adult, never mind a small child who couldn't swim or even begin to appreciate the danger she might be in.

And if she didn't go in the sea, why would her hat wash up later?

Could she have drowned?

Could Sandra be wrong?

Her mobile phone buzzed, and the image went away.

She didn't know the number but she recognised the area code; it was the same one as High Cliffs House. She glanced at David but he was busy talking to Sue, so she let her voicemail system take a message then went outside and then listened to it. It was a woman with a distinctive West Country accent asking her to call back, which she did immediately. The woman worked at the *Herald* and had taken a call from a member of the public who had seen Laura's article on Sandra and wanted to speak to her.

'She *pacifically* asked for you to call her,' the woman said, making Laura want to correct her, but instead she scribbled down the details for a Mrs Upson and called her immediately.

The woman who answered asked to be called Maureen. She said she had given a statement to the police at the time of Jessica's disappearance, which Laura was immediately intrigued by; she hadn't heard of a Maureen Upson or seen her name in any of the articles or police transcripts she'd managed to find online.

'What did you tell them, Mrs Upson?'

'Maureen.'

'Sorry, Maureen. What did you say to them?'

'That I'd seen the little girl.'

'How did you know it was her?'

'Not that many girls her age walking around on their own. And I saw her picture on the telly later.'

'Where was she, Mrs…Maureen?'

'Walking towards the promenade.'

'Away from the water?'

'That's right.'

Laura scribbled a note in her pad and screwed up her face. It didn't make any sense that this hadn't come out before, especially given its relevance to Sandra's theory. There had been no other witnesses that day, Laura couldn't believe the police would discount anything of such potential significance. She asked the woman what had happened.

'I don't think they believed me.'

'Why wouldn't they?'

There was a pause. 'I talk to myself.'

'Talk?'

'Folk round here think I'm a bit...strange.'

'What do you say? To yourself?'

'All kinds of things.'

'When do you do it?'

'When I've had a drink.'

Laura grimaced. She had a feeling that was going to be the answer.

'Had you been drinking that morning, Mrs Upson?'

'I was drinking a lot then, but mainly in the afternoons.'

'Are you drinking now?'

'Do I sound like I am?'

Laura didn't like to say that she did a little.

'And you definitely saw her walking away from the sea?'

'Yes. It was sunny. I was outside. I drink more when it rains, you see.'

'Did the police take a formal statement?' Laura asked.

'The next day, but they still didn't believe me.'

'Why didn't they?'

There was another pause, even longer this time. 'Probably because the day before that I'd told them that I'd taken her.'

'What? On the day she went missing?'

'Uh-huh.'

'Why would you do that?'

'It was in the afternoon. I'd been drinking by then.'

Laura shook her head. David Weatherall would tell her to run a million miles from a witness this unreliable, but she didn't want to.

'I appreciate your calling me,' she said, with doubtful sincerity.

'Just trying to help. Like I was back then.'

Laura pictured a chaotic beach with police everywhere, the parents frantic, volunteers joining the search, divers in the water – and then Maureen Upson turning up saying she was responsible for taking the child. She wouldn't have been surprised if they'd locked her up, so it was very likely that they would have disregarded anything else she told them.

She sighed and told the woman she would get back to her if she needed her again. It wasn't much, but if any of it was true, then it would make the drowning theory a little less conclusive. It didn't prove anything, and it was a long way away from a 'one per cent chance'.

But Laura couldn't stop thinking about what had really happened to Jessica Preston.

33 | Laura

Laura walked into the Devon café.

She had said as little as possible to anyone about what she was doing but her instincts had urged her to at least meet with Maureen Upson and look into her eyes. So she called in and told David she'd been sick overnight, and then told her parents that a last-minute place had opened up on a training course in Birmingham and she'd been on the waiting list. Neither her parents nor her boss had asked any questions, and David had been unusually sympathetic, which had made her feel even guiltier about lying to him.

Her meeting had been arranged for midday, and Laura had left six hours earlier than that so that she could also visit the beach Jessica went missing from. Time seemed to have stood still; it looked exactly as Sandra had described, although the weather was overcast, not sunny, and the sand had no people on it. The ice-cream van wasn't there either. She had walked on to the sand and then gone down to the shoreline and along the edge of the water, trying to picture exactly where the family had been on the day.

By the time she'd got back to the car and driven to the next town, she was a few minutes late. Maureen Upson was waiting for her in the café, a copy of the paper in her hand so that Laura would recognise her but it wasn't necessary – she was the only customer in there. Laura waved to her and ordered a coffee for herself. She took it over to the table and reimbursed Maureen Upson the two pounds, fifteen pence she had paid for hers. 'It's the least I can do. Thank you for seeing me.'

She found the woman friendly and very talkative, and, as far as she could tell, stone cold sober; she'd smelt her breath when she had shaken her hand and given her the coins.

'Why confess to taking Jessica? You must have known it would look bad,' Laura asked after a few minutes of small talk.

Maureen Upson smiled. 'I did a lot of daft things back then.'

'Did it get you in trouble?'

'A ticking-off from Detective Whateverhisnamewas.'

'I bet.'

'When I'd had a drink, I'd say some pretty stupid things, I'm afraid.'

They talked on, and Laura got her to go into more detail about the day that Jessica went missing. Despite the length of time that had passed, Maureen seemed very clear on things, and it sounded nothing like the ramblings of a local drunk.

'So you just walked up and confessed.'

'I'd left before all the commotion, but I saw the news that afternoon and that's when I recognised the girl I'd seen. From her picture on TV.'

'So you called the police?'

The woman nodded and blushed. 'But I'd been...you know.'

Laura nodded, and roughly sketched the timeline on her pad.

'But the next day,' Maureen continued, 'I remembered it clearly. I knew I'd seen her. She had something in her hand – this pink strap or something. It was glistening in the sun.'

'Did you tell that to the police?'

'I called, but they didn't seem happy to hear from me.'

'I guess they had a lot on their plate.'

They talked more. Maureen had been leaving the beach after a mid-morning walk when she had seen Jessica. She'd headed off just afterwards, and gone to her small cottage, where she'd spent the afternoon drinking her bottle of choice – she couldn't remember what that was – and fallen asleep. The woman admitted to Laura that she had had very little recollection of afternoons in those days, and when she'd woken the news was on, she had seen Jessica's picture on the TV, and she'd picked up the phone.

Laura thanked her, bought her another cup of coffee and left her sitting in the café. It was bleak now, with dark grey, rain-filled clouds overhead, and the wind had picked up, so she hurried back to the pay-and-display and collected her car.

But she had no intention of going home.

High Cliffs House was roughly ten miles back along the coast and when she arrived, without an appointment, she was concerned that she might get turned away, but, when the receptionist called the manager in, she was greeted with a smile.

'I hoped you'd be back.'

'You did?'

The manager shook her hand warmly. 'After you talked to her, Sandra was as bright as I've seen her since I started here. I don't know what it was, but you did more good than anything we've tried in the last ten years.'

Laura had been worried that the interview might have had the opposite effect.

'She's just finishing her lunch. I don't think we got properly introduced last time. I'm Violet Stanton.' The manager showed Laura into her office and asked the receptionist to make a pot of tea for two. 'I hope that's OK.'

'Lovely, thank you.'

The manager sat in her leather chair and smiled. Laura sat opposite, awkwardly returning the smile and fidgeting in the plastic chair.

'Can I be frank and ask what your intentions are? With Sandra.'

Laura had anticipated the question. 'I just wanted to follow up after the article, that's all,' she lied. 'I was worried it might have been a lot for her to handle.'

'She's tougher than she looks.'

Laura nodded, and wondered if Violet Stanton knew that Sandra didn't need to be there at all. She looked around at the office, a tidy space with expensive furniture, if only on the manager's side of the ornate wooden desk.

'This is a private unit, right?'

Mrs Stanton nodded.

'It must cost a lot to stay here.'

'About twenty-five thousand a year, give or take. Is it relevant? I thought you'd finished your research with the article.'

'Oh, I have. Sorry, I didn't mean to…' Laura apologised. 'I just wondered how Sandra could afford to stay here. If we're being frank with each other.'

She looked directly at the manager, who didn't flinch. 'I'm not at liberty to discuss patients' financial arrangements,' she said with a smile.

'Of course not.'

'Let's just say,' Violet continued, leaning forward and seemingly enjoying knowing something Laura didn't, 'that there are some generous people about.'

'People? No, I shouldn't ask.'

'An anonymous donor. Paid Sandra's bill ever since her money ran out.'

'Wow.'

The receptionist tapped the door and came in with a steaming teapot and two cups and saucers. Violet stopped speaking and began pouring their drinks as she left. 'I've said more than I should. I wouldn't want—'

'Already forgotten,' Laura said, and smiled. 'As I said, I just wanted to check Sandra was OK.'

'Grab your tea, then. I'll take you through.'

Laura was led into the large room and the manager left her at Sandra's table by the window, winking as she left them alone.

'Hello, Sandra.'

'Thought I'd seen the last of you.' She was staring outside, but Laura heard a softer, gentler tone compared to her previous visit.

'I was in the area.'

Sandra smiled. 'Nice article,' she said, and Laura noticed that a copy of the *Herald* was lying on the table.

'Thanks.'

As they sat and talked, Sandra told her that the article had made her feel, for the first time in twenty years, like a victim rather than the cause of her own nightmare. To Laura she seemed more relaxed, as if a weight had been lifted, and she even allowed Bloody Mary to join them for a cup of tea, although after less than five minutes she suddenly lost interest and ran to the far windows and tried to climb out of one.

'Why don't you get out of here?' Laura said as she watched a nurse tell Mary off.

'What's left for me out there?' She gestured towards the window, towards the sea.

'Family?'

'Todd's didn't want anything to do with me. They blamed me for what happened.'

'How can they have?'

'Not just them. Friends stopped calling round. A few didn't even come to Todd's funeral. There were more bleeding reporters there than friends. No offence.'

'None taken,' said Laura. She took out her notebook and thumbed to the last page she had written on. 'And I wasn't *just* in the area. I was here to see Maureen Upson.'

Sandra smiled and nodded slowly. 'You mean Mad Mo?'

'You know her? She said she saw Jessica before she went missing.'

'How could I not know her?' Sandra snorted. 'She also said she was the one who took Jessica. Did she tell you that?'

Laura nodded. Sandra looked surprised.

'Well, then. She's crazier than Bloody Mary there.' She nodded towards Mary, who had been told off by the nurse and was sulking on one of the sofas.

'She also said she drank a lot. But that she was sober when she saw Jessica.'

Sandra's hand began to shake, making her cup clatter against its saucer.

'Doubt it.'

'If she did see her, then Jessica was going away from the water, not towards it.'

Sandra sniffed. 'That woman doesn't know what day it is.'

'She remembered more than you'd think.'

'Heard on TV, more like.'

'She was really clear about it. The weather, the promenade, even the sparkly strap Jessica was holding.'

Sandra flinched and put her cup down. She continued to stare at the beach, but Laura could see her hands were shaking more than a little now.

'What is it?' Laura asked.

There was a pause that seemed to last for hours. Laura waited for Sandra to speak, her pencil poised on the page.

'She had a toy dog,' Sandra said quietly. 'But I wouldn't let her take it to the beach that day so she took its lead instead, and pretended she was walking it.'

'A pink one?'

'With sparkly little sequins on it.'

'So Maureen Upson really did see her.'

The words hung in the air between them until the silence was interrupted by Laura's phone, on silent but vibrating furiously on the table. It was Sue, so Laura excused herself and answered it tentatively, almost whispering and sounding as if she'd just woken.

'Sorry, Laura, but David wants to know if you'll be back in tomorrow.'

The editor hated paying people to sit at home, and Laura had heard others in the office talk about getting calls when they were off sick.

She looked at a very pale Sandra Preston staring out of the window.

'I think,' Laura said croakily, 'I'm going to need another day at home.'

34 | Danni

The newspaper was a few days old and its corners resembled dog's ears, while two large creases ran across the middle. There was a coffee stain on the front where the passenger opposite Danni on the train had knocked over his not-quite-empty cup as he got off. It had been in her bag since the journey to Southampton, except for the countless times she had taken it out and looked at the article on page ten. No matter which part she tried to focus on, her eyes were continually drawn to the picture, as if it were floating from the page.

The grainy picture of Jessica Preston.

Young. Blonde. Pretty.

Roughly two years old. Smiling.

She'd seen the picture before but hadn't realised it straight away. It had left her mind the instant the police had knocked on the door that stormy night her mother died and turned her life upside down. The events that night had made her completely forget to question why her mother would keep a faded missing persons leaflet in her address book for all that time.

The questions came flooding now.

She wanted to throw the newspaper away, and she tried at the station when she got home from the interview, even folding it in half and putting it into one of the waste bins outside the main entrance, but her hand wouldn't let go and instead she put it back in her handbag until the next time she could read it.

She hadn't dared to mention it or show it to Sam. She knew the reaction it would provoke and that her friend would rightly tell her she was putting two and two together and coming up with a number that almost certainly wasn't four.

Sam's upbringing had been very different from her own and she'd always, Danni thought, been a little envious. Danni had had, by comparison, a perfect childhood, whereas Sam's father had walked out on her and her mother before her fourth birthday. The bitter divorce that followed had eaten up all of her mother's savings, and time she could have been spending with a distraught young girl. Sam had never seen or spoken to her father since.

Danni and Sam had formed a strong friendship at junior school that had strengthened through senior school and beyond and throughout those years, Sam had always wanted to spend time around Danni's parents and immerse herself in their way of life. She'd often said that Danni didn't know how lucky she was that her mum could spend time with her rather than working three jobs, and that she knew her father at all.

So for her to now begin unpicking that life that she'd always taken for granted, and base her doubts on an overheard argument, a newspaper article and a faded leaflet, was not the kind of thing Sam would want to hear.

But it didn't stop her reading the article again, or looking at the photograph.

It was still on her mind at the weekend when she drove the short distance to the family home to collect a few extra items of clothing. When she walked in the front door, her father was surrounded by cardboard boxes in the hallway and he had to unstack the chairs in the kitchen for her to sit down.

'Things are moving quickly,' she said, not hiding her annoyance.

The walls were bare – a strange sight, as her mother had always filled them with paintings when she was alive, and now all that remained were large squares in a different shade of paint that the sun hadn't faded. Her father explained that he wanted to get to the new place quickly – the builder

193

was looking for a quick sale and they'd agreed a cash deal that both parties were happy with – so he was packing up everything he wanted to take with him, including most of the paintings. While in the mood, he had sorted the entire contents of the house into boxes that were now in two neat piles in corners of the living room.

'Can I have some photos of Mum before everything goes?' she asked.

'It's not *going*. That pile is for the apartment,' he said gesturing to the smaller of the two sets of boxes, 'and that one is for storage.'

He began rummaging around in one of the boxes, until he found what he was looking for near the bottom of it, and pulled out a small silver box, which he handed it her. 'I put them all together,' he said, 'so I could take some with me too.'

Danni took the box from him and smiled. She opened it and began to thumb through several plastic wallets, each with the contents of the packet written in black marker pen on the side. A holiday in Florida, several Christmases, a long weekend in Paris when she was fifteen, birthday parties and other occasions. Other packets were more mundane, random collections thrown haphazardly together. She opened one and flicked through the twenty or so prints inside; her mother's beaming smile was on most of them. Danni took out a photograph of her mother, placed it on the table, put the rest of the pack back into the box and continued to check the headings.

'How come there aren't any of me as a baby?' she said.

Thomas laughed. She couldn't tell if it was genuine. 'There must be.'

'Not that I can see here.'

He began looking in the other boxes. 'There must be other packets somewhere.'

Danni's phone beeped; it was another text from Euan, which she read and quickly deleted. 'I thought you put them all together.'

'I've obviously missed some,' said Thomas, but there was a telltale crack in his voice; he was such a meticulous filer of everything that it was very unlikely that he had. He could always lay his hand on a piece of writing, no matter how old or random, at a moment's notice. She felt like pressing the point but stopped herself.

'If you come across them,' she said, 'let me know.'

Her father nodded, but he seemed miles away.

'Did you put Mum's old address book in storage too? The one from the hall? The leather one.'

He looked up and frowned. 'Can't remember seeing anything like that. Is it important?'

She shook her head. 'It doesn't matter.'

Danni left him looking among the larger of the two piles and took the photograph, two clean jumpers, a pair of jeans and some underwear back to Sam's. On the short journey she tried to remember any photographs she had seen of herself as a baby. There had been plenty of her at four, five and older, maybe even some when she was a bit younger, but she couldn't recall seeing any where she was in her mother's arms, or in a pushchair or even just crawling along. When she reached the house she went straight upstairs and opened her handbag, taking her copy of the *Herald* and straightening it out as best she could on the bed until the corners were flat enough for her to open it up and read the article again.

If Jessica Preston was alive, then she had absolutely no idea who she was. She would be a twenty-three-year-old now, she thought, who lived with people she thought were her parents but that were hiding the truth from her.

What if her two and two really did make four?

The next morning, when she woke, she tapped the telephone number of the newspaper's offices into her mobile phone; a few rings later, a man answered.

'I'd like to speak to Laura Grainger,' she said.

35 | Laura

'Do you think Jessica Preston is alive?'

Danni had asked the question before Laura had a chance to introduce herself or find out who she was. The *Herald* had called Laura to tell her that someone else had contacted them about the article and asked for her details. As a matter of policy, the *Herald* wouldn't give out the number, but had passed on Danni's details, and Laura had called her as soon as she was able.

'Can I get some background first?' she said, her training kicking in.

'Please just answer the question.'

Laura bit her lip; not sure what to say. She tried to deflect it. 'Sandra Preston does. And—'

'Do *you*?'

Laura realised that this was the first time she'd been put on the spot about this and she let her answer come out instinctively.

'Yes. I do. Why?'

Now there was an even longer pause.

'My friend read your article,' Danni finally said, slowly, 'and she thinks her parents were keeping some big secret from her.'

Laura scribbled down shorthand on her notepad. She underlined a word. '*Were* keeping a secret?'

'Her mum died. Now her dad's acting, like, really weird.'

'If his wife died, isn't that normal?'

'It's not just that,' Danni said carefully. 'He's avoiding questions, moving house, fighting with her all the time. All sorts of stuff.'

'But why does she think they're *keeping a secret* from her?'

'She overheard them.'

Danni explained the outline of the conversation but as if it had been told to her. 'She thinks they might not be her real parents,' she added at the end.

'There are lots of secrets in families. It's a big leap to get to abduction.'

'She isn't saying—'

'You said there was all sorts of other stuff,' Laura interrupted; she was interested by the call, but she needed more than eavesdropping on a conversation.

'The girl that went missing – she'd be roughly the same age as her, lives close to the beach where she disappeared; she even looks similar and there—'

'Lots of girls would look similar.'

There was a pause. 'OK, look, I know how this sounds. I'm sorry I bothered you—'

'Sorry,' Laura said quickly. 'I'm trained to be sceptical. You were saying?'

'There was a missing persons leaflet, with Jessica on it.'

Laura's eyebrows lifted. She scribbled it down, now very interested. 'Where?'

'In her mother's address book.'

'She has it?'

'No. It's gone.'

Laura sighed. She checked the time. 'Look, I'd like to talk more but I have to get to work.'

She wasn't sure if the girl was disappointed or relieved to end the call, but Laura promised she'd call her again later that day. She checked the time again on her phone. 'Shit!'

When she got into the office, David was standing in his office doorway and made a point of looking at the clock when

197

he saw her. She hesitated, not sure whether to go straight to her desk and hope for the best or acknowledge her lateness and apologise, which would mean going to him and having to lie. In the end she compromised.

'Sorry, David,' she called across the heads of people already into their working day, 'car was playing up.'

The editor gave her a weary look that suggested he either didn't believe her or didn't care, so she threw her coat over her chair and powered up her computer, kicking herself for not having a much better excuse prepared in advance. Her monitor lit up and she entered her password and clicked on the button to load her new emails; there were over fifty. One of them, near the top, immediately caught her eye.

It was from someone using a Gmail account and the email subject was *Please Stop*. It looked like the kind of email she would normally delete straight away, from someone trying to use an intriguing subject line in the hope that she would open the email and attachment, and they had been warned about such emails recently when someone had tried to hack into Kelly Heath's account after pretending to be her bank. But this didn't have an attachment, so she casually glanced around to make sure no one was watching her and opened the email.

Laura read it twice. And then a third time.

The email address of the sender didn't contain a name. She knew the normal practice was to alert David so he could get someone to look into it and maybe even report it to the police, but that would mean having to tell him what she had been doing, and she wasn't ready for that yet, so she filed it in an innocuous-looking folder and carried on with her work.

Occasionally, as the morning ticked by, she opened it and read the words again, questioning herself and her motives.

Did Sandra have a friend outside the unit who might be looking after her interests? Was it the 'anonymous donor'? Was she really doing more harm than good by highlighting Sandra's story? But her article had only retraced an old story and painted a picture of a woman in a very fragile state who refused to accept the version of events that everyone else put before her. Sandra hadn't seemed to be upset by her visits or article, Laura thought, so why would anyone else be?

An image formed in her head. A piece of paper, faded and tatty but with a face on it: the face of Jessica Preston.

She ran down the stairs into the street below the newspaper's office, took out her phone and pressed the contact page on her phone that she had assigned to Danni Edwards.

Now it was her turn to start the call with a direct question.

'When did your…friend's mother die?'

'What?'

Laura didn't say anything and waited for Danni to answer.

'Just under two months ago.'

'How?'

'Car crash.'

'An accident?'

'She went off the road, in heavy rain.'

'Can we meet?'

'You want to meet my friend?'

'We can keep pretending if you want to,' Laura said.

There was another long pause before Danni answered her.

'Where?'

36 | Laura

David Weatherall didn't sound impressed when Laura called him to tell him her car had stopped working completely on her way home and she wanted to book the next day off as holiday so she could get it sorted. But she had plenty of annual leave left and he could hardly say no, as, without her car, she wouldn't be able to do anything outside of the office, so he agreed to it.

It gave her twenty-four hours to meet Danni and see what she had to say.

'Does David know?'

Helen put her car keys next to Laura's. They were swapping cars so that the journey would be more comfortable, and Laura didn't want her own car to be seen on the road, since it was supposed to be in the garage for repairs.

'Not yet. I don't think this is going to go anywhere, but, if it does, I'll tell him then.'

Laura noted the disapproval in her mother's eyes.

'I just need to speak to her first.'

Helen raised her eyebrows.

'I know what I'm doing.'

'OK. I get it.'

For a moment, she considered telling her mother about the email but decided against it. She knew she wouldn't be anywhere near as supportive if she knew someone was trying to warn her off, and she'd insist on her telling David about it. That would lead to a much longer conversation and she didn't have time for that; she was already planning on driving there and back in a day, as staying overnight wasn't an option. Even if she could have afforded it, she needed to be at her desk the next day or David would start to lose patience.

Laura put her breakfast bowl into the dishwasher and gave her mother a hug.

'Let's not mention this to your dad,' Helen said.

Laura looked at her.

'He won't like you lying to David. And he'll only worry if he knows you're travelling so far by yourself.'

Her mother smiled and Laura kissed her on the cheek. 'OK. If that's what you think.'

Laura set off in her mother's estate car, feeling every inch a proper journalist in search of the truth. She knew the odds were against her and she'd even wavered a little in the cold light of day when she got up and thought of the two hundred plus miles ahead of her, but, she told herself, if every reporter turned their back on a story at the first hint that they might be wasting their time, then a lot of stories would go untold.

And the email had really helped to make her mind up to carry on for now.

It was the first time that it had happened to her. Kelly Heath had recounted a few occasions when she'd been subjected to abuse and threats in her career, but no one had taken any offence at Laura's innocuous stories until now.

'It shows you must be on to something,' Kelly had said to her about her own experiences.

As each mile passed, she began to wonder if she *was* on to something.

The email had implied that the writer was looking out for Sandra. But she had spent the past fifteen years in a mental health unit, staring out of the window and no closer to any closure, so she could only benefit from some answers.

Anyone looking out for her would do well to address that first.

Sandra had plenty of opportunity to object; even the unit's manager had said that Laura's interaction had helped.

And, if Jessica Preston had been taken and was living under another identity, surely she deserved to know the truth too.

By the time Laura was on the outskirts of the village, she had reached a conclusion. The only people who would benefit from hiding Sandra's and Jessica's story were the people who had taken her.

She realised that she was now fully convinced that the girl who disappeared from that beach over twenty years ago definitely hadn't drowned.

And she was really looking forward to meeting Danielle Edwards.

37 | Laura

Laura arrived early at the café where she had arranged to meet Danni, and went to the ladies' while she waited for her to arrive. On the way out, she saw her reflection in the mirror.

The girl looking back seemed at least five years older than Laura was, with bloodshot eyes and dark bags under them. She dabbed cold tap water on her face and tied her hair up. The early start and four-hour drive without a stop had left her aching, sleepy and hungry, and she could only do something about one of these things right now, so she ordered the unhealthiest breakfast she could find on the menu and ate it as she re-read her notes from the telephone conversation with Danni.

She finished it a few minutes before their scheduled meeting time and sat watching people as they walked by or entered the café. Laura was used to meeting people without seeing them first – it was an occupational hazard – but she was also used to researching them beforehand. She had, however, soon found that Danni had no online presence at all, and Laura had been unable to find a photograph of her anywhere on the internet, so she was now relying on her assumptions.

And she knew that, if Danni didn't resemble Jessica at all, then the journey would have been a waste of time.

She checked her phone and the clock had moved a few minutes past the hour. She was just beginning to get a horrible feeling in the pit of her stomach that Danni might have changed her mind about meeting her when a girl walked into the café. She was twenty-something, with wavy blonde hair under a woollen bobble hat, and, although she was a few inches taller than Laura had expected, everything else was exactly as she'd imagined. The girl picked up a sandwich and checked the ingredients on the back of the packet, and Laura looked across, hoping to catch her attention. She was impressed by her appearance: a long, expensive coat and high-heeled leather boots; she'd certainly made an effort.

She was about to call her when she heard her name.

'Laura?'

Two girls were standing next to the table. One was a tall girl of mixed race and striking features. Next to her stood a girl who fitted the image Laura had had in her mind of Danni; she was the same height as she was, wearing well-worn faded jeans and a black jumper with her blonde-brown hair tied up in a neat ponytail.

'Danni?'

The girl held out her hand and Laura shook it.

'This is my friend, Samantha.'

'Sam,' said Danni's friend curtly, but didn't offer her hand.

'I brought her along for support,' said Danni. 'I only told her on the way what I was doing.'

Laura smiled; they sat down and the lady from the counter came over to take their order. For a few minutes, until the drinks arrived, they made small talk about Laura's journey and then about the village the girls lived in. Once they were sipping their lattes, Laura opened her notebook to a new page and looked at Danni.

'Are you happy to pick up with our conversation from the other night?'

Danni looked at Sam, as if for approval, and nodded slowly.

'OK,' said Laura, and decided not to mention the email until the time was right.

The conversation was a little more stilted than it was on the phone. Laura wasn't sure if it was Sam's presence or that they were face to face, but Danni wasn't as forthcoming as she had been, and Laura found herself digging deep into what she could recall from her reporter's training, to coax the answers out. And even then it felt to her that Danni was holding something back.

Maybe it was also, Laura thought, because it all sounded a little far-fetched now they were talking about it in person, and she wondered if Danni felt the same. Sam seemed to echo those doubts with her silent hostility.

The initial conversation focused mainly on Danni's father and the way he had shut himself off from her after the accident. Laura explored what had been said and asked Danni to recall the exact words if she could. The subject of the photographs came up, but Laura was quick to put that into perspective.

'It does seem strange, but there could be a perfectly reasonable explanation,' she said. 'They could be mislaid, or lost, or maybe they just didn't take any.'

'Wouldn't that be weird?' said Sam, frowning and seizing an opportunity to disagree with Laura. 'Not taking any pictures of your kid?'

'It was a different time. No camera phones like now.'

Laura looked up at Sam, who stared back, making her feel a little intimidated. She quickly moved on to a new question. 'What about the leaflet?'

Sam looked at Danni again.

'It was in her address book. My dad acted as if it didn't exist but I know what I saw. And why would my mum have it?'

Laura shrugged. That question had been bugging her too. Without it, the evidence was thin at best, but the leaflet added a layer of mystery that she couldn't ignore. She'd driven more than two hundred miles because of it.

'I don't know. I just don't want to get carried away.'

'But what do you *think*?'

'I think we should take it one step at a time. Can I take a photo of you on my phone?'

'What for?' said Sam.

'With Danni's agreement, I'd like a recent picture to show Jessica's mum.'

Laura looked at Danni, who nodded. 'OK, but I need to go to the loo first.'

Laura and Sam sat quietly as she left them at the table, and Laura pretended to write some additional notes on her pad, hoping that Danni would return quickly. To her relief, she did, and Laura could see she had merely tidied up her hair and make-up, so before she sat back down she took a close-up image of her face with the blank off-white wall behind her.

'It would be good to get one of you when you were younger.'

Danni smiled and seemed more relaxed now. 'My dad has them in a box, but I'll get one.'

'Will you go to live with him at his new place?' Laura felt herself empathising with the girl. She couldn't imagine losing her mother or having her father treat her like that, and it was hard not to feel sorry for someone who'd had to cope with both at the same time.

'I suppose I'll have to,' said Danni, glancing at Sam.

'What will that be like?'

'No idea. But I'm out all day and he works in the evenings so I guess that'll help.'

'It won't help your relationship.'

Danni shrugged. 'It can't get much worse.'

'You must be glad to have Sam.'

It was intended as a way of bringing the other girl into the conversation and thawing some of the frostiness, but it didn't work. Danni's friend merely glared at her.

'What about other friends? Family?'

Danni shook her head.

'Boyfriends?'

'Don't go there.'

'Why not?'

Sam was staring at Laura but she resisted looking back directly at her, keeping eye-contact with Danni instead.

'There's only been one, and we split up a few months ago.'

'And he's out of the picture now?'

Sam nodded but Laura saw Danni look down.

'But?'

'I slept with him. After the funeral.'

Sam looked at her but said nothing. Danni shrugged, embarrassed, her cheeks flushed.

'You were grieving,' Sam reminded her.

'And now he keeps calling and texting.'

'How is this relevant?' Sam asked Laura.

'It probably isn't. I just like to get the full picture.'

Laura looked at Danni. She appeared to be drained too, as if she hadn't been sleeping well, which was hardly surprising, Laura thought. She knew it was probably a good time to call a halt to the interview; she had quite a lot of background, and a photo, which she would show Sandra soon, although she wanted to check it against the pictures of Jessica first.

'Can I just ask one more question?' she asked. 'It's a bit random.'

Danni looked up and nodded.

'Do you remember having a toy dog? With a pink sparkly lead?'

'No, why?' Danni said, shaking her head.

'A witness who saw Jessica Preston said she was carrying a pink lead.'

'Witness? I thought no one saw her,' said Danni, and Laura felt Sam's big brown eyes bore into her.

'Maureen Upson.'

Danni and Sam looked at each other.

'You know her?'

'I've heard of her. I heard that she said she took Jessica,' said Danni.

'She says things when she's drunk.'

'How often is that?' said Sam.

'Enough for the police to discount her as a witness. But that doesn't mean she didn't see her.'

'Doesn't mean she did, either.'

'Sandra confirmed Jessica had a pink lead that day. So if she did see her, then Jessica was walking away from the sea not towards it and she might have been taken.'

'Big assumption,' said Sam, and Laura nodded.

'I know. But I'm trying to get all the facts. Danni?'

'I agree with Sam,' she said, her voice colder. 'And, if I'm accusing my dad of kidnapping me, I want to rely on a bit more than a woman who lied about it.'

Sam nodded and stared at Laura, barely hiding a sneer. Laura closed her notepad. It was definitely time to end the interview.

38 | Danni

'What's in this for you?'

They were putting their coats on and saying their goodbyes when Sam asked the question. Danni was about to tell her friend not to be rude when she realised she wanted to know too. She had been surprised at how young and inexperienced Laura was in comparison to the image she'd formed in her head after reading her news story. The article had really made her believe that Jessica Preston could be alive and that her disappearance could have been covered up, but their meeting had made her question it all.

'I won't deny it would be an incredible story if Jessica was found,' said Laura.

'You want the glory,' said Sam.

Laura shrugged. 'It's my job. But I wouldn't be here if I thought there was nothing worth looking into.'

'Because of what that drunk said she saw?'

'It's just one witness. There's a lot to go on and, after meeting Sandra, I think she deserves better. I think she deserves to know what really happened that day.'

'So it's the truth you're after, not the glory?'

Laura looked at Sam challengingly. 'Say what you like, but don't we all want the truth here?'

'And you think you can do better than the police?' Sam challenged right back.

'I'm just worried that the drowning theory is an easy one to settle on.'

Laura paid the bill and they stepped outside into the sun.

'And what do you think now?' Danni asked.

Laura shrugged. 'I don't honestly know. But you called me, remember? So you think things aren't right. I just want to find out if the two things are connected.'

'And then you'd go to the police?' Sam asked.

'Yes. But only if I was sure,' Laura said, and looked at Danni. 'If your dad knew you had contacted me, and that you thought you were Jessica, they'd be no going back even if there was nothing in it.'

Danni nodded.

'So if I investigate, and there's no connection, at least he'll never have to know.'

'And, if there is, you get your big story,' said Sam.

'I've never hidden that. But I have to be sure too, because it's my career at stake if I'm wrong.'

'So what next?' said Danni.

'Give me a week to do some digging,' Laura said, 'and then we'll decide. I'll send you an update in a couple of days. Until then, we keep it between us, right?'

She looked at Sam, whose eyes widened. Danni also shot her friend a glance.

'OK.'

Laura left them at the café doors and began walking to her car. Danni had parked on the road directly outside the café.

'What do *you* think?' Danni asked Sam once they were alone.

'There's something about her I'm not keen on.'

'You'd never tell.'

Sam sniffed. Danni smiled and opened her car door. Her phone beeped and she checked her text messages, shaking her head.

'Euan?' asked Sam.

Danni nodded. He wanted to meet her, and from the way it was worded you'd never know there was any problem between them. There was an earlier message she'd missed from her dad, too, telling her that a letter had arrived for her. She texted back, saying she'd drop by to collect it, and then she deleted Euan's message.

As she drove back to the house, her phone beeped again.

'Let me,' said Sam, ready to type an angry response before calming down as she read it. 'Oh – it's your dad. He says he'll be out but you know where the key is if you don't have yours.'

Danni nodded and a few minutes later they pulled up on the driveway of her house and went inside to find an empty shell: plain walls and carpets with indentations where furniture had been once.

'He hasn't wasted much time.'

Danni was already scanning the space. The pile of boxes that she'd seen on her last visit had gone and just one sat in their place, a stiff cardboard box that had originally been used to package paper and was now full to the brim with a mixture of items: the TV remote, a scarf and gloves, and an opened packet of headache tablets. On the kitchen work surface, a letter with her name on it was propped against the wall next to the kettle, one of the few remaining items unboxed, and she put it into her handbag and walked over to the box.

'Never realised it was this big,' called Sam from the next room as she walked around on the wooden floorboards. Danni moved the items at the top of the box to the side until she could see what was underneath. It was a collection of things that her father had put to one side, or pulled from the other boxes, that were clearly intended for the new flat.

She looked for the silver photograph box in it but it wasn't there.

Near the bottom, she could see a blue folder, creased and tatty, that had been overfilled until it was ready to burst. She reached down and lifted the flap and saw that it was filled with papers, some very official-looking, others still in their envelopes. She tried to lift her hand and make room to open the flap fully, but the items on top were too heavy.

At that moment she heard her father's car pull on to the drive. She snatched her hand away from the box and stepped back into the middle of the room. As he walked in, she pulled the letter out of her bag and clutched it.

'Morning,' he said, as cheerful as she'd seen him for some considerable time. She declined his offer of a cup of tea.

'Like what you've done with the place, Mr E.' Sam came back in and Thomas smiled and greeted her. He nodded towards the letter in Danni's hand.

'Anything interesting?'

'Just trying to sell me something.'

They said their goodbyes and went out to the car. Danni wasn't sure if her father had believed her about the letter but she knew her friend hadn't.

'What is it really?' Sam asked after closing her door.

'It's about the job.'

'What about it?'

'They want me to start in a month.'

Danni clenched her teeth and grinned, and Sam leaned across to hug her. 'That's great, Dan. Congrats.'

Danni went through the motions but wasn't sure if congratulations were in order; she hadn't expected to get the job so hadn't thought there would be a decision to make. She turned the key in the ignition and did a three-point turn in the road to head back towards Sam's. As she moved forward, out of the corner of her eye she saw a figure try to move out of sight – a male, over six foot and dressed in a dark hoodie and even darker jeans. He had been standing to the side of the gate and hadn't expected her to turn the car around.

'Is that Euan?' Sam asked her. Danni knew it was but didn't answer. The tall figure tried to walk away with his back to them. 'Is he following you?'

'Leave it, Sam.'

Her friend was already unbuckling her seatbelt.

'No way. I'm sorting this once and for all.'

39 | Laura

It was early evening when Laura pulled on to the drive, completely exhausted and despondent at the way the meeting had ended; she was glad to have the house to herself for the evening. Her parents were at a fundraiser at the hospital that wouldn't finish until around midnight, and she planned to be in bed much earlier than that, but it gave her time to eat, run herself a bath and collect her thoughts without having to talk to them – and without putting her mother in the difficult position of having to lie about her whereabouts. As she lay in the bath, she wondered how she'd cope in Danni's predicament, if her mother were no longer around, and decided she was just glad she didn't have to.

When she got out, she sent Danni a text to thank her for her time, and to test the water now that she'd had time to reflect on their meeting. She was surprised to get a reply almost immediately, and a friendly one at that.

Hi Laura pleased to meet u 2. hope u had a good journey back. sorry if I was a little off today looking forward to talking to you again Danni

Laura read the text a second time as she lay on her bed. It felt as though it was from the real Danni, without Sam's influence. She spontaneously called her.

Danni answered on the third ring, and was warmer and more talkative than she had been earlier that day. Laura listened as she told her about her father, the box, and the incident with Euan.

'Are you worried about him?'

'He's just a bit intense. He'd followed us from the café.'

'That's creepy.'

'Sam sorted it. He asked her who you were.'

'Should I be worried?'

'About Euan?'

'About what Sam said.'

Danni laughed and Laura laughed with her. 'She didn't like me, did she?'

'She's looking out for me, that's all. You shouldn't worry about either of them.'

'What did Sam do?'

'Tell him to stop.'

'And will he?'

'She has a way with words.'

Danni shared a little background on her and Sam's friendship and how protective she had always been. Laura wished that, in hindsight, the two of them had been alone when they'd met, because it was much easier talking to her like this.

'I did have something else I wanted to ask you about,' she said.

'Go on.'

'We didn't really talk about your mother.'

There was a silence.

'You don't have to,' Laura told her.

'I want to, but it's just—'

'We can leave it.'

'No. Carry on,' said Danni.

'You said when we first talked that she wanted to tell you something.'

'I *think* she did.'

'How come?'

215

'She seemed to be building up to it. Little things – it's hard to explain, but I knew her and how she approached things.'

'Why didn't you ask her? It sounds like you were close.'

'We were. But…'

Laura waited rather than push her.

'I think my dad might have stopped her.'

'Would she have let him?' Laura asked.

'He could – can – be quite domineering at times. I think he persuaded her to keep quiet. That was the impression I got when I overheard them, anyway.'

'And she died soon after that?'

It went quiet.

'Danni?'

'You think they're connected?'

'I'm just asking,' said Laura defensively.

'*No*, you're saying it might not have been an accident!'

'You told me she went off the road.'

'So?'

'Yet you said she was a good driver and knew the roads well. Could someone else possibly have been involved?'

'This is insane.'

More silence. Laura was worried she had lost her again.

'Did you question it at the time?' she asked.

'It was really bad weather. The police and coroner both said she must have lost control and couldn't stop in time.'

'But if she was a good driver she'd have been going slowly, wouldn't she? I read the coroner's report on the internet. She hit three crash barriers and went through the third. Why not stop after hitting the first one?'

'I don't know.'

'I'm just saying, if there was another car on the road, then maybe…'

'This is ridiculous.'

'Can we rule it out completely?'

Silence. Laura waited.

'We can rule out my dad,' Danni said. 'He was with me in the house.'

'Look, I'm not saying it wasn't an accident. I ju—'

'Unless…' Danni interrupted her, and Laura stopped talking. 'Unless he got someone to do it for him.'

40 | Laura

Laura felt the knot tighten in her stomach.

When she'd read them, the police and coroner's reports had both raised as many questions as they answered about Patricia Edwards' death, but she wondered if she'd gone too far by causing Danni to think of the idea of a third party.

'Remember, we're talking about your dad,' she reminded her.

'Like you said, we can't rule it out.'

'We can't make accusations either.'

'It was you who said—'

'I just asked the question. We need actual evidence. And only your mum knows what really happened that night.'

'And the other person, if there was one.'

'*If* there was one.'

'And maybe—'

Laura cut her off and suggested she let her do some more investigation before they said anything else. 'We can talk all night, but it won't get us further forward. Let's sleep on it.'

Danni agreed but, even then, Laura knew it was not going to be an easy investigation. There were no witnesses who had come forward, and no evidence had been found at the scene to suggest foul play.

The email, on the other hand, might, and she knew she would have to tell Danni about it soon enough. Laura ended the call but had no intention of sleeping on it; not right away anyway.

She located the photo folder on her phone and found the one she had taken of Danni. It was a nice picture, clear and in good light. She zoomed in closer, looking at every line and skin imperfection. Danni was a pretty girl, Laura thought. Prettier than her. They were not dissimilar in height and build but Danni's features were sharper and more pronounced, her hair longer; Laura made a mental note to not let her hairdresser talk her into a shoulder-length cut as he had always done in the past.

She emailed herself a copy of the image, flipped the top of her laptop up, and opened it on the bigger screen. She stared at it closely, zooming in on Danni's jawbone and slightly protruding ears until the pixels became too big to see clearly. She went on to Google and found the best image she could of Jessica Preston, taken a few weeks before she had disappeared and put the two pictures alongside each other.

After twenty minutes of looking at them, her head hurt.

She continued to stare at the two images until her eyes began to tire. There was no doubt that there were similarities. On Google Images, alongside the picture of Jessica were some artists' impressions of what she might look like, as a five-year-old, a ten-year-old, and in her late teens. They had a lot of similarities to Danni's photograph, but Laura started to wonder how much of it was wishful thinking.

She copied the image of Jessica aged two and a quarter; the last photograph Sandra had of her, and emailed it to her phone. She'd installed an app called Oldify a day earlier for this specific purpose, and she loaded the image on to it, filling the circle in the centre of the screen with Jessica's smiling face. She pressed the button that would age her by twenty years and watched as a new version of the missing girl slowly took shape. When it was complete, Laura looked at it and shook her head, with disappointment and, even more, with embarrassment. It was essentially the original image, only with slightly wider facial features and a few lines added to the forehead. The app had more or less transposed the same haircut that Jessica had when the photograph was taken, and the final version made Laura slump down in her seat and groan. What had she been thinking? She was using free software on her phone, software designed for children to have fun with. To understand what a grown-up Jessica might look like, she really needed the type of software the FBI used.

But it wasn't just the technology. She had no real under-standing of how a child's face might alter over time, the way the shape of a head might change; how jawbones grew, for example. She knew lots of people whose facial features had completely changed by the time they reached adulthood. And her own limited research had already told her that the blue of Jessica's eyes was a colour shared by not only Danni, but more than half the female population of the UK, including herself.

It all highlighted what a pointless exercise it was, and she slammed her laptop shut and tried to get some sleep instead. But for an hour after she closed her eyes the images of Jessica and Danni haunted her; mocking her inexperience and naïveté, until she was glad of the distraction as a car door slammed. She looked at her clock – it was ten past midnight – and she went to the window and watched her mother and father as they walked from the garage to the house, holding hands and smiling. She listened as they walked in, laughing, and she could tell her mother had enjoyed a few glasses of the complimentary champagne that was always available at those functions. She heard them clumsily get ready for bed, their whispering and giggling; and later she heard them making love: the sound of the springs in their mattress and her mother telling her father to be quiet in case she heard them.

Laura suddenly felt guilty. Not for hearing them – it would have been hard not to – but because they were so present, such a big part of her life, and still very much in love and capable of acting like a couple of teenagers even as they approached their fifties. She realised what Danni had lost, how her life had been shattered, and for the first time she truly appreciated how difficult it must be for her, not knowing for sure who she was or who her parents might be.

And now, Danni was trusting her to give her the answers.

For the first time since she had found the story of Jessica Preston on the internet, Laura began to feel horribly out of her depth.

41 | Laura

Two days later, a struggling Laura reneged on her promise to call Danni back with an update and sent her a text instead to buy some more time. A further two days.

At the paper, David had filled her time with a mountain of mundane assignments, as if he was punishing her for having time off, and she'd had to work later than usual and found herself already tired by the time she got home and began her other research. She also realised how difficult it was in practice to work on the story when she was so many miles from the people involved and the locations where she needed to be. As useful as the internet and mobile communications were, there was no substitute for looking people in the eye and being able to retrace the steps they had taken. But she also knew there was one person she needed to sit down with again before she could take any more significant steps herself, and that was Sandra.

She had to show her the picture of Danni, because that might be enough. Sandra might see, or not see, something that confirmed without doubt that Danni could not possibly be her missing daughter.

Or, she dared to think, she might see something that made her know that it was her.

On the Monday morning, she waited until David and Sue were deep into their weekly planning meeting and printed a large copy of the picture she had taken of Danni, using the office's expensive laser printer rather than her more limited one at home. She put the print in a folder and hid it in her laptop sleeve, taking one more look at the girl as she did. Danni's face stared back at her and made her feel guilty again, and she knew she needed to help her quickly, because it was the not knowing that was hurting her the most. Even if Sandra said she couldn't be Jessica, that would be a step forward, and she could try to discover her parents' secret without this distraction.

The next day began early as usual when Laura's alarm buzzed at six, and, as she dressed in several layers of suitable dog-walking attire, she saw her father roll his car up the drive and off into the misty darkness and towards his bacon sandwich. She went downstairs and opened the back door for Mimark so he could relieve himself while she ate a toasted slice of her mother's home-made bread and sipped on a cup of hot tea. From her window she had already seen the murky coastal fog sitting on the beach, and the weather app on her phone was telling her it was minus five degrees outside, so she wrapped a thick woollen scarf around her neck, zipped up her padded winter coat, put on her fur-lined boots and ventured out.

Mimark didn't mind the freezing temperatures and wagged his tail excitedly by the back gate as she clipped the lead to his collar and led him up the frosty pathway. Before old age had caught up with him, he'd have pulled her up it with sheer enthusiasm and let her jog along to keep warm while he ran alongside. Nowadays he let her pull him, and it took twice as long to reach the entrance to the coastal path and walk down to the edge of the beach and back, because he felt the need to stop and sniff at every bush and tree stump along the way. When she unhooked his lead he slowly criss-crossed the path as he went along it, occasionally stopping to consider chasing a rabbit that had put its head out of a hole, but always deciding against it.

'C'mon, boy,' Laura said as they reached the stile that led on to a small field and another path that stretched down to the steps that would take you on to the beach. The dog squeezed under it as he always did, while Laura climbed over, and they walked in near pitch dark. She had done the walk almost every Tuesday since she was eighteen so it held few surprises, and she'd stopped taking a torch years ago and relied on her eyes adjusting to the darkness in the winter months. If it was a clear morning, the moon would show the way, but on a gloomy morning like this she had to trust her memory and instincts.

As usual, Mimark was proving to be an unreliable walking companion, ducking out of sight and not heeding her when she called him. As they reached the turn, about fifteen yards from the beach, she could hear the waves crashing on to the pebbled shore even though she couldn't see them. She had to raise her voice to call her dog.

'C'mon, Mimark.'

She peered through the gloom but couldn't see the little terrier anywhere, and the noise from the sea drowned out any sound he might make.

'Mimark!'

She knew he'd been heading towards the steps, so she made her way to the top of them and was about to call again when she heard a rustling from behind a thick shrub to her right and stepped forward to admonish the dog for ignoring her.

A tall figure, all in black, stepped from behind it, and Laura jumped. The shadowy figure had its collar pulled up as high as it would go and a woollen hat pulled down to eye level, leaving the thinnest of gaps where the face was visible.

'Whoa, you scared me,' she said, taking a backward step.

The man didn't answer. Laura had done this walk, at this exact time, every Tuesday for five years, give or take a few holidays and one day when she was ill, and she could count the times she'd run into someone on one hand.

'You haven't seen a dog, have you?' she asked tentatively.

The man said nothing. Laura felt an overwhelming urge to run.

There was more rustling, this time from her left, and Mimark came out from behind a bush and trotted towards her.

'There you are,' she said, relieved, and began to step away from the man, but her dog moved past her hands and went up to him instead, sniffing curiously and wagging his tail. The man bent down and Laura relaxed as he patted the top of her dog's head gently.

It happened so quickly.

In one sudden movement the man's hand clamped down on Mimark's collar and lifted him into the air, making the dog squeal in panic and Laura shriek with fright. He held him, dangling in between them, whimpering frantically.

'What—'

'Shut up.'

She could see menace in his eyes but Laura stepped closer to protect the dog.

'Leave him!'

'First, you listen,' the man said, and held Mimark away from her, collar digging into his throat as he hung at head height, whimpering. 'You need to forget about Jessica Preston.'

'What?'

'Otherwise, it won't be the dog next time.'

Laura could feel her heart close to bursting in her chest. 'What do you—?'

The man flung Mimark to the ground and he scarpered, faster than his little legs usually carried him, and with scant regard for Laura as he headed towards the house. The man nodded in the direction the terrier was travelling. 'I know where you live. You *and* your family.'

She was paralysed with fear.

'Understand?' he asked.

Laura nodded, a lump in her throat preventing any words coming out.

'Good,' the man hissed, his face getting closer.

Laura felt a surge of adrenaline and turned on her heels and ran, looking for Mimark ahead of her; he was already out of sight.

She had covered sixty yards before she felt confident enough to look behind her.

Part Five

Five years after she was taken...

The things that happen during your life, where you'll always remember where you were and what you were doing at the exact moment you heard them, are very rare.

In fact, until that day, it had never happened to me.

November the eleventh. Armistice Day. A Saturday and pleasant too for a change; it had rained for weeks, heavy, incessant downpours that had left some parts of the county under several feet of water and put the impact of the weather in the top two or three news stories of the day, every day. But on that Saturday the sun had come out, and the only clouds were thin, translucent ones that gently rolled past in the stiff breeze. There were still a few hardy leaves clinging for dear life to the trees in the garden. I was standing on the step, drying a cup I'd washed and looking out on to the back lawn where our daughter played with a friend on the soft grass while my wife and I finished our breakfast. I had told her to sit and relax while I tidied away.

I remember it distinctly. My wife was worried that the lawn would be too muddy after all the rain but I was telling her it was actually much drier than she thought. The girls were skipping along, singing a song they'd learned at school, while 'A Groovy Kind of Love' played on the radio in the kitchen. Then they went to the hourly news and the person reading the bulletins out covered the usual storm damage updates that accompanied every report and it seemed as if they'd run out of things to say; so the final item sounded like an afterthought.

But for me, it was the best thing I could have heard.

'*And police have officially called off the search for Jessica Preston, who went missing five years ago…*'

I didn't hear the rest. We just looked at each other.

It had been more than five years since my wife had walked in through the door and changed our lives for ever. Five years that had been a mixture of torment and looking over our shoulders and also of joy and happiness as we had watched her grow into a beautiful young girl.

A girl for whom no one was looking any more.

I listened to the reports properly throughout the day after that, and bought every Sunday newspaper the next day and located every paragraph or even individual line dedicated to the story. There wasn't much; it seemed like a footnote in time. The police unit had been disbanded; there was still a telephone number to be used for information, but no one was going to be actively working on the case. It was common knowledge anyway that this team had dwindled down to a solitary detective in the last couple of years. And now that detective was retiring.

The police didn't say so in as many words, but they had given up.

Eager to know as much as possible, I drove to the area surrounding the beach on the Monday and picked up the local editions of the papers that carried the story in more detail, but even still made little fuss of the announcement. One politician was trying to call for a new enquiry but everyone else seemed to want to move on.

Well, almost everyone.

There was one thread of the story that was hard to read. The girl's mother had refused to give interviews until then, or accept the general consensus that she had been taken by the strong currents that day, but one of the larger regional papers had managed to speak to her and get a soundbite about the calling-off of the search. She had managed to get her local MP on her side, but many other people, including some editorial contributors and readers on the letters page, were scathing of her for refusing to accept responsibility for her daughter's disappearance and for, as they saw it, using the abduction claim as a way of protecting herself.

As one of the two people who knew the truth, it was impossible not to feel sorry for her.

But when I looked out on the lawn, and shielded my eyes from the sun to watch the two girls dance and laugh and play, I didn't see the girl from the beach.

She was our daughter now. Not Jessica Preston.

We were parents, with our own worries and issues and responsibilities. My wife had built an incredible bond with that child, much stronger than any that I could ever form. She seemed to know exactly what she needed and how she was feeling; you could be forgiven for thinking she'd carried her for nine months and given birth to her.

And she was a different woman too. So confident, sure of herself, so healthy and happy; completely unrecognisable from the woman who took the child from the beach. I had never seen her look so well or appear so strong. Just to see her walking along, holding our daughter's hand, or soothing her tears when she cried, comforting her if she had a nightmare, or cheering at school sports day, made the bad times we'd had not seem quite so bad.

And now, the radio report had confirmed what we had suspected had been happening for the last two or three years. That child, as far as the rest of the world was concerned, was dead.

We had a daughter; and she was everything we ever wanted.

At that moment, after all we'd been through, it suddenly didn't feel as if anything could go wrong.

I can barely remember what I ate for breakfast this morning, but I can remember exactly where I was and what I was doing when I heard the news.

It was a Saturday, and Todd was sleeping off the night before, a night that had finished long after it had turned into the next morning, and I was putting some washing into the machine in the kitchen so I could dry it in the sun that would be stretched across the back garden by midday. The radio was on in the background and I wasn't really listening because I was too preoccupied with keeping an eye on Stuart, who was standing talking to some of his friends on the corner of the street; I could see him from the kitchen window. He was nearly a teenager but since his sister had gone he'd become withdrawn, distant; he'd stopped talking to me and had turned into a pale shadow of the young boy who had kept us and his teachers on our toes with an endless supply of energy and an eye for mischief. So I worried constantly about him, and watched him like a hawk in case he fell in with the wrong crowd or began to do things he shouldn't.

There was a news bulletin on and the man was talking about the latest storm damage that had hit the country, flooding towns and cutting out the power. That sunny day was a rare break in the bombardment, the calm before the next storm, and the foul weather was coming back, the man warned. Then he read out some more headlines and I tuned out, peering through the gap between the curtain and the frame to make sure Stuart was still there.

'*And police have officially called off the search for Jessica Preston, who went missing five years ago…*'

I didn't hear the rest. I froze to the spot, the words dancing around my head like a playground song, taunting me. It was the worst news that I could have heard.

All the other sounds stopped; there was just me and the radio and the man reading the news, and my stomach flipped and churned and I retched so much that I had to run to the toilet to be sick.

They hadn't even told me.

An hour later a police officer turned up to apologise that the news had been announced before they'd had a chance to contact me. A detective had been due to discuss the case with me before any announcement, but he had been diverted to an emergency and it had, as the officer described it, 'slipped through the cracks'.

Not that it hadn't been inevitable.

No one but me had been looking for her for a long time. I had called the local paper to say as much only a few days earlier, and tried to get them to support a fresh appeal, but they had made up their minds already and they edited my words to make me sound deluded. Our local MP promised to help, but he was a lone voice, and deep down I think he was just telling me what I wanted to hear.

I was officially now the only person who still believed Jessica was alive, and, even though I had a husband upstairs and a son I could literally see through the window, I'd never felt so alone in my life.

Even more alone than on the beach the day she disappeared.

But if anyone had told me that, six months from now, my son would be in care and Todd would be under the ground, I'd have never believed them.

Nor if they'd said I'd wind up in this place.

42 | Danni

Danni ordered her coffee and placed her phone down on the table in front of her. She sipped her drink and watched the device for the next thirty-five minutes, occasionally picking it up to check it was still working and the battery hadn't run out.

'Call her.'

Sam had come into the café, ordered a drink and crept up behind her without her even noticing.

'Don't *do* that!' Danni smiled and shook her head, glad of the distraction.

'You know it won't ring if you look at it?'

She nodded.

'So call! Find out what's keeping her.'

Danni reacted as if the very thought was completely preposterous.

'Text her, then.'

Danni looked at the device but didn't touch it. Sam smiled and changed the subject.

'So have you accepted the job offer?'

'The what?'

'Offer. Remember? It's where a company says *please work for us* and you tell them you want to.'

Danni said nothing.

'Why not?'

'I'll call them tomorrow,' she promised, but without conviction. It had been the last thing on her mind; the letter was still in its envelope in her handbag. Besides, she hadn't wanted to use the phone in case Laura called while she was talking to them.

'They'll think you don't want it,' Sam warned her.

'I said I'll call them.'

Sam frowned at her. '*Do* you want it?'

Danni shrugged. Her world felt as if it was going around in a washing machine and she was on the outside waiting for the spin cycle to stop. Adding another complication into the mix felt like the last thing she needed at that moment. Sam was trying to convince her that the extra responsibilities would be good for her, but they just sounded like more hassle she could do without.

'Just think of the extra cash, then.'

Danni nodded, even though she wasn't sure what she was nodding at.

'I'm sure she'll call if she has something.'

'*If?*'

'Or not. Either way.'

'You don't even like her.'

'I just think you don't know enough about her, Dan.'

'Doesn't mean she's not right.'

Danni had told Sam about the phone call, but her friend had found it pretty far-fetched and hadn't been slow in telling her.

'Just be careful, that's all I'm saying.'

'That's easy to say when you know if your dad is your dad or not.'

As soon as she said it Danni winced. It was a comment born of frustration, and regretted at once, but she could see Sam's expression change, her features harden instantly.

'A lot of good it did me.'

'I'm sorry, Sam. I didn't mean it like that.'

Sam finished her coffee and looked at Danni and her face broke into a smile. 'C'mon. I've two bottles of wine in the car.

Let's go home and drink them while we wait for that phone to ring.'

Danni had limited herself to a glass and three-quarters, but she still felt the dull throbbing in her head when she woke the next morning and opened the curtains to drizzle so fine it all but blotted out the houses opposite.

Sam had polished off the rest of the bottles, but showed no sign of it when she came into the spare room with a black coffee for Danni. They had talked until the early hours, but Danni's shift didn't begin until lunchtime and she'd have been quite happy to stay in bed longer.

'I thought we could go to your dad's new flat.'

'What for?'

'You haven't seen it yet.'

Danni looked at her phone on the chair next to her bed.

'She hasn't called yet?'

Danni shook her head. The idea of going to the flat didn't appeal; the longer she went without seeing her father, the harder it became to force herself to do so. But she did need to get a photograph of her as a child.

'He'll think there's something up if you keep avoiding him.'

'There is something up.'

'And hiding from him won't help. C'mon.'

Sam threw Danni her jeans and left her to get dressed, and twenty minutes later they pulled up outside her father's new apartment, nestled at the foot of the hill, right on the edge of the beach and facing the sea, although the misty, damp weather didn't show it in its best light.

The inside, on the other hand, was immaculate, with expensive furniture and artwork laid out in minimalist fashion among grey carpets and walls with freshly painted brilliant white doors, skirting and ceilings. The place stank of newness, and neither Danni nor Sam could fail to be impressed by it. Thomas had shouted for them to come in when they knocked;

he was hanging a large flatscreen television on to a plate attached to the wall. 'Good timing,' he said smiling. 'I was just thinking I needed someone taller.'

Sam took hold of one side and they lifted it into position. 'Lovely place, Mr E.'

Danni returned her father's smile and walked up to the large patio doors that opened out to dark-lacquered wooden decking and a set of steps that led past the downstairs apartment and on to the sand. She peered out to where the grey sea lapped on the shore about sixty or so yards away.

'I'd begun to think you didn't want to see it.'

Danni snorted unconvincingly. She did actually think it was a lovely place to live, but without her mother it felt nothing like a potential home for her. 'I've just been busy.'

'Deciding whether to say yes to her new job,' said Sam.

Danni glared at her friend. Her father looked at her inquisitively and started asking questions she had little option but to answer. 'What's to decide?'

'It's complicated.'

'It sounds like a great opportunity.'

'That's what I said,' Sam added.

'You two don't have to work there,' Danni said coldly, and stared at them each in turn. 'So *I'll* make the decision.'

'But—' her father began.

'If that's OK with you.'

'Of course.'

Danni walked around, looking outside again. 'Nearly every memory I have of Mum is in the village,' she said softly, almost to herself. Her father looked down in the way he always did when she mentioned her mother.

'It's only an hour or so away,' said Sam.

'The memories won't go just because you move,' Thomas added.

Danni glared at her father. He began tightening the screws holding the TV to the metal plate so he could avoid looking at

237

her. Then, when he was happy it was secure, he went into the kitchen and made them both a cup of tea. He returned with three cups on a silver tray.

'What would your mum want?'

'Huh?'

Danni tensed up. Sam looked up at Thomas, a slight shake of her head trying to warn him not to go there, but he ignored her.

'She'd say take the job, I know she would.'

'Would she?' Danni said sharply.

Sam tried to change the subject by asking about the flat underneath.

'Or is it *you* that wants me to take it?'

'What?'

Sam looked horrified and Danni realised her friend was right: it wasn't the time for this conversation. But, even as she tried to back down and stop herself saying more, it was already too late.

'I'm sick of people telling me what Mum would think and say.'

'Danni,' her father said sternly, but she stared at him.

'I know Mum wanted to tell me something before she died. Why don't we talk about that?'

The silence seemed to last for ever. Sam shuffled uncomfortably, her eyes flitting between both of them as she tried to drink her tea. Danni's father looked at Sam then back at his daughter.

'This isn't the—'

Danni cut him off. 'I know it's not.' She stood up. 'So I'm going. Before I say something we both regret.'

Sam got up too and they left.

Danni had forgotten all about the photograph.

43 | Laura

David Weatherall had a habit that Laura wasn't sure he was even conscious of, where he looked at the door when he thought it was time for someone to leave his office.

He had just done it, and Laura blinked and looked at him, and at the brown folder in her hand. The editor sat back in his leather chair, like some City trader from the '80s but without the cigar, and raised his eyebrows in his trademark *why-are-you-still-here?* style, and she turned to leave, knocking a file off his desk with her thigh. She bent down to pick it up, apologising as his irritation with her visibly grew.

She had no idea what he had said to her in there as she got back to her desk and opened the folder. Her every thought had been about what had happened on the coastal path that morning; it was all she had thought about since it happened.

She hadn't told anyone about it. It changed things; in fact, it changed everything. The only action she took was to open her laptop when she got to the office and order a can of handbag-sized aerosol defence spray from the website of a security company, paying extra for express delivery.

After that she thought about what to tell Danni, because now it was clear that someone had a lot to hide and that both of them, and her family, were now at risk. The email had been one thing, but it had just escalated to a whole new level. As she sat staring at her screen, she knew she had no option but to tell Danni everything.

It just wasn't a conversation she could have on the phone.

She thumbed through the top half-dozen pieces of paper in the folder David had given her and made an assumption about the story he wanted. She looked over at him through the glass partition and for a split second she thought about confiding in him, but quickly dismissed the idea. Whoever said a problem shared was a problem halved had clearly never shared a problem with the *Gazette*'s editor.

The article he expected from her virtually wrote itself; it was as black and white a story as you got in journalism and it allowed her thoughts to continually stray back to Danni and that morning. Eventually she stopped typing and took her private notepad from her bag, turning to a blank page at the back and beginning to list her options. It didn't take long. She could either carry on with her investigation, or listen to the warning and stop. She wrote STOP on her pad with a large question mark. After that, the only other consideration was whether to call the police. She'd almost done that when she'd got back to the house that morning, trembling and with a head awash with thoughts; she also considered telling Danni she couldn't help her any more.

Luckily, she had managed to get ready and leave for work before her mother had got up; she knew that her fear and shock would have been impossible to hide. The office had been unusually full when she got in, and she had found it difficult to conceal her anxiety, so she had kept her head buried in the manila file and the article to avoid conversations. But when she looked up at the bustling environment, with Kelly holding court and the other reporters busy getting their pieces in for print, she knew that they would all give anything to be in her position, with a story that had the potential to catapult her into a different stratosphere. You don't let go of a story like this, she thought. None of them would.

In the early part of the afternoon, she finished her article for David and emailed him a copy to check. A fish-packaging factory on the outskirts of town had allegedly been employing dozens of immigrant workers, and paying below the minimum wage. An employee in Human Resources had objected to being asked to turn a blind eye to the practices and become a whistle-blower, handing over a significant amount of irrefutable evidence to the *Gazette*, hence the thick pile of papers in her folder.

David had conducted an interview with the employee himself, and Sue had transcribed the notes for inclusion in the folder. With so much information, it was an easy article to write, and it was made even easier when her attempts to contact the factory to hear their side were met with a blockade of unreturned calls or a refusal to comment. When she emailed her draft to David she was feeling pleased with it.

With the clock approaching five o'clock, the editor called her back into his office.

'This is good.'

'Thank you,' Laura said out of politeness while she waited patiently for the 'but', because David rarely left one out.

'I must say I was impressed by the way you handled the missing girl story,' he continued, motioning for her to sit down, 'but I'm also worried about you.'

Well, there was the *but*, Laura thought, and it wasn't so bad.

'Worried?'

'You seem a bit preoccupied.'

Laura looked at him. Worried, she thought, was a big departure from his usual mood, and she owed him some kind of explanation.

'I really wanted to do that interview,' she said, 'and I was cut up about it. But I'm OK now.'

'All right,' he said, his discomfort at showing a caring side abundantly clear, and looked back at his screen. 'Well, you've shown what you're capable of. Let's see more of it.'

She smiled and nodded. When she got back to her desk, as most of the staff were already making their way out of the doors, she felt taller and more confident; like a real journalist. She reopened her notepad and looked at her option list, crossed out the word STOP, and closed the pad.

Then she packed up her laptop and left, waving to David as she walked past his office, and when she reached the ground floor she took out her phone and called Danni, who answered just as Laura went out of the revolving doors and into the street. She apologised for having taken more time to investigate.

'Did you find anything?'

Laura pictured the man on the coastal path, holding her dog up in the air. 'You could say that.'

'What?'

'I'd prefer to tell you to your face.'

'Tell me now,' Danni begged. 'Please.'

Laura wanted to. But she had no idea how she might react or what she might do next.

'I can't.'

'When, then?'

'As soon as possible.'

They arranged to meet early the next morning at a neutral venue halfway between their homes – to cut driving time down, Laura told her – but, if she was honest, she didn't want to take the risk of being seen.

Any thoughts of an easy way out had gone.

There was no going back now.

44 | Laura

Laura left the house before anyone was up.

She broke up the two-and-a-half-hour journey by stopping to make a call to David when she knew he would be in his office. 'Women's problems,' she gave as her reason for not being able to come to work, and offered no more, knowing he wouldn't ask. She felt guilty, especially after what he had said the previous evening, but he and the *Gazette* would benefit when the story came out, and she used that thought to justify lying to him.

The services on the M5, near Cheltenham, were the perfect place for the two girls to meet and talk privately. There were more than half a dozen places to eat and drink and plenty of empty tables in quiet corners, so Laura bought two coffees when Danni arrived and they sat down. A member of staff cleared the table of two breakfast plates while they made small talk, and then Laura told her what had happened on the coastal path.

Danni was stunned.

'Has anyone said anything to you?' said Laura.

Danni was pale with shock. She shook her head. 'So Jessica really is alive?'

'He implied it.'

'What do we do now?'

Laura shrugged. 'They only said to forget about Jessica. They didn't mention you or Sandra so I don't know how much they know.'

'We met and talked. Then this? That's too much of a co-incidence, surely?'

'I got the email before we met.'

'Email?'

Laura told Danni about that too.

'Why didn't you say something?'

She wished she had, because she could tell that Danni was now wondering what else she hadn't told her since this had all begun. 'I just thought it was someone looking out for Sandra.'

'And now?'

'It's more than that. Now they've realised the email wasn't enough to stop me.'

'You have to tell the police.'

Laura looked up from her pad.

'You have to,' Danni said. 'They've threatened your family. It's too much.'

'It's not that simple.'

'They need to know too,' said Danni.

Laura nodded her agreement. 'I will tell them,' she said, 'and the police.'

'Good.'

Laura looked directly into Danni's eyes. 'But not straight away.'

'What?'

'I want to show Sandra your picture first. Did you get a photo of you as a child?'

Danni shook her head and explained what had happened.

'The one I've got will have to do. I just need her to see it.'

'But—'

'And if,' said Laura, cutting her challenge off before she could get going, 'she thinks you might be Jessica, then it's a matter for the police and I'll just be the one who breaks the story.'

'*Breaks the story?* This is people's lives.'

Laura lowered her voice and leaned in towards Danni. 'If I go to the police too soon, it will become a circus. They will leak it to their press sources, and it'll be everywhere. We'll lose control, and you and Sandra will be thrust in the spotlight whether you like it or not.'

Danni didn't look convinced.

'Look,' Laura said quietly but with authority, 'I know you think it's about the story, but think about what this will do to you *and* your dad if we're wrong? How will he feel if it all comes out?'

Now Danni seemed to come around to her thinking. 'But what about the man?'

'We keep our heads down. Don't meet up again until I've seen Sandra. No texts, no phone calls until I find out one way or the other if there's a chance you could be her.'

'When will that be?'

'As soon as.' Laura explained that she'd need to get more time off work and that her boss wasn't going to be pleased.

'Shouldn't we just go and see her together? Now?'

Laura had considered it, but she knew it would be a lot for Sandra to take in and she doubted she had the mental strength to deal with it. 'I think a photo would be less stressful for her.'

'You care about her,' said Danni.

'After what she's been through, I'd do anything to not see her hurt any more.'

Danni nodded. 'What do you think will happen? If I am her?'

'Let's not jump the gun.'

'My dad would be arrested, wouldn't he?'

'He would have abducted you, Danni. He'll be in a lot of trouble.'

'Do you think it was him who threatened you?'

'The man was way too young to be anywhere near your dad's age.'

'But he could have—'

Laura put her hand on Danni's. 'Look, one step at a time. I'll go and see Sandra, and you sit tight until then.'

Danni nodded, her eyes watery and wide open.

'Just don't say anything to anyone,' Laura added, 'and try to act as normal as you can around your dad.'

'That's easy to say,' said Danni. 'I'm not sure I'll be able to look him in the eye.'

45 | Laura

'Feet up.'

Laura lifted her legs and balanced her feet on the waste-paper bin as the cleaner pushed the hoover under her desk and then moved away without a word.

'You're welcome,' Laura said under her breath. She wasn't used to sharing the office with the cleaning staff, but then she had never been in the office this early before.

David couldn't hide the surprise on his face when he walked in and found her at her desk. 'Feeling better?' he asked in a tone that sounded as though he knew he was duty-bound to ask the question.

'Yes, thanks, David,' she said, and blushed for effect.

The editor was already beginning to move away, his obligatory health check completed, and Laura didn't make any attempt to stop him. Instead, she buried her head back into the work on her desk until lunchtime.

It was what they all called a 'slow news day' at the paper, with nothing of significance happening locally, or, it seemed, in the wider world. There was never a better time to get up to date with any non-urgent tasks, and, as she filed paperwork and reorganised the documents on her laptop, Laura had plenty of time to think about her meeting with Sandra, whom she called during her lunch break and arranged to meet at the weekend; she couldn't justify taking any more time off.

She began to imagine what would happen if Sandra thought that Danni was her missing daughter.

David had always said that a reporter should be at least two steps ahead of the story, anticipate the outcomes and be prepared for each eventuality. Laura had seen Kelly Heath do this on many occasions: have a strategy that covered different paths so that she wasn't thrown off course by an unexpected turn of events.

If Sandra did make a positive ID, or even anything resembling one, Laura would need a detailed execution plan, because she would have just a tiny window before the national and international media took over. She knew her only real opportunity was to get her name under the breaking news and, after that, try to secure the first interviews with Sandra and Danni. She was in a strong position to do that, but who knew what would happen when the big publications waded in and made huge offers for their exclusive side of the story?

Her afternoon was taken up with crossing items off her task list and daydreaming about the breaking story. She stayed at her desk after all the other staff had left and only David was still in his office; his full attention was taken by Kelly's latest article, so he didn't interrupt her, but she knew he'd be pleased with her commitment to make up for the time she'd missed.

On her way home she stopped at the retail park on the edge of the town to buy a voice recorder from the big stationery chain there. David had never made a secret of his distrust of modern technology and always reminded the staff that, if they must record interviews, rather than use traditional methods, they should use their own equipment, because the *Gazette* wasn't going to reimburse them. That was fine for a local paper and local stories, but Laura knew that if the Jessica Preston story broke it would be far from a small, local story and she would need to be prepared in every way possible – which included not being left behind or disadvantaged because she didn't have the right equipment. So it was after eight o'clock when her red VW Polo pulled on to the drive.

The house was silent; unusually so, because her mother's car was on the drive, and she could see the tyre marks on the frosty ground that her dad had left as he put his car in the garage. She'd have expected to find them talking in the kitchen, or hear the television on in the lounge, but there was no sound. They must have gone to bed early.

As she opened the door to the living room, Mimark waddled out, nudging his head into her shins as he walked past her on his way to his water bowl. The room was dim, with just a small table lamp on in the corner, and as she walked in she expected to find it empty, but her parents were both awake. Her father was sitting up on the chair and her mother on the sofa, and they had clearly been waiting for her.

There was a parcel on the table between them.

'What's up?' Laura said – casually, although she knew something was wrong from their expressions and she had guessed what the parcel was.

'Maybe you should tell us,' her father said.

Laura screwed up her face as if she didn't know what he was talking about.

'I ran into David Weatherall this morning, on my way to work.'

'Oh.'

'He said that he hoped you were feeling better.'

Laura gulped. 'Ri-ight,' she stuttered.

'Why weren't you at the paper?' her mother said.

'What did you say to him?' Laura looked at her father.

'I told him you were.'

'How much time have you taken off work?' her mother asked.

Laura didn't answer the question. 'Thank you, Dad,' she said instead.

'Laura, why have you been missing work?' her mother said.

'I can explain.'

Her father picked up the parcel and passed it to her. It had already been opened at one end and clumsily resealed. She didn't need to open it to know who or where it was from, but she did it anyway, and took out the deodorant-sized, red-topped aerosol can with the words *Attack Defence Spray* in bright yellow on it.

They both looked at her. Her father raised his eyebrows.

'I think you'd better tell us everything.'

46 | Laura

'There's no point my saying I'm not disappointed.'

Her father looked at her. He and Helen had listened without interruption until that point as Laura explained why she had lied to them and to her boss.

'I'm sorry,' she said, because it was the only thing she could think of to say.

Laura was a little intimidated by her father. He wasn't a shouter, not one to rant and show his emotions, and she had always wished he had been, because when he was upset – when the line had clearly been crossed – it manifested in the look he had on his face now: the haunted expression of someone who had failed. She'd have taken him screaming at her any day instead of that.

Usually it was her mother who spoke up on her behalf, but that wasn't going to happen either. Helen was showing no signs of her usual solidarity with Laura, and had the same expression as her husband.

'I thought you could tell me anything,' she said quietly.

'I could. I can.'

'So what was so different this time?' her father asked.

She looked down. The response she settled on was to say nothing. She didn't want to tell them what was in her head: that she wanted to prove to them, or specifically to her father, that she was good enough, smart enough and strong enough. There had never been a doubt with her mother, who encouraged and championed her all the time; but she'd always felt a need to demonstrate to her father that she had what it took.

She wasn't even sure if was just in her head, but it had always been there. She knew it was the reason she'd clung to her goal of becoming a journalist in the first place: because her father had questioned her career choice and her capability. When he'd helped her get the job at the *Gazette*, that had made things several times worse.

So she'd been determined to be the one breaking the story of the missing girl in the shopping centre, and it was the reason she wanted to be the person who broke the story of Jessica Preston being alive to the world.

'You know that I had to call in a favour with David.'

'I know, Dad,' she said resisting an urge to roll her eyes.

'How do you think I felt?'

She wanted to say it wasn't about him or how he felt but about the story, and that, as a journalist, it always had to be about the story, and that sometimes she had to protect herself, her sources and the story itself. But she sat quietly instead.

'And you don't know this girl, or what she might be involved in.'

'She contacted me. And David wouldn't have let me go if I'd asked him.'

'Rightly so,' her father said, a little too smugly for Laura's liking.

'I couldn't not go and see her once I'd set it up.'

'Anything could have happened,' said Helen.

Laura looked at her for more support. She'd known about the interview, after all.

'I can take care of myself.'

'With this?'

Her mother held up the yellow can. Laura had left out a significant detail up to that point; the one that had made her so eager to talk to Danni in person.

'I just wanted to be safe.'

'Safe?'

She explained about the threat on the coastal path and her parents' demeanour changed from one of disappointment to shock. Her mother also turned very pale.

'Goodness,' Robert Grainger said, shaking his head.

Laura let her fingertips run over the can, still wrapped in a plastic coating. 'Journalism can be dangerous.'

'In *war zones*,' her father said sharply. 'You work for the local rag, and you shouldn't ever have to face that kind of threat.'

'This is a bigger story than the *Gazette*.'

'But that's who you work for.'

'Not for ever. This could be my big break.'

'If it's true,' her mother said.

'If I'm being threatened, then I must be on to something.'

Her parents exchanged a look. 'I think we need to get the police involved,' her father said.

'No!' shouted Laura, bolting upright. 'If you do, the story's gone.'

'It's your story,' they both said, almost in perfect harmony.

'It won't be. The police have their own people who they tip off. The *Gazette* won't get a look-in. And David will pass on the scraps we do get to Kelly Heath.'

'He wouldn't.'

'Don't overestimate him, Dad. You might be able to call in favours from him but he wouldn't let me near this, believe me.'

'So you'd rather be looking over your shoulder?' said Helen.

'And have us all do the same?' her father added.

'I need to finish this!' Laura protested.

'Even if it means someone getting hurt?'

'No. But it would change everything for me.' She looked over at her mother, begging for her to back her up. 'It would make me a real journalist.'

'You are one.'

'I mean a *real* one. Not just at some local rag.'

Laura looked at her father, whose face was thunderous.

'She didn't mean it like that,' Helen said hastily. 'The *Gazette* is a real newspaper.'

'Oh, really? Only a week ago, you said I could be studying in America so I could get into a bigger paper,' said Laura. 'Make your mind up.'

Helen looked away.

'This would do more for me than ten years in New York. Can't you see that?'

They paused.

'So, this Danni girl – can you trust her?'

For the first time since she'd walked into the room Laura felt she could see a chink of light, and, although it was still some way into the distance, she was getting through to them.

'I think so.'

'And Sandra Preston?' her mother said. 'Are you sure she can handle this?'

'No,' said Laura, 'but she's saner than most people I know.'

'Have you thought about what it might do to her, if it goes badly?'

'No worse than sitting there and never knowing.'

Her mother and father looked at each other again. Laura had seen this tactic before, their version of bad cop and worried cop where they hit her with concerns and objections in waves until she could no longer hold them at bay. They had used it when she'd said she wanted to become a journalist, and almost worn her down. She needed a counter-punch.

'What if it were you, Mum, and not Sandra?'

'Excuse me?'

'What if I'd been taken from you at that age? What if you were in that place, sitting staring out of the window? Wouldn't you want someone to help you?'

Her parents just looked at her, and the tension dissipated a little.

'Don't use emotional black—' her father finally started, but Laura was expecting it.

'I'm not. It's just a question.'

Silence.

'You've always told me to do the right thing. So which is it?'

More silence.

Laura's father began to speak but her mother shook her head, and Laura decided to quit too while she was marginally ahead. She thought it sensible to hold back the one piece of information she hadn't told them yet.

That she was going to see Sandra again at the weekend.

47 | Danni

Danni and Sam hugged, and that marked the end of the silence between them.

'I shouldn't have done that. I'm sorry,' Sam told her.

'It's OK.' Danni smiled. She knew Sam's intentions were well placed and, although she could be heavy-handed at times, she had been trying to help.

'I just wanted to get you two talking. And the job seemed a good way.'

'I know.'

'And, when this Laura thing is over, you might want that job.'

'If it's ever over.'

'Even if you are this girl, you can still be her in Southampton.'

'If I am,' Danni said, 'then I doubt anything will ever be the same again.'

Sam nodded. Danni hadn't told her yet – this was the first time they'd spoken in three days – but she had contacted the company about the job and explained that she had some family issues to sort out, and they'd graciously agreed to give her until Monday to make her decision.

'Do you think she'll recognise you, just from a photo?'

Danni shrugged. 'Laura thinks it's the best thing to do.'

Sam rolled her eyes.

'What?'

'Forget what Laura thinks. What about what you think?'

'Laura's the one who knows her,' said Danni.

'For, like, five minutes. You shouldn't let her call all the shots.'

'It's just a plan.'

'It's Laura's plan. Why not make your own?' Sam's eyes glistened, the way they did when she got the bit between her teeth on a subject, and Danni listened to see where it went. 'From where I'm sitting,' her friend said, 'it seems that Laura is relying on Jessica's mother too much.'

'She is her mother.'

'But even so,' said Sam, 'she's been in that hospital for years and, besides, you have the answer in front of you.'

Danni frowned.

'Your dad!' cried Sam. 'He knows the truth.'

'We talked about this. If I ask him, I rip us apart. Either way.'

'So don't ask him.'

Sam outlined her own plan, and Danni admitted it was a plausible idea and one that wouldn't do much harm, or necessarily interfere with Laura's.

'So go on, no time like the present,' Sam said.

Danni called her father. They hadn't spoken since she had stormed out and there was a frostiness between them when the call started, but it began to thaw when she told him she was accepting the job.

'They've asked me to send a copy of my birth certificate.'

'Birth certificate?'

Danni looked at Sam, who nodded encouragement. 'Uh-huh. Can I come and get it from the flat?'

There was a pause.

'Is that OK?'

'I'm not sure what got taken into storage. Can you give me a day to look?'

She asked if she could help.

'No, I've got a deadline on an article, so I'll have to do it tomorrow night.'

'Thank you.'

'I've not heard of a company asking to see a birth certificate before.'

'That's what they said.'

They ended the call and Danni relayed the parts of the call that Sam hadn't heard. Her friend thought for a moment.

'It does sound completely normal. He's moved house, there's stuff everywhere, and not being able to lay his hands on it is not that surprising.'

'But?'

'If he doesn't have it, and he never has had it, then he's just bought himself a day to work out what to do.'

'Or he's just a bit disorganised.'

At that moment, the key turned in the door and Sam's mother walked in, wearily kicking off her boots in the hallway and calling out a tired greeting to the two girls as she went into the kitchen to empty her shopping bags.

'Watch,' said Sam and called into the kitchen. 'Mum.'

'Yeah?'

'If I needed my birth certificate, like, right now, could you get it for me?'

'Why do you want it?'

'Just because.'

'I've just walked through the door.'

'Could you get it?'

'It's upstairs in a safe place. Just give me a minute.'

'Thank you.'

They could hear Mrs Newbold cursing under her breath and Sam went into the kitchen to tell her mother she didn't really need her to get it. Danni shrugged when she came back in. 'Doesn't prove anything,' she said.

'You know your dad is a hundred times more organised than my mum,' Sam replied.

'OK,' said Danni, 'so we'll see what he says tomorrow night.'

48 | Danni

Danni walked to the beach and then along the sand until she reached her father's apartment.

It was a thirty-minute journey, at a brisk pace, but she wanted to stretch her legs. When she got there, just after nine o'clock, he was still in his pyjamas and dressing gown and looked shattered.

'Did I get you out of bed?'

Her father filled up the kettle, switched it on and tried to hide a yawn. 'I was up until past two looking for that certificate.'

He made her a cup of tea as he explained that he hadn't had any luck, although she had guessed that the moment she walked in; it would have been sitting proudly on the kitchen table waiting for her if he had.

'I'm stumped,' he said. 'And I can't recall seeing it when I packed all the stuff up to go into storage, either.'

'Is it worth looking, though?'

'I don't remember seeing it for ages. I keep all the important paperwork in a file and it wasn't among it.'

Danni sniffed feigning disappointment, but she was sure he was lying to her.

'I'm sorry, love. Do you want me to email them to explain?'

'No,' Danni replied. 'They'll think I'm a child. I'll do it.'

'Surely it won't affect the offer.'

'Hope not.'

Her father sat down and sipped at his tea.

'Your mother would have known where it was.'

Danni saw his eyes become watery and she hadn't come here looking for an argument, so she changed the subject and they talked for another twenty minutes before she left. She took the beach route back to Sam's and relayed what had happened.

'Do you believe him?' asked Sam.

'Do you?'

'He could have lost it.'

'It wasn't what he said, it was how he said it, and the look in his eyes too.'

'You think he suspects something?'

'I know he does,' said Danni. 'But I'm at square one again. And I can't push it now without being more direct.'

Sam shook her head. 'He told you what to do next,' she said.

'He did?'

'You need to look in that file,' said Sam confidently.

'What?'

'The file! The "important paperwork" one,' she said making air quotes. 'Because, even if your birth certificate isn't in it, who knows what else you might find?'

Danni thought about it and nodded. 'You're good at this.'

'So do you know where it is?'

'I know it's in a box in the apartment.'

'I thought he took it all to the storage place.'

'He did,' said Danni, 'but not that one. I remember he was taking it with him to the new place.'

Sam looked at her quizzically.

'That morning, when we stopped to collect the letter about the job, he had already gone to the storage place, and I saw a box stuffed with folders and paperwork still at the house.'

'Then you've got to find the box when he's not there.'

'You mean break in?' Danni said.

'Don't you have a key?'

'We haven't exactly been on the best terms. But I know where he keeps the spare.'

'There you go.'

Danni began to consider how far she was prepared to go. It had seemed much easier when Laura was calling the shots and she was waiting to be told the next step. 'Laura's seeing Sandra this afternoon,' she said. 'She might—'

'You can't just rely on her!' Sam said. 'After twenty years, whatever Sandra says or thinks doesn't prove anything. And, either way, your dad is still hiding *something*.'

'If he finds out, our relationship is over.'

Sam looked directly into her eyes and Danni knew what she was going to say before she opened her mouth.

'So don't let him find out.'

49 | Laura

'See you tomorrow.'

Laura ended the call on her mobile phone. The wheels were in motion. In a little over twenty-four hours, Sandra would see the photograph of Danni, and that would tell her what to do next.

Sandra had seemed a little offish, she thought, in their brief conversation, but she had agreed to see Laura anyway. Laura had told her that she wanted to follow up the interview with another article, in light of how well the first had been received and because it had awoken some local interest in the story, but she had perceived little enthusiasm and she knew that Sandra was probably wondering what the point of it all was.

The rest of the day was a typical Friday, with everyone at the *Gazette*, Laura included, trying to finish off whatever work they had on their list in time for the weekend. The paper had a skeleton weekend staff, updating the website with any news, while the rest of the staff started with a clean slate on Monday morning. But that all changed at four o'clock when the immigrant workers' situation at the local factory took a turn for the worse. After reading the *Gazette*'s article and the whistle-blower's account, a group of disgruntled ex-employees, who had been laid off and replaced by lower-paid workers, turned up at clocking-off time to protest, and it had quickly descended into a brawl. David got a tip-off just after it started and called in Kelly Heath for an impromptu meeting. Laura saw him nod in her direction and a few minutes later the

Gazette's star reporter was walking over to her. 'David wants me to cover the factory story and suggested you could help me with some interviews in the morning.'

Laura looked up from her laptop and over at David's office. She bit her lip.

'I'm sorry, Kelly. I've got plans I can't change for tomorrow.'

Kelly stood beside her desk, not sure what to do next. It was unheard-of for anyone ever to turn her down if she asked for help. And this story was escalating quickly and had the potential to dwarf the one about the missing girl in the shopping centre.

'I'm really sorry, Kelly.'

She watched as Kelly walked away without a reply and then went over to ask her usual sidekick to help her instead. She received, not a cold shoulder, but a distinctly cool one; no one liked being second choice. Laura felt Kelly's eyes burning into her, and before she left for the evening there was an unmistakable look of disapproval from David and Sue. She felt as though she'd kicked a puppy rather than turned down some overtime. Tomorrow had better be worth it, she thought, as she walked out of the revolving doors.

She was surprised to see a familiar car pull up in front of her.

'Mum? What are you doing here?'

'Quick, jump in,' said Helen through the open window.

Laura's own car was in the car park at the other end of the high street, but there was already a small line of cars backed up behind her mother's, so she opened the door and climbed inside.

'What's wrong?'

'Nothing,' her mother said, and moved away from the kerb just as the driver in the car behind her lost patience and pressed on the horn. 'OK, OK,' she said, raising an apologetic hand.

'So what's this about?'

Her mother took the next left without speaking and then the left turn after that, and they entered a quiet back street with a small number of shops and buildings that had been converted into, among other things, a dance studio, a ladies-only gymnasium and a tattoo parlour. Although she'd worked around the corner for years, Laura barely knew of the street's existence.

'Here we are.'

Helen indicated and parked on the left-hand side of the street in a parking bay that said *Customers Only*. They were in front of the gymnasium, which was owned by someone called Snookie, according to the gold plaque over the door that Laura was reading.

'What are you doing?'

Her mother smiled and took the can of defence spray out of her handbag. 'You forgot it this morning.'

'I didn't. I only got it for when I walk the dog.' Laura took the can and put it in her own bag. She *had* forgotten it.

'Well, if you need a form of defence,' her mother said, 'I thought we'd do it properly.'

'The gym? Are you mad?'

Laura had joined a gym once, when she was nineteen, and had visited it twice and hated it enough to not go again after that, although not enough to cancel her monthly subscription for almost a year and a half.

'They do a women's self-defence class at six,' her mother said, unbuckling her seatbelt. 'And I've booked us both on to it.'

50 | Laura

Laura's cheek struck the floor with a dull thud.

She sat up, rubbed her jawbone and glared at her mother, who was standing in jogging bottoms and a sweatshirt, applauding as a five-foot-tall Chinese girl effortlessly dispatched Laura's feeble 'attack'. Luckily the floor was covered with thick padded matting, so no significant harm was done to anything other than her pride.

'That was fantastic!' beamed the instructor. A thirty-something named Joanna in a tight vest top and even tighter shorts, she had a tendency, Laura had quickly noticed, for exaggerating her praise when someone did well and patronising people when they got it wrong. Laura snorted, but the rest of the group seemed to share Joanna's appraisal.

'Next one up. Helen, isn't it?'

Laura shuffled to the side to wait her next turn, trying to slot into a different place in the queue to avoid coming up against the Chinese girl, who felt as though she was built entirely of muscle. By contrast, Laura already felt beaten up. Less than forty minutes into the class, she had spent most of that time silently cursing her mother for bringing her – and a spare gym kit – here to begin with.

To be fair to her mother, who did as little by way of exercise as Laura did, she had picked it up much more quickly; she put her would-be assailant on to the ground with ease and confidence. Laura grinned at her mother and held both thumbs up as Joanna jumped in with an overly exuberant reaction and then used Helen to demonstrate a slight variation on the move they had just practised.

'I was going to drop out and leave you to it after the first session,' she said as she joined Laura afterwards, 'but I'm really enjoying myself.'

Laura raised her eyebrows. Joanna called for their attention as she started the next part of the class. After an hour, and no further face-on-mat encounters, the instructor called a halt to their night's work and told them to give themselves a round of applause, which Helen forced a reluctant Laura to join in with.

'Well, what did you think?' Helen asked her afterwards as they headed out to the car.

'I think I'll stick with the can.'

'You can make fun, but you should complete the course. You got easily knocked about in there, you know?'

'Hmmm.'

Laura rubbed her jaw again and felt pain on her thigh and elbow. She had no intention of setting foot in the place again, but she didn't say so.

'Want to get a drink?' Helen asked, smiling at her. They threw their bags into the back of the car and walked around the corner to the coffee shop that stayed open until eight o'clock. Laura fetched them both a latte, topped with whipped cream; she thought they'd earned it.

'Admit it: you had fun tonight,' her mother said.

Laura smiled and rubbed her jaw. 'That Joanna was a bit much. And it was painful, even with the mats. Plus I think my jaw is fractured.'

Helen looked at her face and shook her head. 'But apart from that?'

They laughed.

'It was OK.'

'Seriously, though,' Helen said, her face turning very sober, 'you should learn to look after yourself.'

'I'll be fine.'

'This threat thing has shaken me up. And I don't like you travelling up and down the country on your own either.'

'I'm just doing my job.'

The previous evening had ended with an agreement to disagree. Laura hadn't quite convinced her parents that it was a good idea to continue with the story, but they had admitted they understood why she wanted to. The sticking point had been her lying to them, and to her boss; she'd promised she wouldn't do it again.

'I just wish you'd stay more local.'

'You sound like David.'

'And not take risks like this.'

'Now you sound like Dad.'

Her mother nodded. 'He's just very protective. We're your parents; we can't help it.'

Her mother patted her hand and Laura smiled. She wouldn't really want it any other way.

51 | Laura

'You know the worst part?'

Sandra sat in her favourite chair, the only place Laura had ever seen her sit, and she guessed that no one at High Cliffs, patient or staff, had ever tried to take it since she'd made it her own. She was staring out of the window, predictably, her eyes scanning the sand, although Laura hadn't seen a single soul on the beach during any of her visits.

'Go on.'

'I didn't even want to go to the beach that day.'

Laura's new voice recorder was switched on and sitting on the table in front of her. Her bag had a folder with the photograph of Danni inside, but she held it back, waiting until she felt Sandra was ready to see it.

'No?'

Sandra shook her head; her weak smile was sad and full of regret.

'Me and Todd had a row the night before, a bad one. We almost came to blows. But the kids had been asking us to take them to the beach so we got up the next day and pretended nothing had happened.'

'All parents have to do that for their kids at times.'

Sandra shrugged. 'I think that's why Todd was so hard on himself, afterwards. He was sulking that morning and reading his paper. If he hadn't been, he might have seen where she went. We paid a heavy price for that argument.'

'All couples fight. Can I ask what it was about?'

Laura looked at Sandra but the woman showed no sign of reciprocating and gazed straight ahead, pausing for a few seconds as she seemed to wrestle with herself on how far she wanted to go with this part of her story.

'Jessica. Well, not in as many words, but it had been an ongoing fight since she was born. He was fine with Stuart but he'd been different with Jess. Moody all the time and with the shortest fuse you could imagine. It was like a male postnatal depression. These days he would get signed off work, but at the time I just thought he was a miserable bastard.'

'What was different?'

Sandra hesitated before answering. 'He didn't want another baby. It drove a wedge between us. When I told him I was pregnant, he was so mad.'

'So it was an accident?'

Sandra looked down and her face reddened. After a few seconds, she shook her head. 'Not for me.'

'Did he not want you to have her?'

'No,' said Sandra quickly, 'he never said that. But I thought he'd come around to the idea after she was born and he just … didn't.'

Laura let Sandra reflect on her revelation. It had visibly brought her down, though, and Laura needed to change the mood.

'What do you think Jessica is doing now?'

'So you *do* believe she's alive?'

Laura nodded. The heavy frown on Sandra's face went away.

'Doesn't matter as long as she's happy. She'll be doing well for herself. I think she'll make something of her life. She's not like me and Todd. We plodded along. We never tried to be more than we were. And Stuart was easygoing too when he was young, but even at that age Jess was different. She had…I don't know how to describe it. Balls, I suppose.'

Laura smiled.

'Stuart was a little sod, I admit, but only in that he was mischievous. He was also very easy to get in line. *Go to your room.* He went. *Lay the table.* He did it. Jess, on the other hand – she'd stand her ground and argue the toss.'

'I like the sound of her.'

Sandra smiled now. They sat in silence for a few minutes, both watching the waves lap on the sand below with a rhythmic, soothing continuity.

Laura got up to stretch her legs, still aching after the previous night's class, and took their cups to the canteen area in the hallway and made them each a fresh cup of coffee. When she got back to the table she found Sandra with her head pressed against the glass, her eyes locked on the beach. Laura wasn't sure if she knew she had come back; she didn't thank her for the drink or even acknowledge it was there, leaving it untouched as Laura drank hers.

'Sandra,' she said quietly, 'do you think you'd recognise her? If you saw her?'

It felt to Laura that the temperature in the room dropped ten degrees as she finished the question. Sandra's face was stony and grey, the frown back, and her body had tensed in a way that suggested that Laura had better have a very good reason for asking.

'Well, do you?' Laura persisted, softly.

'Why?'

'People responded to the article,' she explained. 'Not just Maureen Upson, but a girl too.'

'A girl?'

Laura could see Sandra fighting the urge to raise her hopes.

'A girl. She called because she thinks there is a chance she might be Jessica.'

Sandra's body was rigid now.

'It's only a small possibility, Sandra. I don't want to raise your hopes because it might be nothing, but...'

Sandra gulped.

'...but she's about the right age, she lives close by and she has a lot of similar features. I've looked at photos of her and Jessica until my brain hurts. And her parents are keeping a big secret from her.'

'Where is she?'

Laura looked around and lowered her voice. 'There is more. But I want you to see a photo of her first, because I think you might know straight away when you look at it.'

Laura could see Sandra was trembling and she knew she had to manage her expectations carefully. She checked the on-duty nurse was occupied elsewhere and slid her hand into her bag, pulling out the manila folder. She opened it so that Danni's pretty face was looking at her off the page. She put it in Sandra's hand.

'Just look at it and tell me what you think.'

The woman's hand was shaking as she put her fingers around the photographic paper and adjusted it on her lap. She looked down and stared at the image for what felt like an eternity and then a single tear plopped on to the sheet, hitting Danni on the neck.

'Sandra?'

More tears dropped and formed little water marks until Sandra moved the page. 'I don't know,' she whispered, her eyes never leaving the photograph.

Laura put her hand over Sandra's and patted it. 'But it could be her?'

Sandra's whole body seemed to shrug. 'I have this picture of her in my head. The one I use when I imagine what she looks like now and what she's doing. I'm so used to seeing her like that, I don't know if my brain will let me accept a different version.'

'I understand.'

'She might look like this for all I know. She's got the same eyes.' She nodded down at the now tearstained image.

'I know it's difficult.'

'What if I want it to be her so much that I see things that aren't there?'

'Anything's possible looking at a photograph,' said Laura with new-found clarity. She could see that, although she'd wanted to spare Sandra the shock, a two-dimensional image threw up even more questions than it answered.

The main thing was that Sandra hadn't ruled out the possibility, or seen something in the photo of Danni that meant she couldn't be her daughter. That made the next step easier. For everyone.

Laura squeezed Sandra's hand.

'That's why I'm going to bring her to meet you.'

52 | Danni

'I have to speak to him first.'

Danni ended the call with Laura and finished dressing for work. She'd had a full update on Sandra's reaction and things were moving now: Laura had asked her to be ready to go to High Cliffs at short notice, as soon as she could get the time off work. She was desperate to see Sandra Preston as quickly as possible but, given that things might happen quickly after that, she felt she needed to try to at least talk to her father, because, if their relationship had any chance of surviving if she wasn't Jessica, they had to get past the latest fallout. So she had sent him a text message asking him to call her that morning.

Her mobile rang at precisely ten o'clock.

'I'm outside.'

Danni pulled back the curtain and looked out. It was a Sunday and a misty one, with low cloud drifting off the sea. Her father was sitting in his car outside Sam's house and she raised a hand to wave.

'Hungry?' he asked on the phone as she looked at him down there. She was.

'Give me two minutes.'

She pulled on her jeans and a jumper and went downstairs, pulling her hair into a tidy ponytail before she got into the car.

They drove to the American-style diner a few miles down the coast. It was a popular place for tourists; a little too popular at times – you had to book ahead at weekends in summer, so the locals tended to go elsewhere.

'The pancakes are supposed to be incredible,' her father said as they sat down and picked up the menus. He asked about the job and the birth certificate.

'They were OK about it.'

'When do you start?'

'I'm confirming tomorrow, so I'll know then. If I take it.'

'You've still not decided?'

'I just want to be sure.'

Danni half-listened as he told about some of the career decisions he'd faced at a similar age. She knew he had always been a hard worker; it seemed as though he'd been chained to either a typewriter, a word processor, or more lately an expensive laptop, for as long as she could remember. But this was the first time she could recall him dispensing career advice to her and she found herself becoming irritated with him, thinking it was a bit late to start playing dad, and he was trying a little too hard.

She let him continue for another minute and was about to interrupt when he mentioned turning a job down when she was very young and she jumped in.

'How old was I?'

'About three. It was the right job but at the wrong time. I didn't want to be away from you and your mum.'

Danni felt her emotions bubbling to the surface; it was rare for him to mention her mother without being prompted.

'Not that she'd have noticed,' he continued. 'She did everything as it was.'

'I didn't know that.'

'She was so good, I thought it was best to just work as much as I could and pay the bills and leave the rest to her.'

'What was I like? As a baby?'

She knew it was a clumsy question the moment it tumbled out of her mouth but she'd had no way of stopping it. Her father had handed the opportunity to her on a plate, and she couldn't let it pass.

'A baby?'

'Did I keep you awake all night? Was I a nightmare? Did I take ages to learn to walk? I can't remember ever asking you.'

'You're not pregnant, are you?' her father asked instantly, either without thought or, she wondered, to deflect the question. Danni glared at him and he held up his hands. 'Sorry.'

There was that look on his face again, she thought: where he had become so uncomfortable that he looked as if he might up and run at any moment. But Danni was having this conversation whether he wanted to or not.

'So what's brought this on?'

'I just realised that I can't ask Mum any more.'

She looked at him: he didn't seem totally convinced by her answer, and he paused as he thought about how to respond. Then he smiled.

'She made it look easy,' he said. 'She was an amazing mother. She could remember who sent you every single birthday and Christmas present, even years later. She knew the exact day and time of every after-school club and you never missed one.'

Danni smiled.

He seemed to enjoy reminiscing. 'I couldn't even tell you the name of any of your friends at school. Your mother knew their birthdays, for goodness' sake,' he said, his voice cracking and his expression turning to one of pain. She could see why he hadn't opened up that much before, and, as he struggled to contain his emotions, Danni felt sorry for him.

'You did other things for me, though,' she said kindly.

'But was it enough?'

'I never wanted for anything.'

She put her hand on his. He managed a faint smile.

'That's just material stuff. Not...'

There were tears in his eyes.

'We should have done *this* more often,' she said.

'We still can.'

Danni watched his face. She thought it looked honest enough, but there was still something, a slight hesitancy when he spoke, that made her feel unsure. She realised she no longer knew if she could trust anything he said, no matter how genuine it sounded.

And he still hadn't answered her question about what she was like as a baby.

The waitress, in full fifties American costume, came to take their order, and when she walked away Danni's father looked at her.

'I'm sorry I haven't been there for you.'

She felt closer to him than she had at any moment since her mother died; and a long time before that too, if she were able to remember that far, but it felt foggy now. Her mother's death had affected them both so much, she wasn't sure which of her memories were real and which were imagined.

There was only one thing she knew with any certainty at that moment.

She didn't want to be Jessica Preston.

'It's OK,' she found herself saying, although she wasn't sure if it was.

They sat in silence until the waitress put plates stacked with pancakes in front of them and Danni began to drizzle hers with maple syrup.

'So will you take the job?' her father asked.

'What would you do if you were me?'

'I don't think it'd do you any harm.'

'I wouldn't see so much of you.'

'It's Southampton,' he laughed, 'not Australia. And we'll have to make time.'

She smiled. The deadline had crept up on her quickly. 'I think I'll probably take it.'

Her father nodded, looking approving. She couldn't help but wonder whether it was in his best interests rather than hers. That was the trouble with knowing that he was hiding something: it cast a dark, unpleasant shadow over everything that was said or done.

'Let me know what you decide.'

'I'll pop round the flat tomorrow after I call them. It's my day off.'

He frowned. 'I've got a meeting in the morning,' he said, 'so if you come round it'll have to be after midday.'

'OK,' said Danni, but in her mind an image was already forming. It was of a file, full of papers; *important papers* that her dad had put in the box to take to his new home and which she could picture clearly now on the kitchen floor of their old house, waiting to be taken.

Whatever he was hiding might be in that box, as Sam had said. And it was somewhere in his new apartment.

If she was going to look for it, she now had the perfect opportunity.

53 | Danni

Danni was frustrated.

Laura had sent a text to her the previous evening to suggest a midweek visit to Sandra, citing work and problems with her boss as the reason for the hold-up, whereas Danni would have liked to see her the very next day and get it over with.

She knew Sam was right in that she was too wedded to Laura's schedule and needed to be more proactive, but in the twenty-odd hours since she'd had breakfast with her father she felt different too. She felt that she wanted to repair their relationship, and spend more time with him, but she could only do that if she knew what he was hiding; and she was certain the box held the key.

Her alarm woke her when it was still dark, but the sky was clear and full of stars, and she could see the dark blue turning lighter and giving way to a tinge of orange on the horizon. She put on her running shoes, with a black hooded top and leggings, and with the hood up she began to jog slowly down to the beach in the semi-dark, and then along the sand, acknowledging the other runners who were out and doing the same thing as her.

But they weren't doing exactly the same thing.

As she neared her father's apartment she looked at it and saw the lights were on and there was movement in the kitchen window. She jogged past, near the edge of the water where the sand was hardest, and carried on for another two hundred yards and then turned and jogged back, almost retracing her footprints. She checked her phone – it was just after eight, and she knew her father liked to set off early for morning meetings in case there were any problems on the roads.

As she neared the apartment again, the kitchen light was off, and she saw the headlights of her father's car as it slipped off the driveway and on to the road. The sky was turning a lighter blue now, but she would still be hard to see on the unlit beach. She turned inland, ran to the steps that led up to the first-floor apartment and looked around. The downstairs occupant hadn't moved in yet; her father had told her that they were due to start their lease in a fortnight, so she didn't have to worry about being seen as she walked up the steps and on to the decking.

Since she was a teenager, her father had always left a spare key, for emergencies, under an odd-shaped rock in a plant pot at the back of the house. On the decking were two plants, one on each side of the decked area, and she walked over to a green Bergenia plant that sat next to the patio doors. She put on a pair of latex gloves she'd taken from the surgery, found the stone that sat on the soil, and carefully lifted it to reveal a gold key on a small ring.

Then she walked back down the steps and around to the front of the property, climbing those steps just as the sun began to rise in the clear sky. She knocked all traces of sand from her shoes and took them off, then wiped the gloves clean and turned the key in the door. It opened to the sound of intermittent beeps from the alarm. Danni took a deep breath, stepped into the apartment and punched her mother's date of birth – the month and the year – into the keypad, hoping her father had continued with another of his habits.

The beeping stopped.

Barefoot, she stepped through the hall and systematically went into each room, looking for a place where the file or the box might be located. She quickly checked all the obvious places – drawers, cupboards, the wardrobe and under beds –

and ruled them out. As her father had bemoaned, there wasn't that much storage space in the apartment, but she was thorough in her search, looking in every room but finding nothing.

She spent more time in her father's study, which he had converted from the smallest of three bedrooms, as it was the place she expected to have success; but the room only had a writing desk facing the large window that looked out to sea, a large chair and a small filing cabinet – which, when she checked it, she found full of contracts and invoices for her father's work. There was nothing that looked out of place, or like the box she had seen at the house.

She knew her father was a meticulous filer and would have put the papers somewhere he could access them if he needed to. But she was fast running out of places to look. Her father had clearly opted for spacious, clutter-free living, and she'd exhausted the few storage options he had. There wasn't a garage, either, so she began to wonder if he'd taken the box to the storage facility after all.

Maybe he had moved it when she started asking questions.

Danni went back into the main living area and took another look around, trying to find anything she might have missed. She checked the backs of cupboards and inside pots, pans and even the microwave. If the file was in the house he'd done a good job of hiding it, she thought, and her mind turned to why he might want to hide it.

Then, just as she was about to give up, she saw it.

It was a small square in the freshly painted white ceiling; an equally white cover that almost blended perfectly with the ceiling but she could just make out the edges. The apartment was on the top floor, but she'd not even considered that there might be a loft with ample space for extra storage.

Or for putting the things you didn't want anyone to see.

54 | Danni

Danni stared up at the ceiling and she knew.

Before she looked inside the loft, even before she opened the hatch door, she knew what she would find in there. It was virtually calling to her: she had no idea why she was so sure, but there was no doubt whatsoever in her mind.

She pulled up a breakfast stool from the kitchen, stood on it to reach the cover and gave the white square a gentle push, gradually giving it more persuasion until it moved fully and she could push it up and back. Then she got on her toes until she could put her head into the space.

She reached down and took her phone from the pocket of her hooded top, switching the torch on. When she lifted her arm into the loft opening, it illuminated the cavernous space, and it looked empty and untouched.

But someone had opened the hatch and placed a cardboard box inside, just a few inches from the hatch door. She held the torch up a little and saw it in the brightness: a box slightly taller and wider than a shoebox and full of files and paperwork; exactly as she remembered it.

Danni slid her other hand into the space and pulled the corner of the box to her, toppling a fraction and having to drop her phone on to the carpet below so she could use her other hand to regain her balance by gripping the edge of the opening. Then she carefully slid the box forward and, using both hands, lifted it out through the hatch.

It was heavier than she'd expected.

She held the box with both hands and lowered herself to the ground, and then put it down on the carpet and began searching through the files and papers, quickly skim-reading each one to ascertain its relevance to her and then moving on, making sure to keep them in the same order as she found them.

The exercise began to eat up time, and the majority of the contents were of no real interest, mainly documents from the old house and some solicitors' and estate agency letters about the apartment. By the time she was three-quarters of the way through it, she checked her phone and saw it was getting close to ten o'clock. This still gave her plenty of time, but she quickened her search all the same and began to listen out for any sounds outside, just in case.

As she reached the last file in the box she began to get disheartened. She had seen nothing that told her anything useful, and there was certainly no birth certificate or important documents; she couldn't understand why her father had made such an effort to put the box out of sight. She thumbed through the pages of the file – the results of a conveyancing survey done on the family house and a list of items that came with the apartment – and then slid it back into the bottom of the box.

Except it wasn't the bottom. There was a piece of cardboard – it looked as though it was made from the box lid – at what looked like the bottom, but a fraction higher than it should be, and balanced on something. Danni carefully lifted the corner and, as she moved it upwards, so she saw an envelope underneath.

Her heart began to thump.

The envelope was brown and had her father's handwriting on the front. *P. Edwards – Hospital*.

Her fingers were trembling a little as she opened the already broken seal of the envelope and slipped out the contents: five folded pieces of paper. They were letters, all addressed to her mother.

She began to read them.

As Danni finished each one she placed it back on to the pile. There was nothing of particular interest on the first two pages, just medical notes and key information on blood group and allergies. The third page was a photocopy of a letter from her own GP. The fourth was a prescription for some tablets.

She picked up the final letter and skim-read it, already resigned to its containing similar information. But then she got to the second paragraph and everything changed in an instant.

Her stomach felt as if it had tied itself into a knot, and she had to swallow hard to stop herself being sick.

She read it again and it said the same thing; she hadn't misread it. Her heart beat so quickly, she felt as if she needed to press on her chest to stop it jumping from out from her body.

Then she was aware of noise – voices, she thought, coming from outside – and she put the letters back the way she had found them and crawled on her knees to the window. Her father's car was on the road outside the gates and he was engaged in a conversation with an elderly woman who lived opposite.

Danni gasped. Another hour had passed, and he was back early too. She quickly pushed the envelope back into its hiding place, gathered the rest of the files and papers into a pile, and put them back into the box as quickly as she could.

She looked again through the bottom corner of the window and they were still talking.

She climbed on the stool, holding the box carefully and lifted it above her head, straining until it reached the mouth of the opening and she was able to rest it on the edge, gather her strength and then push it inside fully. She didn't have time to reset it exactly where it had been; it would just have to be close enough.

Her father was still talking as she pulled the loft cover back across the hatch and positioned it correctly. The join might be slightly more prominent now – she couldn't say for sure – but again there was no time to worry about it. She jumped down from the stool and hurriedly carried it back into the kitchen.

She heard the clanking of iron gates and looked out again to see her father opening them so she scanned the room for leftover clues. There were four faint indentations in the carpet where the stool had been below the loft hatch, and she quickly ran her hands over them to make them go away as best she could.

There was a loud crunch of tyres moving across gravel.

Danni tiptoed to the alarm and took a final look around. Everything looked as it was when she got there. She entered the code into the alarm box and it began to beep at the same time as she heard the gates on the drive close.

As the alarm set itself, she stepped out of the door, closed it and carefully locked it with the key. There were footsteps on the gravel, getting louder and closer, so she picked up her running shoes, quietly skipped down the steps and hid to the side of the property, out of sight. A few seconds later, her father came around the corner and walked up the same steps to his front door, but thankfully not before the alarm had set and stopped beeping.

Danni took in oxygen for what felt like the first time in minutes and bent over, her hands on her thighs, as she caught her breath. She heard her father's keys rattle as he took them from his blazer pocket and opened the door.

'Damn!' she heard him curse. He was coming back down the steps.

Danni stayed where she was but held her breath and waited. He walked back to the car; he must have forgotten something, she thought, so she took the opportunity to run up the steps at the back, on to the decking area and put on her shoes, quickly sweeping the sand off the wood with her hand. She put the key back into the plant pot, placed the stone on top and skipped down the steps two at a time until she was back on the beach; and then she pulled her hood up and began jogging: just another fitness fanatic out for their morning run on a beach that, at that time of year, only they and dog walkers used.

She stepped up her pace a little until she was out of sight of the apartment and then slowed back to a jog. She kept going, her breathing shallow and uneven, until she reached the rocks at the far end of the sand, and stood leaning against them to rest, one hand on her hips and sweat running down her face.

She took a huge deep lungful of cold air.

Then she threw up.

Part Six

Fifteen years after she was taken...

Where did those years go?

Back then, when they called off the search, I knew that we were as good as in the clear. As far as 99.9 per cent of people were concerned, the missing girl was a drowned girl, just one they couldn't find a body for. And people, especially police forces with their resources cut to the bone, don't keep on looking for dead people.

The only problem I foresaw was when that girl reached adulthood. That was when we would have no control; when someone might say something that sparked off curiosity, and we wouldn't know until it was too late.

But it seemed such a long way off. I thought we'd cross that bridge when we got to it.

It's hard to say exactly when we stopped feeling like abductors and turned into parents, but it was around the time that they officially stopped searching for her.

We watched. Watched as her mother was put into that place, watched as her father drank himself to death. Watched as the world forgot all about the missing child and let us breathe normally again.

Years passed. We just didn't notice.

And she grew. In every way possible. She became tall, confident and clever. She became her own person right before our eyes and we watched, as proud as any parent would be.

Then one day, you wake up and it's her eighteenth birthday and she's not that little girl any more.

She's not anyone's little girl any more.

When she walked in on that scorching hot August morning, hiding behind my wife's legs, and sat eating her ice-cream on the rug, she had her whole childhood ahead of her. This day seemed so far away then.

But time passes. You can't hold it back. So, of course, the day had to come. She was a grown woman now. Her childhood was just cherished memories, for her and us. She'd lived it and left it behind. No more piggybacks, no more reading her stories or having her read them to me. No more picking her up when she fell and putting a plaster on her knee. No school, no homework, parents' evenings. No more *Daddy*. Which, bizarrely, in the circumstances, was the one thing I missed more than the others.

No more watching for her to arrive home safely, or waiting for a phone call to say she had got to where she was going. No school discos, ballet classes or just ferrying her around.

All of that was behind us now.

She was all grown up, and we'd more or less done our job in helping to shape a young woman who was ready to venture into the world on her own.

My wife had always wanted that unbreakable bond with a daughter, and she had got one, but suddenly it was different. Our child didn't need us any more. Now she had a choice whether we were in her life or not. She would make her own decisions now. She would continue to grow and learn and ask questions and one day, we knew, she might just ask a question that set off a chain of events that we wouldn't be able to stop.

After fifteen years, as we stood and watched her blow out the candles on her eighteenth birthday cake and make a silent wish, we knew it would never quite be the same again. We'd got to *that* bridge.

And it felt as though we had gone back to being abductors.

Unless you've had a child taken, you can't possibly know how it feels.

It's a crushing, numbing, slow walk along a path that has no obvious start and end, but it's a path you know you will have to walk until death releases you from your pain.

When it comes, finally, it will be a death by at least a thousand cuts.

Cuts that, on their own, you might withstand and learn to build a defence against, but when they hit you, relentlessly, one after the other like waves, there is no respite.

The newspaper columns, the mentions on the radio, the report of another missing child – they are hard enough. But the people who stop you in the street, with their dumb sympathetic faces and even dumber sympathetic questions…they are harder to bear.

How are you feeling?

I'm not, seeing as you ask. I haven't *felt* in a long time.

But you smile and say it gets easier – not because it does, but because it's simpler.

The real cuts are on those significant days of the year that carry only painful reminders of what you no longer have.

Christmas is bad. I stopped celebrating it the year Stuart was taken into care and I've never so much as eaten turkey in December since. When we had Jess, Todd worried how we'd afford to buy presents for both kids. When she'd gone, I'd have given anything to have to worry about that again.

But, compared to Christmas, birthdays are much, much worse. They don't just remind you of what you've lost, they slap you across the face with it.

The first two or three years I tried to use her birthday as a positive: a way of reminding people about her, raising public awareness and trying to drum up more support for the campaigns.

But one day I realised I was the only one who still believed she was alive.

The next few years, I blotted them out altogether with anything I could find to take the hurt away. Alcohol, although it never did it for me the way it did for Todd; and sometimes pills. Some of those birthdays I slept right through. When I was put in this place, it helped; it's easier to lose days in here. Maybe it's the absence of clocks and calendars that makes time and dates seem less important.

From her eleventh birthday, I tried something new. I allowed myself to spend that one special day with her. I pictured what she looked like, what she was doing with her life. I created a little story in my head and kept it there for the whole day, imagining what the last twelve months had thrown her way and how she'd handled it.

A year in the life of Jessica Preston.

It became a slightly happier day after that.

But then, as one particular birthday approached, I realised she was going to be eighteen and it knocked me for six. I couldn't bring myself to picture her, or think about what she was doing that day. I just stayed in my room and cried and cried and cried some more.

My little girl. My Jessica. She's not my little girl any more. She's no one's little girl any more.

And, that day, it slowly occurred to me that I would never see her as a child again.

Wherever she is and whatever she is doing in her life, she'll be doing it as a woman from now on.

My missing child will forever be a missing child.

That day, it was all I could do to stop myself taking that slow journey to death a little sooner.

55 | Laura

'Are you sure?'

It was the kind of question people would ask when they heard something they couldn't quite believe, even though they knew there was no possibility of any doubt.

Not with something so important.

Laura was standing outside the *Gazette*'s offices listening to Danni talk as best she could between heavy breaths.

'There was a letter from the hospital.'

More gasps for air.

'It said she had a hysterectomy in 1989...'

Breathe.

'...which was three years before I was born.'

Laura blew out her cheeks. She'd never taken any interest in her father's occupation, in the medical world – but she knew what this meant.

'Where are you now?'

'Still by the beach,' Danni gasped. 'I rang you straight away.'

'And there's no way your father will know you were there?'

'I don't think so, but I had to get out fast.'

'OK.' Laura thought quickly. 'Can you get back to Sam's?' she asked.

Laura could hear Danni coughing. 'Danni?'

'I think I'm gonna—'

There was the sound of the phone being put down and Danni retching. Laura waited until she came back on the line.

'Sorry.'

Laura knew Danni was in shock. 'You knew they were hiding something,' she said.

'Not this! I thought Sam might be right in the end.'

'Sam?'

'She reckoned you might be full of shit. No offence.'

Laura sniffed.

'But it looks like it's you that's right.'

Laura cautioned her on getting too far ahead of herself. The letter confirmed there was a big secret but they still had a long way to go. 'It explains your dad's behaviour, though, and what you overheard.'

'I knew he was lying,' said Danni, not even trying to hide the bitterness.

'And what your mum said. It explains some of that too.'

'I don't think I can call her *Mum* any more.'

'At least you know. If nothing else, you don't have to listen to any more lies.'

Two of the *Gazette*'s staff came through the revolving doors, and she lowered her voice and smiled at them as they walked past her.

'I want to confront him.'

Laura checked the time. She needed to get back inside before David missed her, if he hadn't already.

'Listen, Danni, you've had a huge shock and I know you want answers. I would too. But please give me a couple of days to get you to Sandra.'

'Days?'

Laura explained that she needed to make arrangements with High Cliffs and find a way of getting yet another day off. Danni was reluctant but she managed to convince her. 'OK. You've got me this far.'

'Thank you. And not a word to anyone. Not even Sam.'

Laura knew it was selfish, and a lot to ask, but she was so close now to a story that would not only make her career but probably define it, and it would only take one loose word to the wrong person to ruin everything for her.

They said their goodbyes and she ran inside and back up the stairs. David was sitting in his office and looked over as she reached her desk. She been handed an article to write about the town's rugby team, who had managed, after a twenty-year battle with the council, to install floodlights on their pitch, only to find themselves in another dispute with locals about how often they could use them; depending on the original planning consent, there was a danger of the club's being forced to tear them down.

She had already made calls to both the club secretary and the man challenging the consent and quickly established that both were unpleasant people who thought they were right and had no intention of ever backing down. She also knew she didn't want to spend any time with either of them if at all possible, so she wrote as balanced a piece as she could, given that her research was limited and her mind completely focused on Danni. She even had to check the internet to make sure she had the club's name right, and correct a dozen other spelling errors, so when she emailed it to David late in the afternoon she knew it was unlikely to make that week's edition, or even the website, without significant amendments and improvement.

Therefore, it was no surprise that she was called into the editor's office at the end of the day. What did surprise her was that it was Sue who gave her the tap on the shoulder a minute or so before five o'clock. That kind of summons was usually reserved for people in *real* trouble, not for a poor article.

As most people had either left or were leaving, she got up and walked to the office and gave the closed door a little tap. David called her in, his voice strained and croaky, and she went in. 'You wanted to see me?' she said meekly.

David had a deep frown line across his forehead. On his desk in front of him was a newspaper opened to a page with a large headline that read: 'Does Life Really Go On?'

There was a grainy picture of Jessica Preston underneath.

Even though it was upside down, Laura had seen the headline and the article enough times to know what it said.

David Weatherall looked up at her, over the top of his glasses.

She *was* in real trouble.

56 | Laura

'I can explain.'

Laura knew it didn't only look bad, but was bad. The editor needed no excuse to get angry with someone whom he felt had let him down and he'd also been feeling unwell after picking up a strain of the sickness bug, although it hadn't kept him from his desk.

'Please do.'

He looked as if he might explode if he weren't so under the weather.

She sat down even though he didn't invite her to, desperate to get to the same eye level and not feel like the naughty schoolgirl who had been called before the headmaster.

'It's delicate.'

'I can see how it might be,' he said, holding the paper up, 'in that it seems that, while I thought you had *women's problems* and *car trouble*, you were really writing for other newspapers and travelling down to the southwest.'

'I only went once on a work day,' Laura said instinctively, and regretted it just as quickly.

'And here I was thinking you'd been taking the piss.'

'Please, David. It's not like that. You know the interview I set up?'

'And cancelled when the girl was found.'

'I was going to. But when I spoke to her, the mother was so upset…'

He looked at her with disdain.

'So I went in my own time, at the weekend.'

'To do what? Not hurt her feelings? Earn more money? Or just to annoy me?'

'It's really not like that.'

'So what is it like?'

Laura took a deep breath and explained as much as she could allow her boss to find out. She was passionate and fought her corner, telling him the article was crying out to be written and none of the local papers had been interested in Sandra's side of things, despite the fact that it was such a tragic human interest story; and she told him that it had been well received by the readers.

'And the money they paid only just covered my travel costs,' she added.

She didn't mention anything about the email threat or the man on the coastal path.

The editor listened without interruption and, when she finished, his frown had all but gone.

'I've tried to do it in my own time,' she continued, 'and, when I couldn't, it was totally unavoidable.'

Laura looked down. He waited for more. 'You'll understand when you know why,' she offered.

David chewed on the end of his biro. Then it was his turn to talk, and Laura sat and listened. He told her he wanted local stories and that he hated it when people lied to him. He said that the paper was still recovering from the sickness bug and the last thing he could afford was to lose anyone to stories that were not connected to the *Gazette*. Laura nodded.

But then he said that he also understood that sometimes a journalist had to follow their instincts and protect their stories and sources.

'Was it worth it?' he said at the end.

'I think it will be.'

'OK,' the editor said, sitting back in his leather chair so that his glasses fell back where they should be. 'We'll draw a line under it. But it doesn't happen again. Not on my time, right?'

'Absolutely.'

He looked at the door, his signal that she should go. She smiled apologetically and stood up to leave.

'And Laura,' David said as she opened the door. 'Nice article.'

Laura smiled again and went back to her desk. She tidied it up, sent a few emails and made a priority list for the next day. Then she got up, making sure David had seen that she had stayed late, and left the building.

She was immediately hit by an icy blast of wind as she walked out of the revolving doors, and she pulled her scarf up around her face to protect it. It was a clear sky, thousands of stars twinkled above, but the temperature had plummeted quickly and she hurried to her car. The *Gazette* was on the town's main road, the last but one building; parking was extremely limited and there were nowhere near enough spaces for everyone. A year earlier, the local authority had introduced a permit scheme that made it impossible to park on the side roads in and around that part of the town, so Laura usually, if she wasn't running late, opted for the more car-friendly side of town even though it was quite a way away.

She walked quickly to keep warm as the wind howled through gaps between the buildings, hurting her face. As she crossed the road and looked both ways, something caught her eye.

Something, or specifically someone, familiar.

A tall man was walking towards her, about a hundred yards away on the opposite side. He was dressed all in black, a roll-necked top pulled up high, almost covering his mouth, and a black woolly hat that was pulled down level with his eyebrows.

Her heartbeat quickened. Even at that distance, she knew she had seen him before.

Laura glanced again and saw that he was crossing, and she opened the zip on her handbag to make sure the defence spray was in there. She slowed down and looked again; he was on her side now and, when she stopped and checked her phone, he stopped too and pretended to look in a shop window. He was fifty yards from her.

She began walking again, quicker now, and, when she turned to look, the gap between them was the same. She was sure he was following her, and at the next set of pedestrian lights she pressed the button and waited until the lights changed and the green man lit up. She put her phone to her ear and pretended to speak, hoping he might think she was calling the police, and crossed the road again.

This would tell her for sure.

When she reached the other side, she switched direction and headed back towards the *Gazette*'s offices. In her peripheral vision she saw the man walk past on the opposite side and she instinctively quickened her steps.

She counted to twenty in her head, stopped outside a shoe shop and looked at the window display, a combination of sale signs and stilettos, and then turned her head back up the street.

He was there. Forty yards, give or take. He had also crossed, and was walking in her direction. She took her phone from her ear and pushed it into her bag.

And then she began to run.

She headed for the offices, hoping the security guard who worked there had taken over from the receptionist on the front desk. But she was still five hundred yards from the building and her legs were buckling.

At that moment a bus passed her and stopped to let a passenger off. She looked around: there was still quite a gap between her and the man following her, and with one short burst of energy and adrenaline she sprinted the last ten yards just as the driver closed the doors. As he indicated to move away, she desperately banged on the door with her hand and the driver looked at her with mild annoyance. She mouthed the word 'please' at him through the glass and he opened the doors and let her get on.

'Thank you,' she panted.

The doors closed behind her and she saw the dark shape of the man run up alongside, but the bus had already pulled back on to the road and was gathering speed along the high street.

'Where to?'

Laura took a two-pound coin from her purse and pushed it into the payment machine.

'Doesn't matter.'

57 | Laura

'Everything OK, love?'

Laura had stood in the area of the bus where mothers would put their pushchairs, and the concerned bus driver had been glancing at her through his rear-view mirror. He asked the question as they reached a stop just over a mile from the high street where she'd got on.

She had stopped shaking, and nodded.

'I can change that for a return if you want.' He indicated towards her hand, which was tightly gripping her ticket.

'Thanks, but this is my stop,' she said, and stepped off back into the cold night air. She looked down the deserted street that led down the hill back into the town and started walking, fast. Her eyes darted all around for signs of the man but there was virtually no one around. It took fifteen minutes to reach the well-lit car park, despite the icy wind pushing her back at times, and she was calmer by the time she had got to the car, checked all around it – including the boot and back seats – and sat inside.

She drove home quickly. Her parents needed to know what had happened, as did the police. She knew it was time to stop taking risks before someone got hurt. The stakes were just too high.

The house was in darkness even though her mother's car sat in its usual position on the drive. She didn't expect her father to be home but her mother was always there at this time, ready to serve the evening meal when he walked through the door.

She checked her phone but hadn't missed any calls. She opened the door and called inside. Not only was it dark but it was cold too, and she went around switching lights on and turned the dial on the central heating so that it whirred into action.

In the utility room, Mimark's tail was excitedly thumping against the washing machine, and she opened the door to let him out. 'What are you doing all alone?' she said, ruffling his fur and giving him a handful of little bone-shaped biscuits from a tin on the shelf. She called her mother and then her father but both phones immediately forwarded her to their voicemail, so she hung up and then sent her mother a text message asking where she was.

She started to boil the kettle and took off her coat as the house began to warm up. She called both numbers again but with the same outcome, although this time she left a message on her father's voicemail. As she put the phone back on the table, it rang. DAD came up on the screen.

'Where are you?'

'The hospital,' he said, almost in a whisper.

'Where's Mum?'

There was a pause.

'She's here. She's been...attacked.'

Laura took a moment to process what she'd heard. His voice was so quiet she could only just about pick out the words, but she realised he was calling from inside the ward.

'*Attacked?*'

'About an hour ago. At the house.'

Laura's heart started beating quickly again. She checked the time on the microwave: it was ninety minutes since she'd been chased and got on to the bus, and it didn't take long to work out what her pursuer had done next.

'I'm on my way.'

She took the ward details. It took her twenty minutes to reach the hospital and another five to find a parking space.

When she arrived on the ward, her mother was in a private side room and was talking to a police officer as her father stood listening. Laura could see she had a bruise on her cheek and a cut under her left eye, and it shocked and upset her so much that she pushed past the officer and grabbed her mother's hand. 'Mum!'

She hugged her tightly and the police officer stood back.

'Laura,' her father said, 'the officer was just—'

'It's OK, Mr Grainger. I'll give the three of you a moment.' He left the room and closed the door.

'What happened?'

Helen looked at her husband, who was visibly trying to stop his anger boiling over.

'There was a knock at the door,' she said, 'and I thought you'd forgotten your key or something and there was this man and he…' She began to cry.

'He did this,' Robert finished for her.

Laura felt sick. 'What did he say?'

Her mother shook her head.

'Nothing,' her father spat. 'Looks like he just wanted to send a message.'

There was a tap at the door and they all looked to see the police officer's face in the glass panel. Robert opened the door. 'Come in. We'll leave you to do your job.'

He looked at Laura, and she followed him into the corridor. He led her down it until they were far enough away from the room for him not to be heard.

'Dad, I—'

His face was red with anger. 'Save it, Laura.'

She looked at the ground.

'We all know why this happened,' he said fiercely.

'Have you told…?'

'The police?' he snapped, and then seemed to remember he was in a public place. 'No. Your mother told them she didn't know anything.'

Laura was about to tell him what happened when she left work, but at that moment the police officer came out of the room and came towards them down the corridor. Laura went back to the side room while her father thanked him.

'Oh, Mum.'

'I'm OK.'

She looked at her mother's injuries. The bruise was shining and looked sore. The cut wasn't serious enough to require a stitch but the hospital had bonded the skin with a Steri-strip.

Her father came back into the room. 'Happy now?'

'Robert!'

'Well, what do you want me to say, Helen?'

'Of course not,' Laura said, still looking at her mother.

'This ends now. I don't care about the story. The police need to handle this.'

Laura nodded. 'Let me call Danni first,' she said, looking at her mother's bruised face. She'd done her best to delay the story coming out, but it had gone too far.

Somebody *had* got hurt.

58 | Laura

'I can't help you any more.'

Laura looked at her reflection in the mirror on her dressing table as she said the words, but they sounded lame and she shook her head.

'I can't carry on with your story.'

She closed her eyes. That was even worse.

Eventually, after a few more unsuccessful attempts to find the right words, she climbed into bed without making the call to Danni and decided to sleep on it and hopefully have more ideas when she woke.

The next morning, the first thing she did was call David Weatherall on his mobile and tell him about the attack.

'Do they know who did it?'

'No idea,' Laura replied, having deliberately kept the details vague. 'She's pretty shaken up, and I said I'd take turns with my dad to sit with her at the hospital for the next couple of days.'

'Of course,' said the editor with genuine concern. 'Do whatever you need to.'

After that, she called Danni.

There was a terseness to her voice when she answered. 'Is it set up?' she asked before Laura had a chance to speak.

'I need to speak to you about—'

'You said a couple of days.'

'My mum got attacked.'

Laura let the sentence sit between them, knowing that Danni would make the connection soon enough; and she did.

'God! Is she OK?'

'Just about. Cuts, bruises and a bit of shock.'

Laura explained what had happened when she'd left work and how she'd avoided the attacker, who had then gone to her house instead. 'I think he wanted to send a warning. Mum was just in the wrong place.'

'I'm sorry.'

'It's my fault. He said this would happen.'

'You can't think like that,' Danni said.

'My dad says I have to end it.'

'I don't blame him.'

There was more silence. Laura searched for the right way to tell Danni that she would have to carry on without her, but it was Danni who helped her out.

'So I'm on my own.'

Laura squeezed her nose and screwed up her eyes.

She could picture Danni clearly, walking into the police station with Sam.

She could see Sandra sitting by the window waiting for them to arrive.

She could picture Kelly's headline in the *Gazette*, a day after the national papers had devoured the incredible breaking news.

She wasn't sure which image was hardest to stomach.

'I'm not stopping.'

'What?'

'If they can do this to my mum, then it shows how afraid they are.'

'But your dad…'

'I'll deal with him. We're still going to see Sandra.'

'Are you sure?' said Danni.

'I've got this far,' said Laura, 'and I'm not stopping now.'

59 | Danni

'Just give me tomorrow to get things clear at work.'

Danni wanted to see Sandra at that moment; to just walk straight out of the dental surgery even though she had only just got there, to get into her car and drive to High Cliffs House, but she knew it was unfair to ask that of Laura with her mother in hospital.

And she didn't want to do any of this alone, so she scribbled *Sandra – Thursday* on the next blank page of the notepad on the reception desk and arranged for Laura to pick her up from Sam's house. She tore the page out and pushed it into her bag.

'I hope your mum is OK,' she said, as they ended the call.

After that, she tried to get on with the day, but it was almost impossible to focus on anything other than the attack. Until then, even though she'd been alarmed by the threat to Laura, she'd felt detached from it. But this was real now, and she knew that, if they were prepared to hurt someone close to Laura, there was no telling who might be next.

In her lunch break, she called her new employers in Southampton to make arrangements for her start date and induction programme, a series of meetings and training sessions that would take up most of her first week, including two days out on the road with a sales rep and an area manager. Her soon-to-be-new boss sounded lovely when she spoke to her and they hit it off immediately; when she said her goodbyes, it struck Danni that they were looking forward to welcoming *her* as a new recruit; but she wondered if they would be so keen to welcome her if she was Jessica Preston.

When her shift ended at three, she went back to Sam's and, old battered laptop on her knees, began looking at places she might rent in Southampton. She was surprised at the cost; even for a basic studio apartment, she quickly calculated, any additional money from her new salary would soon be swallowed up. It hardly seemed worth it.

Danni looked around at the spare room she had called home for two weeks, which was currently covered in piles of clothes as well as the odd bag and a few pairs of shoes, and began to click on to the details of some of the apartments at the lower end of the price bracket. She needed a fresh start; whatever happened next.

An hour later, Sam walked in and Danni heard her kick off her shoes in the hallway the way she had often done when she'd had a rotten day at work. She called out to her.

'That good, eh?'

'Worse,' Sam shouted back, and Danni heard her walk up the stairs. Her friend opened the door and surveyed the scene.

'I'm going to tidy up when I've finished looking at this flat.'

'Sod tidying. Let's have a drink.'

A minute or so later, Danni's laptop was in its bag and they were on the sofa and Sam had poured two large glasses of wine.

'So, bad day?'

'Sometimes, working with family can be the worst.'

Danni smiled sadly. Her friend put her hand on her forehead. 'Sorry. You know what I mean. How's things?'

'I sorted my start date in Southampton,' Danni said.

Sam looked at her suspiciously.

'What?' Danni asked.

'All the stuff you have going on and that's the thing you tell me about?'

Danni snorted. 'There's nothing else to tell.'

Sam emptied half her glass. 'Dan, I've known you how long?'

Danni squirmed in her seat. She'd never been good at hiding things from anyone, and she'd found it practically impossible to hide anything from Sam since they were at junior school.

'Laura didn't want me to say anything.'

Sam laughed to herself and then narrowed her eyes and looked straight at Danni.

'Screw what Laura wants. Tell.'

Danni brought her friend fully up to date with everything, from the letter she'd found right up to the attack on Laura's mother. Sam, unusually for her, listened without interrupting or passing judgement until Danni had told her everything.

'Jesus, Dan.'

'I know.'

'This is a mess.'

Danni nodded.

'Laura's put you in danger.'

'I know you don't like her but she's on my side. And it's *her* mum that was hurt.'

'So go to the police,' said Sam sternly.

'It's not that simple.'

'Why not? Because of "the story"?' She made air quotations as she said the last two words.

'She's got this far. But if we go now and I tell them I think I was abducted, imagine if I'm wrong.'

'I know. It'd destroy your dad.'

'It'd destroy both of us.'

Sam nodded slowly. But she didn't let go. 'But he's been lying to you all this time. He can't blame you for…any of this.'

'I just want to be sure.'

'Isn't this attack the last straw?'

'We don't know he was definitely involved.'

Sam's eyes widened. 'I thought it was me who had the doubts. But ever since we met Laura, someone has been trying to stop you getting to the truth.'

They sat in silence for a minute and finished their glasses, and Danni poured them another.

'So you meet Sandra and then what?' asked Sam.

Danni looked at her. She had played out two dozen possible scenarios in her head already that day, and in half of them Sandra had seen something in her that she recognised. It wasn't the same thing, it was nearly always different things: her hair, eyes, a freckle, a smell, even a smile. She didn't tell Sam this, worried that it sounded as though she had already made her mind up about who she was, and she hadn't.

'Depends on what she says.'

'You must be terrified.'

Danni nodded and lowered her head. Sam put an arm around her shoulder and they sat on the sofa for a few minutes, each with their own thoughts.

'So if she says you are her daughter?'

'*Then* we go to the police,' Danni said firmly.

'And if she says you're not?'

In the other half of the scenarios she'd rehearsed that day, that was exactly what had happened, and it scared Danni because she knew that she'd just want to run: straight out of the room, the building and as far as she could away from everything.

'That's what I want to happen.'

Sam looked at her. 'But it wouldn't definitely mean you aren't her. She just might not recognise you. And there's still all of the other stuff.'

'Whatever happens,' said Danni, 'I need to know everything.'

60 | Laura

Laura had less than thirty-six hours to do a lot of things.

First and foremost, she wanted to spend as much time as possible with her mother, who had been kept in hospital overnight for observation at her husband's insistence. She also had to go the *Gazette* and cross a few things off her list or hand them over to other people, as David had suggested.

And she wanted to set up the meeting with Sandra and get her things packed for the journey on Thursday morning; she had planned to leave in the early hours so that she missed the worst of the traffic, and also because the weather forecast wasn't good for that afternoon.

Her mother was looking and feeling a lot better after her night on the ward. The swelling in her cheek had gone down, and her cut, although still quite nasty, looked much less painful when Laura visited her just before lunch.

'You just missed your dad,' she said, and Laura was a little relieved, as she knew he'd want to check that she had called Danni. Her father had stayed at the hospital overnight too, finishing his shift and then getting a makeshift bed made up in his wife's ward, which was now resting up against the wall.

'Are you staying another night?'

'Your dad's going to talk to them during his break. But I feel fine.'

Laura left at four o'clock and went home to let Mimark out and prepare a meal in case they did let her mother out that evening. She had just put a frozen lasagne in the oven to heat through when her father came in, clearly in a hurry.

'I need a holdall and some fresh clothes.'

'Is she…'

'They've discharged her. But you know your mother: she won't move until she looks her best.'

'I'll get them,' Laura told him, and ran up the stairs and put a set of clean clothes and some toiletries into her mother's overnight bag. When she got back into the kitchen, her father was already in the doorway, his fingers tapping impatiently on the doorframe. 'I'll come with you,' Laura said; she turned the oven down and adjusted the timer, then followed her father out and locked the door behind her.

The worst of rush hour was over, but the temperatures were getting lower by the hour and there were two warnings on the radio as they drove to the hospital about icy roads and the potential for snow. Laura sat quietly and they barely exchanged a word until they were a mile from the hospital.

'It's great she's coming home.'

Her father didn't answer. She tried again, but he only looked at her and then back at the road. The brake lights on the cars ahead all came on. This stretch of road was always busy as ambulances and visitors made a right turn into the drop-off area.

'You can't give me the silent treatment for ever.'

He edged forward and sighed. 'Look,' he said, 'she asked me not to tell you this, but she's terrified of leaving the hospital.'

'What? She said she felt better earlier.'

'What's she going to say, Laura? *Because of what happened, I want to stay in there for ever?*'

Laura looked down.

'She asked me if I could get them to keep her in another night,' he added.

'This is my fault. I'll talk to her.'

314

'Don't! She's embarrassed enough as it is. This has really shaken her.'

'I'm sorry.'

'I wish you'd told us what was going on. All this lying and sneaking around has devastated her. She thought you could tell her anything.'

'Look, I know I've fucked up.'

'Laura!'

She hadn't ever sworn like that before in front of her father.

'I never wanted anyone to get hurt,' she said, her voice cracking. She realised she was trying hard not to cry and she bit her lip. Her father seemed to see, even though his eyes were fixed on the brake lights of the cars in front of them.

'Did you call that girl?'

'Yes.'

'You told her you couldn't carry on?'

Laura hesitated for a split second too long.

'I'll take that as a *no*.'

She had always thought of him as a strict father, with discipline high on his list of traits, and she accepted that as it came with his personality and his profession; a hospital theatre wasn't generally a place for mavericks. And so she'd always tried hard to not give him reason to be angry with her.

But now he was. She saw the hurt in his eyes.

'I thought you said you were sorting it,' he said.

'I was.'

'But?'

They took the final exit at the roundabout and then turned into the hospital grounds, following the one-way system around to the huge pay-and-display car park at the rear, and the staff car park beyond that.

'Danni can't do this on her own, Dad.'

Laura thought he might be angry enough to hit her. He was gripping the steering wheel so hard his hands were going red, and he was taking deep breaths to calm himself. They pulled into a space marked *Reserved* in the staff car park, but, when he turned towards her and saw her face, the anger seemed to disappear.

'I do get it, you know,' he said, more softly than she expected. 'It's a big story. I know they don't come around very often.'

'That's no excuse for what's happened.'

'But if someone wants to stop you that much? Enough to hurt people you love.'

Laura nodded. Surprised. 'I know I'm very close.'

'Close enough to take all these risks?'

Laura hesitated before she answered and then nodded. 'I hate what happened to Mum. But the truth has to be worth the risks, doesn't it?'

Her father thought for a moment and smiled. 'I'm proud of you, Laura. I know I'm angry at what's happened, but I'm proud that you've not backed down.'

A tear trickled down her cheek before she could stop it. 'I want to help Sandra and Danni. It's not just the story.'

He took her hand. 'We always taught you to look out for people.'

'If I broke the story now, it would rip Danni and her father apart. For good. I can't let that happen because of me unless I'm sure.'

Laura's hand was trembling and her father squeezed it gently. 'I get that. But I've got to think of Mum first,' he said.

'Of course.'

'But I can't just ignore your feelings either,' he added. 'I know how much this means to you. What were you planning on doing next?'

Laura's eyes widened, and she told him about her plan to put Danni and Sandra Preston together and that she was trying to keep David Weatherall out of the loop for now because she'd already got in enough trouble at the paper as it was.

'After they meet, if Sandra thinks it's her,' she said, 'then I'll go to the police.'

Her father looked over at the hospital doors and checked his watch. He looked at Laura, right into her eyes.

'OK. I'll cover for you. Go and do what you have to do.'

'Really?'

'Make sure Mum doesn't find out. But promise me that once you get them together…'

'I break the story or I go to the police,' Laura said.

Her father nodded. 'We should be getting inside; she'll be wondering where I am.'

They got out of the car and walked towards the big automatic entrance doors. The hospital staff had thrown large quantities of grit and salt down to stop anyone slipping on the icy footpaths.

'At least if anyone did fall, they wouldn't have far to go.' Robert smiled and put his arm around his daughter.

'Dad…' Laura said, putting her arm around his waist.

He looked at her.

'Thank you.'

61 | Danni

Laura had apologised for calling so early and waking her.

At Sam's house Danni was often the last one to get up, as Mrs Newbold would be pottering about well before daybreak as she got ready to leave for one of her cleaning jobs. Then she would often hear Sam as she got herself ready about an hour afterwards; she would lie under the covers until she heard Sam leave, and use that as her cue to get out of bed.

But Laura's call had woken her and she hadn't heard Sam at all, and it took a few minutes for her to remember that Sam wasn't working anyway. Her boyfriend had a meeting in London and three rare days off afterwards, so she was getting a train to the capital that afternoon and they were going to stay with his parents until the day he flew back to Dubai.

It didn't sound as though Laura had slept at all. She said she had already written a first draft of the article for if Sandra made a positive identification; she told Danni that she needed to have it ready, because, if she did need to submit the article, there would be no time to put it together afterwards; the police and rest of the media would simply swamp them.

After giving Danni the details, Laura told her she was calling the unit to make the final arrangements with Sandra. 'She's not going anywhere,' was her rationale for leaving that part till last.

Danni put her phone down and knew she had to talk to Sam. She went to her room and put her head around the door that Sam always left ajar. 'Are you awake?'

Sam didn't ever lie in, but she'd been up late packing, and Danni felt guilty for disturbing her.

'What's up?' said Sam, peering over the heavy duvet.

Danni stepped into her room and closed the door. Light peeked in through the edges of the curtains and there was a soft red glow from the alarm that said it was twenty minutes past eight o'clock.

Sam sat up.

'I wanted to talk to you before I left,' Danni whispered, even though they were the only people in the house. She sat on the edge of Sam's bed. 'When you get back from London, things might be…you know.'

Sam nodded and smiled. 'Let me know what happens tomorrow.'

Danni nodded but, even in the dim light, her friend recognised her uncertainty and asked her about it. Danni told her that the enormity of the situation was beginning to hit home and she was scared in case she hadn't done the right thing.

'Dan, I think you're well past that point.'

'I know.'

'Look, no one's been more sceptical than me. About Laura and everything.'

Danni nodded slowly.

'But even I admit, too much has happened and you need answers.'

'Even if it tears everything apart?'

Sam shrugged. 'Whatever. You can't go on like you are, can you?'

'No.'

'So it's torn anyway. At least you'll know why.' Sam put her arm around Danni's shoulder and pulled her close to her. 'I know it's hard, but what choice do you have?'

'You're right.'

'I know I am.' Sam smiled.

319

'Next time I see you, who knows who I'll be,' said Danni, trying to make light of it.

Sam saw through the forced smile and looked at her. 'It won't change anything with us.'

They hugged. Danni glanced at the clock over Sam's shoulder. It was almost half-past eight and she had to leave for work.

She had a feeling that, in a little over twenty-four hours, nothing was ever going to be the same again.

62 | Laura

Laura had called the unit at High Cliffs House and spoken to Sandra.

She had told her that she wanted to bring Danni in to see her, but that it was important no one at the unit knew about it because, if they did, there would be reporters and newspapers all over the place.

Sandra made it clear she didn't want that either.

When Laura got to work, a few minutes late, David was too absorbed with something on his computer screen to even notice her, and she got to her desk and began sorting through her notes to find the article she was working on: a story about two local tradesmen who'd been shortlisted for a national competition, but who had a fierce rivalry that was threatening to spill over and scupper both their chances. She was halfway through her second rewrite when she looked over at the editor, still at his desk looking at his screen, his hand slowly stroking his chin. As if using a sixth sense, he seemed to know she was watching him and he turned quickly to face her; too quickly for her to look away. He didn't look pleased, Laura thought, and he stared for longer than she found comfortable.

Then he looked back at his screen and continued reading and Laura watched him, with an inexplicable feeling that something was wrong, and that she was very much at the centre of it.

Laura looked back at her article and shook her head. But when she looked at David a few minutes later he was looking directly at her again and this time he beckoned her to come to his office. She sank a little in her chair and then stood up, took a deep breath and walked over.

'Come in,' he said softly when she tapped the door with her knuckle. 'Sit down.'

Laura sat with her hands on her lap and watched as he tapped some keys on his keyboard and frowned. Then he tilted the screen so that she could see it.

There was an email. Not a recent one; it was a few weeks old and it had been sent to Laura at her *Gazette* email address.

It was from 'A Friend'.

Laura looked at David.

He peered over his glasses and she thought he was waiting for an explanation but he simply tilted the screen back to its original position and did the talking instead.

'I take it that this is what you couldn't tell me about.'

She gulped and nodded.

'And I also presume that what happened to your mother is connected to it.'

Laura began to answer but stopped herself. David was an intelligent man, and he was a step ahead of her already, so it seemed pointless to try to deny it.

'Yes.'

'Sounds like you're playing a dangerous game.'

She nodded because she couldn't think of anything to say that was going to make any of this sound better. David read the email again. 'But you think you're on to something?'

'Yes, but…'

He looked at her, his blue eyes piercing into hers and she coughed and said no more.

'I'm letting you go, Laura.'

'What?'

'I don't have a choice.'

Laura's head began to spin and she thought she was having a panic attack. It felt as if David's face was now no more than a few inches from her face and that the walls were closing in. Her breathing quickened.

'Please don't fire me, David,' she blurted. 'I can explain.'

'I'm not firing you,' he said softly, in a tone that confused her; he wasn't angry at all, and if anything he sounded apologetic. 'I could. The lies, the time off; you've given me plenty of reasons to.'

'What else does "letting me go" mean?'

'It means exactly that. I've a feeling that what you're working on is a bit bigger than the *Gazette*.'

'I don't know that yet.'

'So go and find out. Get to the truth. It'll be there.'

He took an envelope out of a folder on his desk and slid it across the table to her.

'Don't I need an HR person or a union rep or something?'

He smiled as she picked up the envelope and held it in her hand, presuming it was a formal letter that terminated her employment.

'If I were firing you, I guess so,' said the editor, 'but, as I'm not, then I think we can do this without them.'

Laura looked at him. She opened the envelope but there was no letter, just bank notes neatly flattened out, and quite a few of them too. She estimated it was at least a thousand pounds, probably more.

'It'll keep you going,' said David. 'And hold on to your laptop for a week or so too.'

'I don't understand.'

In the past, she'd seen David march employees, ones who had worked at the *Gazette* a lot longer than she had, straight out of the building after firing them, and not even let them keep their security pass beyond his office door. She looked down at the envelope.

'Just go and finish your story.'

She nodded, still unsure what had just happened but pretty certain she no longer worked for David.

'Thank you,' she said, because she couldn't think of anything else.

David smiled and looked towards his door. Laura knew that signal by now, so for the last time she stood up and walked out, stunned.

'And Laura...'

'Yeah?' she said, still in a daze.

'Try to remember the *Gazette* when you do.'

Part Seven

Twenty years after she was taken...

Routinely, every single day, I have exactly one hour of exercise.

It's a regimented but still very welcome release from the enclosure of my four walls: the stretching of legs after sitting or lying down for so long and the taking-in of rare fresh air. But, as welcome as it is, I fear it too because of what follows – what has to follow, because my life is now all about routine, and that routine takes me to the shower block.

It's at the end of a concrete corridor, reached while fellow inmates scream abuse at me on both sides. There are some truly despicable men in here: murderers, rapists, men who have done all manner of unspeakable things; and yet, when I walk that corridor, their crimes seem to pale into insignificance. Even the most heinous of criminals, it seems, draws the line at child abduction. So men who have literally taken another person's life stand in judgement and shout vile things at me, describing in detail what they would like to do to me if they had half a chance, when I have not taken a life but given a child a life she couldn't have dreamed of with her real parents.

But, if the walk to the showers is to be feared, it is nothing compared to being in there.

A man can surely never feel more vulnerable than when he is standing naked in the prison showers, not knowing if today will be that one time – for that's all they'll need – when a warden is distracted, or merely turns away for a moment, and someone is able to do you real harm. All you can do is pray it isn't today, and you pray the same thing every day because you know that, if and when that time does come, there is little you will be able to do.

I'm just not built for life in prison.

I stand there, trying to look left and right at the same time just in case, as the water cascades down my body and I try to finish as quickly as possible so I can get back to the sanctuary of my own cell. Then I hear a noise, a door creaking maybe; it's hard to tell over the sound of the water. Maybe someone is coming.

There are no guards or wardens around. They've inexplicably disappeared.

The footsteps get closer. There is steam everywhere, like a thick fog removing all visibility, until I hear them clearly. Wet, bare feet slapping on the cold, concrete floor, in there with me, just a few feet away. The steam clears momentarily and a mountain of a man, completely shaven head and tattoos on every part of his body, stands in front of me; his face contorted with hatred, and he's got the chance that all the other inmates have craved.

He gets to act on their behalf.

He's holding a blade, glistening under the stark shower block lights now the mist has lifted. He has only one intention, and I let out a terrified scream as he lunges towards me. I jump up, my back straight and my eyes bulging with fear, gasping, and I look around...

I'm in bed, with cold sweat running down my head, producing a vinegary stench that makes me put my hand to my mouth. My wife is lying asleep next to me, and she stirs a little from my sudden movement but doesn't wake.

It was a nightmare.

Years ago I had one like this every few weeks, but they became less and less frequent, until they called off the search for the girl and they went away and stopped haunting me.

Or I thought they had.

I wonder why they have returned. Why now? But then I see the date on the calendar and I know why.

It's twenty years to the day. Twenty years since she went missing from the beach and we made a decision that changed so many lives for ever. I've learned to put any thoughts of that day in a virtually inaccessible room at the back of my mind; and my wife has too.

But a twentieth anniversary is significant enough to jolt it forward, out of that room and to the front of my mind once more.

It's a reminder that we have been incredibly fortunate to keep the secret for so long, yet the nightmare also serves as a reminder too: that things could have been so different.

But we've got this far.

Twenty years without anyone working out what we did.

I'm not going to let anything change that now.

Is that the time already?

They'll be here soon. Where the hell are Stuart and Todd?

She's going to pick up her degree results and then they're heading straight here. I say *they* because she's got a new boyfriend and she's bringing him to meet us for the first time.

I'm nervous.

Just like any other mother when her daughter comes home from university. I know she'll have done well, but I'm still nervous.

Where is Todd? I want to tell him to go easy on her boyfriend, but I know he won't. He'll get all protective like he usually does and ask all kind of embarrassing questions and she'll be 'Dad! Stop it!' but he won't because he can't stop once he starts and I need to warn him because we don't want the poor lad not wanting to come here again.

Was that a car door? They're here.

'Stuart! Todd! They're here.'

I can tell the minute I open the front door that it's good news. She's holding the envelope with her results in her hand but the grin on her face gives it away and she looks at me and raises both hands in the air in triumph.

'Top marks!' she shouts excitedly as they walk up the path to me – I never doubted her for a second – and I put my hands up too and hug her tightly as if it's been years since I saw her.

'I knew it.'

Her boyfriend is standing to her side. He put his hand on her bum when they walked up the path, but she pushed it away because she saw me looking.

'This is Mark,' she says, and he holds out a hand and shakes mine. Strong handshake, handsome boy. Just her type.

'Hello, Mrs Preston,' he says in a posh public school accent that he's clearly tried to soften the edges of but not quite managed.

'Todd! Stuart! Hurry up!'

I usher them in and make excuses for the state of the house even though it's virtually spotless because I've been up since dawn making it that way. It's not every day your daughter comes home with top marks and a new boyfriend.

'I'll put the kettle on. Todd, Stuart. Please!'

She sits down and she's still grinning and she wants to know what we've been up to and I want to know what she's been up to as well. Even though I talk to her every other day on the phone, I still want to know.

'How did you two meet, again?'

She starts to tell me and I want to hang on every word but her dad needs to hear this too; where the hell is he? 'Todd!'

'It's OK, Mum. Let him be.'

But I don't want to let him be. I want him to see her too, all grown up, a university graduate; and a beautiful one too. With her new boyfriend and a carefree smile.

She's happy.

She carries on; she tells me all about how she met Mark and how they have been inseparable ever since and I can see she's clearly already in love, and then she begins to talk about life at university and how much it's made her grow as a person.

'I'm so proud of you, Jess,' I tell her.

She looks at me and smiles but it's not the same smile she's had until now. For some reason it's a sad smile. She looks as if she feels sorry for me and I don't know why. Her eyes are staring behind me, and I hear a noise from the hall.

'Todd. At last.'

But it's not Todd.

Or Stuart.

She watches as Bloody Mary walks in, stomping over until she is a couple of feet away and then standing over her to get a better look before stomping off again without a word.

'What was that about?' Jess asks me. Mark just watches on, bemused.

'Take no notice of her.'

'Who is she?'

'It's just Mary.'

'Who's Mary?' Jess says sadly.

'Nobody important, love.'

But I can already see she's distracted. I try to refocus the conversation.

'Now, where were we?'

63 | Danni

Danni sat in the spare room at Sam's that had become a home from home, although not for much longer.

She scanned the street outside. Her car sat alone alongside the kerb outside the house, but she was really double-checking that Sam's and Mrs Newbold's cars were not there and that she had the house to herself.

She pulled her legs up on to the bed and curled up, her eyes shut tight, and she thought about the person she'd always thought was her mother. She tried to let her mind clear, but it was unable to free itself from the turmoil and questions. She opened her eyes, breathed and then tried again, willing herself to feel the comforting warmth, that sense of wellbeing, but it wasn't there.

There was just a loneliness. A feeling of being abandoned just when she needed her most. But she needed to ask the question anyway.

'Am I Jessica Preston?'

The room was quiet. Danni could hear her heart beating as if it were in her head rather than her chest. Outside, there was the occasional chirrup from a bird but otherwise silence.

'Am I?'

Danni knew she would have to provide the words if she wanted a conversation.

'*Do you think you are?*'

The question actually shocked her. She'd thought of little else, yet hearing someone ask her – even if it was her using a different voice – made it feel as if she was confronting it for the first time.

'Honestly?'

'*Why ask otherwise?*'

'I don't know. Nothing adds up any more.'

'*Then you need to find out why.*'

'I know your secret, don't I?'

'*Are you asking me or telling me?*'

'Why didn't *you* tell me?'

'*You don't know all of the circumstances.*'

'I know you can't be my mother.'

'*That doesn't automatically make you that missing girl.*'

'Then why did you have a missing persons leaflet with her face on?'

'*I worked at a charity shop. I dealt with other charities. It was part of my job.*'

'That's the kind of thing Dad would fob me off with if I asked him.'

'*So ask him to tell you the truth.*'

'And destroy our relationship if I'm wrong.'

'*The way things are going, Danielle, there won't be a relationship to destroy. And he's the only one who can tell you what you need to know.*'

'I wish you'd told me.'

Danni waited for an answer, but her mother didn't have one, any more than she did. She sat up, picked up her phone from the bedside table, called her father, and invited herself to dinner.

64 | Laura

Laura suddenly had more of a spring in her step.

Instead of getting up at dawn and driving towards the morning rush hour in sub-zero temperatures, she could set off that afternoon when the weather and the roads would be better – and she had money from David that she could use to book a hotel room, if there were any left.

She pulled up at the house, called the hotel while sitting on the drive and then ran through the house, stopping only to tickle Mimark's belly and shout hello to her mother.

'You're home early.'

Laura hesitated. She hated lying to her mother but, after tomorrow, at least she wouldn't have to do it again. 'David wants me to cover a big story in Manchester. I'll stay there overnight.'

She ran up the stairs to pack.

'Manchester, eh? I told you that you'd make it,' her mother called behind her. If only she knew, Laura thought as she got to her room and began pulling clothes out of her drawers, because if tomorrow's meeting was positive then she'd *make it* all right; a lot more than anyone could have imagined.

When she got back downstairs with her holdall, her mother was preparing a meal.

'Are you eating first?'

'No time. I want to leave before rush hour.'

Laura bent down and grabbed Mimark's collar and pulled his face to hers, letting him lick her cheek before planting a kiss on the top of his head and ruffling the fur around his neck. 'See you tomorrow, boy.'

It was mid-afternoon and the sky was a blanket of light grey. She had checked the forecasts and they weren't good locally, with lots of snow on the way according to the experts, but it was going to be a little better in the south. Laura ran through a mental checklist of items she needed and double-checked that she had her voice recorder, notepad and purse. She put her hand to the bottom of her bag and felt around until her fingers found the can of defence spray.

'You all right, dear?'

'Of course,' said Laura, 'just running a bit late.'

Her mother stopped preparing food and gave her a tight hug. 'Are *you* OK?' Laura asked. Under the bright kitchen spotlights, her bruise looked a shade of yellowy-purple now, and the scar from her cut had faded but was still visible.

'I'm fine. It looks worse than it is. So much for that self-defence class, though.' She smiled ruefully.

'I'm so sorry, Mum,' said Laura and put her arms tightly around her mother. 'I never meant for anyone to get hurt.'

'You were just trying to do your job,' her mother assured her.

Laura tensed at the words and hoped her mother didn't notice. 'I should have told you, though.'

'You weren't to know what would happen.'

'I should have told the police, too.'

'As long as you've done the right thing now.'

Laura nodded and looked over her mother's shoulder, glad she could hide the guilt that must be written across her face.

'Now, don't let me hold you up.'

Laura stepped away from the embrace and smiled. 'I really am sorry, Mum.'

'Go!' said Helen with a smile.

Laura reached down to pick up her bag but then stopped and hugged her mother again, tightly. 'Love you.'

'Love you too, dear.'

Laura gave Mimark a pat on his head and headed for the door, and her mother followed her to it.

'Bye.'

Laura sensed something in her face, but wasn't sure what it was. If it was doubt, she could hardly blame her, with all that she had put her through. She'd make it up to her when it was all over.

She got into the car and programmed the SatNav that her father had given her to use. It calculated the journey to almost five hours with current traffic conditions, and, on the windscreen, a few tiny flakes of snow were landing, and melting the instant they touched the glass.

She was glad she was setting off early, before any snow began to fall more heavily and slow her down even more – she wasn't going to reach the hotel until well into the evening as it was – and a few minutes into the journey, as she sat waiting at a red light, she put her phone on to speaker mode and called Danni. 'I'm on my way.'

'I thought you said you were leaving in the morning.'

'I changed my mind. There's heavy snow forecast here.'

'Where are you staying?'

'I got the last room at the hotel by you.'

'OK.'

There was an awkward silence. Laura sensed Danni wanted to tell her something. 'Are you OK?' she asked, and Danni hesitated before answering her.

'I'm going to dinner with my dad tonight.'

'That won't be easy,' Laura said, a little surprised.

'I arranged it with him earlier. I can't do this without at least seeing him first.'

Laura knew she couldn't stop her. 'Just be casual.'

'It feels like the Last Supper,' said Danni, and laughed nervously, unable to help it. 'Just before I stab him in the back.'

'It's a meal, and you aren't stabbing anyone anywhere.'

The conversation turned to Sandra, and Laura gave Danni a quick reminder of the arrangements. 'Just one thing. Don't take it personally if she spends all the time staring out of the window. That's just what she does.'

'I guess she's got no choice but to look at me,' said Danni.

Laura laughed. It was a really good point.

65 | Danni

Danni knocked on the door at her father's apartment.

She felt like a door-to-door saleswoman, and she had no emotional connection to the place, but she realised it was more than that: it was her too. She felt nothing like a daughter at that moment.

'Come in, it's great to see you,' he said as he opened the door, a navy and white butcher's apron covering his crisp light blue shirt, and a bottle of red wine in his hand.

Danni sat down on a kitchen stool while he continued preparing the food: beef Stroganoff. He had chosen one of her favourite meals, and the smell that was wafting around the apartment was making her hungry. He put a glass of wine in front of her and poured a water for himself.

They talked, mostly about her father's work and her new job in Southampton, until the oven clock pinged to say the food was ready. Thomas warmed the rice in the microwave and served up a big plate for each of them. Over the meal, they talked more, but Danni found herself wanting to ask the questions that sat on the very tip of her tongue.

When she finished her wine, her father topped up her glass and refilled his water. 'I'll run you home later.'

'I can get a taxi if it's easier.'

She had walked there, a journey of little over a mile by road, but that had taken longer than she'd expected because a strong wind was whipping in from the sea and she had been walking straight into it. Light rain had begun to fall just as she reached the apartment. The rain was much heavier now, and, as her father took some bread from the cupboard and put it between them, they could hear the large spots bouncing off the decking outside.

'Is it OK?'

Danni nodded. 'Lovely, thanks.'

Danni finished all but the tiniest portion of her meal and her father suggested they go to the living room to eat dessert. The room was a huge open-plan area with a lacquered dark wooden floor and the minimal amount of furniture he could get away with. There were two large grey suede sofas and they each sat on one. Other than that, there was the large flatscreen TV on the wall that Sam had helped him to put up, and a tiny table in the corner with a lamp on it.

'You've really settled in here. It looks nice.'

She meant it. It might never feel like home to her, but her father had done a fantastic job of making it homely and inviting.

'I like it. If I'm going to write all day, I might as well have a good view.'

'Do you miss the house?'

He looked uncomfortable and sighed. 'Of course I do.'

Danni nodded.

'But I was right to move.'

'Why?'

He looked into his half-empty glass as if the answer was somewhere inside. 'Too many memories in the house. It was hard to see them every…more wine?'

Danni tried to cover her glass but he insisted.

'Surely the memories are good ones,' she asked.

He smiled sadly. 'Of course. But that doesn't make it easier.'

'I want to remember her all the time.'

Danni knew she was goading him into a discussion he didn't want, but she couldn't help it. Her mouth was saying words before she had time to think about them.

'I can remember her in here,' he said, and tapped his chest, 'but, in the house, it was one constant reminder of what was missing from it.'

Danni felt a tear form in her eye. 'I still find it hard to believe she's gone.'

'I know,' her father said, and sank back into the sofa. The rain sounded heavier still, battering against the patio windows while the wind howled in from across the beach. It reminded Danni of the night they had sat waiting for her mother to come home.

'Do you think Mum really *did* lose control of the car?'

His back visibly stiffened and he frowned at her. 'What?'

'Do you think it was an accident?'

'Of course it was.'

He seemed annoyed with her, but her mouth seemed to be making decisions on its own and she noticed her third glass was already finished.

'We don't know for certain.'

'She must have lost control, Danni. She went off a cliff.'

'Or someone made her?'

'What?'

Danni looked him directly in the eye and didn't reply.

'Why do you insist on torturing yourself?' he asked her. 'It was an accident.'

'That's what *they* say.'

'Accidents can be terrible, but they still happen.'

'She was a great driver.'

'Great drivers can go off the road. The weather was worse than it is now, the roads…we've been over this so many times.'

'But what if someone was there? What if someone made her lose control?' Danni's head was spinning a little.

'The police and the coroner both—'

'I don't give a damn what they said.'

'Danni!'

'They weren't there.'

'Neither were you. No one was.'

'So you keep saying.'

Her father looked at her, angry but also, she thought, a little sad. Danni's eyes glistened as she looked straight into his. 'Why are you hiding things from me?'

'What? Why would you say that?'

She took a deep breath. 'What did Mum really mean by *she'll find out eventually*?'

He took a deep breath. Danni noticed his hand was trembling. 'I can't remember her ever saying that.'

'Bullshit!'

'Danni!'

'No. I'm not leaving here until you tell me.'

They stared at each other. Her father looked down and sighed. His eyes welled with tears and he took another deep, long breath. 'OK, OK...' he muttered, and breathed in, so hard that Danni thought he wanted to suck all of the oxygen from the room.

'Well?'

'You had an older sister,' he said; she was sure he didn't mean it to but it sounded incidental and matter-of-fact, the way it came out.

Danni's pulse quickened. 'A what?'

He put his head in his hands. She waited for him to continue.

'You were too small to remember her. Your mother had her when she was young.'

'What?'

'But she died when you were just a baby. Your mum always blamed herself and couldn't talk about her. It made her so depressed. That's why the funeral was so hard for me: it brought it all back. That's why I don't have photographs of you back then; it was a hard time.'

Danni stared at him, shaking her head. 'What was her name?'

'Julie.' A tear rolled from his eye.

'I don't believe you.'

'What?' he said. He looked more shocked now than upset.

'You *just* decided to tell me this now? I'm not having it.'

'Danni?'

'You're hiding something else. I know you are.'

'Why would I lie about something like this?'

'I don't know, but you're not telling me the whole story.'

He looked away but, before he did, he looked as guilty as she imagined anyone could.

'Mum isn't really my mum, is she?'

'What?'

'Is she?' Danni screamed the question, her eyes filling with tears of anger.

'What's come over you?' He stepped towards her.

'Did you have her killed?'

The question hung in the air for what seemed like minutes. Danni held her stare but she was shaking. Her father's breathing had become erratic and he was shaking too, unsteady on his legs; as if he was about to have a heart attack.

'Did you?'

Her father looked down and then back at her. He had stopped shaking but he looked different, his expression contorted with anger. His eyes looked as red as her wine.

'How dare you.'

'Did—'

He lunged forward, his eyes bulging and wide. He had never hit her in his life, but he seemed to want to now. She rolled to one side to avoid him and jumped to her feet, stumbling a little on unsteady legs and ran to the patio doors.

He moved towards her, his hands in front of him, seemingly out of sync with the rest of his body. It was as if they had decided to strangle her, no matter what the rest of him wanted to do. Danni desperately pushed her hand down on the handle, and it opened and she fell out on to the wet decking, only just

343

managing to stay on her feet as she scrambled towards the steps.

'Danni! Stop!' her father shouted, but she ran to the corner of the decking and down the steps on to the heavy sand.

The wind was so strong it almost knocked her off her feet. She had left her coat hanging in the hallway of the apartment, and her shoes on the shoe rack, and the cold rain lashed against her bare shoulders as she started to run away from the steps and towards the middle of the beach.

'Danni!' she heard her father call, but it was muffled by the wind and rain.

She didn't turn around but kept running, her feet sinking into the cold, wet sand, as the rain soaked her clothes to her skin. It was too dark to see where she was stepping and the rain was driving into her, slowing her down; after a few minutes she stopped and gasped desperately for air. She reached the end of the sandy part of the beach, and the street-lights from the village gave her some sense of her bearings. She put her hand into her pocket and pulled out her phone, dropping it on to the grass verge that separated the beach from the road.

She picked it up and wiped it dry with her sleeve. She found her recent calls list and pressed the name LAURA.

'Where are you?' she panted before Laura had a chance to say anything more than hello.

'An hour away – what's wrong?'

'Just hurry.'

'Why?'

'My dad's trying to kill me.'

66 | Danni

Even in the few minutes she'd been on the beach, the storm seemed to have worsened, and the rain was near-horizontal as it swept along the coast, with a wind that was as cold as it was fierce.

Because of her bare feet Danni kept to the grass verge as much as she could, but it was quickly turning into a bog underfoot, and eventually she had to move on to the footpath as she pushed on against the driving wind towards the lights of the village, half a mile away. The rain was already beginning to change into sleet and hurt her face and shoulders as it hit her, thrown by the seventy-mile-an-hour gale. Her feet hurt on the concrete and then became so numb from the cold that she lost any feeling in them, other than the sharp throb from her little toe, which she'd struck on a rock as she climbed from the beach to the road and which was now split and bleeding and forcing her to walk on the other side of her foot.

She stopped to take a breath and checked the time on her phone. It was almost ten o'clock and she knew the village would be busy at that time, and that she'd be safe when she got there, but it still looked a long way off and every step was becoming a challenge.

There was only one road in and out of the village on this side, a winding single carriageway that led up and out along the coast until it reached the houses where her father lived, and split into two wider roads. It had poor drainage, or at least it did when there was a deluge like this, and not only was the sleet beginning to stick to the tarmac, but the edges of the road, where it met the footpath on one side and grass on the other, were now hidden by flowing water; every few feet the footpath was completely covered, and she had to splash through it.

Danni looked back down the road towards her father's block. With so much rain, it was impossible to see anything except the dim glow of street-lights and lights in the row of three buildings. As she watched, breathing heavily, she saw the headlights of a car coming down the hill from that direction, moving slowly and still at least five hundred yards away. She checked her distance: she was roughly halfway between the village and the houses, and she decided to try to flag the car down and ask the driver to take her the rest of the way, or, better still, to the police station.

But, as the car got closer, she recognised it.

It had distinctive headlights, with a row of smaller lights along the top of the glass so that, when the headlights were on, each looked just like an eye and a narrow eyebrow.

It was her father's car.

It was crawling along, and she stepped back off the footpath on to the grass behind it and watched as the car rolled along towards her. It was going very slowly, and she knew that that wasn't because of the treacherous conditions but because the driver was looking out of the windscreen and windows on both sides.

Looking for her.

It was about three hundred yards away now and she had nowhere to go. The footpath was exposed, and when the car made the next bend she knew she would be visible in its headlights, so she looked beyond the grass. It was so dark she couldn't see any more than what appeared to be a narrow ditch running adjacent to the road, probably dug to house pipes or cables that hadn't been installed yet. She scrambled towards it, and, as the car straightened after the bend, she climbed into the trench – which was just over two feet wide – and ducked down out of sight.

The ditch was three-quarters full of ice-cold water. It was dirty water that had been topped up by the rain, and it took her breath away as her shoulders went under and only her head remained above the surface. Her teeth chattered furiously and the coldness began to bite her limbs until she cried out in pain.

The car was close now, and she kept her head as low as possible so as to not get picked out by the beam of the headlights, and listened as it rolled past.

He hadn't seen her.

She heard the wheels splosh through the rainwater that covered the kerb and move on without stopping, so she waited until it sounded as though it was a comfortable distance away, and then pulled herself up out of the water, her fingers digging into the fresh mud on the side. She was so cold, she felt as if her body was paralysed, but now she was out of the water she began to regain the feeling in her arms and legs.

The car continued its slow journey towards the village and she realised that it was only a matter of time before her father worked out that she couldn't possibly have got that far so quickly, and turned around. If and when he did, she would have to hide again, and she couldn't bear the thought of getting back into the ditch.

She took her phone from her pocket. The screen was black and no matter what buttons she pressed it stayed like that. As she wiped the water off the screen she saw tiny bubbles forming around the edge and knew it was hopeless.

Calling Laura, the police or anyone else was now not an option.

'Shit!'

She looked at the car. It was no more than four hundred yards in front of her and its brake lights came on, bright red through the gloom. It stopped, and then began to make a three-point turn. It was coming back. He'd worked it out.

Beyond the ditch was a fence and then a field. It was too dark to see anything more, but in the distance, maybe another quarter of a mile, she could see the faint, flickering neon sign outside a building that could only be the hotel. It was the only one the village had, and she remembered that Laura had told her she'd booked a room in it.

The car began to increase speed. The field didn't look much more inviting than the rain-filled ditch but she knew she had no choice. She jumped across the trench and climbed over the fence. When she landed on the other side, her feet sank into thick mud, which felt both horrible and comfortingly warm.

Her jeans were sodden, heavy and stuck to her thighs. Her thin top was soaked right through and her arms and shoulders were beginning to go numb. Ahead, all she could make out was a black, square shape that stretched as far as the hotel, and she began to move forward, her feet sinking with every step as if she were wading in treacle. For what seemed like hours she ploughed on, the mud sucking her feet down and making her use muscles and strength she didn't even know she had. Then, at last, the neon sign, which for minutes on end had seemed to stay the same distance away no matter how hard she pushed forward, finally got closer, and eventually she reached the fence in front of it and climbed over, collapsing in a heap on the other side.

Her breathing was heavy and erratic. She could see the hotel building, just beyond the sign on the other side of the car park, but her exposed and shattered body wanted to give up, and she lay on the grass as the icy mix of rain and snow battered her, almost to submission. There was no one around. Everyone was inside sheltering, and, although the entrance was so close, it felt as if even one more yard was beyond her limits; her body had begun to shut down as her final reserves of energy ran out.

She closed her eyes and put her head on to the wet grass and groaned. There was a noise; a car engine. When she opened her eyes, the hotel building was fuzzy and blurred.

Then brightness.

Headlights from a car. Forcing her eyes shut as the glare temporarily blinded her.

It had entered the car park and was driving towards her.

67 | Danni

Through the rain, the blurry glare of the headlights made her blink.

Danni tried to curl up and make herself smaller, like a mud-covered ball, but her arms and legs hurt so much she could barely move them.

The lights got closer. Came into focus.

They were normal headlights, she saw, not ones that looked like thin eyebrows.

She staggered to her bare feet and stumbled forward, across slippery wet grass and then the gravel of the car park, crying out as the open cut on her toe scraped against the uneven, unforgiving surface.

It was a smaller car; driving around the car park looking for a parking space as close to the building as possible. There was a girl inside; she could make out her shoulder-length hair as the wiper blades cleared the glass for a moment, and, as the car's headlights hit Danni full on, the girl inside the car stared at her, not believing what she was looking at. The tyres ground to a halt on the gravel and the driver jumped out and ran towards her.

'Danni?'

She almost collapsed into Laura's arms. The young journalist took her coat off and wrapped it around Danni's exposed shoulders. 'Let's get inside,' she said.

Ten minutes later, Danni was in Laura's hotel room, standing with her hands against the bathroom wall as the jet of hot water from the shower struck her body, and dirty, muddy water ran from her feet, body and hair and down the plughole. In the corner, her jeans, top and underwear lay unrecognisable in a filthy heap surrounded by a filthy puddle.

It took several minutes before she felt warm enough and clean enough to stop the shower running and step out of it. She wrapped the large white towel, which Laura had laid out for her, around her body, and another smaller one around her head.

Laura was waiting outside the bathroom with a cup of steaming tea.

'Better?'

Danni sighed and nodded. The water had increased the circulation in her arms and legs, and the feeling had returned to her face and fingers too. She sat down and sipped her tea while she told Laura exactly what had happened from the moment she had arrived at her father's house.

Laura didn't interrupt, and the shock on her face was enough to tell Danni how it must sound.

'Where do you think he will look for you?'

'He'll go to Sam's,' said Danni.

'We need to warn her.'

Danni nodded, then shook her head. 'She's not there. She's in London.'

'Well, he won't look here, so we should be OK.'

Laura looked at the clock which was fast approaching half-past eleven.

'You should have seen his eyes. I've never seen him like that.'

'You're safe now. That's all that matters.' Laura unzipped her bag and pulled out a T-shirt and threw it to Danni. 'Sleep in this,' she said, 'and I've got some sparc clothes you can wear tomorrow.'

Danni went back into the bathroom and came out a minute later with Laura's T-shirt on, and her hair wrapped in a fresh towel. She took the hotel's hairdryer from its holder and plugged it into the wall socket.

'We have to call the police,' she said.

Laura was sitting on the edge of the bed. She nodded but was only half-listening, and trying to process what Danni had told her. 'We're this close to it all coming out.' She held her fingers less than half an inch apart.

'I was that close to him finding me in that ditch.'

'But he didn't. And now he's probably making a run for it because he knows we're on to him. If he has any sense, anyway.'

'I don't know, Laura. The police—'

'We don't know what the police will do. Let me take you to High Cliffs first. We can go straight to the police from there.'

'I just want it to be over,' said Danni.

Laura nodded. She did too, but she also wanted to get the story on the website. She felt guilty for making that a priority, but she hadn't got this far to stop now. She took her laptop from her bag. 'You need to rest. Take the bed; I'll be OK on there.' She nodded towards a sofa.

'And then?'

'And then, first thing tomorrow, I'll take you to Sandra.'

68 | Laura

The alarm on the phone sounded angry, a beeping jab in the ribs, and Laura silenced it quickly.

It was dark outside; too dark, it seemed. She thought it couldn't possibly be morning yet, despite the red digits of the TV's clock saying it was. She picked up the phone from the floor beside her and it confirmed the TV was indeed correct. The sky outside was dark grey; almost black, with thick layers of cloud, and heavy rain was lashing against the hotel room's window, as it had for much of the night. Laura felt as if she had not slept for more than two or three hours. She sat up and untangled her legs from the sheets and extra blanket, and glanced at the bed.

Danni's eyes were open.

'Morning.'

Danni half-smiled. 'Sleep well?' she asked.

'Not really,' said Laura, and she stood up, stretched, and took the cheap plastic kettle into the bathroom; when she came out, she put it back on its stand and switched it on at the wall. After a few seconds, a gurgling hiss came from it; while she waited for the water to boil, Laura opened her laptop and checked the news and weather.

'Great,' she said, and Danni looked over at her. 'This rain is turning to snow later. It's already hit most of the country.'

The news page had several articles on it. Locally there had been a fair bit of storm damage, but over the rest of the UK snow had fallen or was falling and weather warnings were now in place, the ones that advised people to only make journeys if they were absolutely necessary.

Danni got out of bed and yawned.

'I think we should just get to Sandra as soon as we're dressed. Before the snow reaches here,' said Laura.

'OK.'

Laura sat with the computer on her lap and clicked on a tab at the bottom of her screen. The document she had worked on after Danni had gone to sleep was almost finished, and she began checking it, making minor amendments and tidying up the last section, the part she had been working on when exhaustion had finally beaten her and she'd rushed to complete it.

Danni went to the bathroom, and when she came out she sat on the makeshift bed next to her. Laura jumped and clicked back to the news page instinctively.

'What was that?' Danni asked.

'Nothing.'

'It was something.'

'I didn't want you to see it. Not yet.'

'See what?'

Laura pressed the tab and the article filled the screen. Danni began to read it.

'I had to get it written so I could send it to the paper asap. If it's true, of course.'

Danni blew out her cheeks. Laura knew that, seeing it in writing, the enormity of what they might be about to do was beginning to sink in.

'Sorry. I didn't...'

Danni waved her apology away. 'This is really happening, isn't it?'

Laura nodded.

'What do *you* think she'll say?'

Laura had thought about little else before and after the sleep she'd had.

'I'm really not sure.' And she wasn't. Just about any outcome seemed possible at that moment.

'What time do we need to leave?'

Laura looked at the digital clock on the TV. It was almost half-past seven but still middle-of-the-night dark outside. The rain was still falling, but not as heavily now; it had begun to ease, a gentler pitter-pattering on the window.

'As soon as you're ready.'

'Will *she* be ready for us?'

'She's got nowhere else to go.' Laura shrugged. She'd originally arranged to be there at midday, but she doubted Sandra would care how early she got there and she hoped the manager would not interfere. 'You OK with that?'

Danni nodded, and Laura opened her holdall and took out a spare T-shirt, knickers, jumper, leggings and trainers and threw them on to the bed. 'I'll wear what I had on yesterday. You can have these.'

Danni picked them up and went into the bathroom to change. Laura quickly pulled her creased clothes on and went down to the hotel's restaurant, where she collected a napkin full of mini croissants and pastries; when she got back to their room, Danni was dressed and had rinsed her muddy clothes. She was wringing them out over the bath and dropping them into a plastic bag. Laura doubted that they could be saved but her spare clothes fitted her well.

'Lucky we're the same size,' she said.

Danni smiled and dropped the plastic bag by the door.

They ate the food and left the room to check out at the reception. The rain was heavier again and bouncing off the car park surface, and off the bonnets and roofs of the cars. They stood in the hotel's entrance watching and waiting for a break in it to run to the car, but it was soon apparent that there wouldn't be one. If anything, the weather was getting worse.

'C'mon.'

Laura held the one coat they had over both their heads and they ran as fast as the surface water allowed until they were inside the VW Polo parked in the far corner. Laura opened the glove compartment, took the SatNav out and found the address for High Cliffs in the 'Previous Destinations' section. It quickly calculated the journey to a precise twenty-one minutes.

Danni looked at her quizzically as she put her seatbelt on.

'I've never driven there in the dark,' Laura said. 'Ready?'

'Ready.'

Laura turned the key and the engine slowly spluttered to life, as it tended to do when it was cold. The temperature on the car's display said it was three degrees, but it felt much colder with the strong wind. She drove slowly to the car park exit, put the validated ticket into the machine, the exit barrier lifted slowly and they rolled under it. At the junction they turned on to the main road, its white lines hardly visible under the rainwater, and as they left the village – even though the car's clock was telling them it was fourteen minutes to eight – on the unlit sections of road it was still very dark. Laura kept to a low speed as they drove along the coast, the headlights only just showing her the way through the rain. On her left she could see a slightly lighter horizon and knew that the sea was out there somewhere but it was impossible to make it out.

'I can't believe this weather,' she said, trying to make conversation and break some of the tension. Danni stared out of the window but didn't answer.

Behind them, a few hundred yards away, a car pulled on to the road. Laura didn't see it because it had no headlights on. It was much too dark, and the conditions far too dangerous, to drive without lights but that was what it did, slowly gaining on them but holding a distance that was far enough back to remain unseen.

Laura braked to slow down on a tight bend, and the other car also slowed, but it did so without braking, so as not to illuminate the blackness with its red lights. The next section of road was a series of tight bends, a half-mile stretch that ran perilously close to the cliff edge and which had a long set of metal safety barriers to keep drivers away from the drop beside them. Invisible to the eye, there was a seventy-foot sheer drop on to the jagged rocks that ran the length of the shoreline separating the sand from the cliff face.

There was just enough room for two cars, but in the dark, with so much surface water on the road, it seemed narrower. Laura took her foot off the accelerator and the car's speed fell to twenty miles per hour; she kept the main beam on, to give them as much light as possible and so that she could see the barriers clearly.

The car behind them picked up its pace and closed the gap to around a hundred yards.

Laura still couldn't see it.

Then it really began to increase its speed.

69 | Laura

The remaining distance to High Cliffs House was a fraction over five miles according to the SatNav.

Laura slowly negotiated the next bend. The sky was beginning to get a little lighter, but the rain was so heavy that the fastest wiper-blade setting wasn't quick enough to clear the windscreen for Laura to see properly, and she had to lean forward and peer out to make sure she wasn't too close to the edge.

Danni felt sick. Since her mother's death, she'd tried to avoid driving on roads like this and her frequent dreams always seemed to end with her driving on the edge of a cliff, just as they were now. She closed her eyes, hoping it would settle her stomach.

Their speed was down to fifteen miles per hour; they were virtually crawling along, and Laura hardly applied pressure on the pedals as they rolled along, the tyres sloshing through several inches of water.

Crash!

'What the...'

There was no warning, no sound, but a hard forward jolt as they were hit from behind, and they both let out a shocked cry at the exact same second.

Laura's car grazed the barrier on her left-hand side and she clung to the steering wheel, correcting it to turn them back towards the centre of the carriageway. She glanced to her right, into her side mirror, but could only see a dark shape in the blackness behind them; the raindrops on the windows and mirror blotted any detail out. She thought for a split second that they had been involved in an accident.

Crash!!

Danni screamed. Laura knew then that it was no accident.

The dark shape had hit them again but much harder this time, and the momentum and the other car's speed pushed the VW into the barrier, making a horrible grating sound as the thin metal of the car doors scraped along the thicker steel.

Laura put her foot on the accelerator instinctively, trying to get away from whoever was behind them and pull the car away from the barrier, but her wheels spun in the water and they slid along instead, slowly zigzagging along the drenched tarmac.

The dark shape came again, faster and alongside them, its left front corner leaning into their rear side, forcing them back into the barrier, but with more force; instead of grinding along it, this time one of the panels buckled and broke off, sailing down to the rocks below as Laura pushed her foot down again and got back to the middle of the carriageway.

'What are they doing?' Danni yelled, but Laura ignored her. She knew she had to stay in front of the other vehicle, because if she let it get alongside her again it might be her car and not a barrier that went over the edge next time.

Crunch!

They were hit again from behind and it almost caused the VW to spin, but its front wing clipped another barrier and Laura was able to correct her position just in time, although the barrier crumpled and snapped off at one end and was left hanging over the precipice.

She managed to get them back towards the middle, for a brief moment, then the other car hit them again, side-on this time and much harder than before, and they smacked with a ferocious clanging into another barrier.

Danni was screaming hysterically now.

The VW hit one of the barrier posts, knocking it out of the ground and over the edge, and Laura tried desperately to straighten her car as the next post loomed before them, but she shunted into it and sent it flying over the cliff edge.

'We're going to die!'

Laura ignored her, focusing her every thought and action on staying on top of the cliff.

Crash!!!

They were pushed back against the next barrier with incredible force, so much that Laura felt the barrier give way and one of her wheels drop over the side of the cliff, making the car start to spin to the left in a way that she knew would take it over the edge. She pressed her foot down on the accelerator as hard as she could and the VW lurched forward, its errant wheel finding solid ground; they moved a few yards ahead, the other driver having backed off, expecting them to go over. Laura tried to get into the middle again, but the other driver seemed to guess this time what she was going to do and the car came hard down her flank, aggressively pushing its wheels alongside hers and forcing her over to the left and back against the metal barriers again. Two more barriers came off under the force and weight of her car, and she knew that, if both her wheels went over the edge together, she wouldn't be able to get them back on to the road the way she had when it was just one. The other car would then only need to nudge them and that would be it.

The other driver was dictating everything, and she didn't know how to stop them, because their car was clearly faster and bigger than hers, and, from behind, they could see her but she couldn't see them.

She was fast running out of ideas.

Unless…

She slammed her foot on the brake.

It was desperate and she had no idea what might happen but it worked. The VW went into a sideways skid, the tyres sliding across water, but the friction as the back of the car scraped against the barrier slowed them, and then they bounced off one of the posts and spun completely before coming to a halt in the middle of the road.

Their pursuer hadn't anticipated Laura's actions and their car went past on the outside, trying to slow down too but sliding in the wet, slaloming away from where Laura's VW sat.

Laura was now facing in the opposite direction. Danni had her eyes closed and seemed oblivious to what had happened, as if she'd accepted they were going over the cliff and was still waiting to hit the bottom. Laura looked in her mirror as the black shape, brake lights lighting up the darkness around it, came to a halt about sixty yards or so away, up against the barrier.

She gasped. For the first time since they had been struck, she spotted a way out. She pushed the gearstick into first gear and pushed her accelerator down. Her wheels spun furiously but the car stayed where it was and she looked around, sure she had done something wrong, and then realised it was just the water. Her wheels were spinning too fast to hold on to the road.

She glanced in the mirror again. The other car's reverse lights came on.

She pushed the stick down into second gear and they jolted forward, slipping one way and then the other but moving. Laura put her foot down as far as it would go and the tyres finally found some grip and the VW shot off on to the gloom. She ignored the conditions and poor visibility and raced back along the cliff road.

Danni's eyes were open now. She clung to her seat as they raced around bends and flew down the straights as if Laura knew they were on a track and couldn't come off. She didn't and they weren't but Laura could not have cared less. She just focused on putting as much distance between them and the other car as possible.

'Is it still behind us?'

'I don't think so,' Laura replied, checking her mirror again, but she couldn't be totally sure in the dark. She wasn't even confident, with the damage they must have sustained, that her car wouldn't fall apart at any moment.

They turned on to the wider road and she went faster still until she reached a dual carriageway and finally a stretch of road that was lit, and then she eased her foot off the pedal and relaxed her shoulders.

The voice from the SatNav was telling them to take a U-turn, but Laura kept going.

'How do we get to Sandra now?' said Danni.

Laura shook her head.

'We don't.'

70 | Laura

'What?'

Laura checked her mirrors again and decreased her speed to eighty miles per hour, although they were still in the outside lane and overtaking anyone else that was on the dual carriageway.

'They were waiting for us.'

Danni looked at her in disbelief. Laura kept her eyes on the road. It was a little lighter now; the grey clouds still filled the sky, but somewhere behind them the sun must have come up.

'They had to be. They knew we were going to High Cliffs.'

'Shit.'

Laura drove in silence for another five minutes, allowing the car to slow down a little.

'Where are we going?' Danni asked.

'We're getting out of here.'

'What about the police?'

It was the obvious answer and Laura knew it, but she didn't reply straight away. She kept looking in the mirror, expecting the other car to come hurtling up behind them at any moment, although with every mile that became less and less likely.

'They would rather kill us than let you meet Sandra,' she said, glancing at Danni.

'You think I don't know that?'

'Then you know what it means?'

Danni looked ahead. Laura glanced at her again.

She knew.

Laura could also see that the story of a lifetime was slipping from her grasp. If they went to the police now, they'd be questioned for hours, and in that time the incredible news was bound to leak out. She'd put her life on the line, literally, for this story, and it didn't seem fair. She needed to get the article to press, and she couldn't think of anyone better than David Weatherall to help her with that. And she'd earned the right to see this through to the end.

The motorway junction was ahead. They passed a sign that said they had a mile and a half before they reached it.

'Whoever that was isn't going to stop,' she said, 'and we're lucky to be alive.'

The slip road loomed on their left. Laura indicated, and they pulled on to it and approached a roundabout, from which they exited on to the M5 and Laura headed north.

'What are you doing?'

'Getting as far away as possible. I don't trust anyone around here. And that's the second car that's chased you.'

'You think that was *him*?'

Laura had been thinking it since the attack started. 'I couldn't see. It was too dark,' she told Danni truthfully instead. She settled into a comfortable speed in the left-hand lane. 'But we can't rule anything out. You said yourself that your mum wouldn't have lost control.'

Danni didn't answer. Laura could see that she had been thinking exactly the same thing, and when she did speak she was holding back tears.

'They're not my mum and dad.'

They drove in silence for the next fifteen miles until they reached the next services. Laura took the exit and found a quiet corner of the car park with no one around them; the drivers of the few cars there had parked as close to the building as possible to avoid getting soaked in the downpour.

'Good God.'

Danni had got out first and stood looking at the damage on her side of the car. Laura was shocked when she joined her. In near daylight, the VW looked as if it had been all but written off. The whole left side was filled with dents, and so much of the paintwork had been taken off that it was hard to tell what colour it originally was. The lights, front and back, were smashed, and on both wheels there were deep, shiny fresh gashes in the alloy. It was incredible that the passenger door had opened at all, and Laura worried that it might not close now.

'We were more than lucky,' she said.

They ran through rain that was beginning to thicken into sleet, to the main building, and Laura bought some sandwiches and several chocolate bars. They stood in the entrance to the services building and Laura checked the time. It wasn't quite half-past nine.

She took her phone from her pocket.

'I need to call Sandra and my boss.' She pressed the button on the phone to wake it from its sleep mode. 'Shit.'

'What?'

'My battery is at one per cent. I meant to charge it, but with everything…can I use yours?'

Danni shook her head. 'Totally dead.'

Laura grimaced and looked back her phone screen. 'I can't risk it. If I call and it dies on me, she'll not know what's going on.'

'Charge it in here,' Danni suggested.

Laura looked behind them. There were a café and a fast-food counter with a seated area. If she found a socket, she could charge the phone and send an email with the article to David. She looked out at the car park and it was now snowing, thick flakes driving horizontally across the fields and already sticking to the car roofs and grass verges.

'I think we should get to my house.'

Danni frowned. 'That's miles away.'

'If we go now, before this gets any worse, we can do it in less than two and a half hours, three at most,' said Laura. 'And at least we will have shelter, food, and my parents to help us.' She decided not to mention that they could also go to the *Gazette* and get David to break the story.

Danni looked unconvinced. 'I don't know.'

'If this snow carries on, we'll be trapped. And then what will we do?'

'Go to the police.'

'We can go to the police from mine. And call Sandra.' Laura knew if they went now and were lucky, they could be at her house by the early afternoon.

Danni shrugged. She had no phone, no clothes, no money, and she was pretty sure the person she'd always thought was her father now wanted to kill her. 'Whatever you think.'

'I think that, right now,' said Laura, 'we need to be with people I trust.'

71 | Laura

'Listen carefully, Mum, because my battery is about to die.'

There was a 'low battery' warning beep. Laura knew that she had to be quick; if she only managed to tell her mother half of what had happened and then got cut off, she would leave her out of her mind with worry.

'What's wrong?' said Helen, her voice full of concern.

Laura gave her enough details that she understood the gravity of their situation without wasting any seconds as the phone beeped another warning. She heard her mother gasp when she finished.

'We're not hurt. The car is in a bad way, but I think I can make it back.'

'Then get here as quickly as you can.'

'I will.'

Her mother told her that the weather forecast was for heavy snow in the afternoon. Laura looked up at the sky: a thick light grey blanket had replaced the rainclouds, and the snowflakes were beginning to settle in any empty spaces on the car park.

'It's snowing here too.'

'Be careful. We can sort it all out when you get here.'

'Is Dad there?' said Laura.

'I'm going to call him at work right now so he'll be back before you get here.'

'OK.'

'We have to go the police.'

'I know. I'm sorry for all the trouble, Mum.'

'Just get home.'

There was another beep in her ear: a final warning that the battery had run out.

'I'll see you…'

Silence. Laura looked at her phone but the screen had gone black. 'Let's go,' she said to Danni, and they ran to the car, their hair and shoulders covered in snow in the few seconds it took to get inside.

The engine started at the second attempt. The temperature was falling sharply, down by three degrees on the car's display compared to when they had set off that morning. Laura checked the fuel gauge: she had half a tank, probably enough to get back but she'd stop for more if she needed it.

'What happens with Sandra now?'

'I'll call her from home and I guess the police will take care of things after that.'

'Will I still get to see her?'

Laura nodded, but she had no idea what would really happen. That part was out of her hands now.

Danni put her head back and closed her eyes, allowing Laura to concentrate on the road, which was getting busier with other traffic, and, although the snow wasn't settling yet on the motorway, the fields either side were already white all over. Danni was drifting in and out of sleep, fidgeting and lightly snoring, and for the next fifty miles they travelled in silence until Laura switched the radio on to listen for weather reports.

'Your mum sounds nice.'

'Huh?'

Danni had woken up and stretched her arms in front of her. 'Nice. Your mum.'

'She is,' said Laura. 'She's great.'

'That's good.'

Laura didn't answer. There was a bitterness in Danni's tone.

'I feel like I've been lied to all my life.'

The snow was swirling outside, getting much thicker the further north they went, and Laura began to worry that this hadn't been such a good idea after all. The traffic was building up too, and she hadn't been able to go faster than forty miles per hour for quite a while.

'I can't imagine what that feels like.'

Laura had tried to imagine, but it was hard. How did you cope with suddenly finding out that everything and everyone you believed in was not what and who you'd thought they were?

Danni closed her eyes again and Laura had to slow down as the brake lights of the vehicles in front of her came on. There was snow on the roads now, on the hard shoulder and where the white lines were. When she checked the SatNav, they only had another seventy miles to go, but those miles weren't going to be covered quickly.

Danni managed to get some more sleep for a while, mumbling incoherently and flinching occasionally, and Laura felt for her. She knew she had done the right thing, especially after what had happened that morning, and Danni deserved to know the truth about her past, but now, watching the obvious torture she was going through, it didn't make Laura feel better.

The orange fuel warning light came on. Laura checked the SatNav. Forty miles to go, but they were down to a slow crawl now and the only parts of the road without snow were the wet black tracks the vehicles had cut through it. When they reached the exit for the next services, she pulled off and into the petrol station and put twenty pounds' worth of fuel in the tank, using the money David had given her. When she opened the car door, Danni was woken by the chilled air that was sucked in.

'I got you more chocolate,' said Laura, and handed her a bar. They had eaten the sandwiches and other bars already.

'Thanks. How far to go?'

The SatNav was plugged into the car's cigarette lighter, and was jolted from its sleep mode when Laura turned the key into the ignition.

'Twenty-five miles. Forty minutes, maybe a bit more in this.'

She pulled back on to the motorway to make the final leg of the journey. The snow was swirling around in an energetic flurry now, and the wind had picked up. The whole scene was completely white. There was a line of cars moving at little more than twenty miles an hour when Laura joined them in the left-hand lane, and they slowly trundled along as the wiper blades worked overtime to keep the windscreen clear.

'I'll be glad to get out of this,' said Laura.

Danni bit into her chocolate bar and opened Laura's can of Coke and handed it to her.

Neither of them had any reason to notice that a dark-coloured car had left the services a few seconds after they did and carefully slipped into the nearside lane between a lorry and a van about a dozen vehicles behind them.

It was covered in snow, which hid some of the damage to its left-hand side, and it slowly followed Laura's VW as it made its way up the northbound carriageway.

Part Eight

The present day...

Do you know, there was a time when I thought I could avoid this?

It seems inevitable now, but at one point I thought I might be able to stop it – stop them digging, so that the truth could remain hidden.

The email. I admit that was a mistake; amateurish and counterproductive. No journalist with anything about them will drop an investigation that easily.

Getting someone to scare her: I thought that might work, especially by including her family in the threat, but they just kept going; even hurting her mother didn't stop her, and the more I tried to scare them, the more determined they became.

But wasn't this exactly the way it was always going to turn out?

When that little girl came into the house that day, holding my wife's hand with her cute smile and blonde curly hair – that's when I should have put a stop to this. But I panicked instead, allowed myself to think about what my wife wanted – needed – and not what had to be done. We should have got rid of her that day. However we decided to do it, we should have ended it then and there and faced the consequences.

But I was too hasty; too soft. I allowed my heart to rule my head.

That day is still so clear, even now. I have a crystal-clear image in my mind of them standing there in the doorway. The hot sun shining outside; my wife's face looking at me, *you'll-go-mad-when-you-know-what-I've-done* written all over it.

But I knew exactly what she'd done.

And why she'd done it.

It's obvious now, in hindsight, that I should have screamed at her, made her pack that child straight back into the car and take her back to the beach, or take her anywhere; somewhere where they'd never trace it back to us.

We should have done it while we still could.

But hindsight's fantastic, isn't it?

My wife was broken, and this child seemed to instantly begin to mend her. If we'd done what we should have done, she'd have been even more broken than ever but we'd have got past it, found a way to blot out the pain in other ways and emerge from the other side.

Maybe the experience would have made us into better people.

Maybe she'd have healed eventually anyway, even without the child.

And we could have avoided all this.

You see, now I'm out of options. Out of choices.

They already know far too much. Both of them.

Pushing them over that cliff felt like a last resort. They were about to uncover everything I have worked so hard to keep hidden for all those years. If they'd gone off the edge, they'd never have survived. And the secret might have died with them.

Sandra Preston would never have got to see her daughter again. And even if she said anything, they'd think it was just a crazy old woman in a psychiatric unit rambling on, unable to let go.

Either way, it would buy me time.

Because I can't go to prison.

I'm not going to prison for someone else's child. That's the thing, you know – that's the advantage I have, in her not being my flesh and blood.

It makes what I am going to do easier.

It's unthinkable, sure, but it won't be the first time I've done the unthinkable.

Not taking that child straight back to her parents or to the police, that day. That was unthinkable.

Taking her summer hat to that beach and leaving it to be found washed up on the shore so they'd be convinced she drowned. That was unthinkable.

Raising her as our own; that was pretty unthinkable too.

As was paying to keep her real mother in that mental health unit all these years.

Thinking that we could keep it all a secret for ever. Not just unthinkable, but also unrealistic.

So, you see, that's why I can do the unthinkable one more time.

And finally get rid of that child once and for all.

It's going to be her.

It's strange, because, when I looked at the photograph the journalist showed me, I didn't see Jessica; not the Jessica I had in my head, anyway. But I've spent so long imagining, picturing in my head, how my little girl has turned out, it's hardly surprising is it?

But something inside me knows. It knows; I'm not sure how, or why, but my gut is telling me that the day, the one I didn't dare to believe in, is finally going to happen.

When she vanished that day, from that beach, I knew she was alive, even though all the other people said she must have drowned. It's that same feeling now: a voice deep inside telling me, guiding me. It's the same voice that told me on the day that she'd gone in the other direction, away from the water.

It was the one that told me that she had been taken.

When the divers searched the water that morning, I watched them, but I wasn't ever worried they'd find her. I never expected them to drag her body from the waves. You don't find someone when they aren't there.

When the police tried to tell me she might be dead, or when people tried to persuade me to move on, to get some closure and stop trying to fool myself – that's why I refused to accept what they said. It's why I fought them.

I knew they were wrong.

And yet, though I knew she was alive, I still didn't expect to see her again.

The voice also told me that whoever had taken her wouldn't bring her back.

You don't go to those lengths to take a child only to do that. They were always going to carry on, keep her hidden until no one was looking for her any longer. So I prayed – although that's not the best choice of word because I stopped actually praying – that she would be all right, that whoever took her had given her a good home and raised her to be a decent person.

I thought that was as much as I could possibly hope for.

Until that journalist turned up.

What brought her to me? She was looking for another child, in a different era; a different place. Another missing child that had no business with my daughter. She had no reason to look for me, let alone find me and talk to me, a crazy old woman in a mental home; one who can't let go of the past.

Yet she did. She wrote that article.

She believed me.

And now, because of her and against all the odds, I am going to see my Jessica again.

I just know it.

All these years, years sitting in this chair, looking out on to that beach, I knew that I couldn't ever give up; not completely. That voice deep inside said I had to believe there was a chance. However unlikely it seemed.

And now I know why.

Because she's coming back.

My daughter's finally coming back.

72 | Laura

Laura indicated that she was taking the next exit but they were moving so slowly, even though they were so close to the slip road, it took them another ten minutes to reach the roundabout at the top of it.

The heater was coughing out hot air on full power. Outside, the conditions had become atrocious, a blizzard of strong winds and swirling snow that covered everything except the tracks made by the car tyres. All the drivers in each vehicle could do was to follow the one in front, placing their wheels with absolute precision into the grooves in the snow and hoping there was no need for a sudden stop, because that had become almost impossible.

Everyone was relying on everyone else to keep moving.

Laura's head ached from the concentration needed to carry on and the stress of the journey to that point. The three hours she had anticipated had become a morning and most of the afternoon; it had now turned dark and the snow on the roads was already starting to freeze.

The speed with which the snow had fallen had caught the local authorities out, and, although some roads had been gritted, this had little effect because the snow had become so deep so quickly. Every road leading from the roundabout was equally chaotic; each of the four exits were jammed with stationary vehicles and bright brake lights.

They took the fourth one, the single carriageway that led to Laura's town. As they edged along, with all the other cars, they saw abandoned vehicles at the side of the road, where they had either got stuck or else the driver had left their car and made the rest of the journey on foot.

Danni shook her head. 'This is bad.'

Laura nodded. Danni had been asleep from the petrol station to the motorway exit; not a good sleep, a fitful one where she squirmed around, occasionally mumbling to herself, the odd moan and indistinguishable word as she drifted in and out of the chaos inside her head. Laura had been happy to drive without having to talk; it had been hard enough to drive with her pounding head as it was.

'We'll be home soon,' she said.

Danni sniffed dismissively. 'Home?'

'I didn't mean—'

'Your home, your parents. I don't have either, remember?'

'That's not what—'

'No!' snapped Danni. 'It *is* what you meant. It *is* your home. And don't tell me how hard it must be for me, or that you can imagine how it feels. Because you can't and you never will.'

'Danni, I—'

'Your mum and dad will take care of everything now. Just like they always have.'

Laura glared at her as they slowed to a halt behind the lorry in front. 'That's not fair.'

'Isn't it?'

'No.'

'This is a story for you. Don't deny it. It's why you've avoided going to the police. It's why you wanted to come here. It's all to protect your precious fucking story. You can send it off to your paper to tell the world and then live off it for the rest of your life.'

'Hang on—'

Danni cut in and Laura let her. She knew she needed to get this off her chest whether she wanted her to or not. 'You'll never know what it's like to find out your whole life has been bullshit! That everyone you know, or thought you knew, was just…fucking *bullshit*!'

'How could I?'

'You live this sheltered life. Everyone there to do whatever you need. Popular at school, lots of friends, good grades, good job, steady boyfriends, you name it.'

Laura bit her lip. She wanted to tell Danni that she didn't know anything about her at all. That she had tried for months to get the good job her grades – *her* hard work – deserved but that in the end she'd had to rely on her dad to help her and had never been allowed to forget it. She wanted to tell her that she'd lost that job *because* she'd put the story first. That she had put helping her and Sandra ahead of her job. And she'd done all she could to stop Danni destroying her relationship with her dad before they knew the whole truth.

She wanted to tell her that she hadn't had a proper date, let alone a boyfriend, for more than a year because her dad scared all of them off.

And she wanted to point out that she'd never asked Danni to read her bloody article and contact her in the first place.

But Laura didn't want an argument any more than Danni needed one. This was about her saying all the things that had bounced around in her head for days, maybe weeks, so Laura let her talk.

'My real parents couldn't even look after me for one day.'

Laura gulped.

'You have your perfect family. I go from the one that can't look after a child to the one who can't have a child and take someone else's. Then when, shock, it all goes wrong, they…'

Danni stopped, tears rolling down her cheeks.

The snow was so deep. All of the cars heading in the same direction as Laura were having the same difficulties and the drivers were carefully shunting forward and then braking gently as the red lights lit up on the car in front. Laura had to put the car into second gear to get up the incline ahead of them and the lorry in front struggled more than she did and she worried for a second that its wheels would lock and it would slide back down into them.

Danni sat with her head buried in her hands.

'Christ, I didn't mean that,' she said after a few minutes.

Laura shook her head.

'You aren't the one I should be shouting at.'

'You needed to let it out,' Laura told her.

'Not at you, though.' Danni scrubbed at her eyes.

'Forget it.'

'I couldn't have got this far without you.' Danni held out her hand and Laura took it. Danni gripped it tightly until Laura needed to change gear. 'I didn't mean those things.'

'I said forget it.'

Behind them, ten cars back, a black car crawled in the line of vehicles, and when Laura and the car behind her both turned off down a smaller, narrower road a mile later, a road that led towards the coast, the black car followed but stayed back, out of Laura's view.

On this road, where there had been far fewer cars, deep snow had already built up on both sides and there were no wet black grooves to drive on. Laura felt her wheels slide over hardened snow and she let the VW crawl in first gear and left a larger gap – a few car-lengths – in front of her, until after another mile they turned again and then one last time, and then the wheels were crunching through fresh, undisturbed white powder and they reached a small cul-de-sac with four picturesque houses and a field to the side that led down to the sea.

It was like a postcard. Three of the houses had lights on, and thin plumes of smoke drifted from their chimneys. Everything was white, except for the soft orange glow of the street-lamp. Heavy snow covered the roofs and all the trees and the tops of the fences.

'We're here,' said Laura.

When they reached her house Laura got out, kicking two feet of snow away from the base of the black iron gates to be able to move them. As she climbed back inside, the door opened and Helen stood on the step watching as Laura slowly rolled down the slope and eased to a halt next to her mother's car.

Helen ran outside to greet her. 'I've been worried sick.' She hugged her tightly. As she moved back from the embrace, snow covering the tops of her Wellington boots, she looked at the car. 'My goodness.'

Laura turned to look too. 'You should see it in the light.'

Danni got out of the other side and stood awkwardly until Helen's attention was diverted from the car's damage and she smiled at her.

'You're Danni.'

Danni nodded and smiled back.

'Now let's get in out of the cold. You must be starving.'

A little way up the street, the black car had rolled into the cul-de-sac but parked at the top, near the entrance, and switched off its lights. Its driver watched from that distance, looking down at the four houses, and one in particular, as Helen Grainger greeted the girls on the drive.

He watched as the three of them went into the house and closed the door.

73 | Laura

'Where are you? Hang on.'

Helen stepped into the hallway so that she could hear properly. The kettle was boiling and a saucepan of soup warmed on the hob. She came back into the kitchen after a minute and gave it a stir.

'He's on his way,' she said to the girls, who were sitting at the table. Laura's mother had given Danni one of her thick cardigans and Laura had fetched a jumper from her room. 'He wanted to be back for when you got here,' she continued. 'But there's been an accident on the bypass, and they asked him to stay and help.'

'It's fine.'

'He's been worried half to death. And now most of the roads are blocked.'

'It's a nightmare out there,' said Danni.

Helen took the soup from the heat and sliced up a crusty loaf for them; she left them to eat while she gathered extra blankets from the airing cupboard, made up the bed in the spare room, and filled the bathroom with fresh towels. When she came back down, they had almost finished, and she tried to give them more soup but Laura shook her head.

'Mum, stop fussing. We ate on the way.'

Helen went to the window instead. 'It's getting worse out there. I hope your dad's not stuck.'

Danni smiled at Laura and used the bread to mop up her remaining soup. There was a familiar whining from the utility room; Laura let Mimark into the kitchen and he playfully danced around them, flopping on to his back every so often to let Danni tickle his belly.

'He likes you,' laughed Laura.

'They usually growl at me.'

Outside, the snow had settled over their tyre tracks and a drift was building up against the wall around the driveway. Helen put a cup of tea in front of them and left the room, leaving Mimark to enjoy the extra attention. Danni bent down to play with him until her back felt stiff and she stood and stretched, unable to stifle a yawn.

'It's been a long day,' said Laura, and walked to the window. She could tell from the way a few flecks danced in front of the street-light that the snow had almost stopped falling.

'So what now?' said Danni.

'We wait for my dad to get back,' said Laura confidently, 'and see what he says.'

Helen put her head around the door. 'The fire's on in the living room,' she announced. 'Do you want anything? More tea, toast, hot chocolate?'

Danni looked at Laura.

'Hot chocolate sounds good, Mum.'

'Two?' She looked at Danni, who nodded. 'Coming up.'

Laura led Danni to the front of the house, into the huge living room with an open fireplace and a portrait of the Grainger family hanging above it. It had been painted by a local artist when Laura was fifteen, and had been Helen's present for her husband's fiftieth birthday; it took pride of place in the house. Danni looked at it before she sat down on one of the two large brown sofas that faced each other. Laura sat on the other one, feeling guilty about the picture: smiling, happy family portrait faces that the artist had made even happier than they were on the photograph he had painted from.

'It's nice,' said Danni, sensing her discomfort.

The fire began to spark and spit as the flames took hold of the dry logs that Helen had put on it. She had also put a fresh blanket on each sofa, and Danni covered her legs with hers.

Laura's mother brought in two steaming cups of hot chocolate, topped with cream, and a plate of biscuits, and put them on the table while Mimark spotted an opportunity and followed her through the open door and found a cosy spot by the fire.

Outside, the wind had picked up again and the few flakes of snow still in the air were being blown around like confetti rather than falling to the ground. Helen walked over to the window, looked out and pulled the curtains together before joining her daughter on the sofa and asking all kinds of questions of Danni.

'It's not an interrogation, Mum.'

Danni smiled and Helen apologised, although Laura was glad she'd avoided asking anything about her parents or home life. But it was still a relief for Laura when she heard the engine of a car, the clunking of the iron gates, a car door closing and then the crunch of tyres on snow. Helen stopped her questioning and stood up expectantly. They heard the sound of feet stamping outside the back door and then the door open.

Robert burst in, his face full of concern. He looked at his daughter and ran to her, wrapping his arms around her and holding her tightly. 'Thank God you're all right.'

'I'm sorry, Dad.'

He held her at arm's length, his hands on her shoulders and looked at her. 'I'm just glad you're safe. It sounds like you were very lucky.'

He looked at Danni, who had stood up.

'Dad, this is Danni. Danni, my dad.'

'Hello, Mr Grainger.'

'Robert, please,' he said, and shook her hand warmly.

Everyone sat down, Laura's father next to her with his arm around her shoulder. He told them that the roads were getting so bad that they would have to be closed if the snow started to fall heavily again. Eventually, he began to talk about what had happened.

'I couldn't believe it when your mum told me.'

Laura nodded. She had little appetite to go through it again but she sensed he wanted more detail.

'We're safe now,' she said. 'Can we talk about what to do next?'

'Call the police, surely?' said Helen. Danni agreed.

'One hundred per cent,' said Laura's father, nodding too. He looked at his watch; it was after eight o'clock. He stood up and took the home phone from the cradle and dialled a number.

'Keith Houghton, please?'

He stepped into the hall. They could hear him from the living room.

'Dad's known him for years,' Helen told them.

'Yes…yes. OK,' they heard Robert say. Danni looked at Laura, who smiled at her reassuringly. 'OK,' said Robert. 'OK, I'll do that.'

He stepped back into the living room.

'Keith is dealing with the accident. They've got everyone out because of the weather and there's only a desk sergeant left, and they're going to close all the roads in an hour because the snow's starting to freeze.'

'That's not good,' said Helen.

Her husband nodded in agreement. He went to the window and pulled the curtain to the side; heavier snow was starting to fall again.

'It'll be hopeless trying to get there in this. I think we should all get a night's sleep; you two look as though you need it. Then, in the morning, I'll call someone from CID.'

'CID?'

'Someone tried to kill you, Laura. This isn't something the local station can deal with.'

She nodded. Danni nodded too.

'Good,' said Helen.

'Now I'm putting the cars away. Any chance of some of that hot chocolate when I come back in?'

Helen smiled, stood up and went into the kitchen while Robert went outside to first drive her car into the garage and then come out and put his own in too for the night. The wind had completely dropped and the snow was falling straight down, big flakes that settled on his head as he kicked several inches of snow away from the garage door before he could even open it.

Helen watched him from the window.

She didn't look up the hill to see if there was a black car parked at the top of the cul-de-sac, or if the driver was still watching the house.

74 | Sandra

Sandra sat waiting.

Bloody Mary had been on her feet for an hour, a nervous, fidgety figure yet still imposing; her mass of grey hair went in all directions and had not seen a brush in years. She had attempted to get on to the radiator and then the windowsill three times in that hour, each time prevented by the increasingly bad-tempered nurse, each time acting as though she was sorry, embarrassed even, and would never do it again; only to repeat the exact same process within a quarter of an hour.

Sandra watched her, wondering what she was thinking. Wondering if she *was* thinking or whether she just repeated the same routine out of habit, much like the nurses whose job it was to look after her. She glanced over at Old Tony, watched as he moved his eyes right and left to see if the nurse was around, not ever realising how obvious or silly it made him look, before thrusting his hand down his trousers and underpants.

For once, she didn't watch the beach through the window. She didn't need to. Not today.

But it was now dark. She could see the white flakes of snow against the dark backdrop, and her reflection in the window, and she could remember eating at least once, maybe twice. Hadn't she said they were coming at midday?

She was suddenly aware of someone close and looked to her left to find Mary hovering in the way she sometimes did. Hunched over, not sure whether to speak or run.

'What do you want, Mary?' she asked her.

Mary shrugged. Her hands were covered in tiny cuts where she had tried to grip the windows in an attempt to climb out of them, despite the fact they were locked and hadn't been opened for years. Almost every day she reopened the wounds on her palms and fingers, and the dried blood would remain on them until a nurse washed it off before she went to bed.

'Sit down if you want to?' Sandra said, and to her surprise Mary did, like a naughty schoolgirl, eyes darting all over the place – anywhere but at the person opposite her.

Sandra looked at her. She didn't look at anyone as a rule, she hated eye-contact – had from the moment Jessica went missing and everyone started looking at her in the same accusing way; but there was no danger of that with Mary.

'My daughter is coming today,' she said, and Mary's eyes opened a little wider than they normally did, although Sandra had no idea if she had understood her or not. 'You don't know her, Mary. I don't either. I haven't seen her since she was this tall.'

Sandra held her hand at knee height. Mary seemed to shrug, but it might have just been a nervous twitch because she did that a lot too.

'I knew she was alive, though.'

Bloody Mary looked at her.

'I knew she hadn't drowned. Todd thought she had, but what did he know? He was reading the bloody paper when they took her. What do you say?'

Mary snorted and Sandra smiled.

'Exactly. But I knew she'd been taken. A mother knows, Mary. They said I was mad, can you believe that? That's why they put me in here.'

Mary looked uncomfortable and as though she was gearing up for another escape attempt.

'But I never gave up. Not in here.' Sandra put her finger on her chest where her heart was. 'That's why I stopped arguing.

That's why I stayed here, Mary. So I was in a place she could find me if she came back.'

Sandra looked outside again. It had been dark for a while now, she wasn't sure how long. Had the evening meal been served? She couldn't remember eating it if it had.

The nurse came over. Sandra looked around and, other than her and Mary, the room was empty, although she hadn't noticed a single person leave.

'Time for bed, ladies,' the nurse said, and Mary got to her feet obediently, like a well-trained Labrador, and shuffled off towards the corridor. 'And wash those hands. I don't want blood all over the bedclothes again.'

The nurse looked at Sandra.

'It's bedtime?'

The nurse nodded impatiently.

'I have to wait for my visitors.'

The nurse sucked her cheeks in, anticipating a difficult situation. 'I think it's a little late for visitors now, Sandra.'

'They've probably been held up, with this weather and everything.'

'I don't think they're coming now,' the nurse said.

Sandra's grip on the side of her armchair tightened. 'You don't understand. Someone important is coming today.'

The nurse raised her eyebrows and looked towards the door for back-up.

'They told me not to say anything,' Sandra continued, talking in little more than a whisper. 'But it's my…daughter.'

She waited for the nurse to display her amazement at this. But she only smiled. 'Come on, now, Sandra. It's after ten o'clock.'

'The reporter is bringing her. She promised she would.'

A member of staff from the reception opened the main doors and looked inside, exchanging a glance with the nurse.

'We'll talk tomorrow,' the nurse said, anxious to avoid a scene, 'but it's late and we need to get you to your room.'

'I'll go when I'm ready,' Sandra hissed, and pulled her hand away as the nurse tried to take it.

'Sandra! Please.'

'Leave me.'

The nurse looked at her and walked away. Sandra sat in her seat, determined not to move, but knowing full well that the nurse was right. No one was coming now.

The door opened, and the nurse returned with the receptionist and the manager. Sandra saw their reflection in the window. She didn't turn around.

'Takes three of you, does it?'

'Sandra, we can find out what happened in the morning.'

'I have to be here. What happens if they arrive and I'm not here?'

'Sandra!' the manager said loudly, losing patience.

'Just piss off!'

The three women exchanged glances and the receptionist took a small white box with a red cross on it from behind her back and handed it to the nurse. Sandra caught sight of it and her nostrils flared.

'Just let us help you,' the nurse said softly.

Sandra was suddenly aware that they were either side of her, and she felt an arm on hers, applying downward pressure; she tried to lift it but the receptionist held her in her seat.

'Stop!' She struggled, but they were too strong. 'Leave me…'

The nurse bent down and rummaged in the small white box. She stood upright, a syringe in her hand.

'You don't get it!'

'I know,' the nurse said softly.

'I need to be here when Jessica arrives.'

Sandra felt the briefest of pricks, sharp, in her arm and then the sensation of a soothing liquid coursing through her veins. 'No!' The room became blurry; the nurse's face became even blurrier still. 'You don't underst…'

Her head was heavy; beginning to fall to the side. She could just make out the out-of-focus image of a person, moving towards her. She heard the rumble of wheels. Felt them lift her up and lay her down, and then someone was pushing her, rolling her across the carpet.

She tried to speak but couldn't, and she gave up and let it all go black.

What was the point?

No one had cared twenty years ago.

Why would they care now?

75 | Laura

The top half of Laura's body shot upright in bed.

Sweat ran down her forehead. She reached around in the dark, panicking. Her eyes adjusted and she saw she was in her own room and the previous night began to come back to her. She'd gone up early, exhausted, and couldn't even remember getting into her pyjamas or putting her head on to the pillow.

'Shit!'

She was wide awake now. The image of Sandra being wheeled away made her feel like throwing up. She had forgotten to call High Cliffs; it had gone to the back of her mind when she'd seen her parents and she was so tired, it had stayed there.

The clock said five past one; there was nothing she could do until morning, so she lay there and then tried to go back to sleep but her brain was whirring with emotion and anger at her stupidity. She thought about Sandra, about how she'd have sat waiting by the window, about how she'd have wondered what was going on.

After an hour, she needed to go to the toilet. Her mother had supplied an endless flow of soup, tea and hot chocolate since she'd pulled up on the drive. She tiptoed out of the room, past the spare room – she couldn't even recall Danni going to bed – and into the bathroom.

When she got back to her bed she slowly climbed under the covers and tried to get back to sleep but it was too late: she could hear it, the low whining sound from below. The sound of four padded feet, the expectant tap-tap-tap of a tail against a door. She pulled her duvet over her head to drown it out, but it only seemed to get louder.

She stepped back out of bed, pulled her polo-neck jumper over her pyjama top and quietly crept downstairs so as not to wake anyone. When she opened the utility room door, Mimark was impatiently scratching the back door, and she tapped his backside and told him to shush. She kept a pair of old fur-lined boots in the cupboard for exactly this purpose, and, as she began to put them on, the dog excitedly headbutted her shins and wagged his tail.

'OK, OK,' she whispered. 'Give me a chance.'

She unlocked the door and turned the handle and the spaniel stepped cautiously through the opening and into the fresh snow in the garden, so deep in places that, when he stood still, his legs sank right in and he had to jump like a kangaroo to move around, which he managed to do, until he reached the garage. He relieved himself against the wall and then stopped and sniffed at the door, nudging his head against it and whimpering.

'What is it?' Laura called from the doorway.

Mimark didn't like anything coming into his garden and he had probably caught the scent of a cat or a squirrel, but she flipped the utility room's light switch so that enough light was cast on the garden to see what he was doing. She called him back but he ignored her. Sighing, she walked down towards the garage, trudging through the fresh snow that came up to the tops of her boots. There was nothing to suggest anything had been there, certainly no footprints in the fresh, undisturbed snow, and when she got there the dog had already forgotten it and was circling, ready to pee against the garage wall again, putting his head into the snow and eating mouthfuls before spitting them out.

Laura checked the door for her own peace of mind.

It was shut fast.

'Hello?' she said quietly, and felt foolish. She knew that if it was an animal they were hardly going to answer her. She grabbed Mimark by his collar. 'C'mon, pest,' she said, and led him back to the back door, stepping in her own footprints so no more snow fell into her boots. Inside, the dog climbed back into his basket, circled and lay down with a yawn. She locked the door, switched off the light and went back to bed.

But she was still awake two hours later.

It felt as if she'd been lying there for ever, and the image of Sandra was too heavy on her mind to let her rest. She got back up and went downstairs again, letting Mimark into the kitchen to stop him scratching the door, and started to warm some milk on the hob.

As she drank it, she stroked Mimark's ear as he sat beside her, and looked out of the kitchen window. The grey, snow-laden clouds had moved on; hundreds of flickering stars had replaced them, and a three-quarter moon lit the blanket of white on the ground. It was a sight that you rarely saw: no clouds, the clearest of skies, and snow, which only fell like this every two or three years. She went through to the utility room and opened up the back door to look properly. Mimark slid past her legs to have another wee.

'Beautiful, isn't it?' she said.

Mimark was at the garage door again, scratching and sniffing the ground around it. She called him in but he ignored her.

Laura cursed under her breath and pulled on her boots again. She didn't have her jumper on this time, and when she stepped out into the garden the chill of the clear night air took her breath away. The temperature had fallen another few degrees and the cold cut right through her pyjama top as she retraced her previous footsteps.

'Come on,' she said as she pulled Mimark's collar and yanked him towards her.

The dog pulled his head away, unimpressed by her intervention, and began sniffing the garage door, whimpering softly. Laura hesitated and looked back towards the house. 'Enough now,' she scolded, the icy chill hurting the exposed skin at her neck, and grabbed his collar again. As she leaned down to do so, she saw the footprint nearest the door.

It wasn't one of hers.

It was too big. It was in exactly the spot where she had stood, but a larger foot had made it; she could see that the edge was an inch wider than her original print.

She bent down to look properly, but when she got too close her body blocked the light from the moon and she had to find the right angle, almost on her hands and knees, to look at it with enough light to make out the tread.

It was a man's shoe.

She stepped back towards the house. Mimark had moved around in the snow so much that he'd erased most of the other prints but, as she checked each one that was still left, she found another that wasn't made just by her boot. And then another.

Laura stood still, her heart thumping in her chest. She slowly stepped back towards the garage, put her hand on the door handle and carefully pushed it down.

It opened. The door moved away from her, just a few inches and she held the handle tightly to stop it opening any more.

It had been locked when she tried it before. Hadn't it?

Her mind felt as if it was playing tricks on her.

Were they fresh prints, or had they been there before and she just hadn't noticed?

Laura's fingers trembled on the handle.

Then she pushed the door fully open and went inside.

76 | Laura

'Is anyone there?'

Laura stood just inside the entrance to the garage. Mimark trotted in too; she could hear his breathing and his paws on the concrete floor but it was pitch black in there beyond the doorway and she fumbled around with her hand for a light.

It struck her that she didn't know where the light was; she didn't know where anything was because she never went in the garage – never really had need to. Her eyes began to adjust; just corners and generic shapes were visible in the darkness at first, but she got a sense of where things were, and found the light switch half hidden by a large tool cupboard.

The strip-lights, two of them, one on each side of the large space, buzzed and came on. The light from them was dim at first, until the two lights warmed and began to get brighter and let her see properly.

It had originally been two garages, separated by a brick wall that the previous owners had put up, only for Robert to tear down when they'd bought the place in order to build head-high storage cupboards on one side. Typically, he had done the job with precision, with enough room for her mother's estate car to be able to fit neatly on one side, with the row of cupboards full of medical journals and Christmas decorations above it, while her father's own larger car was parked up against the nearside wall, reversed in to the width of a wing-mirror away so that there was enough space for them both to open their driver's doors and get in and out.

'Hello?'

Mimark let out a low growl and then sniffed the air and went back outside. Laura looked around, scanning the corners of the garage. To make herself feel better, she opened the tool cupboard positioned against the back wall and picked the largest item she could find – a heavy wrench – and closed the door.

She stepped forward.

'If anyone's here, the police are on their way.'

She listened. The only sound was from Mimark outside. She looked all around the garage again, trying to detect any slightest movement, but there was none. She felt foolish; her father had probably left something in the car and made the prints ages ago.

But something didn't feel right. Something was bothering her – her gut instinct was telling her to stay alert – so she walked over to her mother's car and looked inside, on the front and back seats, but it was completely empty. She stepped over to her father's car and looked through the driver's window, but it was also empty, the only movement the tiny red blinking light of the alarm.

Laura moved to the back window. This was harder to see through because it was tinted glass, and she had to put her face right up against it to see inside, but the back seat was empty too and she breathed out, gasping for oxygen as she realised she'd been holding her breath.

There was a noise behind her.

She spun around, the wrench rising to head height, ready to strike.

Mimark stood in the door, his tail wagging. Fresh snow all over his snout.

She let out a nervous giggle and breathed out, then put the wrench back in the cupboard. Water dripped from the dog's soggy coat as he walked past her and sniffed around. He lined up his body and lifted his hind leg, ready to pee up against the back wheel of her father's car, and she jumped towards him. 'Mimark, no!'

The dog looked up, stopped before he had done anything and then came back to her indignantly, and trotted back outside. She shook her head, took one last look around and turned off the light. The room was black again.

Something still wasn't right.

She put the light back on. The strip-lights buzzed and brightened much more quickly this time.

The garage looked the same. Her eyes darted around, and she thought that her eye had been caught by something but she wasn't sure what it was.

Her heart began to pound.

She looked into the corners. Her eyes scanned every inch, not seeing anything but her instincts were pushing her to continue looking. She went to her mother's car, stood behind it and bent down to look underneath.

Nothing.

She looked over to her father's car. Nothing looked any different. She went on to her haunches to look underneath. Nothing.

She went back to the door and shook her head, putting her hand on the light switch to plunge the garage back into darkness when, in the corner of her eye, she saw it. The back indicator light of her father's car.

There seemed to be a crack in it. It was barely noticeable: a jagged line across the orange plastic. Laura walked towards it.

The car was only a few inches from the wall, and there were some training weights and a gym bag on the floor, which she had to stand on and lean over to see properly.

It was definitely cracked. It was clear now and she followed it with her finger, tracing the line of it until she could no longer see it and had to rely on touch. The crack became a hole. She could feel the sharp edge of the plastic and, when she put her finger inside, she could feel the exposed bulb.

Laura stepped over the weights and put her head against the breeze block wall the car was parked against, just enough to see the rear wing of the car.

It was scratched. Paintwork was missing.

Her breathing became shallow.

She ran around to the front of the car. The headlight on the passenger side was also broken, as was the orange indicator casing next to it, which was smashed completely. There were deep gashes in the paintwork on the front wing, and when she put her ear against the wall and looked down the side of the car, as best she could with it being so close to the side wall, she saw dents and missing paintwork that stretched from the front wheel arch as far back as the rear one. It looked as if someone had taken to it with a wrecking ball.

Among the damage, she could just make out the tiniest flecks of red paint.

Her stomach tightened as if someone had tied a knot with it. She had to put her hands on her knees and her head down to steady her legs.

After a few moments Laura managed to lift her body back up. Her head was light and her legs swayed as she tried to move. She put her hands on the workbench to steady herself and hot tears began to fall slowly down her cheeks.

She tried to control her breathing.

Her mind was racing, her heart beating so quickly it hurt her chest, and she staggered towards the open door.

As she got to it, a dark shape appeared in the doorway.

It was Robert Grainger.

77 | Laura

Laura opened her eyes but her vision was blurry, everything around her had a fuzzy, unreal feel about it.

She coughed, and the taste in her mouth, sharp and surgical, made her want to be sick. She tried to move her hand to her mouth but it wouldn't budge. Both of her hands were behind her, and as she pulled them she realised that they were bound together; the more she struggled, the tighter whatever was holding them became.

Laura looked forward, the blur beginning to sharpen at the edges. She could make out a dashboard, a windscreen and a mirror. She was in a car – her father's car; she recognised the softness of the leather seat – and her legs were tied as well, at the ankles. She instinctively tried to get them free, but this made the bonds tighten around them as well.

She tried to pull herself upwards and forward, but there was another shackle, a bandage that had been put around her neck and the headrest, like a loose-fitting scarf; when she tried to move, it held her head in position, and stopped her moving it more than three or four inches forward. That was enough to see into the rear-view mirror, behind the car and towards the garage door, but there was no movement in the dimly lit space.

She called out but there was no reply.

Laura sat still, trying to think. Her head was throbbing and the smell of the chemical substance used to knock her out reeked throughout the car, so she could only take small intakes of breath. She strained her ears, trying to pick up any sound, and for a while there was nothing at all, but then she heard a faint shuffling and what sounded like a door closing. She turned her head to the right, and looked across to the wing mirror, which gave her a better line of sight to the doorway.

She saw her father come in, backwards. He was dragging something inside, something heavy from what she could make out. She cried out to him but he ignored her and continued what he was doing. Laura couldn't see any more until he got closer, under the strip-light, and rested his load on the concrete floor.

It was Danni. She was unconscious.

Laura gasped and watched as he stood up, straightened his back and moved away from her motionless body. When he came back, it was with more bandages, and he began binding her wrists and ankles.

'What are you doing?' she pleaded, but he worked on as if he she hadn't made a sound, tightening the bandages with several knots until it was impossible to undo them without a sharp object. Then he lifted Danni up by putting his hands under her armpits and dragged her to the car. He opened the driver's door.

'Dad!'

He looked at her, for only the briefest of moments, and then began lifting Danni up on to the driver's seat. The surgical smell that had begun to slowly leave the car returned with a vengeance and Laura felt vomit in her throat. Robert positioned Danni's body on the seat and swung her legs in under the steering wheel.

'Dad. Stop. Please.'

This time, he didn't look at Laura at all. He took another bandage from his pocket and put it around Danni's neck, feeding it around the back of the thin, metallic-coated supports that held the headrest in the seat, and tying a knot.

'Please, Dad.'

Emotionless, he leaned into the car and pushed the key into the ignition and turned it once, and all the dashboard lights came on, a mix of red and orange symbols.

Laura tried to keep as calm as she possibly could. 'Dad. You don't have to do this.'

Her father pushed the button to open the electric window behind Danni's head. He let it go down a fraction and then back up until there was the smallest of gaps, and then went to his tool cupboard at the back of the garage.

Laura strained her neck to see him as he reached up to the top shelf, and when he turned around he was holding a long piece of flexible rubber tubing, tightly coiled.

She struggled in her seat, the bindings around her wrists digging in more as she moved her hands from side to side, hoping to find a way to prise them free. She looked at Danni's face, peaceful and oblivious, and for the briefest of moments she felt envious.

Then she tried to scream, but the drowsiness from the chloroform made it sound more like a pitiful yelp.

Robert didn't flinch. He walked to the back of the car and after a few seconds she heard the unmistakable sound of tape being ripped off a roll. Laura watched through the side mirror, tears beginning to slowly trickle down her face, as he came from behind the car and went to the rear window and fed the rubber pipe into the thin gap he had made in the back window.

'Dad!'

He paused, or at least she thought he did, then walked back behind the car.

'Why are you doing this?'

'Doing what?'

The voice was groggy, confused. Laura turned her neck and saw Danni's eyes opening, blinking rapidly, no doubt encountering the same blurred shapes she had seen a few minutes ago.

'Danni.'

Danni tried to turn, but the binding around her neck was tighter than Laura's. She coughed and gagged as the smell and taste of the chloroform invaded her senses. 'What…?' She struggled to free her hands and legs, writhing on the seat, her knees hitting the steering wheel.

'Don't. It just makes it worse.'

'What's happening?'

Danni was getting her bearings. Her eyes widened as she saw the inside of the car. She turned her neck as much as she could to see Laura in the same predicament as she was and her face seemed to cave in on itself, as if her brain had imploded with an overload of information that made no sense whatsoever.

'What's happening?'

Laura turned her head to face her.

She didn't know what to say.

78 | Danni

Danni struggled desperately in the seat.

She tried to pull her hands apart and slide her left ankle away from the right, but the bindings dug into her skin and got even tighter.

'I told you it's no use.'

Laura felt calm. She'd had a little longer to see what was happening but there was also a level of understanding that Danni didn't yet have. Laura had seen it all unfold; not just this but the email, the threat, the chase, the attack on her mother.

It had all been for her.

'We lost. I lost.'

'Lost?'

Danni wriggled, trying to get her knees upwards, on to the seat. She was upset; scared witless but more angry, and Laura saw a wildness in her eyes she hadn't seen before.

Robert opened the driver's door. Danni's eyes widened and she slumped momentarily, as if this was yet more new information in a sea of detail that she already couldn't comprehend, then she heaved her shoulders forward, trying to bite his arm. The noose around her neck stopped her.

He turned the car's key one extra rotation.

The engine came to life.

Laura took a deep breath.

'You don't need to do this, Dad. We can work it out.'

There wasn't a flicker of emotion on his face. There was sweat, Laura could see it on his brow and smell it; but then he had carried Danni from the house. His face looked exactly as it always did, but she couldn't recognise anything else about the man. His eyes were lifeless, fixed forward but looking at nothing. Laura knew he didn't want to see her, look in her eyes; that would make it too real.

'Robert! Dad! Please!'

The first trace of exhaust fumes reached her nose and she gasped, closing her mouth tightly and looking at her father, or at least the man she'd always thought of as her father. In her head, all she could recall was an article that Kelly had written a few months ago about a local councillor who'd tried and failed to commit suicide. She remembered Kelly telling her that she'd researched and found that more modern car engines were not as effective a method of taking your own life as older models, because of all the EU-imposed emissions regulations. She remembered Kelly holding court and recounting the facts to the rest of the office, and the sidebar to her story that explained how the regulations had saved the man's life.

If Kelly's article was accurate, she knew they had a few minutes, maybe as many as seven or eight, before they lost consciousness.

Danni was screaming now.

'Don't scream, you'll take in more fumes.'

Danni stopped and looked at Laura, unable to understand her relative calm demeanour. 'Why is he doing this?'

Laura realised she still didn't know.

'He's keeping the truth about Jessica hidden.'

Danni heard it but Laura wasn't sure she understood.

'What's that got to do with…?'

'Danni, *I'm* Jessica!'

Laura could see her eyes acknowledge it, but she still made little sense of things. 'So why did my dad—'

Laura cut her off as she felt her throat begin to fill up with the toxic fumes that were drifting around the car, making their heads feel lighter by the second. 'This has nothing to do with you or your dad.'

Danni closed her eyes. Laura knew she had realised that she was going to die for nothing. That she wasn't even connected to Jessica's disappearance. Laura hoped it would comfort her if her final thoughts were to know that her father hadn't taken her from a beach and lied to her for more than twenty years.

'You…?'

Danni's head began to slump. Laura felt the drowsiness began to take her too. She lay back in the seat and held her breath. In the side mirror, she saw Robert standing in the doorway.

Watching them die.

She wanted to hate him; but, for a reason she didn't even know, she couldn't. She felt sorry for him, and even sorrier for Danni. The other girl had stopped crying and had closed her eyes; Laura suspected she'd accepted what was going to happen and just wanted it over.

Laura knew she might as well do the same.

She took one last look at the man in the door and was about to close her eyes.

Then Robert suddenly lurched forward, stumbling into the garage behind the car. He was staggering, arms flailing at first, and then he put his hands to his face and let out a cry. Laura stretched every muscle in her neck to see what was happening.

In the doorway, she could see Helen.

Robert put a hand on the back of his car to steady himself. Laura saw Helen move towards him. She held something up in the air, red at the top with yellow writing on it: the defence spray. She sprayed Robert in the face again and he screamed out and was trying to walk towards her, his arms out in front like Frankenstein's monster, trying to feel his way forward.

Laura took the tiniest gasp of air into her lungs and held her breath again.

'Danni! Hold your breath!'

Laura watched as Helen easily sidestepped her husband's blind attack. The woman she had always believed was her mother calmly opened the tool cupboard behind her as Robert turned at the door and made another attempt to reach her.

'Danni!'

Laura watched as Helen brought something down on his head and saw Robert's body fall to the floor in a heap.

Danni opened her eyes. The car was full of fumes now but suddenly doors were opening, the front one first and then the rear one, and much-needed oxygen raced inside. Laura gulped as much of it as her wide-open mouth could take in.

Helen put the wrench on to the floor, leaned inside the car and turned off its engine. Danni spluttered and coughed, sucking in cleaner air. Helen put her hand in her pocket and took out a small kitchen knife and began cutting the bandages.

'It's over,' was all she said to them.

79 | Helen

'The police are on their way. If they can get through this snow.'

Helen helped Laura out of the car. Danni was already out and standing behind them, her hands holding on to the tool cupboard as she tried to control her dizziness. She coughed as if she was trying to bring something up, but nothing came.

Beside her, Robert lay unconscious, blood already drying in his greying hair and matting it together. Helen bent down and tied one of the discarded bandages around his ankles. 'Just to make sure,' she said, looking at Laura, who was leaning on the car bonnet with both hands until the feeling came back in her legs.

Laura looked around at Helen, and then at Robert's body on the floor. She wasn't sure how, but she was calm – certainly calmer than Danni, who was crying again and demanding answers from no one in particular.

Helen was avoiding looking at Laura, and was tying extra knots in the bandages to give her something to focus on.

'Why?' Laura said quietly.

Helen stopped what she was doing and looked down.

'I always wanted a little girl,' she said in little more than a whisper. 'Nothing I can say excuses all this but I was in a different place back then. Miscarriage after miscarriage, expensive IVF treatments, but I'd never given up hope. But then they said I couldn't, that I would never...'

She looked up, risking a glance at Laura.

'I don't know what I was thinking that day. I was supposed to be at the shops, but something drew me to that beach instead. Then I saw you, walking on your own.'

Laura stared at her.

'I spoke to you. You looked like you were lost. Or maybe I wanted you to be lost, I don't know, but I talked to you and I held your hand and, something just…well. So I took you.'

'Just like that?'

Helen nodded.

'I just shut out everything. I put you in the car, drove off, and next thing I knew we were on the drive and you were asking for the ice-cream I'd promised you.'

Laura sniffed. It sounded so simple the way she said it: more like an oversight than abduction.

'Your father was…'

'My father?'

Danni looked over. Laura stared at Helen and she took a while to answer.

'Robert was shocked. I don't think I'll ever really know what I did to him that day, but he did what he did to protect me. It's not his fault.'

Laura looked at him, lying on the concrete. 'He was going to kill me.'

'He got desperate. He'd tried everything. He tried anything to stop you finding out. He sent the email. Got that boy to threaten you. He never wanted it to come to this.'

Laura looked at the tiny trace of a fading scar on Helen's face.

'Did he beat you up?'

Helen looked down. 'We thought it might work.'

She seemed to wince. Danni snorted behind them and Laura shook her head. 'You must have known it might come to this.'

'At the beginning, we thought something might happen just about every day. We lived in constant fear; didn't let you out of the house for two years. We moved hundreds of miles away, we lost our accents, got false ID for you. He tried to cover every base. Then…'

'Then?'

'It got easier,' she continued, head down. 'People stopped looking for you. They thought you were dead.'

Laura thought about Sandra, sitting in her chair, looking out on to the beach. 'Not everyone.'

'That was what we'd dreaded. We'd done so much to keep it hidden, and then that girl went missing and you went to work on the story. We didn't know what to do, and then you said you were going to see that woman.'

'*That woman* happens to be my mother.'

Laura felt a sudden anger rise through her body. She could see Helen was crushed, not caring what happened to herself now, and she couldn't help feeling sorry for her.

Helen took a deep breath; she looked ashamed. 'Sorry. Your m-mother,' Helen stuttered; the words sounded painful for her to say. 'We couldn't believe it was happening.'

'You didn't try to stop me.'

'What excuse could we have given for not wanting you to go? And it would only have made you want to even more.'

'It would.'

'We just hoped that nothing came of it. That you'd write your story and it would all be forgotten about in a few weeks.'

She turned and looked over at Danni.

'Then I came forward,' Danni said flatly.

Helen nodded. 'We knew you'd not stop after that.'

'Unless you stopped me.'

'You'd found your story.' She looked across, her face ashen. 'You just didn't know how much it really was *your* story.'

Laura closed her eyes.

'It's why we never wanted you to be a journalist. We knew that, if you had a job where you were always asking questions, you might ask the right ones eventually. When you wouldn't give it up, your dad got you a job with David so you were local and we could…'

She looked down again.

'Keep an eye on me?'

The sound of vehicles interrupted them. A siren, and what sounded like at least two cars, maybe more.

'They're here,' Helen said, and looked at Laura, tears filling her eyes. 'I'm sorry. I just want you to know that.'

Laura could see a flashing blue light reflecting off the snow in the gap under the garage door and footsteps outside, crunching over frozen snow. She heard some outside the door, while others filed off towards the gate and the back door.

'This is the police,' a voice called loudly.

Laura went to the front of the garage and pressed the button that opened the door electronically. It rolled up and three police offers clambered in before it reached anywhere near head-height – only to find that the scene was far from the one they anticipated. Two of them ran past Laura towards Helen and Danni, while the third stopped to check Laura wasn't hurt as another officer, a female one, joined them. She asked questions, but Laura's head spun and she only heard a garbled noise as she stumbled out on to the drive with the officer steadying her arm.

There were two cars parked at the top of the drive, and an ambulance behind them waiting for the occupants of the front car to clear the snow and open the gates. As one of them did it, another car arrived, a 4x4 with its lights flashing, and three more officers jumped out and ran down to the house. They quickly established that the scene was already secure.

'Are you hurt?'

The female officer was looking at Laura and she shook her head. They walked up the driveway and the officer helped her into the back of the police car nearest the house. She sat there and closed her eyes, feeling the soreness on her wrists and ankles, and when she opened her eyes again she could see the red grooves where the bindings had dug into her skin and scraped some of it away.

Another officer led Danni from the garage, a blanket wrapped around her shoulders, and helped her into a different car. She looked over at Laura but was expressionless. In the other three houses in the cul-de-sac, Laura watched curtains and blinds moving as the neighbours feasted on the unfolding events.

They would have no idea what was happening, she thought. But they would soon find out, and they'd be shocked that a child missing for more than twenty years would turn out to be the girl next door.

Helen Grainger was handcuffed and being led up the driveway towards the 4x4 by two officers. She looked over at Laura, and their eyes met for a second, but then Laura looked away and Helen put her head down as she was helped into the back seat and the door closed behind her, the tinted glass hiding her now, and the 4x4 pulled away.

The car Danni was in left shortly afterwards, allowing the ambulance to reverse down the driveway and stop just outside the garage door. Laura watched as the paramedic in the garage knelt over Robert and then one of his colleagues joined him and they began moving the unconscious man on to a stretcher.

The female officer had been talking to two other officers, who were now stationed outside the house. She walked over and climbed into the passenger seat.

'We're off,' she said.

'My dog, is he OK?'

'He's in good hands, don't worry.'

Laura gave her a weak smile. The officer buckled up and the driver started the engine. The snow was deep and they had to carefully stay within the tracks that were there as they began to move away from the house, while a third officer outside the house began sealing up the area with yellow crime-scene tape.

Laura glanced back, just in time to see the paramedics bringing the stretcher with Robert on it out of the garage and towards the back of the ambulance.

She closed her eyes and the police car pulled out of the cul-de-sac.

80 | Laura

The snow made the short journey to the police station into a much longer one.

It was still fairly dark when they pulled up outside, but the first hints of sunlight creeping up over the horizon were evident as the female officer helped Laura from the car and into the small local station, a rectangular building near the centre of the village that was little more than a series of offices around a main reception area.

Laura looked for the other cars, the ones with Danni and Helen in, but she couldn't see them; she wasn't even sure they'd be brought to the same place anyway, and probably not to somewhere as small as this.

The clock behind the reception desk said it was a few minutes after seven as Laura was led straight through the door into the inner sanctum and put in a small waiting room with three chairs around a cheap wooden table that had a copy of the previous day's *Gazette* on it. Against one wall was a small blue sofa, and Laura sat down on it and waited, drifting off occasionally when she put her head back on to the soft cushion, only to be woken by her dreams: the faces of Danni, Helen and most of all Sandra, until an officer put his head around the door and asked her if she'd like a drink while she waited.

'What's happening?' she said. The officer said he didn't know but ran through a list of drinks available from the station's vending machine, and she asked for coffee, which he

415

brought. Another hour passed and she only saw the officer once more, when he collected her empty cup and said someone – he didn't know who – would be with her shortly.

After another forty-five minutes he came in again but couldn't give her much more of an update. 'The snow's caused havoc on the roads,' he offered as a reason, and left it at that.

The room was square, windowless and stuffy. There was a noticeboard behind the sofa with a few addiction helplines and business cards pinned to it, and Laura began reading them to pass the time, but her head wasn't ready for reading. It was a full of questions, feelings, contradictions; things she didn't even want to think about and tried to force back out of her mind.

The officer came in again, this time with a cup of tea in a white china cup, rattling on a white saucer. 'I made you one. Better than the rubbish from the machine.'

'Where's Danni?'

The officer placed her cup down and gave Laura a look that told her he wasn't in a position to answer. He was tall and slightly overweight, with an ill-fitting shirt, a salt-and-pepper beard, and kind eyes that looked as though he would like to say more if he could.

'Is she all right? Is anyone with her?'

The officer smiled and looked around, to visibly demonstrate to her that he was revealing information he wasn't supposed to. 'She's at another station.'

'Can I talk to her?'

'I think they want a statement from you first.'

'When? I've been here for hours,' said Laura, frustrated.

'There's only two of us on duty. We don't normally see anything like this, so they're sending in the big boys from the city.'

Laura raised her eyebrows.

'I'm sure they'll be here soon.'

Laura sipped her tea. The officer hovered around for a few more seconds and then left her alone. She slumped back on the sofa and groaned. Fatigue was trying to take over her body. She didn't want to sleep but it was impossible to stop herself; it felt as though the last time she'd slept soundly was a week ago or more, and after a few minutes she fell into a fidgety slumber, the kind you had just before you woke in the morning, where your dreams were so vivid it was impossible to tell if they were real or not.

She was standing on golden sand, with the sea no more than a hundred yards away and seagulls filling the air with their cries. It was a sunny day, not a single cloud in the sky, and she could feel the heat from the sun on her skin. There were people everywhere, a silly number really, too many for the size of the beach, moving in all directions; she was trying to get through them but it was like being on a packed underground train, and she was unable to move, unable to get to where she wanted to go; she wasn't sure where that was anyway.

Then the crowds cleared. Almost by magic. It was just her now, her bare feet on hot sand, powdery between her toes, looking towards the horizon where the sun was in the sky above the green hills.

Only she could no longer see the sun. It was blocked. A dark silhouette was standing in front of it, getting closer, covering the bright ball of light behind it until only a golden glow could be seen around the edge. The silhouette spoke to her. 'Hello, sweetheart. Are you lost…?'

'Laura, Laura.'

The police officer was in front of her, blocking out the light.

She jumped up and felt moisture on the side of her mouth; she had dribbled as she'd slept and she wiped it with her sleeve. The officer was close; his beard was moving, his mouth opening and closing, but she couldn't quite work out what he was saying or where she was. There was someone with him – not a police colleague. It looked like a nurse; they had an apron on.

'What's...?'

'They need to take a DNA sample,' the officer said, resting his big hand on her arm.

Laura looked at the nurse.

'I need a swab from your mouth,' she said.

Laura looked at the police officer, who gave her a reassuring nod. The nurse had something in her hand and was approaching from the side. 'Open wide.'

Laura closed her eyes.

81 | Danni

With more than a dozen abandoned cars and several minor accidents to pass, it had taken more than an hour for the police car with Danni in it to reach the station, a modern, newly built eco-building on the edge of the nearest main town.

They'd pulled into the car park just as Helen was being led from the 4x4 she'd been in and through the main doors, and Danni noted that the driver deliberately waited a minute before pulling into a space, to allow time for the older woman to be processed and taken out of sight before Danni was also ushered through the reception area. She was shown into a small windowless office which looked as though it belonged to the station manager. It had a desk, with a smart leather chair on one side and a less fancy one on the other. There was a metal filing cabinet next to the door and a photograph of a man and woman with two small children. Danni sat and waited, occasionally having drinks brought to her, for almost two hours.

'Has anyone spoken to my dad?' she asked the constable who had been tasked with bringing in the refreshments.

'Someone will be with you shortly.'

'Where's Laura? Is she OK?'

Same answer.

Danni buried her head on her hands. Although she'd had time for everything to sink in, it didn't seem to make any of it better. That she'd almost died was almost the last thing on her mind; it was the damage she'd done before, which was maybe irreparable, that was really bothering her.

Another drink. More questions. No answers other than for the constable to stall for more time. Then after another hour she heard voices outside, coming up the corridor. She stood up and put her ear to the door, trying to listen to them, but they had stopped. Then the handle turned and she jumped back. An officer showed someone inside.

It was her father.

'Dad!' she shouted, and dived into his arms.

'I'll let you have some time together,' the policeman said, and left the room, closing the door behind him.

'I came as soon as they called.'

Danni held him tightly for a few minutes, not wanting to let go, but he stepped back and put his hands on her shoulders, looking into her tear-filled eyes.

'I'm so sorry, Dad,' she said.

'No, I am,' he replied. 'I shouldn't have reacted like that.'

'I should never have said what I did.'

'I tried to find you. I looked everywhere.' He took her hands and squeezed them. 'Danni, what you said…you must know I could never have hurt your mum.'

'I got it into my head that it wasn't an accident. I got a lot of things into my head.'

'It's natural to want to find someone to blame in those circumstances.'

'And when the car tried to run us off the road I couldn't help but…'

Her father smiled sympathetically and squeezed her shoulders. 'You were grieving. We both were.'

Danni cleared her throat and the tears rolled down her cheeks. If ever there was a time for complete honesty, this was it.

'I thought you'd done another terrible thing too,' she gulped. 'I thought you and Mum had abducted me.'

He didn't look as horrified, or surprised, as she'd thought he would.

'I know about Mum's operation,' she added, and he nodded slowly. Danni didn't elaborate on how she knew; that didn't matter now. 'So I know she wasn't my real mother. And if you didn't abduct me, then what? Am I adopted?'

She thought he looked like a waxwork at Madame Tussaud's: a lifelike replica of the man she knew but frozen in the moment, staring ahead but not seeing, listening but not hearing.

'Dad?'

He seemed to suddenly realise where he was, and blinked several times. He looked at her, his face a mass of frown lines and anguish. His grip on her hands became firmer, his skin sweaty and clammy.

'She said you'd have to find out one day,' he whispered, finding it difficult to look at her but clearly knowing he had to.

Danni felt a chill; it ran from the top of her neck right down her body, and her stomach churned. Pieces of the jigsaw puzzle began falling into place. Then, as quickly as it came on, her insides settled and she felt a calm inner peace settling over her, as if she'd been looking for one final piece and suddenly, it was right there; under her nose all the time.

She looked at her father – a tear had started rolling down on to his cheek – and she nodded.

'Julie,' she said softly. 'She's my mother, isn't she?'

82 | Danni

It wasn't a question.

Or, if it was, it was a rhetorical one. She didn't need his confirmation, although it was written in his eyes anyway. She'd saved him having to tell her. The only thing left was to understand what had happened.

Her father sat down. Danni wasn't sure if he looked as if his world had come tumbling down, or as if a weight had lifted from him, but either way he looked older, weary and beaten. He took three deep breaths, each time trying to speak and then pausing and breathing again until he finally felt ready. Then he put his hands on his face and dragged them down until they reached his chin, stretching the flesh on his cheekbones.

'We never wanted you to find out like this.'

'You didn't want me to find out at all.'

'It's not like that, Danni. How do you tell a girl that her mum isn't really her mum? Or that the sister she never knew was? It's not as straightforward as you think. Your mum and I could never agree on it. And when she died...'

His voice began to crack.

'What I told you about Julie was true. Your mum was very young when she had her, we struggled to bring her up, she got into a lot of trouble and she died.'

Danni didn't say anything. She pulled the other chair from behind the desk until it was in front of her father and sat down on it, and took his hands.

'Your mum always blamed herself, thought she should have been a better mother.'

'She was young. You both were.'

'In those days, there wasn't the support people have now. We did our best but, as Julie got older, she became...' he mumbled '...rebellious, lost; angry.'

Danni gripped his hand a little tighter.

'We had always wanted more children. We even thought a brother or sister might calm Julie down. But with all the problems, even though we tried, it didn't happen.'

Danni nodded.

'Then, one day, your mum started having a lot of pain – you know, down there. They said it was related to having Julie when she was so young and they did some tests.'

'And?'

'They said her ovaries had been damaged and she was unlikely to get pregnant again.'

'So she had the hysterectomy?'

He nodded sadly.

'A partial one. We'd all but given up on having another baby anyway, and, although it broke her heart, the operation was for the best. She was in so much pain.'

'It must have been terrible.'

'The pain went away and instead she became more and more depressed. She thinks that was what drove Julie away in the end.'

'Away?'

'She was a wreck. She couldn't look after a teenage daughter, especially one who had so many issues. Julie was sixteen, she'd been virtually kicked out of school, was mixing with the wrong people who had got her into all kinds of drugs, and then there was all this going on at home. One day, she said she had an interview at the Careers Office, left the house and we didn't see her again.'

'Ever?'

He shook his head. 'She'd taken some clothes and emptied her building society account. We searched for her, got in touch with everyone in her circle of so-called friends, but they either didn't want to tell us or they didn't know themselves. She didn't want to be found.'

'So Mum contacted a missing persons charity?'

'What?'

Danni's body was shaking. She didn't answer and let him continue.

'So for two years we heard nothing other than a card at Christmas saying she was all right and not to worry. But the next Christmas, there was no card.'

'What happened?'

'I said she'd probably decided to make a complete break, but your mum knew it was more than that. We called people and tried to find a way to contact her but it was hopeless. And then, on the New Year's Eve, in the afternoon, there was a knock at the door.'

He composed himself. A tear formed in Danni's eye.

'It was this lad, eighteen maybe, with this little girl in his arms.'

A large tear ran down his face. Danni fought back hers.

'Julie had left because she was pregnant. She was scared to tell us so she and this lad went to live with his mother in Weston. They had lived hand-to-mouth but she just couldn't stay off the drugs. She'd become an addict, he told us.'

'Is that how she died?'

He nodded. 'She overdosed. The day before. Died before the ambulance got to her. This lad's mother said he had to come and tell us, and that he should bring you with him.'

Danni winced. Her whole body was shaking.

'He told us what had happened, what hospital Julie had been taken to, and he more or less begged us to take you and of course we did. He handed over this bag with a few clothes and a doll and we never saw or heard from him again.'

Danni wiped her eye.

'Mum took you upstairs, gave you a bath and put you to bed. You were not even three years old and you didn't make a fuss at all. I went to see Julie's body at the hospital and, when I got back, we sat up all night talking about what to do. We'd lost a daughter and found out we were grandparents in all of about five minutes. But we knew Julie would have wanted us to make sure we didn't make the same mistakes as we did with her, so that's what we set out to do.'

Danni's eyes widened.

'Your mum said it was a second chance; that we owed it to Julie. We always said we'd wait till you were old enough to really understand and then tell you.'

'But?'

'The older you got, the more you became our *daughter*. We never thought of you as anything else in the way we raised you. When you got to fourteen, Mum said we should tell you, but it was me that persuaded her to leave things as they were.'

'How come?'

'You were happy. It seemed wrong to just rip up everything you knew and believed, and I couldn't see what good would come from it.'

'You did what you both thought was best.'

'What *I* thought was best. We hadn't told anyone. We moved house and just kept up the pretence; no one knew any differently and I began to think it was better, for you and for us, if you never knew.'

He hesitated. Another tear formed in his eye and began to roll down his cheek.

'Your mum wasn't comfortable with it. It really made her so unhappy; she always hated living with the secret. The longer it went on, the worse she got; I worried what she might do. She thought that you had the right to know, which was true of course, and we ended up disagreeing about it, which made her feel even worse. I said that we should wait. And then, after her accident, I didn't know what to do. You'd already lost your mum. How could I tell you about Julie after that?'

'I don't blame you.'

'Then you began asking questions, understandably, and I didn't have the answers. No birth certificate that I could let you see, no photos. I knew you had to know the truth, but I didn't know how to tell you.'

'I understand.'

Danni wasn't sure he even heard her. He was staring ahead, his eyes glazed over as he opened his heart up. A tear fell down her cheek too and she looked at Thomas. His eyes were hollow. He looked completely crushed.

'I was scared I would lose you too.'

'You won't lose me. You did the right thing.'

'What?' It seemed as if he was finally hearing her.

'I needed parents. Of course I wish Julie hadn't died, she gave birth to me, but she couldn't look after me. I never knew her or...'

'We just wanted you to have a normal life.'

'And I did have. You and Mum couldn't have done any more for me. When I needed it most, you gave me everything and more.'

They both stood up and began to cry as they hugged each other tightly.

'As far as I'm concerned,' said Danni, pulling him closer, 'you're my dad. You always have been and you always will be.'

83 | Laura

Laura sat on the sofa, her tongue constantly finding the side of her mouth where they'd taken the swab from, the way it always did for the few hours after you'd had treatment at the dentist.

She waited, although she was no longer entirely sure what she was waiting for, and she could still smell the surgical bag they'd put the blue cotton-tipped swab-stick into, even though it had been more than twenty minutes since the bearded policeman had shown the nurse out. Another half-hour passed; she began re-reading some of the stories in the paper, and she was about to call out and try to get some answers when the bearded officer came back in with a friendly smile.

'You OK, love?'

'Not really.'

He smiled sympathetically and nodded. 'Thought not. You'd better come with me, then. You're on the move.'

He led Laura into the corridor and to the reception area she'd first arrived at, which now seemed a long time ago. A blonde woman with a sharp face who introduced herself as Detective Constable Wicks was standing next to the desk. She held out her hand and shook Laura's, while apologising for the time she'd been kept waiting, blaming procedure and the snow. She also told Laura they were taking her to another station, a larger one, where she could see Danni and finally give a statement.

'What about Sandra?' Laura asked.

'We're working on that.' The detective refused to commit and ushered Laura towards the exit door.

'You take care now,' the friendly officer called as she left the building, and she gave him a nod and goodbye wave as DC Wicks closed the door behind her.

The drive was only twelve miles, but the problems on the roads made for a slow and frustrating journey. The detective spent much of it muttering under-her-breath expletives at other drivers who weren't as capable in the snowy conditions as she was.

'What happens now?'

The detective glanced at Laura in her rear-view mirror. 'We need to get a statement, first and foremost,' she said, 'and, after that, I suppose we just go from there.'

'Go from there?'

The detective smiled. 'This is a new one for me, for everyone actually, so one step at a time.'

Laura nodded. It was new for her too.

They pulled on to the gritted black tarmac car park of a shiny new police station and Wicks led Laura into its reception area, where they were greeted, logged in by a desk sergeant and shown to a door at the side of the reception hatch that he buzzed open. It opened on to a corridor with three doors on either side. 'Room Four,' he said to the detective, and they walked down towards the last one on the left.

'Don't I get a phone call?' Laura said as they reached it.

Wicks laughed. 'You're not under arrest.'

'So can I make a call?'

The detective looked around; they were alone in the corridor and the door had closed behind them. She took her mobile phone from her pocket and handed it to Laura. 'Nothing controversial. Just a quick *hello and I'm all right*, OK? Do you know the number?'

Laura nodded. She dialled the *Gazette*. Sue answered; her surprise at hearing Laura's voice was obvious.

'Is David there, Sue?' Laura knew he would be. It was almost nine and David would have been at his desk for at least an hour and a half by that time. She asked Sue to transfer her, telling her it was important, and David's PA obliged.

'Laura? How are—?'

'David. I can't speak for long. I just needed to tell you something.'

Wicks looked at her and frowned.

'Yes?' said the editor.

'I'm Jessica Preston.'

The words, almost shouted rather than spoken, caught in her throat. Wicks tried to swipe the phone from her grasp but Laura ducked away. Through the handset, David Weatherall's voice was asking her to repeat what she had said. The detective glared at her, grabbing her wrist and holding it in a vice grip.

'Jessica Preston! I'm the child that was taken, David. Print it!' she shouted as the detective yanked the phone from her hand and ended the call.

'What are you playing at?'

'I wouldn't be here if it weren't for him.'

Laura stared at the detective, who shook her head and put her phone back in her pocket and shrugged. 'I guess it's going to come out anyway.'

They walked down to Room Four and, as Wicks pushed the door open to let Laura in, another door opened at the top of the corridor behind them and the desk sergeant came through, surprised to see they were still there. Wicks looked at him and tried to usher Laura inside the interview room, but she heard a voice and shrugged her off.

'Can someone tell me what I'm doing here?'

The voice was so distinctive. It was a woman's; weary, and more than a little angry too. Laura had heard it so many times recently, she didn't need to look, but she did anyway.

Sandra Preston walked through the door at the end of the corridor, followed by a uniformed officer.

'If we can just get to the interview room, Mrs Preston,' the officer said softly, 'we can explain everything in there.'

Sandra looked up. At first she didn't react when she saw them, and was about to argue with the officer, and then she did a double-take. 'You!'

Laura froze to the spot.

'Mrs Preston,' the officer was saying, looking up and seeing Laura and the detective still in the corridor ahead of him. He tried to put an arm on Sandra's shoulder but she pulled clear and began marching towards them.

DC Wicks stood in front of Laura outside Room Four.

'You!' Sandra shouted loudly, quickening her steps. 'Where is she?'

'Mrs Preston...'

The officer was a couple of paces back now and DC Wicks stepped into Sandra's path, communicating with a simple look for the officer to leave her be.

'You said you were bringing my daughter to me!' Sandra Preston reached Wicks and looked over her shoulder at Laura, her eyes raging with anger and frustration. Laura realised she'd never seen her face like this before – she was usually looking out of the window and sideways on, but now she could see all her features. She was only a few feet away, and Wicks stepped aside. 'You said you were bringing my daughter!' Sandra shouted, her words echoing around the corridor. 'You said you'd bring her to me!'

The policeman and the detective looked at each other but didn't move.

Sandra stopped right in front of Laura. She put her face right up close, and Laura stood her ground, staring back, unable to find any words.

And, for the very first time, Sandra Preston looked directly into her eyes.

Epilogue

You know, now I'm actually here it's not as bad as I imagined it would be.

I'm in a cell of my own and I spend hours in the library reading, or on the computer, or talking to the librarian, Mrs Aston, and so far she hasn't judged me or, if she has, she's not shown it. The routine's there but I also get to exercise for at least an hour a day. There are no monsters screaming my name in the dark, or ambushing me in the showers.

OK, so it's only been three months; who knows how I'll feel after a year or more? But this is my new home now – for the next ten years with good behaviour – so thank goodness it's not the hell I've seen in my nightmares.

When I came around in the ambulance, and found my hands in cuffs and fastened to a stretcher, and as one of the police officers in there with me read me my rights and informed me that I was under arrest for the abduction and unlawful imprisonment of Jessica Preston, I was actually thankful that I wasn't under arrest for her murder.

I had no recollection of what had happened – the last thing I remembered was Helen standing in front of me in the garage doorway – but I felt the pain from the cut on my head, which ended up taking eight stiches to close, and the stinging in my eyes from where she'd sprayed me. I think the police officers must have thought I was mad, grinning like the proverbial Cheshire cat, as we reached the secure hospital where they sewed up the opening in my head.

But then, they didn't realise I was finally free.

Free from the lies. Well, almost. I just had one more to tell.

In the hospital room, the police hung around while the doctor stitched me up and told them I probably needed to rest before they began questioning me. No, I told him, I was ready to tell them everything.

I began by saying that my wife had been suffering with severe depression when she took the child that day. Which was very true. She'd had three miscarriages in the previous two years, we'd had all the tests, tried IVF, and then she'd finally been told she'd never be able to have children, so she hadn't been in control of her actions on that beach. I told them that when she got back, when I saw what she had done, I was the one who had said we should keep her even though she begged me to take them both back to the beach, or to the police, at that very moment. I told them that she had wanted to confess her crime then, and for more than twenty years since, but that I had always stopped her. That I had been desperate for a child, but also because I wanted to keep us both out of prison. I told them I was a controlling and intimidating husband of whom she lived in perpetual fear, so much so that she would probably try to take the blame herself when they questioned her. I admitted that when the truth began to surface she had wanted us to hand ourselves in, even that late on, but that I had threatened and eventually beat her to prevent that happening. The medical records were there to prove it; they just needed to check. I told them I had become consumed by the secret and would have done anything to keep it hidden. That I had long since crossed the line, and would have continued to cross it had my wife not had to use a wrench to stop me. My wife had saved lives.

Because of what I said, and her intervention, they gave Helen less than two years – just under ten months' jail time if she co-operates – for her part in this. And of course she'll do as she's told. It's a chance to start again. Without me. I don't think she'll ever put a foot out of line again.

Everything I did, it was for her. As I told you at the start, I love her. Always have.

What would you have done?

I can't believe it's already been three months.

Three months since I walked out of High Cliffs House with my dusty suitcase – a suitcase that still had plenty of room in it after I'd packed everything I owned. Three months since I began the process of reintegrating into a society I'd long left behind and hadn't thought I'd ever return to.

It hasn't been easy. You can quickly become institutionalised, even when it's you who has exiled yourself in that institution to begin with. But, three months ago, the only thing I had to live for was the tiniest sliver of hope that my daughter might one day find me again.

Now I have so much more to look forward to – and I'm playing catch-up as it is – so everything they've put me through – it's all worth it. I've been through three months of counselling – we both have, actually – plus heaven only knows how many psychoanalytical tests, assessments and role plays; not to mention the endless bloody form-filling, just to get this far.

But you don't simply pick up where you left off when you haven't seen someone for twenty-one years; that was never realistic. It was always going to take a lot of work, and it has, and we're not completely there yet, but it's a landmark moment this afternoon.

You see, today, we're seeing Stuart for the first time in what seems like for ever, and it more or less is for his sister. He's twenty-nine now, with a wife and a young baby of his own, can you believe?

Am I scared? Of course. Most things are scary these days – but in a good way.

And I've had worse days, put it that way.

Now, my daughter and I are building our relationship from scratch. One piece at a time. I didn't expect her to be able to just waltz into my life, and I haven't been able to waltz right into hers, but we're working on it, and we'll get there.

It's wonderful but also weird. They can't prepare you for some of the obstacles that come up almost every day – for instance, what I should call her, and her me. She's been Laura her whole life; the part she can remember, anyway. It's who she is. You don't lose that.

So, one step at a time. She's moved into an apartment, she and her dog, and we only live a few miles apart. She's had so many job offers she's lost count – she could work for virtually any newspaper in the world right now – but she wants to see how she feels when all the media attention has settled down and she's adjusted to the changes in her life.

We get together a few times a week, and talk every day on the phone, and we rebuild piece by piece. She's making a new life for herself, meeting new people, and I'm trying to do the same. In that sense, we're both starting from zero. I've had to learn to look at people again, but it's a lot easier now.

I still go to High Cliffs House, but as a visitor. I went to see Violet Stanton – we're on first-name terms now – and we've set up a programme to help the patients interact more and not get so disconnected from the world outside. At the moment I'm teaching a group, including Mary and Tony, how to play poker. Tony's quite good – he can bluff with the best of them. Mary's rubbish, but at least she's stopped climbing on the windowsills quite so much.

But this afternoon feels like a big step into a new world.

The powers-that-be believe that not only am I ready to rejoin society, but I can see my son again.

My son. Her brother. She can hardly believe it.

She'll be here any moment now.

I can't help thinking about what she's been through, or if, when she looks at me, she thinks I should have taken better care of her. That she was just a small child and I let her down by allowing that woman to take her.

But I don't think she does. She doesn't work like that. Neither of us works like that. Everyone I speak to presumes that I'll never forgive those people for what they did, but, every time I look at my daughter, I find myself grateful instead.

Grateful because they took such good care of her and made her the person she is today.

I sense my daughter has that same confusion, not knowing if it's right to feel the way she does when logic says she shouldn't. But they loved her as if she were their own for more than twenty years; you don't wipe that away at a stroke. She even wrote a letter to the court asking the judge to pass the most lenient sentence he could. She asked me beforehand if I was OK with it, because if I wasn't she wouldn't do it.

Was I OK with it?

I thought it was one of the most beautiful things I'd ever heard.

We can't waste time being angry at the twenty-one years we lost; we have too much to look forward to, and catch up on.

There's the door now; she's right on time as usual. I don't know if she's as excited at seeing Stuart as I am. Or as scared?

Either way, it doesn't matter. We'll do it together.

Anyway, I can't stand here all day talking to you. I'd better buzz her in before she wonders where I am.

'Hello?'

'Mum? It's Jessica.'

Acknowledgements

If anyone told you, right at the outset, just how hard it is to write a book and get it published, you'd most likely never bother trying.

If they explained to you, in grisly and graphic detail, about the long hours, countless re-reading and edits; about how repeated rejection feels and knocks your confidence, you'd wonder if it was actually worth it in the first place.

Luckily, by the time I found these things out, it was already too late, and, even more fortunately, I also had an amazing bunch of people who helped me on every step of the way.

This book, like most of the things I do in life, wouldn't be possible without my wife, Luisa. If I ever think writing is hard, I only have to remember that she not only has her own career but also balances everything else in our lives to give me time to do it. And, as a bonus, she's full of great ideas and is brilliant at filling the various plot holes I can sometimes dig my way into.

But I would still have never have got this far if it weren't for Maria Turner, whose unwavering support and belief has allowed me to persevere when it would have been much easier to give up. And there have been plenty of others who've done their bit too.

Carl Jarvis has been, and continues to be, a constant source of sound advice, encouragement and enthusiasm while also managing to keep my feet on the ground. Madalene Aston and Sara Bradley were vital too, with their honest feedback and healthcare knowledge respectively.

Dan Evans, who gave his time and considerable expertise to turning my fanciful idea of a book trailer into more than an idea, deserves a special mention, but also Leanne and Ava, and Ben and Carron too, for their part in making it happen. I can't thank them enough.

But even so, after all that effort, you still only have a lot of words on a laptop until someone makes it into an actual book and Heather, Clare and Anna at RedDoor came along at just the right time to turn my dream into reality. Their consummate professionalism, expertise and know-how shines through at all times and I really couldn't have done it without them.

I also need to mention Linda McQueen, Liz Garner and Gillian Stern too for adding their unquestionable experience, advice and ideas at various points along the way, which have, like those from RedDoor, always made perfect sense and improved the book.

I got here in the end. It was definitely worth it. Thank you.

And, last but not least, a big shout out to 200 Degrees Coffee Shop in Nottingham. Not only do they serve great coffee, but, without them, I wouldn't have had anywhere to sit.

About the Author

Darren Young lives in Nottingham with his wife, Luisa, and their two children, Alessio and Emilia.

Away from writing, his background is in helping organisations improve their customer service, working initially in financial services and then as a consultant in the UK and Europe. He has a master's degree in business administration from the University of Wolverhampton.

He's always enjoyed writing – he used to chronicle his family holidays as a child – and had an ambition to try to complete a novel for a while, but didn't think there was enough time in his already busy life to fit it in. Luckily, he found a sympathetic coffee shop and plenty of encouragement from those around him, and he began working on *Child Taken* at the end of 2014 after hearing a radio news bulletin while in the car. The story – ninety-five per cent of which made the final version – was complete in his head before the end of that journey. He is especially interested in how ordinary people deal with extraordinary situations that 'could happen' but that, thankfully, few of us ever have to face.

Darren is currently writing his next novel.